*Was Alan part of* ... *life...?*

"Someone would have to get up pretty early in the morning to think they ever owned me—other than the Lord, that is."

The remark sparked a hearty laugh from Alan. "I can see that! I guess that's what I find so fascinating about you." He leaned over, took her face in his hands, and kissed her softly on the lips. "I've been wanting to do that ever since I gave you mouth-to-mouth resuscitation on the banks of the Swansea River."

"You have? I mean, you did?" She felt weak, like a little kid with a stomach full of butterflies.

"Mm hm. I have, and I did. Both."

# Cater
# to a Whim

*Norma Jean Lutz*

*Heartsong Presents*

To Jean:
      Sister-in-Law
      Sister-in-Love
      Sister-in-the-Lord

A note from the Author:
*I love to hear from my readers! You may correspond with me
by writing:*

      **Norma Jean Lutz**
      **Author Relations**
      **P.O. Box 719**
      **Uhrichsville, OH 44683**

**ISBN 1-55748-563-1**

**CATER TO A WHIM**

PRINTED IN THE U.S.A.

# one

Bandy pulled the van to a stop beside the massive, old stone church two blocks off the main street of Pembrooke. Her van was filled from floor to ceiling with all the makings of a memorable wedding. She looked over her shoulder at the van's contents, savoring the air-conditioned air for a moment longer before she switched off the ignition.

She turned and gazed up at the church's bell tower. The Mississippi July sun bathed the structure with gold. *If those stones could talk*, she thought, *such stories they would tell. Of past weddings, of stately ladies in hoops, crinolines, and ruffled parasols.*

"Lands, girl. What are you thinking about?" asked her friend and assistant Millie Atkins. "Are you just going to sit here all day?"

Bandy looked at the ripples of heat that shimmered off the brick-lined streets though it wasn't even noon yet. "I was wondering why any bride in her right mind would opt to get married in the middle of a hot Mississippi summer," Bandy replied.

Millie gave a little laugh as she rubbed her arthritic knee. "Who can explain brides? You've been in the business long enough to know they take leave of their senses once they fall in love and begin making wedding plans."

"You're right about that." Bandy pointed to Millie's bad knee. "That thing bothering you? There's no storm predicted."

Millie rubbed her knee again, then looked up at the bright, cloudless sky. "There's a storm brewing somewhere," she

5

said with a smile. "This knee is never wrong."

A tap on the side of the van made them turn toward the window. Gena Karr, Bandy's talented florist, smiled in at them. "Did you two pass out in there? Hadn't we better get moving?"

Behind Gena stood her newest boyfriend, Brian Farlow, one of the local university football players. Bandy was pleased to see he'd agreed to help them unload. Gena, too, was a university student and worked for Bandy's Bridal Boutique only part-time. Bandy was glad to have her work for as much as she could get her; the girl could turn out flower arrangements that rivaled the work of a ten-year veteran.

Bandy pushed her door open and gasped as the heat assaulted her. "Whew. We'll all be wringing wet before this is over." She hopped down to the sidewalk. "First we'll unload the flowers at this side entrance, then I'll pull around the back to unload the catering supplies."

Across the street the magnolias on the courthouse lawn were heavy with waxy blossoms. The fragrance wafted gently on the heat-filled air, mingling with the thick honeysuckle that cloaked the church's entryway. The building covered almost a full half block, and Bandy was thankful the wedding was to be held in a smaller chapel, rather than the cavernous sanctuary. That would simplify the decorating.

"Brian," Bandy said, "would you come around here and help Millie out first?"

"Sure."

The burly young man leapt to help Millie down from the van, but Millie tossed her gray head and pulled her arm from his grip. "You'll do no such thing. I can still get myself in and out of this van, thank you. And I'll be sure to let y'all know when I can't."

Bandy looked up at Brian and shrugged. Brian grinned, then pulled open the side door of the van and reached for a container of flowers.

"The air conditioning system in this old mausoleum is archaic," Bandy warned them. "I'm guessing there will be a million fans sitting around, so keep an eye out for cords on the floors."

"Don't call it a mausoleum," Gena said softly.

Bandy looked at the girl as she too leaned into the van to grab an armload. Gena was dressed in a trim blue halter top and matching shorts. Her long brown hair was twisted neatly into a french braid. "Why not?" Bandy asked. "Don't you think it looks like a gloomy building from some old horror movie?"

Gena shook her head. "I think it's beautiful."

"To be perfectly honest," Bandy leaned closer to Gena, "I think so too. But it's not a very practical place to have a wedding in the heat of the summer."

Bandy grabbed yet another box and followed the two in through the big double doors. Looking at Gena's neat hairdo and gorgeous tan made Bandy more aware of her own flyaway copper curls. Now that the humidity had risen, each tendril stubbornly demanded to go its own way. And her skin was sun-burnable ivory, her freckles legion. "Some trick You played on me, Lord," she muttered as she maneuvered up the steps.

They took the altar and pew flowers into the chapel, and the bouquets, boutonnieres, and corsages to the bride's room. From there they would leave Gena to her work in the chapel and Bandy and Millie would begin work in the fellowship hall.

"Is Denise coming to help?" Gena wanted to know. Denise Jepson, Bandy's accountant and secretary, was usually exempt from "field" work.

"She promised she'd be here," Bandy answered. "Reluctantly, but she did promise."

When Bandy had hired Denise, she had stressed that her outfit was small and everyone had to pitch in to make it work. That meant that on occasion Denise would be called on to help out in ways other than secretarial. Denise hadn't care much for the idea, but she had agreed. Ellen Persell, the sales associate in the bridal boutique, was the only one who was never asked to leave the store.

"Will Denise be working in here with me?" Gena wanted to know.

"Looks like that's where the most help is needed."

Gena rolled her eyes.

"Now, Gena," Bandy warned. "Try to be civil."

They all knew that Gena did not like Denise. But Denise was a crackerjack accountant, and Bandy needed her services.

"I do try." Gena's lips were tight. "But she winds up telling *me* how to do *my* job. Every time, she does it! Every time."

"I know, I know. Keep trying, okay?"

Gena groaned softly and began fastening flowers to each pew. Bandy looked around the little chapel. The room was accented with carved rosewood, and tall stained glass windows cast soft-hued patterns across the wine carpeting. The padding in the pews matched the carpet, blending perfectly with the pink and wine floral arrangements that Gena was putting up.

As she watched Gena work, Bandy thought about how bossy and snippy Denise could be; unfortunately, she upset Bandy's entire staff. Usually Bandy hired another college student to assist Gena, but in the summer that wasn't easy to do, since only a few kids stuck around for summer school. This weekend no one had been available. Brian had even tried to get one of his buddies to come, but the attempt was futile, and Bandy had been forced to ask Denise for her help.

Gena was so gentle and soft spoken, Bandy was often afraid Denise would scare her off. Gena had once remarked, "If Denise were the boss, I'd never work here."

Brian interrupted her thoughts by coming up with the last box of flowers. "Want me to drive the van around? You can meet me at the back door. That way you won't have to go back out in the heat.'

Bandy glanced over at Gena. ' Shall we keep this guy?"

Gena's cheeks turned pink. "Sounds good to me."

Bandy tossed him the keys and made her way through the many hallways to the fellowship hall in the back of the church. Millie was already there working in the kitchen.

When Brian came around, Bandy kept a close eye on him to see how he handled the fragile items. She watched as he gently placed each box of crystal on the two-wheel dolly—not stacking them too high, and keeping one hand on the top box as he wheeled them into the kitchen. He was a good worker.

Bandy had been right about the fans. They were everywhere. This church must spend a fortune on them. Box fans, round fans, oscillating fans, large fans on stands. And they did provide merciful relief from the dead air spaces—especially in the kitchen.

The kitchen was old, but spacious. She and Millie had done two other weddings in this church, so they were familiar with the facilities, and Millie briskly unloaded her delicate hors d'oeuvres and placed them in the large commercial refrigerator at one end of the kitchen.

The older woman continually tested recipes to upgrade their line of condiments and party trays. Millie's loving hands decorated each bridal cake, as well as prepared their exotic punch. Bandy often commented that Millie's culinary skill was the key to their success in the community.

Bandy was showing Brian where to put the various sections of the punch fountain, when Denise breezed in the door.

"Hello, everybody," she announced with a smile. "Sorry I'm late."

One would never know by looking at Denise that the day was miserably hot. Her black hair, styled in a short, severe cut, was precise and unruffled, and her white sundress, trimmed with black piping, was crisp and unwrinkled. She pulled off her sunglasses and perched them atop her head.

"Where do y'all want my able assistance today?" Denise asked, looking around at the activity.

"The chapel," Bandy told her. Somehow, with Denise's arrival, Bandy suddenly felt rumpled and sweaty. Although she would be changing before the wedding, for now she had on her usual "unload the wedding" attire: jean cutoffs, a loose T-shirt, and tennis shoes. And of course she could do nothing with her wild tangle of red curls. She sighed and mentally shrugged. "Gena's already in the chapel setting up," she told Denise.

"The chapel it is," Denise said, turning to head down the hall.

"Oh, Denise," Bandy called after her. "Have you met Brian?"

Denise turned around to take a better look at the boy she'd walked by a few moments before. "No, I don't believe I have." She twirled and backtracked to where he stood, looking him over from stem to stern. "Is this a new addition to the staff?"

"He's Gena's friend. Just helping out today. Brian, this is Denise Jepson, the accountant for the boutique, and my personal secretary. Denise, this is Brian Farlow."

Denise looked up at the ruggedly handsome football player. "I'm pleased to meet you, Brian." The words were honeyed with her deep Southern accent. She took his large hand in both of hers. "How wonderful to see that our little Gena's taste in men is improving."

A bright blush bloomed from Brian's neckline to the tips of his ears. Before he could think of an answer, Bandy said quickly, "Speaking of Gena, she needs help. Like right now."

"Sure, sure, I'm going." Denise looked back up at Brian, patted his hand, and smiled. "Bandy's such a slave driver. If you hang around with us, you'll see what I mean." She sauntered off down the hall toward the chapel.

"Let's get these tables set up," Bandy told Brian. Denise's open flirting had embarrassed them both, but dismissing it without comment seemed the best route to take. Bandy knew she should be used to it by now, but though she'd lived in the deep South since she was twelve years old, she'd never learned to turn on the charm and flirt like a genuine Southern belle. Southern girls seemed to be born with the aptitude, but Bandy had too much New England blood flowing in her veins to bother with such an impractical pastime.

She and Brian quickly set up tables for the reception area. "These tables must have been purchased before the war," Bandy commented. "But I'm not sure which war." Each leg folded separately, making the tables unwieldy to work with.

"This one seems to have a loose leg," Brian announced as they set the last table upright.

"Let me see." Bandy knelt down to investigate the problem. "It's the locking piece that's missing. The leg will hold up, but it won't lock." She was accustomed to such predicaments. Church furnishings were seldom in peak working order, especially in a church this old. "Take a quick look around and see if there's an extra one not in use, would you, Brian?"

He returned shortly with the report that all other rooms were locked tight. Bandy sighed. "We'll have to use the bad table for the hors d'oeuvres, and possibly the groom's cake." Quickly, they set it up and began spreading the wine-colored cloths and lace coverlets. "I think it'll be okay," she said half to herself.

She glanced at her watch. "I'll have to go change in a minute. Here, Brian, let me show you how to put the punch fountain together. It's simple once you get the hang of it."

Before they had the fountain fully constructed, Julie, the bride-to-be, came rushing in. She'd purchased her gown at Bandy's shop, and it was one of Bandy's favorites, a regal satin with an Elizabethan neckline and basque waist. Beaded lace covered the bodice, sleeves, and train.

Julie's eyes sparkled with excitement as she surveyed the room. "Miss O'Sullivan, everything is more lovely than I ever dreamed. How can I ever thank you?"

Bandy gave her a hug. "Don't forget—all this is done to your exact specifications!"

Julie laughed. "I know, but you took my specifications and did wonders with them. And you and Ellen helped me pick out the most wonderful dress." She turned about slowly so Bandy could see the train with the perky bow in the back.

"You look gorgeous, Julie. Absolutely gorgeous." Bandy stepped closer to straighten the veil. She never tired of the excitement of seeing a happy, satisfied bride on her day-of-all-days.

"I'm due back in the sanctuary for photos," Julie said. "But I told everyone to wait. I just had to come and see you first." She flashed another bright smile and was gone again down the hall.

Millie had the towering cake nearly all assembled, Bandy noted before she turned back to helping Brian with the fountain. She nodded her head toward the hall where Julie had disappeared. "Doesn't that put you in the wedding mood?"

Brian glanced at her, obviously to see if she was kidding. "Hey, I'm just a pup," he said. "Too young to be thinking of such things. However," he added with a slow grin, "I'm told Professor Wyler will probably be here this afternoon. Maybe it'll give him a few ideas."

From the other table, Bandy heard Millie giggle. "What're you laughing at?" she demanded.

"You better watch your step," Millie said. "Here's a fella who can throw it right back at you."

"Thanks, Millie." Professor Jordan Wyler and Bandy had dated off and on for about year, but she had had no idea their relationship was the talk of the campus. Bandy busied herself arranging crystal punch cups on a rolling cart behind the serving table. "So what does the professor have to do with anything?" she asked with a shrug, baiting him.

Brian looked at her with a deadpan expression. "Didn't you know he has your photo taped up on the door of his office?"

"What?" Bandy straightened up so fast she almost knocked a cup off the tray.

Brian laughed. "Just kidding, just kidding. Actually Gena happened to mention that you two were an item." He threw up his hands. "That's all, honest."

Millie was still giggling. Bandy shot her a sidelong glance. "And what's so funny?"

"I told you to watch your step."

Turning back to Brian, Bandy said, "Remember what I said about keeping you around? I think I've changed my mind."

"I think he's pretty funny," Millie said. "I vote to keep him."

Bandy ignored her. "So why would the professor come to this particular wedding anyway?" she asked Brian.

"Dave, the groom, is one of his star history students."

"Is that right?" Jordan hadn't said anything to her about coming today. Not that they discussed everything in detail. But she had thought their relationship was growing. Then at other times, she wasn't really sure.

Bandy turned and saw a long-legged, thin young man entering the reception room. She often had to chase out members of the wedding party, or guests who moseyed around gawking—or worse, foraging in the precisely-arranged mint trays. This young man, who looked to be the age of Brian, was preoccupied with a gadget in his hand, which Bandy recognized to be a photographer's light meter.

"Hey!" she called to him. "You'll have to wait in the foyer. You're early for the wedding and much too early for the reception."

"Gotta get this reading just right," he mumbled, moving about the room. "Let's see now, it's lighter over the cloth-covered tables."

"Please," Bandy persisted. This guy must be a shirt-tail cousin or something. "You'll have to leave this area."

The young man scowled. "I have as much right to be in here as you do. I'm making light readings."

Bandy pressed her lips together. She had no time or patience for this. "See here, young man. . ."

"Don't panic, lady. I'm following orders. Just one more reading here and I'll be. . ." He moved to reach his meter over the lace cloth and his knee met with the unlocked leg of the shaky table. Bandy's heart went wild as she saw everything begin to slide toward the floor in haunting slow motion.

# two

Bandy ran toward the table. Guests were already arriving in the foyer, and she forced herself to swallow her scream. She was quick enough to rescue the groom's cake, and Brian grabbed a tray of hors d'oeuvres, but the silver coffee server was rolling and tumbling, spreading a trail of russet coffee across the lace. Another tray of hors d'oeuvres followed it as though in pursuit.

The wide-eyed young man clutched the corner of the table, saving it from total collapse, but the coffee server hit the floor, filling the room with a heavy aroma. Bandy clenched her teeth against the harsh words she would have liked to use.

"Hayden, what's going on in here?" Another man, older than the first and better dressed, strode into the reception area. A shock of light blond hair fell across his forehead, and a large camera hung from a strap around his neck. "Hayden, let these people clean up their own spills. I need you in the sanctuary!"

By now the thin boy named Hayden had firmed up the table leg with his foot. He turned to the taller, blond-haired man. "Yes, sir, Mr. Brockhurst."

Bandy whirled to face the second intruder. "For your information, Mr. Brockhurst, or whoever you are, your friend here is the one who *caused* this spill." A mishap like this could ruin her reputation permanently. She moved the groom's cake to another, sturdier table, biting her lips to hold back her anger.

"Hayden did this?" Mr. Brockhurst took a closer look at

the steaming coffee on the carpet and the strewn bits of cheese, ham, and black and green olives.

"I'm awful sorry, Mr. Brockhurst," Hayden said meekly. "I took a light reading just like you told me and my knee hit . . ." He pushed a little at the leg to demonstrate and Bandy lunged toward him.

"Don't do that!" she yelled.

"Hmm." Mr. Brockhurst moved to examine the leg. "Missing locking mechanism," he announced. "Pretty risky to use it that way. I suggest you find another table that's more reliable."

"Brilliant. What a simply brilliant suggestion!" Bandy's words were tight and deliberate. "For your information, there *were* no other tables, and we *knew* there was no lock. What we didn't know was that someone would come in here and kick it down while taking a light reading!" She turned to take the wet towels Millie was handing her. The older woman gently patted her arm, warning her to calm her fiery temper.

"I'll get the extra tablecloths from the van," Millie said softly. They'd learned long ago always to carry extras.

Bandy was now down on all fours mopping madly. Mr. Brockhurst grabbed a roll of paper towels from the kitchen and assisted. "I'm Alan Brockhurst, photographer for this distinguished occasion."

Bandy studied the tanned smiling face and the lively blue eyes. "I'd shake your hand," she said coolly, "but I seem to be otherwise occupied."

"And you are. . .?"

"Bandy O'Sullivan." She took the towels back to the kitchen sink to wring them out. What a mess. She should be changing her clothes at this very moment. And obviously this photographer should be in the sanctuary taking photos.

"Bandy?" he said from the kitchen door. He tossed coffee-soaked paper towels in the large trash bin. "You said your name was 'Bandy'?"

She glared at him. Any remark about her name at this point and she knew she would scream. "Yes," she said. "Bandy. An old family name—Bandy."

"Okay, Bandy," he said calmly, "let's get this place in order. Hayden, get that coffee server and take it to the kitchen and clean it up. Got any more coffee, Bandy?"

"Plenty of it." She pushed her contrary curly hair away from her face with the back of her hand.

"Hear that, Hayden? Refill that pot, then get these other towels rinsed out for Bandy."

Hayden pushed his glasses up on his nose. "Yes, sir."

Millie returned with the table cloths and Alan helped her spread them—first the wine-colored cloth, then the lace over it. From the kitchen, Bandy heard him say, "Why not turn the table around so the bad leg is toward the servers? You can warn the servers—and then no unwary guest will lean against it and get the same surprise Hayden did."

Bandy noticed a little lilt in Millie's voice as she answered, "Good idea."

"Good idea, my foot," Bandy muttered. She would be delighted if this pushy guy departed permanently.

"Actually," Alan continued, "when you stop to think about it, it was better to have the incident happen now than during the reception. Right?"

"I guess you're right," Millie answered as Bandy returned from the kitchen.

"Wrong," Bandy said. "It would have been much better if it hadn't happened at all. I'm almost late, and this could have caused me to lose an account. You should be in the sanctuary taking photos, and you hang around here suggesting this was all for the best. Pretty nervy, if you ask me."

Alan Brockhurst looked over at her from where he and

Millie had the lame table almost restored to its original beauty. His eyes twinkled as he said, "Nervy? That's a great word to use to describe me. I've been called worse."

"I can believe that," Bandy retorted.

"The place still smells like coffee," Millie interrupted, obviously intent on quelling their squabble. "How about room spray, Bandy?"

Bandy wheeled around and retrieved a can of air freshener from their supplies in the kitchen. From across the room she tossed it to the vain Mr. Brockhurst. She was disappointed when he made a perfect catch.

"Ah, jasmine," he said. "My favorite."

Bandy ignored his bright grin. "I'm going to go change, Millie. Be back in a minute." Hopefully, when she returned, he'd be gone.

Quickly, she made her way down the hall to the ladies' room where she'd left her navy satin dress. She took a moment to splash cool water on her face and freshen her makeup. As she slipped into her dress, she wondered about the brash photographer. She'd never seen him before, and she knew nearly every photographer in the city. If this was any indication of how he conducted himself while on the job, he wouldn't last long around the fussy patrons in Pembrooke.

A few moments later, she felt like a new person as she emerged into the hall. The detached organza bib-cape riffled softly in clingy folds about her arms as she walked.

Strains of music floating throughout the old church let her know the wedding had started. Shortly, she would be helping Julie and her new husband set up the receiving line. Then she would be instructing and helping the servers. And, of course, Millie would be keeping a steady stream of delicacies coming from the kitchen for hungry guests.

She was startled from her thoughts by a terse voice

calling her name. She whirled around to see her stepmother Claire O'Sullivan striding toward her. Bandy's heart caught in her throat. She hadn't seen Claire for several months. On this very hot day, her stepmother was dressed in a pale yellow suit, replete with gloves and a matching veiled hat.

"Why, Claire, good to see you." Bandy strained to make her voice pleasant without sounding phony. She held out her hand, but Claire ignored it.

"I should have known you'd be lurking about back here."

"The word is 'working,' not 'lurking.'" Bandy quipped with a slight smile.

"Don't get smart with me, Bandy O'Sullivan. You should be in attendance at this wedding as part of this family rather than rummaging around back here with the kitchen help."

"Kitchen help?" Bandy could only assume she was referring to Millie who used to be a housekeeper and cook for Claire before the death of Bandy's father. "First of all, I *am* the kitchen help. And I'm in attendance at this wedding as much as you are—and perhaps even more so."

Claire seemed to bristle at that remark. "For your information, Julie is the granddaughter of very dear friends of the family. And the groom—Dave—happens to be a distant cousin descended from my grandfather's family on my father's side. If your father were alive, he'd have attended with me as our family ought to attend—in the church, *not* in the kitchen doing servants' work."

"Well, you seem to be attending this wedding in the back hall. And from the sound of the music, I believe they're playing the recessional. Now if you'll excuse me, I have business to attend to." Bandy turned to go, then paused. "Good to see you again," she said as an afterthought.

Through the years, she had tried not to be rude to Claire, but was usually unsuccessful. Her very proper, very Southern stepmother had never agreed with Bandy's choice of catering for a business, and she had fought Bandy every step of the way. Claire hated the thought of her stepdaughter stooping to cook and serve the friends and acquaintances Claire had known for a lifetime. Claire never seemed to grasp the fact that Bandy's boutique was much more than a catering service.

Bandy sighed and pushed the thought of her stepmother from her mind. She made her way back to the fellowship hall and found that Gena, with Denise's help, had transformed the room into a wonderland of flowers. Gena was carefully lighting the tapers on the tables, when Bandy came up behind her. "Super job, Gena. Everything looks wonderful."

Gena smiled her thanks. "Don't you think we'd better move these fans back against the wall?" She pointed to the two large pedestal fans located about the room.

"It's going to be suffocating in here once it fills up with people." Bandy studied the location of the tall fans. "It's already warm now. Guess we'd better leave them where they are."

"Brian and I are going to escape for a few minutes. Is that all right?"

Bandy could see Brian waiting outside the back door. "Sure. Be my guest. Just be back in time for clean-up duty."

"We will." Gena stretched to reach the last taper.

"He's a nice guy."

"Brian?"

"Uh huh."

Gena smiled. "I think so, but I'm glad you do too." She blew out the match in her hand, and her smile faded. "Bandy, I don't mean to complain, but could you do something about Denise?"

Bandy steeled herself. "What's the matter with Denise?"

"I probably shouldn't say anything." Gena was obviously

uncomfortable.

"If there's a problem, I need to know."

"It's just—" Gena sighed. "When it's happening, it seems so hateful, but after it's over, it seems so trite."

Bandy knew Denise was curt and short with Gena, but she felt helpless to rectify the situation.

"She talks to me as though I were a child," Gena went on. "Condescending and patronizing. And then she infers that I don't know what I'm doing. At first I just put up with it, but it's getting so I hate to work with her." Gena's eyes were imploring. "Could you just talk to her?"

"I don't know how much good a 'talk' will do, but I'll sure give it a try. I'm sorry she gives you such a hard time. I appreciate all your hard work *and* your talents." She saw Gena's expression brighten. "Now you two go find an air-conditioned mall and enjoy a cold soda, then get back here to help us clean and load up."

"Sure thing." Gena skipped out the door.

Bandy felt certain the problem wasn't going to be solved by a talk. Denise was a difficult person to understand. She was extremely business minded and efficient, yet she had another side to her that was continually teasing or flirting. Come to think of it, Bandy hadn't seen Denise since before the wedding began. No telling where she was.

But Bandy had no time to think about trivial matters, as the receiving line was ready to be organized. Within minutes, the large hall was alive with buzzing, chatting guests milling about waiting for the cakes to be cut and the toasts to be made.

In the midst of attending to a score of tiny details, Bandy noticed the tall blond photographer was back on the scene. And there beside him, chatting and holding his camcorder for him, was Denise Jepson. Bandy might have known.

The glowing bride and groom were now cutting the cake

and feeding one another. Twitters of laughter filled the room. Alan Brockhurst moved about the room, maneuvering to get the best shots, while Bandy tried to keep the guests out of his way. Denise caught Bandy's eye, lifted the camcorder she was holding and winked, but Bandy ignored her.

Alan's young assistant dogged his heels as though he were studying his boss' every move. If they were not both such pests, Bandy thought, the scene would have been almost amusing.

Alan moved in for several close shots, then stepped back again. Hayden was so close behind him that he had to jump back to avoid being stepped on. As he did, he backed squarely into one of the large pedestal fans. Before Bandy could react, the fan came crashing down on her. A sharp pain stabbed her shoulder, and then she and Hayden and the fan were in a heap on the floor.

She must have hit her head and lost consciousness for a time. When she opened her eyes, she found two faces hovering over her—Alan Brockhurst and Professor Jordan Wyler.

## three

Through a fog, Bandy heard Jordan calling her name, his voice soft and anxious. When she tried to lift her head, he reached out his hand to stop her. "Better lie still a moment. You had a bad bump."

People were standing about gaping at her, she realized, and humiliation and anger burned inside her. She struggled to sit up. "I'm all right. Please. Help me up."

"Isn't this the point in the movie where they slosh the bucket of water in the victim's face?" Alan asked with a grin.

"No, sir," said Hayden, who was standing behind him. "That's before they wake up."

"Very funny," Bandy muttered. She clearly remembered Hayden falling down on top of her, but he looked none the worse for the tumble. Her lovely chiffon cape was bunched around her neck, the satin skirt tangled between her legs. She felt Jordan's arm slip under her neck to help ease her up. The sensation was rather nice, in spite of the fact that the room instantly tilted before her eyes. Jordan helped her to her feet, and she was glad he kept his arm around her.

She realized Millie was clucking over her, trying to get her to go to the kitchen and sit down with an ice pack on her head. Jordan's dark eyes looked at her. "You should, you know," he said.

"Back away, people," Alan told the crowd. "Just a little mishap here. Nothing to gawk at. Let's form a line. There's plenty of food and punch for everyone." He deftly herded the crowd away from Bandy and back toward the food-laden tables.

"I'm fine," she told Jordan, as she smoothed her dress, while Millie straightened the cape from behind her. Bandy could see that the culprit fan had now been moved over against the wall. She should have taken that precaution in the first place—but how could she have predicted what would happen? Something must be done about this accident-prone kid named Hayden, before he turned the wedding into a total disaster. She reached back to feel the bump on the back of her head. As she lifted her arm, a stab of pain in her shoulder made her wince.

Jordan's hand covered hers. "Millie's right about that ice. That's a nasty bump."

"Maybe I should go sit down for a minute," she said.

"Good idea."

"Meanwhile, would you please ask the photographer, Mr. Alan Brockhurst, to meet me in the kitchen? I need to talk to him."

"The kid who knocked over the fan—is he with the photographer?"

She nodded. "The problem is, that's the second mishap he's caused."

Jordan gave her a look to let her know he understood. Millie helped her to the kitchen, and Jordan went to fetch Alan Brockhurst.

Millie made a makeshift ice pack with cubes in a small towel. Pain throbbed through Bandy's head as she pressed the coldness against the bump.

Presently, Alan poked his head in the doorway. "A guy out there said you wanted to talk to me. You need to make it quick, we're about to take the photos of the garter throw." The look of pain that crossed her face must have made him pause. He walked over to where she was sitting. Standing this close, he seemed taller than before. The ironic gleam in his eyes softened. "Hey, I'm sorry about the fall you took. Are you okay?"

"My health, or lack of it, isn't what I want to discuss with you. It's your assistant."

"Hayden?"

"Hayden. Have you ever considered getting a new assistant? That kid is a walking disaster."

Alan gave a little laugh. His wide shoulders fell almost imperceptibly. "Actually, he's a distant relative of some kind. My aunt back in Biloxi insisted that if I moved up here to Pembrooke, I was to let Hayden work with me. He's a student at the university, and the kid's wild about photography."

"I thought I recognized him," said Jordan from the doorway.

"And who're you?" Alan asked.

Jordan stepped forward and offered his hand. "Professor Jordan Wyler." Beside the tall and lanky photographer, Jordan appeared shorter, more stocky. His dark hair and serious dark brown eyes contrasted with Alan's straw-colored hair and bright gaze.

"At the university, I take it?"

Jordan nodded.

"So you know Hayden?"

"He's not in any of my classes, but I recognize his face." Jordan slipped off his gold-rimmed glasses and dropped them in his coat pocket. Bandy smiled; she often teased him about his indecisiveness of whether to take his glasses off or keep them on. The typical Southern male, he hated the word indecisive.

"If you take the time to look around, Mr. Brockhurst," Bandy put in, "I'm sure you'll find a more able assistant. Especially after school starts again in August. But meanwhile, would you keep him under wraps until this thing is over? I'm afraid he'll wind up being dragged behind the wedding car along with the tin cans."

Alan ran his fingers though the shock of blond hair, pushing it off his forehead, though it instantly fell back. "He may seem all arms and legs now, but he's still just a kid. Everybody needs a chance."

Bandy sighed. "Very well, Mr. Brockhurst. But if he has one more mishap, I'm going to give Julie permission to order him out of here. Better yet, I'll do it myself."

Just then Hayden appeared at the door, his face red. "The garter throw, Mr. Brockhurst! They're ready for the garter throw. Want me to take this one?" Hayden now had the large camera around his neck. As he turned, it smacked against the door frame.

"No, thanks, Hayden. I'll take care of it." Alan tipped his head toward Bandy. "Excuse me. Thanks for your help and your kind advice." And he was gone.

"What an arrogant snob," Bandy said.

"Probably not," Jordan said.

"Not? What do you mean he's not?"

"More likely, he just doesn't like being bossed around by a woman."

Bandy looked up and studied Jordan's summer-tanned face; as usual, though the afternoon was still early, he sported a four o'clock shadow. He was putting his glasses back on now.

"Most men don't," he said mildly, avoiding her eyes.

"Millie." She turned to her friend for help. "Did you hear me bossing anyone around? Wasn't I merely making a wise suggestion, which would save both me *and* Mr. Brockhurst further grief?"

Millie lifted another food-filled tray destined for the tables in the reception room. "Maybe you did come on a mite strong. After all, the boy's his kin."

"Ah, yes, kinfolk." Bandy took the ice pack from her head and tossed it into the sink. "I keep forgetting I live where kinfolk ties are stronger than super glue. *And* where men can't stand to be corrected by a woman, no matter how right she might be. Nope, they wouldn't want to risk having their masculinity threatened by listening to a woman's advice." She hopped up. "I've got work to do."

As she moved toward the door, Jordan gently caught her arm. "Wait a minute, Little Red, calm down. I didn't say I agreed with the guy. I merely made a simple observation about him. You're right, the boy could become a real problem. But let Mr. Brockhurst find out for himself."

"I certainly will," Bandy retorted, pulling her arm away. "If I live that long."

The squeals and catcalls told Bandy the garter and bouquet were being thrown. Time to make sure the birdseed-filled lace bags were ready and available for the guests. She also took a moment to talk to the maid of honor to be sure all of Julie's things for the honeymoon trip were packed and ready.

Presently, the crowd spilled outside where the searing heat rose from the concrete sidewalks and hung thickly in the air. Ladies fanned themselves as the men loosened their ties. A gleaming silver limo waited at the curb.

Bandy noticed that Alan had stationed himself just outside the door to get the first shots of the couple. Beside him stood the ever-present Hayden. But on the other side of Alan, holding the camcorder, ready to shoot, was Denise. *Perhaps blood wasn't that thick after all,* Bandy thought.

The string of cans, cleverly tied to the axle, made a terrible clatter as the limo pulled out with the blissful couple safely inside. The wildly-tossed bird seed was scattered about the sidewalk, crunching under the shoes of the guests. The squares of lace lay limply where they fell, unstirred by even a breath of breeze.

As Bandy turned to go back inside, Jordan came up beside her. His jacket was slung over his arm, and his tie loosened. Sweat glistened on his upper lip. The gold-rimmed glasses were back in his shirt pocket. He stood there, squinting against the glaring sun, obviously wanting to say something.

"Yes?" Bandy said finally. She was too hot to wait for him to figure out how he was going to say whatever it was he was planning to say.

"I hope your shoulder is okay."

"It only hurts when I move," she joked weakly.

"Perhaps I was a little rude in the kitchen earlier. If so, I apologize."

*Good old Professor,* Bandy thought. *Can't stand any friction.* "No apologies needed. I've already forgotten it. You were probably right anyway."

"I'm having a few people over next Friday night for a backyard cookout. I'd like you to come."

The "few people" usually meant other professors from the university and their families. Bandy didn't feel she had much in common with them, but she did enjoy being with Jordan. She gave a quick nod. "Sure. I'd love to come. I'll bring a few of Millie's famous snackies."

His dark brows went up, and a slow smile spread over his face. "Sounds fine. About seven. I'll see you there."

She watched him walk away before she went up the steps to the cool interior of the church. Gena and Brian had returned and were in the kitchen, cleaning up and packing and loading. Bandy hurried to change into her cutoffs so she could lend a hand.

When she arrived back in the kitchen, Gena said, "I heard you had a little accident. Are you all right?"

Bandy nodded as she began washing the punch cups. "Of

course I'm all right. It takes more than a falling fan hitting me between the eyes to slow me down."

Millie put her hand on Bandy's shoulder where the fan had made its crash landing. Bandy jumped when the tender point was touched. "It didn't hit her between the eyes, Gena. It hit her shoulder, and, yes, she should have it looked at. Could have cracked your collarbone, my dear," she added softly to Bandy. "To say nothing of a possible concussion."

"I'm fine, I tell you." She turned to Millie, her hands dripping soapy water. "I'm a tough New Englander, not a fragile Southern belle. I didn't call for my smelling salts." She plunged her hands back into the water with a splash. "And don't forget," she added, remembering the humiliating scene all over again, "the dear gentleman named Mr. Brockhurst didn't even have to pour a bucket of water on me, although he very kindly offered."

"He was kidding, right?" Gena asked with a look of surprise.

Bandy shrugged. "From what I've seen of him so far, who knows?"

"He was kidding," Millie calmly reassured Gena as she handed her another box to carry to the van. "He was trying to distract the gawking crowd." When Gena was out of earshot, she added, "Mercy, Bandy, don't be talking about people like that."

Bandy pushed copper curls out of her eyes with the dry part of her arm, and gave a deep sigh. "Of course, you're right, Millie. I'm sorry. What a crazy day this has been."

"Land's sake, girl. Things can't go perfect all the time. You own a business you love, and do work that you love. You have a beautiful shop in a splendid shopping center. God's pouring blessings out of heaven on every side. How can you be mumbling and moaning?"

Bandy dried her hands and then gave Millie a hug.

"Thanks, Millie. That's why I keep you around. You always keep me in line."

Millie returned the hug. "Does the new job description mean a raise in pay?" she quipped.

"Not till you learn the job a little better," Bandy shot back, returning to the sink full of soapsuds.

"Now that's a tall order."

Bandy looked at her friend and smiled. "Keeping me in line? Yes, I suppose it is."

Later, as Bandy helped load the van, she overheard Gena and Brian discussing Hayden. Obviously, they too knew him from school. "He's a nerd, plain and simple," Brian was saying.

"Not necessarily," Gena retorted. "Just because someone doesn't fit your preconceived notions doesn't mean you have to brand him with some trite label."

"That's not a trite label, ma'am. Just facts," Brian said. "You should have seen him slam-banging into that table. Then he almost creamed Miss O'Sullivan. Sounds pretty nerdy to me."

"Hayden was in my English lit class last year. And he's not a nerd. He's brilliant. Someday he'll be the head of some great university and you'll come to him looking for a coaching job."

"I don't think so," Brian said with a scowl.

"Hey, hey," Bandy interrupted their little spat. "Is the heat getting to all of us? All's well that ends well. Everything is fine. So let's forget the boy named Hayden. Okay?"

"Sounds good to me," Brian agreed.

"He's still not a nerd," Gena said, successfully getting in the last word.

Finally, everything was loaded. As Bandy turned the key in the van's ignition and turned on the air conditioner, she chanced to see Alan Brockhurst and Denise congenially chatting beside Denise's parked car. Denise still looked crisp and composed. Of course, she hadn't helped in the scrubbing or the loading, so why wouldn't she? Bandy was feeling a bit miffed with her trusted secretary; she sighed, reminding herself that Denise really hadn't done anything out of the ordinary. Bandy really had no reason to feel as annoyed with her as she did.

Millie climbed into the van, once again rubbing her bad knee.

"See there," Bandy said as she put the van in gear and drove off, "your knee *was* wrong. There's not a storm in sight."

"I beg to differ with you, my dear." Millie jerked her head back toward the church. "There were a number of storms brewing back there all afternoon."

Bandy thought about Millie's words for a moment, and then she was forced to agree.

# *four*

On Monday, Bandy was attempting to straighten her cluttered desk at the end of the day, when a call came through. She was hungry for her supper, and she almost didn't take the call. She would have been very sorry if she hadn't, for she had been waiting for this call, or one like it, ever since they had moved the boutique to its present location several months ago.

"It's a Mrs. Gilchrist for you, Bandy," Denise's voice had said over the speaker phone.

Instantly, Bandy pulled herself up straighter and rummaged among the papers and photos for a note pad. "Did you say Gilchrist?"

"I did," Denise replied. "Does that mean something special?"

Bandy pulled open the top drawer and finally found the note pad she'd been looking for. "There might be other Gilchrist families in Pembrooke, but there's only one who lives on Enderlin Drive. Could be we're finally in."

She took a deep breath and pushed the button to connect her to the flashing line. "This is Bandy O'Sullivan. May I help you?"

An all-business voice, rich with a Southern accent, sounded on the other end of the line. "Thank you, Miss O'Sullivan, you may. This is Mrs. Edward Gilchrist speaking."

Bandy gripped the pen tighter as she copied down the name. This was the right Gilchrist. She felt a little shiver of excitement, and struggled to keep her own voice equally business-like. "How pleasant to hear from you, Mrs. Gilchrist."

"Our daughter Nan saw your shop in the Harwood Heights Shopping Center," the voice continued. "Nan has recently become engaged. I understand you cater weddings as well as merchandise bridal gowns and accessories."

This was it! Bandy could almost taste the success. After all this time.

"That we do, Mrs. Gilchrist. Bandy's Bridal Boutique offers a full service for the entire wedding, from the gown for Nan, the attire for her wedding party, right through your flower needs—plus the most elegant and memorable reception you could ever want. All customized to your specifications, of course."

Bandy had no need to exaggerate. She'd been producing exactly that for brides of Pembrocke and the surrounding areas for almost eight years. Quite successfully.

"Mm, I see. May we make an appointment for you to meet with Nan and me in our home to discuss your services?"

"Certainly. Please hold a moment while I speak with my appointment secretary." Calmly, Bandy pressed the hold button and waited, smiling to herself. She reached up to unclasp the barrette from the back of her curly hair and shook her head, relishing the looser, more free feeling.

For a moment she studied the framed scrap of paper hanging on her wall above her desk. When she had first started her business in her father's garage, he had written out Proverbs 16:3 on a sheet of his old letterhead and given it to her. The words scrawled out in his bold handwriting, "Commit thy works unto the Lord, and thy thoughts shall be established," had meant a great deal to her over the past few years. Surely that's what was happening now—the Lord was establishing her thoughts, making real the dreams she'd had for so long.

She smiled and clicked back into the open line. "I have an opening tomorrow evening, Mrs. Gilchrist. How does seven-thirty sound?"

"Perfect. The address is 127 Enderlin Drive. Please be prompt."

"One twenty-seven Enderlin Drive." Bandy repeated, writing it neatly on the pad. "I'll be there."

Her hand rested on the phone after she hung up, and she sat staring at it for a time. Enderlin Drive—one of the broad tree-lined avenues that meandered through Harwood Heights, the exclusive district of Pembrooke where the large old homes and the "old" money was located. Bandy wasn't sure if the Gilchrists were in the *core* of Pembrooke's high society, but if not, they were close enough to know all that was going on.

Bandy had taken a sizable risk by moving the shop from the small shopping center where it had been before to this high-rent district. But her dream had always been to be an exclusive shop catering to high income clientele. She'd studied other nationally acclaimed stores carefully, and she had noticed that once the market was secured in one community, clients would begin to come from far points, due to the elite nature of the shop. Bandy had visited extensively with a store owner in New Orleans whose clientele now included celebrities from New York and Los Angeles, and Bandy dared to have dreams that were just as lofty.

Perhaps one day her shop would be housed in a renovated Southern mansion—a unique location all its own. There would be a sweeping drive flanked by sprawling live oaks and tall straight cedars, laced with delicate Spanish moss. No doubt she could probably find such a place—but to find such a place that was zoned for business would be an absolute miracle. Southerners were picky about their old mansions, and most were designated as state museums or converted to a bed and breakfast. She could still dream, though; who knew what might happen?

But first, she thought as she returned to straightening the messy desk, she had to make a go of it in Harwood Heights. Recently she'd seen a rash of articles in her business magazines about the inefficiencies of a cluttered desk. Such articles always gave her a guilty pang. She felt she was doing just fine in the clutter, thank you. But then she would wonder how much more efficient she might be if everything were in its proper place. Secretly, she hoped the persons who wrote such articles had desk tops that were stacked high with junk.

Methodically, she sorted through the papers and made neater, more organized stacks. Under a fat trade magazine she found the worn, blue leather Bible which had belonged to her mother. Bandy pulled it out and ran her fingers over the soft edges of the yellowed pages.

At one time, the pages had been crisp and white, their edges gold, but no longer. Her mother had made marks, underlines, notes, and smudges through long years of loving wear. That Bible had been constantly by her mother's side during the last days before she died.

Bandy has been only sixteen at the time, a difficult time to lose a mother. Later, her father had suggested she have the Bible rebound, but she loved the floppy worn feel. She loved touching the very cover her mother had touched. She placed it on the shelf above her desk where it would be handy to grab when she needed it.

As she turned, her eye was caught by another reminder of her mother and father. On the credenza was her parents' wedding picture. Caven O'Sullivan had been a dashing, handsome, young, red-haired Irishman. She could well understand how her mother had fallen in love with him.

Bandy placed a stack of catalogs beside the picture and then picked up the frame to study the couple more closely, though she'd looked at the picture a thousand times before. She touched the smiling faces with her fingertips. The sharp pain of losing them both had diminished into a dull ache that never seemed to go away. How she missed her father's wise business counsel; she missed her mother's tender spiritual counsel just as much. She set the picture back in its place and sighed. No time for self pity.

Slipping her stockinged feet back into her pumps, she strolled out of her office to Denise's desk. Her secretary's desk, she noticed, was as neat as the magazine articles said it should be.

From the enclosed mezzanine offices, Bandy could look out the one-way windows and survey the activities in the shop below. Ellen was helping a young customer, who was dressed in one of the newer gowns, to step up the pale blue carpeted steps to the circular mirrored area. The girl was obviously overwhelmed at her reflection, and Bandy could almost hear her gasp.

Once she saw that Ellen had everything under control, she sat down in the chair opposite Denise's desk. Her secretary glanced up. "Well? Was it the right Gilchrist family?"

"It sure was. I believe our little shop has finally been noticed in Harwood Heights. I'm expected at 127 Enderlin Drive tomorrow evening at seven-thirty."

Denise punched a few more numbers into the computer accounting program. "You hadn't begun to doubt had you? About making it here in this area?" She kept her eyes on the bright color monitor.

"Doubt? What an awful word!" Bandy gave a little laugh to discount the idea. But the account still wasn't in the bag. Mrs. Gilchrist simply wanted to discuss matters. *Had* Bandy been doubting? She'd tried hard to keep up her strong semblance of confidence, but after all these months, they were still doing mostly smaller, middle-income weddings in homes and in the suburban churches. Maybe she had been having a few niggling doubts.

Carefully, she changed the subject. "I noticed you were running the camcorder for Mr. Brockhurst Saturday at the wedding. I didn't know you had experience in photography."

Denise looked up and her brown eyes took on a little sparkle. "Wasn't that Alan just the cutest thing? I found out he's kin to the Longmonts of Biloxi."

Denise said the name as though any fool should know who she was referring to. But Bandy did not. "And who are the Longmonts of Biloxi?"

She knew what was coming next. Denise raised her dark brows. "You don't know? Why I thought everyone knew about the Longmonts. I keep forgetting you're not from here." She gave a dramatic pause. "The newspaper barons of Mississippi. All them Longmonts have been running newspapers for about as long as there's been a South, I suppose."

"That long, huh?" Bandy commented absently. It figured. Mr. Brockhurst was a spoiled child of some wealthy newspaper magnate. He certainly filled the role. "But you and the camera. Was this just beginner's luck? He just handed you the camera and trusted you with it?"

Denise gave a trilling little laugh. "Mercy me, no. I've done a little photography before."

"How little?"

"I was a photographer's assistant for a time."

Bandy shook her head in disbelief. "You were a photographer's assistant and you never told me?"

"You never asked."

This remark was discarded by Bandy as just another comment stemming from Southern female mentality. "Do you have enough photography savvy to help update our catalogs?"

Denise's eyes widened. "Catalogs? What's wrong with our catalogs? Why, they sure look good enough to me."

"Other than the fact that they're about two years old, out of date, and originally done by rank amateur, I guess nothing. For Harwood Heights, I need something current and professional."

"Oh, I didn't know." Denise's voice went soft as though suddenly the ineffective, out-of-date catalogs were all her fault.

Bandy bristled. How could this intelligent woman melt from a crackerjack accountant one moment into a lump of humble, apologetic female the next? Bandy was not only bewildered but irritated. "You didn't have to know, Denise. That's my department. I'm asking if you can remedy the situation."

"Me?" Privately, Bandy marveled that she didn't say, "Li'l ole me?" Denise shook her head. "Good heavens, no. I was just a measly assistant. I'm sure you'd need inside shots, right? That means precise lighting techniques. That's tricky. Lighting and shadows are real tricky. I could never do that. But why don't you ask that nice Mr. Brockhurst? He's real professional. I know he'd be glad to work with us."

Bandy caught the word "us." She shook her head. "I don't think so. I probably can't afford him anyway. Surely there are other good photographers in town."

Denise turned back to her computer. "You didn't like him, did you?"

"What makes you say that?"

"Woman's intuition," she said, as though that explained everything. "It wasn't his fault his assistant was a clumsy little kid. He was awful sorry about the mishaps."

Bandy wanted to make the point that Mr. Alan Brockhurst had the freedom to choose a competent assistant *and* stress the fact that Hayden was not a little kid, but she refrained. "Whether or not I like Mr. Brockhurst has nothing to do with the subject at hand."

Thankfully, the phone buzzer sounded, preventing Bandy from getting herself into more hot water. She was now sorry she'd even mentioned the subject of photography to Denise.

"It's Gena," Denise announced. "She wants you in the back."

"She's probably finished with the flowers for the Taylor girl and wants a standing ovation. Tell her I'll be right down."

Denise relayed the message, hung up the phone, and gave a slight smile. "If that little gal were any more encouraged, she'd go into orbit."

Bandy tried to envision Gena's reaction at being called a "little gal." Bandy stood to her feet. "I wish I had half her energy and maybe a third of her creativity." She paused a moment, as the thought crossed her mind to bring up the subject of Denise's working relationship with Gena, but just as quickly she dismissed the idea. Somehow, this didn't seem like the right time. Instead she said, "By the way, I'll need our latest profit and loss statement as soon as you can get it to me."

A look briefly crossed Denise's face which bordered on embarrassment. Bandy wondered what she'd done to cause her secretary to feel uncomfortable. "Is there a problem?"

"I had asked to get off a little early this afternoon."

Bandy slapped her forehead. "Goofy me. I totally forgot. Doctor's appointment?"

Denise rubbed her jaw. "Dentist," she said, wrinkling her nose.

"By all means, go. I always wait until the pain is excruciating. Can I have the report in the morning?"

Denise shut down the computer. "First thing," she promised as she slipped into her suit jacket, grabbed her matching handbag, and ran down the stairs which led to the shop.

*Goodness*, Bandy mused as she moved toward the back stairs, *what a fast exit*. She pushed open the heavy door and stepped out onto the wide iron catwalk that surrounded the warehouse portion of the building.

The storage area was what originally sold her on this location. She needed the space for storing her catering supplies. In the beginning she had rented such items, but slowly she had built up her own inventory of punch bowls, flatware, platters and servers, ranging from the most casual styles to the most formal.

On the floor below were racks of gowns, dresses, crinolines, and veils. After she and Millie had come back from market, new shipments of inventory had been arriving on a regular basis. As she made her way down the metal stairway to Gena's corner workshop, the sight of her well-stocked inventory filled Bandy with satisfaction.

She and Gena had carried most of the supplies up these metal steps themselves. She wondered if Brian might be a prospective candidate to help them more through the upcoming school year. But then, he was on the university football team. Obviously a busy guy.

She stepped lightly down the stairs and around the corner to the door of the workshop and gave a light tap. The door was open, and Gena was there in the midst of all her creative genius. The spacious, well-lit workroom was strewn with silk flowers, ribbons and lace. Gena's favorite Christian posters plastered the walls.

Gena worked mostly with silks, but when fresh flowers were ordered, Bandy had contracted with a local florist to allow Gena to work in their shop to fill the order. Her father would have been proud of this set up, she reflected. He'd always told her she had a good business head.

Gena looked up from her work, then wordlessly held up a massive bridal bouquet in pinks, lavenders, and pure white, with cascading satin ribbons and touches of frothy baby's breath. "That's the most beautiful one yet," Bandy told her. "How do you do it?" She reached out to take the delicate arrangement and ran her fingers down one of the silky ribbons. "You just keep outdoing yourself."

The girl blushed slightly and waved off the compliments. Bandy doubted that Gena understood what a skilled craftsperson she really was. "You're ahead of schedule on this order," Bandy said. Carefully, she grasped the bouquet's handle with flat hands and held it close to her waist, as she taught all her brides to do. At times, in the midst of all this wedding mania, she had to wonder if she would ever be holding her own bouquet and walking the aisle. She shook away the pesky thought. "How're you coming on the Johnstons' order?"

"I've been on the phone with Sara almost every day." Gena's young face revealed concern. "She's doing the usual—trying to please Granny, Cousin Ida, Great Aunt Harriet, and Mom, all at the same time."

Bandy smiled her understanding and handed back the bouquet. She too had worked diplomatically with brides to draw them out and help them realize that the wedding did not belong to the entire family. "So what stage are you in now?"

Gena gave a little chuckle. "The stage where she gasped at the photo of the theme we did last year for Margie Nichols. At least now I know what she *truly* wants."

"Hm. The photos, huh? They're a great help, aren't they?"

"Well, you know the old adage, 'A picture's worth a thousand words.'"

"But our albums are so amateurish. And our catalogs are

horribly outdated," Bandy said almost to herself. "I must get busy and get them redone."

"Amateurish or not, they did the trick with Sara Johnston."

"By the way," Bandy said, still thinking about the catalogs, "I have an appointment tomorrow on Enderlin Drive."

"Terrific. Up there in the ritzy district, right?"

"Ritzy is as good a word as any. Do you think you could work with those folks?"

"Work with them?" Gena shrugged. "Sure. They're just people, aren't they? No different than anyone else."

Bandy stifled a giggle which came out like a snort, then she gave Gena a little hug. "That's what I needed—a fresh outlook on the situation. Of course they're people. They're people who need exquisite weddings, just like every bride does. And. . ."

". . .and we're just the ones who can do it," Gena finished for her.

"Have I said that before?"

"A few thousand times."

"Imagine that." They both laughed. Bandy started for the door. "I'm on my way downtown to the post office so I'm leaving a bit early. See you tomorrow."

Gena gave a little wave and turned back to her work. As she did, the wall phone jangled and she answered it. "For you." She extended the phone to Bandy.

Since Denise was gone, no one was there to screen her calls. Otherwise, Bandy would have never answered it.

"Alan Brockhurst here, Miss O'Sullivan," the deep masculine voice sounded on the other end. "I was calling to see how you're doing after your fall Saturday. I hope there were no after effects."

*My* fall, she thought to herself. Strange wording, seeing as how the mishap had been *his* assistant's fault. She wanted to say, "Oh, you mean the fall your clumsy helper gave me."

Instead, she carefully chose her words. "After two nights of Millie's liniment rubs and sleeping on the heating pad, I seem to be faring fine. Thank you for asking."

She sensed he gave a little sigh of relief. "Good. I'm grateful to hear that. That was our first time working together. . ."

"Obviously."

"With a little time, a little training, I'm sure Hayden will work out fine. He's just young."

Bandy couldn't agree with that remark, so she let it pass in silence.

"I have something I'd like to talk to you about, Bandy. May I call you Bandy?"

"You may. So talk—I'm listening." Somehow she sensed he wanted more than to check on her state of health.

"Not now. I mean, not on the phone. How about dinner together Friday evening? I can pick you up after work."

"I don't think so. I'm very busy." Whatever could this man want to talk to her about?

"I assure you, I won't take much of your time. I'm leaving town for a week or so. Newspaper assignment. I was hoping to talk with you before I leave."

So he wasn't just a wedding or portrait photographer. How could he juggle both? she wondered. "Really, I. . ."

"Just dinner. I can pick you up at your boutique, or I can meet you somewhere."

Boutique? This man called her shop a boutique. No man she knew ever called it a boutique. Even Jordan still called it the "store." She felt her resistance softening. "Well, I suppose I could."

"Great! Pick you up there?"

Suddenly, she remembered Denise's rapt attention to this man, and she felt an inexplicable need to keep him away from the premises. "Not here. This place is such a zoo. My house would be better. I could rest a moment and change."

She quickly gave him the address.

Gena's expression clearly showed the question she didn't ask, as Bandy handed back the phone.

"Just a friend," Bandy said. Did she want the whole world to know she was going to spend time with this guy?

"Right. A tall, blond friend who was at the wedding Saturday?"

Bandy felt herself blush. Why on earth should she be blushing? She hadn't made a date with the man, only a business meeting. "Keep it quiet, will you?"

"I didn't hear a thing."

"Thanks."

"Incidentally, I think Alan Brockhurst is gorgeous."

Bandy closed the door to the workroom and hurried away as though she hadn't heard. She was in her car and halfway to the post office before she remembered Friday night was her dinner engagement with Jordan. Her grip tightened on the steering wheel. Now what was she going to do?

# *five*

Her mind was in a dither as she pulled up in front of the post office and ran inside with her packages. She was so preoccupied she wasn't looking as she came flying back out; as a result, she nearly tripped over a long dog leash. There in front of the post office was Jordan, with his beautiful blond Labrador, Goldie.

With quick action, Jordan gave the leash slack and grabbed her arm to help keep her aright. "In a hurry, Bandy? I thought the work day was over. You can relax now."

Bandy gave a weak smile, as Goldie gave little whines of recognition and slobbered on her hand. "Oh, hello, Jordan. You too, Goldie." She patted the dog's wide head and stroked her strong, thick neck. "I guess I never slow down."

Jordan smiled. "I can attest to that."

Should she say something about Friday night—or let it go until she had thought about it some more? Surely she should be able to break a date with Jordan without hurting their relationship. After all, he didn't own her. But on the other hand, she didn't want to offend him. Quickly, she prayed for wisdom.

"Where are you and Goldie off to?" The dog whined at the sound of her name, and her wagging tail bumped against Bandy's leg.

"Stay, Goldie," Jordan said firmly, and the dog obediently moved back beside her master and sat down on her broad haunches. "We waited for the heat to lift before coming down to pay bills and pick up a few office supplies."

Although Pembrooke had its share of suburban shopping

centers, some loyalists, like Jordan, still insisted on doing most of their business on Main Street. He particularly enjoyed patronizing the old office supply store which still had oak hardwood floors. Jordan liked it, he said, because it still "smelled" like an office supply store should smell. She remembered he had said the same thing about the book store as well, and he had once chided Bandy for ordering her office supplies from the new company in town.

Bandy fanned herself with her hand. "If the heat has lifted, I'd not noticed," she joked, still thinking about Friday night. She could simply tell him she had other plans. But what if he asked her about those plans? She couldn't lie. But then, why shouldn't she just tell him the truth? Why should she feel so embarrassed and uncomfortable about a mere business meeting?

"I should have said when the heat 'lessened' rather than 'lifted,' right?" Jordan smiled. "So, how's business up on the hill?"

"Funny you should ask," she said, resenting his description of her location, but glad for the distraction. "I have an appointment with Mrs. Edward Gilchrist tomorrow evening at their home. Her daughter Nan is getting married." She watched closely for his initial reaction, and she saw what she thought was a flicker of recognition. "You know them?"

"I know them. Rather I should say, they are known."

That remark answered her question better than any other could have. If they were "known," they were in contact with others who were "known." In spite of the heavy heat, she felt a quick chill of excitement.

The tower clock on the courthouse chimed, and she jumped. "Goodness, I need to be getting along. Millie will wonder what happened to me."

"Give her my best," Jordan said, as he gave a slight tug on Goldie's leash.

"I will." She turned to go.

"Bandy," he called over his shoulder. "Don't forget Friday night. I'm inviting the new English professor."

She was at her car door, but she could still stop him and tell him no. Oh, phooey, she would rather call Alan and break off the meeting with him instead. After all, she didn't even know the guy, and she had no business she was interested in discussing with him. She didn't owe him anything after all.

"I won't forget," she called back to Jordan.

Methodically, she drove the mile or so from the center of town and turned into the residential district toward the lovely, old, two-story home her father had so wisely, and so generously, deeded to her before his death.

Even after several long heat spells, flowers bloomed thick in this neighborhood, and, for the most part, in all the neighborhoods in Pembrooke, a community full of gardeners and flower-lovers. Now as she drove by house after house, she saw sprinklers spurting and spraying in every yard.

The beautiful flowers were one of the first things that fascinated her about living in the South—blue columbine, pink foxglove, golden coreopsis, creamy daisies, snow-white hydrangeas, and, of course, roses. Hundreds of roses everywhere. They came on early and stayed so much later than in her home state of Massachusetts.

She was deep in thought as she drove under the canopy of massive trees that dripped Spanish moss over the shady street. One moment she was sure she would call Alan and cancel her meeting with him Friday night. But then curiosity overtook her, and she was sure she should back out of the cookout at Jordan's with all the stuffy professors. For the millionth time, she wondered what Alan Brockhurst wanted to talk with her about. Much to her surprise and embarrassment, every time she thought of him she saw his blue eyes and the boyish shock of blond hair falling across his forehead. How silly of her. One would think she was becoming as man-crazy as Denise.

As Bandy turned in the driveway, she noticed that Waldo had obviously been working on their flower beds again. Everything looked trimmed and clipped, with not a weed in sight.

Waldo was one of Millie's cousins. Shirt-tail cousin, of course. The elderly man had been a much-sought-after gardener and yard man in his younger days. Now he tended only a few residences. She and Millie were lucky to have their yard benefit from his talent and creativity.

Bandy pulled her car into the small garage at the back of the property. Although there were outside back stairs to her upstairs living quarters, she seldom used them. Millie never minded her coming and going through the front, even though the downstairs was Millie's domain.

As soon as she entered the front door, she knew Waldo must be staying for supper. A fruit tray was in the center of the dining room table, with places set for three. A tantalizing aroma of grilled chicken floated out to meet her.

Bandy was thrilled to see Millie enjoying her own place. She remembered how her friend had argued when Bandy first suggested that she live here with Bandy.

"That's your house," Millie had protested. "You don't need any old widow lady cluttering up the place. Why should you squeeze yourself into the upstairs when you can have the whole house?"

Bandy only laughed. The upstairs was huge. The entire house was huge. In fact, a family of six had rented it before Bandy had taken over residence several years ago, and they had had plenty of room. So Bandy ignored Millie's protests, and had the upstairs remodeled—by another one of Millie's cousins who did carpentry work—and added a small kitchenette area. She seldom needed it, though, since Millie insisted on cooking for the two of them. Other than the nights Bandy worked late, they nearly always took supper together.

Bandy felt she had the best of both worlds. A private living space—far away from her stepmother Claire—plus the motherly company of Millie. The arrangement had turned out to be even more perfect than she'd first hoped.

"Bandy, is that you?" came Millie's call from the kitchen.

"No. Just your friendly bill collector." Bandy went through the dining room into the kitchen and gave Millie a hug.

"Not *my* bill collector," Millie countered with a laugh. "Since some particular person, who shall remain nameless, sees to it that I live rent-free, and still pays my salary, the bill collectors ignore me."

"That's just the way it should be. Where's Waldo?"

"Now how did you know Waldo was here?"

"I'm a sleuth! Actually it's pretty obvious. The flower beds look like a page out of *Southern Living*, and the table is set for three."

"I forgot I'd set the table already," Millie said with a chuckle. "The yard and flower beds do look spiffy, don't they? We're so blessed. Well, hurry yourself and get changed and come eat with us."

"I wouldn't miss it. I smell that wonderful grilled chicken!"

Bandy always enjoyed visits with Waldo. He was more like the community historian than a gardener. He'd probably been in the back yards of the best places in town.

After the blessing was said over the food, and the fruit tray was being passed, Millie asked, "How was business today, Bandy?"

"Why, I thought you'd never ask," Bandy retorted, remembering the phone conversation with Mrs. Gilchrist. "I have an appointment on Enderlin Drive tomorrow evening with Mrs. Edward Gilchrist."

"Well, that's nice, Bandy." Millie smiled, though Bandy had hoped she would look more impressed. Millie bit into a slice of melon. After a moment she asked, "From up on Harwood Heights?"

Bandy nodded eagerly, but Waldo gave a little grunt as he pushed his white bushy mustache with the back of his weathered hand. "Whatcha want to be meeting with them Gilchrists for?" He cut himself another piece of honeydew melon and chewed vigorously.

"She may be my client, Waldo. Do you know them?"

"You know better than to ask Waldo that question." Millie passed the platter of grilled chicken breasts.

Bandy looked back at the old man. "You do know them?"

"I know pert near everybody in them hills, and mostly how they got there."

"Meaning?"

Waldo speared a chicken breast, looked at the several left on the platter, and decided to spear a second one. "Meaning, whether it was honest or dishonest. Whether they're true Southerners or if they was Yankee-helpers after the war. . ."

Bandy started to interrupt, but he lifted his hand. "Or if they *was* Yankees," he finished.

Bandy smiled; she often wondered if the old man thought of her as a Yankee, but she never dared ask. "Frankly, I don't care how they got there," she said. "Before long, they may all be clients of mine."

"I can't see why you'd want 'em," Waldo said past a mouthful of chicken. "Throw 'em in a bag with a bunch of regular folk, shake 'em up, dump 'em out. I swear, you couldn't tell one from another."

"Don't swear," Millie chided.

"Aw, you know what I mean, Millie." He gave a wave of a wrinkled hand. "Always seem to me like them no-'count folk have mush instead of gray matter, and ice water in their veins."

Bandy gave an involuntary shudder. This conversation wasn't doing anything for her courage. "People are just people," she said, repeating Gena's comment. "Isn't that what you just said?"

"What I meant was they're no better than the rest of us." For a moment, Waldo gave his full attention to a big helping of fried okra. "Might be those folk up on that hill are a sight worse, though."

"Don't pay him no mind, Bandy," Millie said. "You'll be fine tomorrow night. I'm sure Mrs. Gilchrist will be quite impressed."

"I wish my catalogs were more current."

Millie reached over and patted her hand. "*You* do the selling, dear, not the catalogs."

"We need sharp clear photos of the great work Gena's been creating lately," Bandy went on as though Millie had not spoken. "And the last few cakes you've done—each one is more breathtaking than the last. And your party platters. We should have photos of all of them."

"Why not call a few photographers and get estimates?" Millie suggested.

"I don't think that kind of talent is in Pembrooke." Bandy dumped two spoonsful of sugar in a crystal glass, stirred it thoughtfully, and took a sip of the mint-flavored ice tea. "The lighting needs to be just right. The background too. Coloring, textures. It's a different kind of photography, that's all. I need a real professional. I might have to have someone come up from Jackson. But I just can't afford it right now."

"Why not ask that nice young fellow we met last Saturday?"

"Alan Brockhurst?"

"That's his name. Alan."

Bandy shook her head. "Funny, Denise suggested the same thing. But I hardly think that 'nice young fellow' would be a likely candidate. He seemed more like a rank beginner, stumbling around with his clumsy little helper. And then handing the camcorder to Denise."

"Did you ever think maybe he could put you in touch with someone? Surely photographers know other photographers."

"Hm. Perhaps."

Waldo was clearly bored with the way the conversation was going, and took advantage of the lull to tell Millie more of the latest gossip he'd heard over the back fences of Pembrooke.

Later, after Waldo was gone and Bandy was helping Millie clean up, she mentioned to Millie about Alan's invitation for Friday night.

"Well now, how nice. You getting together with that fine young man."

"First of all, it's only business." At least Bandy hoped it was only business, though she couldn't guess what business Alan could have with her. "And secondly, the big problem is, I've made a date with Jordan that night. He's having several professors over for a cookout. I even promised to take a few of your goodies for them."

Millie scrubbed off a plate before placing it in the dishwasher. "And we all know what a rollicking good time you always have with them professors. Right?"

Bandy chuckled. "They're not so bad."

"Not so bad, huh? My vote is to go with the cute, tall fellow with the pretty, gold hair. I can take the goodies over to Jordan's house and keep your promise."

"Oh, would you?"

Millie gave a sweet smile. "I surely would."

Bandy leveled a look at her elderly friend. "Millie, I don't know what you're thinking, but please keep in mind this is only a business meeting."

"I hear you, honey. And I got it in my mind. Don't you worry. Sure would be nice to see you come up out of that rut you got yourself in."

"Rut? What rut?"

"That rut of working too hard and then just hanging around with Professor Wyler. He don't seem to know what he wants half the time. Beautiful sweet girl like you. Why, I'd have thought he would have proposed to you long before now."

Bandy hung a wet towel on the rack above the sink and turned to go. "Millie, I'm perfectly happy in what I'm doing and where I am in my life." She gave Millie a little hug. "I'll see you in the morning."

"I'll still be glad to see you get out of that rut," came Millie's barely-audible mumble as Bandy headed for the stairs. "You're so busy, you don't even teach Sunday School or attend Bible study anymore."

Bandy felt a stab of guilt whenever Millie pointed out how she'd backed out of her church work. But there were so many demands at the boutique's new location. Although she'd never admit it to Millie, even her own personal quiet times with God had suffered. She just didn't have the time anymore. Surely God understood that once everything returned to an even keel, she'd jump right back in again.

Now it was time to call Jordan and break that date.

# six

Bandy showered first and changed into her nightgown and slippers. Millie was right in one way, she mused as she brushed her red curls to a sheen. Jordan did act indecisively at times, in bigger ways than just never knowing whether to keep his glasses on or off. And yet she enjoyed being with him. He was a sweet, likeable guy.

Picking up the phone, she settled on the soft cushions in the window seat. Outside, the moon was playing softly on the stone-flagged steps that curved around the flower beds to the gazebo. In the semi-darkness, the brilliant colors were softened to pastel shades. Saturday mornings, she and Millie enjoyed eating breakfast in the gazebo, surrounded by the floral fragrances and the many birds who gathered at the nearby feeder. Bandy sighed; Friday night came before Saturday morning, and she needed to call Jordan. She punched in his number, still trying to figure out what to say to him.

He must have been sitting on top of his phone, for he answered after the very first ring. "Bandy. What a surprise. Didn't I just talk to you?"

"You did at that. Are you busy with lessons?"

"Always. Summer school," he said. "What a misnomer. The very essence of the word summer denotes slowing down and relaxing. But actually, summer classes are more concentrated and fast-paced. I seem to have triple the amount of papers to grade."

"You're supposed to use hunt and guess tests—the ones that take only a few minutes to grade." Those were always her favorite kind when she was taking business courses at the junior college.

Jordan gave a little grunt. "So I'm told by some of my colleagues. I maintain, though, that a student will never learn the material if we teach them to guess and not to dig for the real answers. But I'm a prisoner of my own devices. The desk top is now filled with five-page reports, all complete with end notes and bibliographies."

"When do you have to have them graded?"

"Tomorrow morning." She heard him sigh.

"Well then, you need to get back to work. I just called to tell you I can't make it to the get-together at your house Friday night."

"Oh, really? What's up?"

Bandy strained to hear a tone of disappointment in his voice. She wasn't sure if it was there or not. "I hate to renege after I've committed, but I have a business appointment that's suddenly come up."

"Business before pleasure, they always say. Whoever 'they' are." She could hear papers shuffling as he spoke.

"Right. Well, Millie offered to deliver a few goodies to your house anyway."

"You don't say." His voice brightened. "That's gracious of her. Tell her I'd be extremely appreciative. And I'm sure all the other guests will feel the same."

A moment of awkward silence slipped by. She thought he might say he was sorry she couldn't be there. Or even that they would make another date for another time. Nothing. "Give Goldie a pat for me," she said at last.

"I'll do it. She's right here under my feet." More papers shuffled.

"I guess I'd better let you get back to your work."

"There's a ton of it."

"Sorry to let you down about Friday night."

"Don't worry your little red head a bit about that. Hope

your business appointment goes well."

"Thanks."

She clicked off the cordless and laid it down beside her. So much for that. Now she knew why she'd been so bothered by making the call. She hadn't been afraid he'd be upset, but rather just the opposite—that he wouldn't be. She rose up from the window seat and strolled out on the balcony that led to the back steps. Pink and lavender petunias overflowed the hanging planters and filled the night air with their heavy perfume. She leaned against the railing and heaved a big sigh.

For all the time she'd known Jordan, she'd never known him to get excited or over-react about anything. Surely that was good, wasn't it? That aspect of his personality, she'd always told herself, was what she liked most about him—his easygoing manner and quiet demeanor. But tonight she had, for a split second, wanted to hear him get a little upset. Upset enough to say something like, "Oh, Bandy, I'm so sorry you can't make it. It won't be the same without you there. Are you *sure* you can't come?"

Maybe Millie was right about her being in a rut.

❧

The drive to the Gilchrist home flooded Bandy with memories. Her father had been crazy about azaleas, and nowhere in Pembrooke were there more azaleas than in Harwood Heights. In the early spring, in the peak of the blooming season, he had made almost daily trips up here in the hills to drive about and drink in the profusion of pink, white, red, and scarlet blossoms of the azaleas. Bandy had often accompanied him.

One stretch of road she remembered in particular was lined with massive sprawling live oaks, underplanted with banks of azalea bushes. Her father never tired of gazing at the tall curling branches draped with Spanish moss forming a canopy over the colorfully lined roadway.

"You have to give the Southerners credit," he'd say. "They sure know how to make a Northerner's heart melt."

Bandy often wondered if her father had wished he'd been born south of the Mason-Dixon line. In fact, she thought perhaps that's why he'd married Claire—because she was so dyed-in-the-wool Southern. But Bandy had never pressed him to explain his feelings for Claire, and now she had lost the chance to ask him.

Although the azaleas were not in bloom now, the drive was still magnificent. Bandy turned in the long, narrow driveway at number 127. The homes here, as Waldo had explained to her, were mostly built by northern industrialists who came South after the war to make their fortune off the misfortunes of the wounded South. Although not antebellum in style, the houses still had a magnificent grandeur. The sweeping lawn of the Gilchrist mansion was terraced, neatly trimmed in formal walkways and closely clipped shrubberies. A small bridge spanned a quiet lagoon that perfectly mirrored the flowers and trees growing on the banks. A fountain sounded its soft gurgling in the background.

Bandy felt her hands growing clammy as she pulled up in front of the broad entrance. Suddenly her car, her clothes, and even her catalogs seemed paltry.

"They're just people," she whispered as she gathered the catalogs in her arms. "Lord, help me to remember they're just people. They need the services I have to offer. And I have the best in the city." The dialogue with herself continued under her breath as she climbed out of the car and up the wide, brick-lined steps to the front door. As she rang the bell, she admired the ripples of lavender phlox spilling over stone-lined flower beds.

She fully expected a butler of some sort to greet her, but it was Mrs. Gilchrist herself who opened the door. She was a tall, graying woman with a stern expression. After a quick, reserved introduction, Bandy was led through the vast front entryway. Their footsteps clicked and echoed on the terrazzo floor tiles. By the second or third turn through the hallways, Bandy was sure she'd never be able to find her way out alone.

Mrs. Gilchrist led her to a sunny atrium overlooking a formal garden. Their footsteps softened as they descended the few carpeted stairs to the sunken room. A brightly colored oriental rug covered half of the sunny room. Bandy glanced around at the array of urns, fragile statuettes, ornate tables, old books, and artifacts, obviously collected from the far corners of the world.

Brusquely, but not unkindly, Mrs. Gilchrist directed her to a wing chair covered in floral fabric. The cheery colors and friendly tone of the room put Bandy at ease. Somehow her imagination had envisioned a dark, moldy library with damask draperies drawn shut. But this room had no draperies at all, allowing sunshine and light to fill the room from two walls of windows.

"Nan will be down in a moment," Mrs. Gilchrist said as she sat down nearby. "We're eager to get her plans made as early as possible. I detest having to rush or hurry." She drew a long cigarette from a gold case and proceeded to light it from an oriental brass lighter sitting on the marble coffee table. Carefully and slowly she blew smoke away from Bandy's direction.

Bandy was somewhat allergic to cigarette smoke; she wondered if she would be rude to mention this fact or if she should disguise her distress. Before she could decide, a portly woman came in with a large tray carrying two pitchers, several glasses, and a smaller plate of assorted crackers and cookies. The tray was placed on the marble table among the books, magazines, and vases of cut garden flowers.

"Thank you, Madge," Mrs. Gilchrist said. "Lemonade or iced tea?" she asked Bandy.

"Lemonade is fine," Bandy said.

As Madge poured the drinks and set them on coasters, Bandy remembered how Millie used to wait on Claire's guests. While Bandy realized such an occupation was no dishonor, still she never felt Millie was treated fairly by Claire. Seeing Millie have to obey Claire's commands had increased Bandy's determination to help Millie find a better life, and Bandy was glad she'd done so. But Claire had never forgiven her.

Bandy chose two small crackers from the plate offered to her. "When is the wedding date?" she asked, feeling the need to get down to business.

"November." Mrs. Gilchrist waved Madge away. "I had hoped for a spring wedding, but you know how impetuous youth can be. Nan wants it in the fall."

"Has the engagement been announced? Is an announcement party planned?"

"Sort of." Mrs. Gilchrist nibbled on a cracker and, thankfully, left the cigarette to smolder in the ashtray. She gave a slight smile. "Of course most of our friends know. We've talked about the engagement party. Nan's not sure. . ."

"I'm not sure about what?" A young woman breezed into the room, her face as fresh and bright as the flowers that bloomed outside the windows.

"Oh, hello, Nan," her mother said. "I was just commenting that you weren't yet convinced there needed to be an engagement announcement party."

Nan rolled her eyes and sat down on the brocade couch opposite them. "As if I had a choice."

"Nan, we always. . ."

"I know, I know. We always. So I must always, too!"

The stern Mrs. Gilchrist let a crack show in her demeanor.

"Please, Nan. Not in front of Ms. O'Sullivan."

Nan's face brightened. "O'Sullivan? You're from the boutique in the Heights Shopping Center?"

Bandy nodded. "You can call me Bandy."

Nan reached across the broad table to shake Bandy's hand, nearly knocking over a vase of flowers. "Your shop is splendid," she said wrinkling up her nose as she smiled.

"I'm glad you like it."

"But you have more than the shop, Mother told me."

Bandy nodded. "Our boutique services include complete consultation throughout all the wedding planning—from the announcement, showers, and rehearsal dinners, to the very wedding itself. We can do the flowers—either fresh or silk, catering, and all the dresses. What we don't have in stock we can easily order."

Nan's eyes lit with interest, and Bandy relaxed as they moved into discussing the things she knew and loved. She pulled out the catalogs and showed the masterpieces created by both Gena and Millie. Bandy felt sure this job was clinched. And she was elated.

Bandy grabbed her day planner and began marking dates. Before the visit was over, she presented various contracts, and they were duly signed by Nan and her mother.

As Bandy was gathering her things to go, Mrs. Gilchrist surprised her by asking, "Are you familiar with a photographer in town by the name of Alan Brockhurst?"

Bandy hesitated. "Brockhurst? The name sounds familiar. Why?"

"He's kin to the Longmonts from Biloxi."

If Bandy heard that statement one more time, surely she would scream.

"I've heard," Mrs. Gilchrist continued, "that the boy's uncle sent him up here to work with Mr. Griscom at the *Pembrooke Chronicle* as a photojournalist."

Boy? Could this be the same Alan that Bandy had met? Surely he was near thirty.

"But I hear he's doing wedding photography as well." Mrs. Gilchrist crushed out her second half-smoked cigarette. "I've not tried as yet to locate him, but if you hear of his whereabouts would you put us in touch with him? Nan's father and I would like to help out any kin of Rupert Longmont."

"Of course," Bandy said, mulling this information over in her mind. Alan was obviously the offspring of a family somewhat like the Gilchrists. A family who was still looking after him when he was long past the age of being able to care for himself. Bandy wondered how she would feel if she had people going before her, preparing the way, instead of doing all the hard work by herself.

She pushed the thought of Alan Brockhurst out of her mind. As she drove home with the large retainer check in her purse and the signed contracts in her portfolio, she felt light as air. What a marvelous beginning!

Millie was still up when she came in, and Bandy spilled over with the good news. Together they scratched notes of ideas for the engagement party, which would take place in September at the Gilchrist estate.

"Nan seemed to warm up to everything I showed her," Bandy said, still shivering with the excitement.

"And why shouldn't she? We do good work." Millie laughed.

"If they like us, Millie, I know the word will spread. And these are the kinds of people who know people in other cities and states. One day we'll be *the* boutique to come to in the South."

"If it's God's will, it'll come to pass."

"And speaking of knowing other people, Mrs. Gilchrist asked me about Alan Brockhurst."

"I can believe that. I hear he's kin. . ."

". . .to the Longmonts of Biloxi," Bandy blurted out. "Not you too. Does that make him some sort of royalty?"

Millie laughed. "Sort of. The Longmonts not only were war heroes. . ."

"And I don't have to ask which war," Bandy put in with a touch of sarcasm.

"Of course you don't. It's the only war we really know about since it was fought in our back yard." She smiled her soft, loving smile. "Anyway, where was I? Oh, yes, the Longmonts were war heroes and also, by some miracle, they wound up with a fair amount of money after the war which they used to help their fellow citizens who hadn't fared as well. Then they began one of the biggest newspapers in the South. Which has quite a large holding yet today."

"So the Boy Brockhurst is still being pampered by all his kinfolk across the state? How convenient."

"Can a man help what family he's born into?"

Bandy gave a sigh. "I guess not. But it seems pretty unfair at times."

"Since you and I have citizenship in heaven, what should it matter? I'd take the blessings of my Heavenly Father over all the rich kin in Pembrooke."

Bandy felt a pang of shame at Millie's reprimand. She thought of all the blessings the Lord had showered upon her in the past few years. "You're right, Millie. As usual. Forgive my sniveling."

"Forgiven."

"And now, I'd better let you get to bed." Bandy jumped up and headed toward the stairs. From the stairway, she called back. "Millie? It's not wrong to be so excited about such a large account is it?"

"Heavens no! The Word says to be diligent in business, and you are. Just remember to keep your priorities right.

It's okay to make money, but there's things that are more important. Never forget that the Holy Spirit shines through you no matter where you go, no matter what you do. There are plenty of people up in the Heights who desperately need that Light."

"Thanks, Millie."

## seven

At the staff meeting the next morning, while she was reporting the good news about the Gilchrist contract, Bandy decided she wanted to do something for all her staff. They'd worked so hard since the move, and Labor Day weekend was coming up; that would work perfectly as an occasion for a little getaway. She knew her sales clerk Ellen had a family cabin at Swansea Lake, so she asked Ellen if she knew how and where they could rent cabins.

They were all sitting around Bandy's office before the store opened. Millie was present as well, since she always came to the store for the weekly staff meetings.

"Why, I know of a marvelous place," Ellen said. "Are you familiar with the Swannanoa Lodge?"

Bandy shook her head, but Denise said, "Oh, honey, everybody knows about the Swannanoa Lodge. Been there for years. It was a swank hideaway in the thirties and forties for all the rich Yankees. But now it's back in the hands of Southerners who've breathed a breath of life back into it. Just like everything else, the Yankees deserted it when it stopped making tons of money."

Bandy wasn't expecting a history lesson, but she faked a smile of approval. "Sounds like the place we need."

"Our cabin is located a few miles from the lodge," Ellen said. "It's beautiful up there. Picnic grounds, swimming at the lake, paddle boats, float trips down the Swansea tributary."

"Float trip?" Gena's eyes lit up. "Bandy, are we going to

be able to invite guests to this shindig?"

Like a fellow teenager, Denise piped, "That's a great idea. Can we, Boss?"

Bandy hesitated a moment. This hadn't been in her plans. But what was the harm? After all, Ellen's family would be there with her. Bandy glanced at Millie, and Millie gave a slight nod. "Guests will be welcome. . ."

"Awesome!" Gena's smile was wide.

"Ooo, nice," Denise added.

". . .but only if they pay their own way," Bandy finished her sentence. "The boutique can't foot the bill for a mob."

Gena gave a flip of her hand. "No problem."

Denise elbowed Gena in the ribs and gave a little giggle as though the two of them had been bosom buddies forever. "We can handle that. Right, Gena?"

For quite some time Denise had been dating a man who owned the local exterminating company. Bandy had seen him once, and she had been surprised; he was a small man with a bland personality, not at all the sort of man she would have imagined would attract Denise. Filthy rich, though, Millie had said. But he seemed like a non-threatening guest for the weekend. Gena, of course, would want Brian there. Bandy couldn't blame her.

"Ellen, can I count on you to secure these rooms?" Bandy asked.

Ellen was taking notes on her ever-present note pad. "I'd be glad to."

"You can get the names of the guests later. We'll meet up at the lodge on Sunday afternoon and return Monday evening."

"How about having a cookout at our cabin on Labor Day afternoon?" Ellen suggested. "There's plenty of room, and our property goes down to a dock and beach area. I know

John and the boys would love to have y'all come."

"I can help coordinate the food," Millie said to Ellen.

Ellen nodded her agreement.

"Marvelous. Thanks for the invitation, Ellen." Bandy glanced over her clipboard. "Now, that's taken care of, and we need to get on to more important business." The rest of the staff meeting was taken up with discussing the ramifications of the upcoming Gilchrist contract and how it would be handled in the most expeditious manner.

Later, alone in her office, Bandy thought about inviting guests for the Labor Day get-together. Perhaps the idea wasn't such a silly one. Maybe—just maybe—Jordan would want to come. Maybe the romantic surroundings would relax his academic starch. It was a nice thought.

⁊⁊

Bandy stood in front of the mirror in her bedroom, studying the emerald turtleneck dress. She adjusted the bloused waist over the belt. She'd already changed clothes three time trying to decide what to wear—and Alan was due any minute. The evening was so warm, and this dress would be too heavy. Back over her head it came.

From the heap of clothes on her bed, she went back to the hunter-green poet's shirt with the soft shirring and blousey sleeves. To that, she added a long, brightly-flowered skirt, slipped into leather sandals, and was brushing her thick curls when she heard the doorbell. She knew Millie would get it. She grabbed her purse and stopped to take a breath. No sense in running down the stairs like a girl to the prom. Purposely, she slowed her pace.

Alan was standing at the door chatting with Millie when she appeared on the landing. He looked up at her and smiled, a boyish smile—almost a grin—with laughing eyes. As usual his blond hair lay carelessly across his forehead. He was dressed in a pale blue jacket and slacks, his shirt open with no tie.

Although Millie was still talking, his eyes followed Bandy down the stairs. With a polite "hello" and a few amenities to Millie, he was quickly escorting her out the door to his car.

Somehow she had envisioned Alan Brockhurst driving a bright little sports car with a sun roof. Or perhaps even a convertible. Something in the "playboy" line. The practical blue compact surprised her, though it was nearly new and spotlessly clean.

"You're looking mighty pretty tonight, Bandy," he said as he opened the door for her.

"Thank you." She carefully gathered the flowing skirt in before he closed the door.

"Prettier even than I remembered from the wedding that afternoon," he continued as he opened his door and folded his long legs inside. "Although you did look sorta cute all laid out there cold as a cucumber in your pretty frilly dress."

"Please. I'd rather not be reminded." She'd thought his compliment was sincere, but here he was teasing again.

"Hey, it takes a real lady to know how to fall gracefully."

"It takes a real lady not to strangle the one whose fault it was that she fell."

"That too." He gave a little chuckle. "But you might be interested to know that Hayden was with me on another job recently, and there was only one minor mishap. He *is* doing better."

Actually she wasn't at all interested in the problem child named Hayden, and she was beginning to wish she was with Jordan instead of Alan Brockhurst. "That's nice," she managed to say.

He looked over at her with smiling eyes. "Well, actually

there were two, but who's counting?"

Suddenly she realized he was trying to pull her into the joke, and she couldn't help but snicker. "Two and two. What a track record."

"But my aunt in Biloxi is happy. So what else matters? You know how it is with kinfolk."

"Actually, I don't. I seem to be lacking in that area. Or they're not as thick where I come from."

"But I thought Millie. . . Isn't Millie some kin of yours?"

Bandy shook her head. "She's my dear friend, but no relation."

"Don't that beat all. I could have sworn she was an aunt or your father's third cousin once removed, or something. Thick as you two are."

"Any of my father's cousins, removed or otherwise, would be somewhere in New England, and I wouldn't care to spend much time with any of them."

Alan nodded as he let the information sink in. "So why are you living with Miss Millie?"

He steered the car through the winding hills just outside Pembrooke. The air was cooler here than in town. Bandy breathed deeply of the clean pine fragrance. "Actually, Miss Millie lives with me," she explained. "I insisted she take the downstairs because of her arthritic knee."

"Don't that beat all," he repeated. "You two act more like kinfolk than real kinfolk."

"And without a Hayden thrown in."

"Touché." He laughed as though he enjoyed the joke being thrown back at him. His ready laugh was contagious, and Bandy found herself smiling too. He was so different from Jordan who seldom joked about anything.

Alan pulled up in the parking lot of Giustino's Italian Restaurant. Bandy had heard good things about this place, how

the Giustino family had been told they could never make it
in the heart of Dixie, and yet their restaurant was thriving.
Even now, though the hour was late for dinner, the parking
lot was crowded as Alan drove slowly through, searching
for a space to squeeze the little compact.

"Have you eaten here?" he asked as he found the spot he
needed and quickly parked the car.

She shook her head.

"Good. I always like being the first one."

Whatever that was supposed to mean. She didn't ask. He
came around, opened her door, and helped her out.

The rotund man who met them at the door introduced
himself as Papa Giustino. "Welcome, welcome," he said as
he ushered them in with great gusto. "Don't tell me, don't
tell me." He looked them over. "This is your first date together. Right?" He looked up at Alan with a questioning
look, but waited not a moment for his answer. "And so everything must be a little special. I have that right. Right? So
come this way. We have just the thing." He turned to lead
them through the spacious restaurant to the garden terrace
in the back.

Alan looked down at Bandy and stifled a laugh. He took
her hand and tucked it under his elbow. "Let's not break his
bubble. Just a little special, right?"

"I guess a little won't hurt."

"That's the spirit."

By now they were both trying to smother their giggles as
they followed the little man out the back door.

The restaurant was tucked snugly into the side of the hill,
and the back was built out cantilever-style from the hillside. The view was magnificent. They could see clear across
the wooded valley to the next range of hills. Stately pines
grew thick and tall all around the restaurant and flowers

bloomed in pots and planters along the edges of the terrace. Papa Giustino led them to an umbrella-covered table close to the railing.

"The perfect spot, no?"

"Perfect, yes," Alan said, and the older man gave a deep belly laugh.

"I give you the privilege," he said motioning to the chair that would be Bandy's.

Alan quickly stepped around and pulled out the chair for her and gently scooted her up as she was seated. Almost before Alan was seated, large colorful menus were placed in front of them. "Someone will be with you in a moment. Meanwhile," Papa Giustino gave a sweep of his chubby hand, "enjoy our lovely view." With a wink to Alan, he added, "Which includes more than the countryside, no?"

Alan looked at Bandy for a moment—long enough to make her cheeks flush. "Yes," he agreed, returning the wink. "What a fellow," Alan said when the old man was out of earshot. "No wonder he's doing so well. Only an Italian could be more of a romantic than a Southerner."

Bandy realized that of course Alan was right. Southerners were hopeless romantics, and Papa Giustino had simply beaten them at their own game. Suddenly the thought hit her—what worked for Giustino could work for the boutique as well. Perhaps she'd become so business-minded, she'd forgotten the most important part. She should be able to find a way to include more touches of romance in her own business. She'd make a point to talk to Millie about it as soon as she got home. In fact, Denise and Gena might have a few ideas as well.

"Where'd you go?" Alan broke into her thoughts. "Don't you like Italian food? I should have asked you first."

"What? Oh, I apologize. Yes, I adore Italian food and never

get enough of it. Millie abhors pasta, so it's one thing she never makes. She insist it's nothing but flour and water. She'd rather have a mess of grits, she always says, than a mountain of spaghetti."

"Ah yes." Alan chuckled. "A true woman of the South. My mother, aunts, and cousins would all say the same thing if asked. They should have never let me go north, though. I lived on pasta at college. That and pizza."

"You went to school in Yankee-land?"

He nodded. "Harvard. An enlightening time in my life."

"I'm sure." Bandy could hardly imagine this spoiled child of the Southern wealthy existing in New England. But obviously he had. She studied him as he mused over the menu. High cheekbones gave him an aristocratic appearance, but the ruddy color hinted that he was out of doors a great deal. Blond brows knitted together in concentration, and the shock of golden hair fell across his forehead. A smoldering light of laughter constantly glowed in the blue eyes.

He glanced up and caught her gaze. He smiled and said, "You've made up your mind already?"

"I'll just order whatever you're having," she said, embarrassed at having been caught staring.

"That keeps it simple." He folded his menu and then took hers. She was relieved when he ordered sliced veal parmigiana with fettuccine alfredo. There were a few items listed she didn't care for, and she would have regretted her impulsive words if he had picked something like eggplant or tripe.

Alan made small talk, asking her more about Millie and how they came to be living together. She told him bits and pieces, only briefly mentioning Claire. As they talked, soft music spilled out into the fragrant night air. Dusk was beginning to settle across the valley, lending a faint blue haze, which deepened as the sun slid over the far, tree-studded hill. The view was entrancing. She'd almost forgotten to wonder why he'd invited her out this evening. The food was delectable. Probably too heavy and too filling for a hot summer night, but she ate nearly every bite.

During a lull in the conversation, she thought she saw something in the last rays of the setting sun, something tall and rectangular below them among the trees. She leaned a bit to get a better look.

Alan turned to look. "What do you see?"

"I don't know. Could something be standing there among those trees?"

"I think I see what you mean." He scooted his chair nearer to her and tried to look from her viewpoint. She caught the heady fragrance of his cologne as he put his arm across the back of her chair. "To the west of that little clearing about halfway down that hillside?"

"That's it. What could it be?"

"Looks like a set of chimneys. Probably another lost, abandoned plantation house."

"Really? There are such things?"

"All over the South."

"Just left to rot?"

"More or less. Why? Are you interested?"

"Very." An abandoned plantation just sitting out here? She could hardly fathom such a thing. She felt hesitant to share with this stranger her dreams of the future Bandy's Bridal Boutique. But city planners had said the city of Pembrooke was moving in this direction. Papa Giustino was obviously already making good out here.

"Want to go find it?"

"Tonight?"

"Sure. Why not?"

"I'd rather not. Not now. In the dark. I'd want to see it in the daylight."

"Tomorrow afternoon then. After you close the boutique?"

Suddenly she felt pushed and pressed. She gently scooted her chair back away from the table, away from him. "No, really. It's probably nothing. Probably ravaged by transients."

"You'll never know until you see for yourself."

"On the phone the other day, you said you wanted to talk with me about something." She changed the subject firmly, moving the conversation to where she was again in control. "I've yet to hear what that something is. Surely you didn't bring me up here just to talk about my past."

"It wouldn't have been a waste if I had," he said, eyes twinkling. "But you're right. I do have a matter in mind that I want to discuss with you." He crossed one long leg over the other and took a sip of his iced tea. "It's a business deal, actually. I've observed your setup, and it's incredible the amount of services you're offering with such a small staff. No wonder you're making it in Harwood."

Bandy felt a twinge of discomfort. What could he be wanting? Since he'd just paid her an obvious compliment, she mumbled a thank you.

"The only missing ingredient seems to be a photographer." He leaned forward and toyed with the silver spoon. "I'd like to propose some type of little merger."

So that was it. The muddy waters were beginning to clear. "I thought you were deep into newspaper photography. Isn't your family all newspaper people?"

The blond brows raised momentarily. "They are at that. And, yes, I'm working for the newspaper as my uncle has directed. But my heart isn't there."

"Are you trying to tell me your heart is in wedding

photography?"

"Well, yes and no. I mean, more so than in photojournal-ism. I wouldn't take up much room. I just need a place to get started with minimal investment. Denise said you have all kinds of space in the back of the boutique."

Bandy felt herself stiffen. "Oh, Denise said that, did she? And how did you happen to discuss this matter with her first?" This man was sounding more nervy by the moment.

"I admit I was snooping a bit, asking her leading ques-tions, but I never let on why I wanted the information."

But as savvy as Denise was, she probably quickly guessed. Bandy couldn't help but wonder if Denise had suggested this little get-together in the first place. She was beginning to feel set up. Conspired against. "Really, Mr. Brockhurst. . ."

"I may be suggesting a business deal, but can't we stay on first name basis?"

"Alan, then. I have no need to enlarge my staff just now. I've just moved into Harwood, and the new expenses are enormous. Besides, I barely know you. All I know is what I saw of you at Julie's wedding."

"Which wasn't too flattering, right? Look, Bandy, I know it's not easy keeping everything in the black. I could be a great asset to your business. By letting me come on board, you can say you have one more service for the bride. An-other service that she doesn't have to go looking for. I'd like to become an actual working part of your business, but barring that, I'd agree to simply pay rent and set up shop in your back room for a while. Until we see how it works out."

She was shaking her head as she took her napkin from her lap, folded it, and placed it on the table. "The answer is still no."

"But you need a photographer. And I'm acquainted with

many of the families who live in Harwood Heights. What accounts I get, you get, and vice versa. What a great mutual deal."

Bandy felt a million sirens going off inside her. She wanted no part of working with this man. The audacity of him even suggesting such a thing.

"I think we'd better be going."

"We haven't had dessert yet," he protested.

"I couldn't eat another bite. . ."

From behind them came a high, cheery voice. "Hello, Bandy. Hello, Alan."

Bandy turned around to see Denise Jepson strolling across the terrace toward them.

# eight

"Bandy, I declare. Fancy meeting y'all here," Denise cooed as she and her escort came closer. "What a teeny, weeny, little world it is."

Bandy managed a weak hello, wondering how Denise had happened to show up here, on this night, just as they had mentioned her name.

Denise introduced them to Wendell Whitmarsh of the Whitmarsh Exterminating Company of Northern Mississippi. While the thin, balding man stood quietly by, Denise explained the extent of his fleet of trucks and number of employees. "Why, he's practically got the whole of north Mississippi sewed up, don't you, Wendell?"

"Pert' near," Wendell answered with a satisfied smile. Bandy wasn't sure if the satisfaction stemmed from the business—or from having Denise at his elbow.

"It's so nice to see you two here having a good time together," Denise went on. "Have you asked her yet, Alan?"

"Aha," said the beaming Wendell. "Is this a private little moment? Perhaps we should go, my dear, and leave these two lovebirds alone."

"I thought you said you hadn't discussed this with anyone," Bandy demanded of Alan.

"Really," Wendell said, pulling on Denise's arm. "Don't mind us. Denise insisted we try this great new restaurant. We're just passing through."

"I didn't tell her anything, Bandy," Alan protested.

Denise pointed to her head. "My little mind quickly deduced why you were asking me all the questions the other day." She pulled back against Wendell. "It's not what you think, Wendell. Just a little business dealing." She looked around the terrace, taking in the scene. "And what a lovely place to talk." Bandy had no idea how Denise could make the word "lovely" sound like it was coming from the deepest part of her throat.

"I need to be going," Bandy said, rising.

"We really need a good photographer, Bandy," Denise said. "I wouldn't be too quick to make up my mind if I were you."

Bandy was now standing, looking directly into Denise's dark eyes, which seemed to be glittering with the delight of her little joke. "As long as the boutique is still in sole ownership, I guess I'd better continue to make the business decisions on my own."

Denise smiled. "Don't forget, I know the facts and figures."

"I haven't forgotten. Did you divulge that information as well?"

"Oh, heavens, no, Bandy." She pushed the idea away with a wave of her hand "You know I'd never do that. But I do know you could use a good photographer. And he's good." Alan too was standing now and Denise looked up at him with her alluring eyes. "He's *real* good. Come on, Wendell. I'm getting mighty hungry."

"Me too, Pet. Good to meet you folks."

Bandy was walking across the terrace back into the restaurant almost before Alan could take care of the check. Papa Giustino was just as boisterously friendly on their departure as he was on their arrival, but Bandy ignored him. Alan hurried behind her to grab the door and open it for her.

Silence filled the car as they drove back to Bandy's house. She was struggling to sort out her thoughts. Alan's request alone had been difficult enough for her to deal with, without having Denise come barging in to side with him. Bandy had seen the way Denise looked at Alan. Perhaps Denise had her own reasons for wanting him tucked away in the back room of the boutique.

As soon as she thought it, Bandy hated herself. But Denise was a puzzle of contradictions. Acting flighty as a bird, but always beneath the surface, wily as a fox. Bandy found her disconcerting to say the least.

Alan pulled into her driveway and turned off the ignition. "I'm sorry," he said. "I had no idea that gal was outguessing me. I only asked her a couple of questions before we left the wedding that day. She was so helpful to run the camcorder for a little bit. It freed me to do the stills. And they turned out great."

"I'm sure they did. So tell me, did she suggest we go to Giustino's?"

Alan looked at her. "Might I remind you this is *your* secretary you're talking about? I said nothing to her about asking you to dinner."

Now there was an edge to his voice, and this time she apologized. "Forgive me, Alan. I'll retract my kitty claws. I don't like being pushed or cornered, and that was the feeling I had this evening."

"I can't help what your employees do, but I'm still very much interested in merging our mutual interests. Will you at least think about it?"

"I promise, I'll think about it. But I'm sure the answer will still be no."

Alan reached over and took her hand. "If you promise to think about it, that's all I can ask. Thanks. And thanks for agreeing to come with me tonight. I had a wonderful time getting to know you."

There was a sweet softness in his touch. A gentleness. She carefully pulled her hand away and opened her door.

Alan moved to get out, but she stopped him. "No, please don't. I'll see myself to the door. Good-bye, Alan." She was out before he could protest.

"A Southern gentleman would never let a lady walk to the door alone."

"I'll survive." She turned to go, then paused. "And so will you."

Bandy started to go around to her back entrance and then hesitated. If she did that, Millie would think something was wrong. But if she went in the front and Millie saw her face, Millie would *know* something was wrong. Bandy sighed; might as well go in the front and face the music. Maybe she could gloss it over somehow. She didn't want Millie to know how upset she was with Denise.

Sounds of the TV spilled out from Millie's bedroom. As soon as Bandy stepped into the front hall and closed the door behind her, she heard the set click off.

"You home already?" Millie called.

"Home already."

"Come in and tell me about it."

"I have a better idea. Meet me in the kitchen. I need to find an antacid to settle my stomach." Plus she needed a few more moments to regain her composure. By the time Bandy had taken two tablets with a glass of water, Millie came in, shuffling in her slippers, and tying the belt to her robe.

"Eat too much?" Millie asked.

"Even a little Italian food can be too much in this heat."

"Why, y'all must have driven up to Giustino's." Millie pulled out a chair as though she were planning to stay a while.

Bandy leaned back against the kitchen counter. "You're right. We did."

"Did you like it? I hear tell it's a real nice place."

"'Real nice' is an understatement. That restaurant set me

to thinking, Millie. We need more romantic touches in the boutique."

Millie's eyebrows arched. "So it was a romantic evening?"

"Don't get any ideas. It's the *place* I'm referring to. The Giustinos know how to weave romantic touches throughout their restaurant. It's wonderful. You and I need to pool ideas and think of a few ways we can do the same."

Millie rose and went to the refrigerator to pour a small glass of milk. "Just bring it up at the next staff meeting," she said, her head in the refrigerator. "What Gena can't think of, I'm sure Denise can."

"That's for sure," Bandy answered too quickly.

Millie set down her glass. "And just what is that supposed to mean?"

"Nothing. It meant nothing. Just that I'm sure those two could think of something." Bandy sat down at the table. "Pour one of those for me, please. It may help put the fire out."

Millie took her time fetching another glass and filling it. Then she sat down across the table from Bandy. "Don't tell me 'nothing.' I knew you was riled about something the moment you came in."

"You didn't," Bandy countered, but she knew different. Millie could read her like a book. No sense in arguing.

"Now what could Denise have done to work you up into such a dander? I thought it was Alan you were with."

"But she showed up at an inopportune time."

"Denise? At Giustino's?"

"Yes, and yes." Bandy fought to keep the anger from her voice.

"Why do I feel I'm getting only a smidgen of the story here? Want to begin at the beginning?"

Bandy heaved a deep sigh, then attempted to calmly explain Alan's interest in coming into the boutique as a business merger, and how Denise knew all about it. But somehow when she described the incident, it sounded like nothing had happened out of the ordinary. In fact, she could tell from Millie's questioning look that she wasn't making herself clear.

"You say that Alan explained that he didn't divulge any information to Denise. Denise said she didn't divulge any information to Alan. You said no to Alan about a merger. You made it clear to Denise that you still make the decisions and she went off with her rich, but wizened, little escort. Have I got all that right?"

This was ridiculous. Now it sounded sillier than ever. "You just had to be there. It was a terribly awkward moment."

"Awkward perhaps, but nothing to get so upset about."

How did Millie do it? She always seemed to shrink things down to their proper perspective. "I guess not," Bandy agreed. "But I sure don't want that Alan Brockhurst to come and park himself inside our boutique. No telling what might happen."

"Well then, we could hire a few armed guards to keep him out." Millie's eyes twinkled. "One of Waldo's boys is a crack shot when it comes to rabbit hunting. . ."

"Millie, please."

Millie rinsed the glasses and set them in the dish drainer. "I'm sorry. Just couldn't resist a little teasing. You sound as though poor Alan was one dangerous customer."

"You're right." Bandy sighed. "Again. I overreacted. But I have this strange feeling. I'm still not fully convinced either one is telling the truth."

"Back to your first statement—you were talking about adding more romantic touches to the boutique. I'm all for that. And no matter how you feel about Denise, I think she's the best one to ask."

Suddenly Bandy felt bone weary. "You're probably right.

Thanks."

Millie came around the table and put her arm around Bandy's shoulders. The familiar aroma of her wild rose lotion lingered in the air. "I have no earthly notion what it is you're feeling. But the Lord can show you if you'll let Him."

Bandy clasped Millie's work-worn hand. What was it Alan had said? She and Millie were more like kin than real kin? At least he was right about one thing.

⁂

Much to Bandy's delight, plans for the Labor Day weekend were progressing nicely. She wondered why she'd never thought of a staff outing before. Teamwork was imperative for the business to thrive. She hoped this time away would knit all of them together and create stronger unity.

Ellen announced that her husband had agreed to have them at the Persell's cabin for a cookout on Monday. Each staff member seemed eager to help with the food.

Following that order of business, Bandy broached the subject of ways they could weave a greater aura of romance into the boutique.

Denise leaped on the lines almost before Bandy finished speaking them. "My, my. One little old dinner at Giustino's and now finally, y'all are thinking about romance." She gave a light little laugh. "I didn't think there was room in your business mind for soft, mushy thoughts of moonlight and roses."

Bandy flinched, but was prevented from responding as Gena jumped in. "That's not fair, Denise. How do you know what goes on inside Bandy's mind? Just because she doesn't hang all over a guy like some people. . ."

"Wait a minute," Bandy broke in. "I didn't bring this up to turn it into a discussion about me. I've asked for ideas. Plain and simple."

"Food," Millie suggested. "Let's begin placing silver trays

of homemade mints, and tiny wedding cookies on the coffee tables."

"Pipe in soft music," Ellen added. "Instrumental arrangements of love songs. And not just the pops. Classical numbers as well."

Bandy jotted as they were talking. The ideas were soon flowing, and she had a page full of notes. She was pleased, but at the same time, she still felt the prick from Denise's caustic remark. Briefly, she found herself wondering how much she should take from this woman before considering firing her.

But later, when it took Bandy several days to build up the courage to invite Jordan to the Lodge for Labor Day weekend, she was almost ready to agree with Denise; maybe Bandy did spend too much time thinking about business. Bandy was convinced Denise would have been plagued with no such hesitation. Were Southern women born knowing how to pursue men?

She and Jordan were on their way to a movie one Friday evening when she finally accomplished the seemingly impossible task. To her surprise, he quickly agreed. "A getaway weekend sounds pretty tempting right now," he said. "I've barely caught my breath between the summer session and the beginning of the fall term."

The car windows were rolled down and the heat of the August day still hung heavy in the air. The air conditioner in Jordan's car had given up the ghost earlier in the summer, and as yet he had no extra money to have it repaired. Bandy was anxious to go and sit in the cool theater, but she kept herself from complaining as she quietly studied Jordan's serious face. The gold-rimmed glasses were on now, and his dark hair as usual was neatly combed back. A calm stillness reflected in his dark, almost-black, eyes. That calmness gave her a contented sensation. She never felt she had to outguess Jordan.

He gave a little smile, indicating he felt her watching him. He reached over, took her hand in his, and gave it a little squeeze. "Sorry about the air conditioner, Little Red. By the time I can afford to get it fixed, the heat will be over. Such is the life of a college professor."

"I'm fine," she insisted. "It wil be cool inside the theater." The air seemed as hot now with the sun low in the sky as it had at noon.

At the theater, Jordan hopped out and came around to open her door. As he reached for the handle, a trim, blond-haired woman was walking across the parking lot toward him with quick, deliberate steps.

"Jordy! Oh, Jordy. Hello."

Who in this city would dare call Professor Wyler, "Jordy"? Bandy watched Jordan as he turned toward the approaching stranger, who, as it turned out, was not a stranger at all, at least not to Jordan.

Jordan put out his hand to greet her. "Hello, Lena."

Bandy watched as this Lena took Jordan's hand into both of hers. "It's so good to see you again," she said. "Our paths never seem to cross now that the term has started."

"Oh, Bandy," Jordan said, as though he suddenly remembered she was standing there. "This is Lena Brookneal. She's the new English professor I wanted you to meet a few weeks ago."

## nine

This was a professor? Quite a change from the usual group of stuffy men Jordan hung out with. Lena's soft blond hair was perfectly pulled back and fastened with a pink bow at the nape of her neck. Her scoop-neck dusky rose dress clung to her tiny waist. Of course Bandy had met other women professors at the university, but they looked nothing like this. Bandy was painfully aware of her own fly-away red mane as she shook hands with the new English professor.

"I wanted you to meet her when I had the cookout," Jordan was saying. "That was the night you had the business meeting come up at the last minute. Remember?"

"I remember."

"Lena's new in town. I thought if you got to know her, you could sort of show her around Pembrooke."

Bandy formed the words to answer, but Lena spoke first. "Now, Jordy," she said in a voice that reminded Bandy of Denise's, "don't you worry none. I'm a big girl. I don't need a baby sitter." She gave his arm a friendly little pat and hardly gave Bandy more than a glance. "Why, I'm finding my way around Pembrooke just fine. But thank you for your sweet concern. And after you gave me the personal tour of the campus, I'm finding my way around there too."

"Were you going to the movie?" Jordan asked.

For a split second Bandy held her breath. Was he going to invite her to come along?

Lena glanced around at the theater. "The movie? Oh, no. I was at a little shop at the other end of the shopping mall. When I came out to my car I just happened to see you over here and came to say hi. Gotta run now. 'Bye." She gave his arm another pat and waved, even though she was standing right next to him. As she departed, she paused and turned. "Nice to meet you too, Brandy."

"Bandy. The name's Bandy," Bandy called after her. But the English professor was too far away to hear. Or didn't want to hear.

"Come on," Jordan said. "We'll miss the movie."

"Coming, Jordy," Bandy answered in sing-song. "Jordy. I can't believe you let her do that."

"Do what?"

"Call you that."

"It makes no difference to me what she calls me. She's a good instructor. All the students seem to like her."

"Especially those of the male gender."

Jordan pulled her to a stop a few feet from the ticket window. "Why, Little Red. I do believe I hear a hint of jealousy in your voice."

"A personal tour of the campus?"

Jordan shook his head. "It's not like it sounds. I ran into her outside the history department. She was totally turned around. So I showed her the way to the administration building. Simple as that."

"She probably had a campus map right in her hand."

"Actually she did," he said stepping up to the window and paying for the tickets. "But it was upside down."

Suddenly she realized Jordan was cracking a joke. A dry joke, but a joke. She laughed. Not only at the joke, which was funny, but at the very thought of him saying it. Jordan was chuckling as well. The movie was a comedy, so their laughter continued. By the time the evening was over, the two of them were in high spirits.

When Jordan walked her to the door, he took her in his arms. His good-night kiss was warm and gentle. "I'm looking forward to Labor Day weekend," he whispered.

Usually, Jordan kissed her and released her. But tonight he stood for a moment, not moving. Contentedly, she lay her head on his shoulder. "Mm. I'm glad you want to go."

"Two workaholics who need to get away."

Her head came up. "I'm not a workaholic." Denise's words came back to her—that she was so business-minded, she never thought of romance.

"We both are, Little Red. Just as well face it. But yours is the worse case."

"How can you say that?"

"What do you think of besides the success of that store up there?" He jerked his head in the general direction of Harwood Heights.

"Lots of things."

"Name one."

"What I think about is none of your business, Professor Wyler."

He quietly kissed her again. "It would probably do you good to put a little balance in your life and have some play time."

"I will if you will," she challenged.

"It's a deal." He chuckled, kissed her on the nose, and told her good night.

Thoughts of the English professor were miles away, until later when she was alone in her room getting ready for bed. What was it with these women who had the audacity to barge in where they weren't wanted? She failed to understand how they could do it. If only they were as dumb as they acted. Bandy would have never guessed by looking at her that Lena was a college professor.

She gave a shrug and crawled into bed. What did it matter anyway? The Gilchrist contract was in hand. The future looked great with the boutique, and her evening with

Jordan seemed more special than ever before. And now she had a wonderful holiday weekend to anticipate. Why should she be upset over anything?

She grabbed her Bible and read some Scripture, but she couldn't concentrate. When she finally fell asleep, she dreamed of beautiful women pushing and shoving her around, pressing her into the midst of a crowd until she could hardly breathe. She woke up shaking, then rolled over and slept again.

&

The week before Labor Day, storms came to northern Mississippi. Sheets of gray rain broke the spell of stifling heat, lifted the faces of the daisies and roses, and cleared the air so every living thing could breathe again. The rain fell so hard and so long, Bandy wondered if they might have to cancel the weekend event. But early on Saturday the clouds parted and the sun broke through. The air then turned into a sauna, but at least the dust had settled once again.

Bandy had hoped she could travel to Swannanoa Lodge with Jordan, but that was impossible. The foodstuffs she and Millie were taking had to be loaded in the van, and besides, Millie needed a ride. No, Jordan would have to come alone, while Bandy drove the van the fifty miles from Pembrooke to the Lake, following the easy-to-follow maps Ellen had sketched to both the Persell cabin and the lodge.

Bandy and Millie had most of their packing done and loaded in the van Sunday morning before church. Following church, all they had to do was eat a quick lunch, load the refrigerated items, and be on their way.

The drive out of Pembrooke took them past Giustino's. Bandy was anxious to know what Millie thought of the place, so she took a few minutes to pull in and drive through the parking lot, letting Millie get a look at the overhanging terrace in the back. Rain-washed red and pink flowers shone and sparkled in the sunlight, spilling their colors over the outdoor tables.

"You're absolutely right, my dear," Millie said, approval in her voice. "It does have a romantic touch."

"The inside is just as pretty. I'll bring you up here for dinner sometime."

"Just as long as I don't have to eat that no-'count pasta stuff. Such a waste!"

"They have other things. By the way," Bandy pulled back onto the highway, "do you know anything about a forsaken plantation anywhere out in this area?"

"Honey, those things are everywhere. Some out in the sticks so far, it'll be years before they're all found."

"When Alan and I were eating, I thought I saw something just across the valley behind Giustino's. How could I find it to see if it has any possibilities of being a future home for the boutique?"

"So that what's on your mind."

"That's always on my mind."

"Business, business, business. This is your weekend off. Time to kick up your heels and have a little fun."

"Now don't you start in on me, too. Would Waldo know anything about that place?"

"Like as not, he does. Now let's forget business."

"Can't forget it completely. Remember we're having a staff meeting tonight in the Swannanoa Lodge meeting room."

Millie groaned.

An hour or so later, they saw the sign for the turnoff to the lodge. Winding through a few more steep hills on a narrow gravel road, suddenly the valley opened up. The sight made them suck in their breath, Bandy slowed the van so they could drink in the view. Below them lay a small protected inlet of the lake. At the point of the inlet, the lodge seemed to rise up from the still blue water in haughty majesty.

The lodge was nothing like Bandy had expected. Later, she tried to conjure up the way she had first pictured it. Rough-hewn logs perhaps. Definitely small and definitely rustic. But in reality, it was just the opposite. The wise designers of the lodge chose a site on the side of a broad hill directly overlooking Swansea Lake. The building was pure white, shining in the September sunlight. The front veranda stretched from one end of the massive house to the other, fat, gothic pillars reaching from the base of the veranda to the third floor. White, wooden, deck chairs and cane-back rocking chairs were placed here and there on the veranda. The many chimneys told of a time when fireplaces had heated the various rooms.

Slowly they wound around a few more curving stretches of road before pulling up in front of the lodge. Now they could see that behind the lodge were a series of individual cabins, providing further accommodations for guests. The gently sloping front lawn faded into a sandy beach where scores of people were laughing and playing in the blue waters of the lake. The squeals and giggles of the children rang through the air.

"What do you think?" Bandy asked Millie.

"I think we should have thought of a getaway a long time ago. As soon as I get unpacked and settled, I'm coming out here and sit in one of these rocking chairs on the veranda and stare at the trees and the water and do absolutely nothing."

"A splendid idea, Millie." She spotted Brian's car in the parking lot, so Gena was already here. Bandy was looking for Jordan's car. The first thing she wanted to do was take a long walk with Jordan through the woods. Or perhaps take a swim together. Or maybe just lie on that sandy beach area and soak up the sun. She'd show Denise a thing or two about being romantic.

An attendant came out and helped them unload their things. Crossing the wooden veranda, they entered into the front entryway. A curving stairway mounted up to a second story balcony which overlooked the vast foyer. Dark oak gave the interior a rich hue.

After checking in, they followed the attendant up the wide stairs to the second floor. Bandy and Millie had agreed to share a room to keep their costs to a minimum. Their room was bright and cheery, outfitted with antiques, including a massive four poster bed and a china washbowl and pitcher perched primly on a slender stand. Lacy curtains floated on the lake breezes that drifted in through the open windows.

Bandy hurriedly changed into her swim suit. She felt like a little kid, giddy and excited.

"You go ahead," Millie said as she sat down on the edge of the four-poster. "This looks so inviting. I think I'll take a little nap. When I've rested enough, *then* I'll go relax on the porch."

Bandy laughed. "Sounds like a good plan." She grabbed up the tanning lotion and a couple of beach towels, slipped into her thongs, and was out the door. "See you later."

She was descending the stairs when she saw Jordan coming in the front door. He glanced up and shot her a grin. The approval in his eyes gave her a quick shiver.

"Hey," he said as she approached, "you look really great. I think I'm even more glad I came."

"Does it take a swim suit to make you glad?"

"It sure doesn't hurt." The glint in his eyes told her he was teasing.

She smiled. "Don't stand around here gabbing. Get changed and come out and enjoy the water."

"Be right there." He turned to go to the front desk. "By

the way," he said over his shoulder, "I took Goldie over to Ellen's house. Ellen said it would be fine for her to stay there tonight."

"Sounds great. Goldie needs a change of pace as much as we do."

Bandy was crossing the entryway to the front door when she saw Denise tripping up the front steps. Bandy stopped dead in her tracks. Accompanying Denise was not the thin, little, homely Wendell Whitmarsh Bandy had expected to see. Rather, following Denise up the wooden steps, effortlessly carrying two suitcases, was Alan Brockhurst. Bandy felt a little catch in her throat as she watched him. He was dressed in white shorts and a dark blue knit shirt. His tan was as deep as a Californian's, and his blond hair shone in the afternoon sun.

What in heaven's name was he doing here? On this of all weekends? But even as she wondered, she knew. Denise had invited Alan to be her guest rather than Wendell. But why? Why would he even want to come? This was crazy.

They spied her immediately and Denise came rushing over. "Oh, Bandy, there you are. Honey, isn't this place every bit as lovely as I told you it would be? Don't you love every teeny square inch of it?" With a quick breath she added, "And I'm just tickled pink that we could have guests. Alan and I have been wanting to get together for ever so long. And now we have our chance."

Alan set the suitcases down and came toward Bandy with his hand extended, his eyes sparkling. "Hello, Bandy. What a great idea to give your employees such a generous gift. Wise employer you are." He clasped her hand in both of his. "I'm pleased to be able to be a part."

*I bet you are*, Bandy mused, remembering his desire to be linked up with the boutique. "Welcome," she said, as she gently pulled her hand back. "I hope you have a nice weekend."

Turning away, she saw yet another startling sight. Coming up the steps, struggling with a suitcase, a garment bag, two camera cases, and two tennis rackets, was the young Hayden.

"Your counterpart?" she asked Alan.

"Oh yeah. Well, you know. . ." He gave a shrug and a chuckle. "He won't be any trouble. He's been a big help lately, so I'm giving *my* 'employee' a weekend getaway as well."

"They have attendants to help with the luggage."

"He wanted to bring it."

"I see." Bandy looked again as Hayden stopped twice to readjust his load. She shook her head and stepped on out through the front door, barely giving Hayden a nod.

Bandy marched down the stairs, across the lawn, and out across the warm sand. All the brightness seemed to have drained from the day. She spread out a towel and flopped down on it. If she'd suspected for a moment what Denise was scheming, she'd never have agreed to let her invite a guest.

Gena and Brian were down the beach a ways, playing catch with a neon green frisbee, their laughter drifting to where Bandy was sitting. Gena saw her and came running toward her.

"Bandy! You finally got here. What took you so long?"

"I went to church first. Remember?"

"Oh, yeah. Well, I skipped church. Brian and I wanted to get up here as fast as we could. Isn't this place awesome? Thanks so much for thinking of this. It's going to be a great weekend."

"Hopefully."

"Say, did you see Denise arrive?"

"I did."

"Did you see who she brought as her guest?"

"I did."

"Were you surprised?"

"Shocked is more the word."

Gena looked back to where Brian was waving for her to come back to their game. She waved back at him, then turned once more to Bandy. "You don't sound very happy about it."

"Why should I care who she invites? I didn't specify that guests had to pass prior approval. I just hope little Hayden doesn't destroy the place."

Gena scowled. "Now you sound like Brian. He said the same thing when he saw Hayden unloading their gear. Give the guy a break. He just had a little bad luck that day."

"Maybe so. We'll see. I'm assuming he'll be at our picnic tomorrow."

"Now if you'd been quicker on the draw, things could have been different," Gena stated.

"What's that supposed to mean?"

"You could have beat Denise to the draw and invited the exciting, handsome Mr. Alan Brockhurst rather than the stuffy professor."

"Why, Gena Karr! Of all the nerve." Before the girl could move, Bandy whacked her soundly on the fanny with her thong.

Gena yelped, but she was laughing as though she thought her little joke was quite funny. Bandy didn't think it was a bit funny. She could only hope Gena did nothing throughout the rest of the day to embarrass her.

As it turned out, Gena and Brian were out and gone for most of the afternoon. They swam, took trail hikes, rode the paddleboats, and seemed quite contented to stay away from the rest of the group.

At least Gena didn't hang around to be able to say, "I told

you so." Jordan's idea of a restful afternoon was closely related to that of Millie's. He did swim with Bandy a couple of times, but the rest of the time he spent stretched out on the sand, napping or reading a book. Bandy suggested a paddleboat trip out to the small island situated in the neck of the inlet, but Jordan nixed the idea.

At last, she left him and joined in a rousing game of volleyball with a group of strangers. At one point, she noticed Alan standing by watching. When a player dropped out, Alan joined in. He put everything into the game, and obviously was no stranger to the sport. Bandy found herself at the net, looking eyeball to eyeball with him. She thought he might humor her by letting up some, but she was glad when he didn't. He played as hard as ever. After the game broke up, he came over to her.

"Great game you play," she told him.

"You don't do too bad yourself."

"I seldom have the opportunity to play much. I felt pretty rusty."

His eyes lit up as he smiled. "I don't think I'd want to be opposite you when you weren't rusty."

"I don't think I'm that big a threat. Where's Denise?"

He looked around. "Beats me. She was out here a while ago." He hesitated, then looked at Bandy with an odd expression in his eyes. "Look, our original partners seem to be preoccupied. Want to take a paddleboat ride? They're great fun."

Bandy looked down the beach at Professor Wyler lying with a book over his face. "I don't think so," she said. "That game nearly wore me out."

"I'm not tired at all. I can do most of the work. What say?"

Bandy hesitated. Everything in her wanted to agree. Wanted to go off and have a good time. But it wouldn't be fair to

Jordan. Or to Denise. Alan was asking the impossible. "It's getting late. I still have details to finish up for the staff meeting tonight."

"I understand." She saw the disappointment in his eyes. "Maybe another time."

She nodded. "Another time." Deftly changing the subject, she asked, "Where'd Hayden get off to?"

"He's working with the macro lens on his camera. I think he took one of the trails. He wants to try his hand at a few close-up nature shots. Wild flowers, insects, that sort of thing."

Bandy had difficulty imagining the boy handling such expensive equipment while concentrating on such small details. Perhaps she *had* misjudged him.

"While y'all are in your meeting," Alan went on, "Hayden and I are going to set up our tripods on the veranda and work to get shots of the sunset across the lake."

Bandy looked up at Alan with new interest. "That should be a beautiful scene."

"Breathtaking."

"Maybe I'll come out and check on you before I turn in." Alan gave a little nod. "Please do. I'd like that, in fact."

## ten

Bandy had assumed no one would be able to keep his mind on business, but the staff meeting went surprisingly well. Everyone seemed super-charged with creative ideas, as though just getting away from the boutique had infused them with energy. Bandy outlined the sales promotions planned for the winter months.

"We need to cease thinking of spring as traditional wedding months," she explained. "Statistics are showing winter weddings, especially around the holidays, are more popular than ever. In fact, for the first time, there will be a fall bridal fair at the Pembrooke Civic Center."

She passed out the promo brochures which had been provided to her by the fair sponsors. "I've already chosen our booth space—close to the front door. As soon as possible I'll have a schedule of times when each of you will work in the booth."

"I hope it's not too close to mid-term finals," Gena said.

"We'll work around your study schedule," Bandy assured her. "Ellen, I'll need you to help me design a great promotional idea for the booth and a giveaway for the drawing. Something a little different than we've done before."

Ellen nodded and scribbled in her notebook. Denise too was taking notes. This was something new. Bandy wondered why the sudden attention. Usually Denise filed her nails during staff meetings.

Bandy studied the calendar before her. The fall schedule

already seemed crammed full. Following the fair, she and Millie would be making a trip to the Dallas market, but that would be the very time when follow-up from the bridal fair would be needed most. Maybe she could turn the follow-up task over to Denise. Maybe. Bandy started to say something to that effect, but changed her mind. There would be time enough to decide later.

After the meeting, as the others were filing out, Ellen came up to her. "Professor Wyler was over at our cabin checking on Goldie when I left. He and John were in a deep discussion about the university football team."

"Oh, really?" Bandy wasn't sure what she was supposed to say. She had wondered where Jordan had gone. Perhaps Ellen realized he might not have told her.

"Our boys love having Goldie there. She's such a good dog. They've always wanted a dog, but their dad keeps saying no."

"Maybe when he sees how much fun they have with Goldie, he'll change his mind," Bandy offered, wondering how long Jordan would stay at the Persell cabin.

"Maybe. But you know how men are. Once they've spoken, they hate to be shown they're wrong."

"Mm. I suppose so." Actually Bandy didn't know at all. She never remembered her father caring whether or not he was in the wrong. He was always willing to admit when he'd made a mistake. But then, she guessed there weren't many men like Caven O'Sullivan.

They planned for Ellen to take the coolers of food to her cabin that evening to be ready for the picnic the next day. As they were in the parking lot, transferring the coolers, Alan came to lend a hand.

After Ellen drove off, and Millie went back in, Bandy and Alan found themselves on the veranda alone. She noticed his camera still on the tripod aimed toward the lake. Only a few wisps of pink were left floating in the warm summer sky, and Bandy realized the meeting must have lasted longer than she had planned. She hadn't anticipated, though, how much material they needed to cover. She was thankful her staff was so cooperative.

"Did you catch the sunset?" she asked Alan, nodding toward his camera.

"Perfectly. I'll show you the prints when we get them back."

"I thought Hayden was helping."

"He was. We had both cameras up for a while. But now he's out in the bushes again. He has his heart set on photographing a firefly or perhaps a moth."

"A tiny lightning bug?" She thought about that for a moment, as she followed Alan down the length of the veranda. She watched him lift the camera off the tripod and pack it in its case. "What a challenge. I hope he's slathered in repellent. The mosquitoes are terrible." She slapped at her arm as she felt another bite.

"I'm sure he's slathered," he answered.

Bandy could tell his mind was elsewhere as he carefully folded up the legs of the tripod. She wondered where Denise had gone off to. Gena had said something about her spending time with the owner of the lodge, but Bandy had seen nothing to substantiate that. She assumed Denise simply became impatient with all this photography nonsense.

Alan set the packed case on the floor and sat down on a wooden deck chair. "I've been wanting to talk to you ever since we were together at Giustino's the other night."

Bandy leaned back against one of the pillars of the veranda. "About what?"

"I can see now that I was too forward. Sometimes I do

that—rush in too fast when I see an opportunity. 'Nervy' was probably the right name to give me. The idea of our combining efforts seemed like such a good idea to me—I guess I just assumed you'd jump at it."

"Does one acquire that trait by being kin to the Longmonts?"

He gave a wry smile and shook his head. "Who fed you that morsel of information?"

"You should ask who hasn't. It seems to be common knowledge."

"The funny thing is, actually I'm not."

"Not what?"

"Kin to them."

Bandy considered this bit of news. "Then why. . ."

"I'm like the grafted branch referred to in the Scripture. Although I'm sure the Lord accepts His grafted branch much more warmly than I've been accepted among the Longmont clan."

"Are you saying you're adopted?"

A buzzing speck circled his face. He slapped his hands together, making a loud smack that startled the still air. "Got him." He flicked the dead pest from his hand. "I was three when my widowed mother married Jacob Brockhurst, nephew of Rupert Longmont. My step-father was a gentle man in a rough family. Had he lived, my life would have progressed differently, I'm sure."

"You lost your father, then your step-father too?" Bandy thought of the loss of her own parents, but at least they had been there for her in her tender, growing-up years.

"My step-father, too. But not before he had legally adopted me. Therefore, in Uncle Rupert's eyes, I was a Longmont. By the time I was eleven, he was busy transforming me into the newspaper man he wanted all the Longmonts to become.

That might not have been so bad—except I wasn't interested. But that didn't matter. As far as Uncle Rupert was
concerned, I didn't have a choice. He was a hard, cold man."
Alan shook his head. "When I was growing up, he barely
gave me room to breathe."

"What about your mother? Didn't she have something to
say about it?"

He shook his head. "She sort of made a trade-off."

"She forfeited her right to interfere in her own son's life?"

Alan looked up at her. "You're pretty perceptive. The
trade-off was for her to have a comfortable lifestyle. I can't
say I blame her. It's not easy being widowed twice."

Bandy felt a sudden anger at this mother who obviously
thought more of things than she did her own son. "I would
have gone hungry first," she said fiercely.

He smiled and nodded. "I have no doubt about that, Bandy
O'Sullivan. But unfortunately, my mother didn't happen to
be blessed with that kind of fortitude."

"So you're here working on the *Chronicle*, still striving
to please Uncle Rupert?"

"I've been making the break from my uncle for several
years. But I keep searching for ways to break away and yet
keep peace. I believe that's what the Lord wants me to do.
With a man like Uncle Rupert, that's not easy."

Bandy was surprised to hear Alan refer to the leading of
the Lord. She had never thought that he might be a Christian. "What is it you want to do? Not just wedding photography, I take it."

He shook his head. "No, but that comes closer than working for the *Chronicle*. I'll never fit into that world of chasing ambulances and meeting deadlines. Now that I'm older,
I don't begrudge all that Uncle Rupert forced me to learn—
it's been a great training ground."

"Training for what?"

Alan thoughtfully toyed with the strap on the camera bag. He seemed to be choosing his words. "Photography to me is an art form, Bandy. My lenses are like an artist's palette. I express myself through the photos I take. To me, my photos are works of art, and I treat them as such." He gave a short laugh. "Poor Uncle Rupert can't bear to hear me talk like this. He calls it unproductive and unprofitable."

"But if that's the area of the work where you excel, given time, it would become productive *and* profitable." She recalled her own early years of struggling with her small business, working out of her father's garage. But she always had his support.

Alan's eyes twinkled. "That's what I've always said. I guess that's why I jumped at the chance to work with you. I thought you might understand."

"But you didn't tell me any of this."

He stood up, taking a deep breath of the cool evening air. "I told you I'm too impetuous. I didn't even take the time to prepare the ground to make it fallow, did I?"

Suddenly, she was acutely aware of the moonlight casting its mellow light on Alan's soft blond hair and chiseled features. His clear blue eyes seemed to be searching her face. "Not that it would have helped," he went on. "You might have thought I was trying to take advantage of your sympathies. I didn't want that either."

Bandy wasn't sure what to think. She could say "yes" to him now easily, but she still had a niggling feeling of caution deep inside. "I can help you in one area," she said. "Mrs. Edward Gilchrist asked about you."

He gave a low chuckle. "Mrs. who? Oh, let me guess. Someone who's heard that Rupert Longmont's nephew might be in the area."

"Bingo."

He leaned down to pick up his case and tripod, then placed his free hand on her shoulder to guide her back toward the front door. Bandy dug in her feet, not sure she was ready to go in just yet and resenting the push of his hand on her back. "The mosquitos are going to eat you alive," he told her.

She relaxed and moved easily along with him, aware of the warmth of his touch. "Do you want the Gilchrist's phone number?"

"Sure."

"Even though it comes through your uncle?"

"Can't help that. The deciding factor will be whether or not they give me a referral afterward. What all's involved? A wedding?"

They paused midway along the veranda. Soft aromas and sounds floated out from the restaurant just inside the front entrance.

"The engagement party and a wedding. Maybe a shower." She ran through the highlights of the social events surrounding the prestigious community wedding and the work she was doing for the Gilchrist's.

He reached down and slipped her hand into his. "Perhaps, if I secure the account, we could attend the engagement party together?"

"I'm not sure. I'll be pretty busy seeing to all the details."

"Then we could be 'pretty busy' together."

"We'll see."

"I'll accept that. At least, it's not a 'no.'" Not releasing her hand, he turned again toward the entrance. "By the way, did you ever go searching for the deserted plantation house in the valley?"

Bandy shook her head. She had made a phone call to

Waldo from the lodge, but his answer had been disappointing. "Waldo said it wasn't worth it. He said only the chimneys are standing."

"And who is Waldo. An authority?"

She nodded and smiled. "Quite. He's one of Millie's shirt-tail cousins who's lived here forever, and knows history back at least twelve generations."

"I know the kind. The South is full of them. Are you thinking of eventually putting your boutique in an old plantation home?"

She stood still and looked up at him. "How could you know that?"

"Well, I sure didn't think you were going to live in it. It's a great idea, but it would cost a fortune to renovate one of those old places."

She released a short sigh. "I know. I would have to have investors."

"It's not impossible."

"Nothing's impossible."

The large double doors of the lodge suddenly flew open, and Jordan came out onto the veranda. "Bandy? Is that you out there? I've been looking all over for you. Couldn't figure out where you'd gotten off to."

"Me?" she said curtly, pulling her hand out of Alan's grasp. "I've been here all evening. You're the one who ran off."

"Hey there, Alan," Jordan cordially addressed the tall photographer. "I know I was remiss in staying so long, Bandy. I only went to check on Goldie. . ."

"I know, I heard. Football got in the way?"

"John Persell played on the university team, and his father and uncle before him. I found it most intriguing."

"Certainly sounds intriguing. Doesn't that sound intriguing, Alan?"

"Don't pull me into this." He gently pushed passed Jordan and grabbed at the front door. "I'll see y'all tomorrow."

"I'm sorry I was gone, Bandy, but I figured you'd be busy all evening with the meeting."

"You're absolutely right, Jordan. I was busy all evening." She too pushed past him, giving a little Professor Brookneal wave. "See y'all tomorrow."

# eleven

The Persell's cabin, like the lodge, had a sweeping view of the lake, but rather than being in an inlet, the cabin faced miles of water; Bandy felt as though she were looking out across the ocean.

Ellen's husband John had barbecued ribs on the charcoal grill. As Bandy picked up a piece of meat, dripping with sauce, she couldn't remember a time when she'd enjoyed herself more. The outdoor picnic, the panoramic view, the delectable food, the happy bantering of the guests, everything combined to make a perfect occasion.

After the meal, the older people were languid from all the food, and from the heaviness of the afternoon heat. Ellen's two boys, ages four and five, were still lively, however—as were Gena, Brian, and Hayden. The five of them ran Goldie on her leash down the length of beach in front of the cabin, and then they set up a makeshift game of volleyball. Bandy didn't see how they could find the energy. Even Denise was somewhat subdued, stretched out on a chaise in her two-piece swimsuit.

Bandy hadn't changed into her swimsuit as yet. She'd moved from a lawn chair to a blanket spread on the grass, and was sitting up hugging her knees, watching brightly-colored sailboats skim across the lake. Her thoughts drifted peacefully.

Millie, who rarely sat still, got to her feet and began to clear plates and dishes to take back into the kitchen.

"Oh, leave it be a while," Ellen told her.

"The flies will have a feast if I don't get these inside,"

Millie retorted, and she carried two dishes in through the back door. The screen door slammed, loud in the dead air.

The lake was glassy still and the sun's reflection brilliant. Bandy looked up through the dense shade trees, thankful for the covering.

The laughter of the younger members of their party grew nearer. Bandy glanced over to see Hayden in the lead coming up the sloping bank from the lake. Actually Goldie was in the lead, and Hayden held the leash. Just as Hayden started to come around the still-laden picnic table, Goldie heard Jordan's voice and decided to lunge in the opposite direction from Hayden. With a sense of *déjà vu*, Bandy saw the table begin to tip.

She sprang to her feet. "Hayden, stop!"

Alan must have seen it at the same moment. He and Bandy both lunged toward the table to steady it. Their eyes met and instantly laughter bubbled up.

Hayden halted in mid-stride and managed to reverse his steps. Bandy heaved a sigh of relief.

"We must stop meeting like this," Alan said, still laughing.

Bandy moved dishes back from the edge of the table. "Tell me this isn't happening."

"Sorry," Hayden called over his shoulder.

"Quite all right." Bandy shot back at him. "Happens all the time."

Alan was moving toward her, looking as though he were going to say something. She never found out what it was, though, since at that moment Gena touched her elbow. Bandy turned away from Alan toward Gena.

"I thought we were all going on a float trip this afternoon," Gena said.

"Yeah," Brian echoed behind her. "We're ready."

"We've barely digested our dinner," Bandy said. But she

too was ready, now that she been jerked so rudely out of her relaxed state of mind.

"You can't get me in one of those teeny, weeny, little things." Denise's voice was slow and lazy.

"And I'd better stay here and put the boys down for a nap," Ellen put in.

"You're not going in one of those canoes are you, Bandy?" Jordan asked.

Bandy hesitated. She'd been hoping she and Jordan would be going on this little excursion together. "Of course I am. I thought you were too."

He shook his head. "No canoe for me. Give me a nice broad-bottomed fishing boat any time. At least they stay right side up. I don't care to swim with snakes, thank you."

Bandy couldn't believe this was coming from the fearless hunter Jordan claimed to be.

"Like I was saying," Denise put in, "them teeny, weeny, little things are just too dangerous. I like the water right here." The wave of her slender arm took in the quiet lakefront.

"You can ride with Hayden and me," Alan offered.

Bandy shook her head. "I can float one alone easily. My dad and I used to take float trips several times each summer. I can handle it myself."

"We'll put your boat between us," Gena suggested. "Brian and I can take the lead, and Alan and Hayden can bring up the rear."

"Whatever," Bandy said, fighting to keep the disappointment from her voice.

They all piled into Brian's car. As they drove the dozen or so miles to where the tributary offered float trips, Bandy struggled with her feelings. Why should she care what Jordan did or didn't do? After all, he'd never given her one indication that he was serious about her. But she had to admit to herself that she'd hoped this weekend would work to draw them together. Realizing that, she felt like a guilty manipulator.

Unlike the lake, the tributary was not glassy still. The week of rains before Labor Day had swollen the river which flowed out of the mammoth lake.

As planned, Bandy's canoe was the middle one. Before they poled off, Alan repeated his offer to let her ride with them. "I think I just want to be alone for a while," she told him. He nodded, but his eyes caught hers again. Somehow she felt he understood. The look in his eyes gave her a strange sensation deep in her midsection. A feeling best to be ignored, she told herself as the little canoe began to move silently down the tributary.

About thirty minutes into the ride, she knew this was exactly what she'd needed. All was quiet and peaceful. Hayden had his camera, so he and Alan were making stops along the way in order to take pictures. Gena and Brian enjoyed the fast rush of staying in the center of the river, riding the more rapid currents, and they were soon out of sight. Bandy stayed toward the side where the water flowed a bit slower. Presently, she was quite alone, with only the gurgling of the water, the soft buzz of insects, and an occasional bird call to keep her company.

She didn't even try to pray, although that's what she'd told herself she wanted to do out here. Pray and try to seek a few answers. But now that she was quiet, she simply let her mind drift along with the water. Even praying seemed like too much effort.

Closer to the bank, the trees cast a blessed shade. She had on a broad-brimmed sun hat to save her ivory skin from a nasty burn, but she was still thankful for the coolness among the shadows. Where the water widened, the current was even smoother, and she took a moment to pull a cold soft drink from her insulated bag.

Ahead, she could see a curve to the right. The river looked narrower there, but she couldn't tell for sure because of the curve. Quickly, she swallowed the last of the cool drink, and took the paddle in her hands once again.

The river had indeed narrowed, and the water flowed faster now. As she approached the curve, she maneuvered the paddle as best she could. The little canoe rounded the curve, and she saw too late the log jam along the right bank.

A tree had fallen into the water, and the bare branches were acting as a net to catch any debris coming down the fast-flowing river. "I can get around it," she told herself. "I can make it."

Her own words startled her. If she'd been in the center of the river at the bend, she would have easily missed the tree. But since she had chosen to float so close to the bank, now she had to push hard to get around the log jam.

Unfortunately, the fallen tree and debris were causing a whirling and sucking movement. Struggle as she might, she couldn't make the canoe move where she wanted it to go. If she were only a few feet further over, she thought, then the center flow would catch her and pull her safely past.

Well, so what if the boat gets caught in a few limbs? she told herself. Alan and Hayden were close behind. They could help pull her out. Nevertheless, her panic was growing. Faster now and still faster, the little boat was being pulled and turned like a tiny leaf. It rammed the log jam with an impact that jarred Bandy to her bones. She tried to push the paddle against the logs and force herself away toward the center of the river, but the water's suction refused to let her go.

Studying the situation, she considered climbing out of the boat onto the logs and making her way toward the bank. On her hands and knees, she could probably make it. She tightened her life jacket securely and stood up to examine the logs. As she did, somehow her movement and the strong current worked together. The boat flipped, and she plunged into the swirling, murky water. Later, she remembered being thankful for the life jacket—and then wondering why it wasn't helping. The sucking current had her imprisoned against the logs. Could a person actually drown while wearing a life jacket?

Frantically, she pulled and grabbed at limbs, trying to pull her body free from their clutching fingers. Instead, she found herself being slammed deeper in the water against the rough limbs. She held her breath, but soon her searing lungs screamed for air.

Again, she grabbed for a limb, grasped, and pulled. But just as she felt herself moving toward the surface, the limb broke, and she was again buffeted by the angry current. Again and again, she grabbed and pulled, only to be dragged back down again.

Finally, she knew she could stand it no longer—and at that moment, she saw another figure beside her in the water. She felt arms about her, pulling her free. And then she blacked out.

❧

How strange that she should be thinking about the broad-brimmed sun hat. She hazily pictured it being swept gaily down the river without her.

She must have spoken her thoughts out loud, for a calm voice told her not to worry about the hat. She would be all right now, the soft, deep voice assured her, sounding far away. Gentle hands rubbed her arms, and the hands, like the voice, made her feel safe—safe and sleepy.

Later—how much later she could not have said—she opened her eyes enough to see the relentless sun trying to push through the leafy boughs above her head.

"Bandy?"

She strained to open her heavy eyelids.

"Bandy? Talk to me."

Now the voice was clearer, and she realized that it was Alan's. *His hands*, she thought, *his voice*.

"You? You pulled me. . ." She didn't want to think of the terrifying force of the waters dragging her. How had he pulled her free? "Thank you," she whispered.

"Hayden went on," Alan was saying, as though continuing an existing conversation. "Help will be here in no time."

She was wrapped in beach towels. Where they had come from, she had no idea. Later, she learned that downstream, past the dangerous log jam, Hayden had thrown them to the bank, and Alan had sprinted through the underbrush to fetch them.

She never did think she needed an ambulance, but of course she wasn't in much condition to be the one to say. Alan was there in the ambulance as well, talking softly to her the entire way. Much of the talking, she realized, was praying. Perhaps that was why waves of peace swept over her, pushing out the fear.

The ambulance sped her to a small area hospital. "Treated and released"—isn't that what she always heard them say on the news? It sounded so neat and tidy. No broken bones, only multiple bruises, they told her. Some of which, the doctor said, would not be discovered until tomorrow. Surely, she thought, there could be no more bruises; she already had no place on her body that didn't hurt.

Before she was released, Millie came with a fresh change of clothes for her. Feeling more like herself, Bandy looked from Hayden to Alan. How could she ever thank them enough?

Alan's wrist had been sprained during the rescue, and the hospital staff had wrapped it. Like Bandy, he too was covered with ugly red welts and scratches where he had been slammed against the underwater branches.

Back at the cabin, they tried to convince Bandy to stay the night at Ellen's, but she refused. She thought sure either Denise or Jordan would be saying, "I told you so," regarding the canoe, but they were strangely quiet.

Gena continued to apologize that they had sped off and left her. "We should have stayed within sight and earshot," she said over and over. "We never should have left you alone. Please forgive me."

Of course Bandy forgave her. But she was so woozy, she couldn't talk very well.

With very little discussion or planning, Hayden decided to drive Millie in the van, while Alan took Bandy home in his car. Denise rode quietly in the back seat. Since Bandy had been given something for pain, she was too groggy to talk much. In fact, later she could barely remember the ride home, or Alan helping her up the stairs to her room.

❧

The doctor had prescribed a few days of bed rest, but one day was enough for Bandy. She was back in the boutique by Wednesday. The most difficult task was walking up and down stairs. That was when her body reminded her of the terrible pummeling it had suffered.

Her first task back on the job was to instruct Gena to create special floral arrangements to send to both Alan and Hayden to thank them. Bandy smiled as she listened to Gena; because of the incident, Hayden had obviously become a hero of sorts.

"Most people would have simply floated on to the pickup point," Gena explained to Bandy, "but not Hayden. As soon as he found a place to tie up, he left the canoe and ran to find help. In all that underbrush," she added dramatically. "Luckily he found people at a nearby cabin where they phoned for the ambulance."

But Bandy knew luck had nothing to do with this rescue. She was praising the Lord for sparing her life. Later, when she talked to Alan, she was even more convinced that the Lord's hand had been at work.

When she asked Alan how he did it—how he had pulled her from the water—he said quite simply, "I don't know."

"You don't know? How can you not know? You were right there." They were sitting in the back yard in the gazebo. The apricot sun was about to set, and the air was beginning to cool. Their glasses of lemonade dripped little puddles on the white wooden table.

Alan shook his head. "Bandy, by rights, we both should have died in that mess. The current under that log jam was so intense that logically no one could have gotten out."

"Then how. . .?"

Alan smiled. "You believe in miracles, don't you?"

"Sure," she said quickly. She realized, though, how glib and automatic the answer was. She believed in miracles for other people, that was what she really meant. But for her?

"I pulled off my life jacket before I dove in," Alan told her. "I knew it would only impair my movement in the water. And of course, I said a quick prayer. That's all there was time for."

"Why did you dive in? Why didn't you guide the canoe over?"

"And trap Hayden as well? He was our alarm. He had to stay free to fetch help."

She shook her head in disbelief. "But the current was so strong, like giant arms pulling."

"All I know is, I was struggling to pull you up to the surface, when suddenly the current seemed to let you go. The awful pulling stopped. As soon as I felt it, I was able to gain leverage against a big limb and lift you up onto that fallen tree." He smiled and the blue eyes twinkled. "Some of those purple bruises might have been from me slamming you around."

She politely laughed at his humor, but she was still in awe. Perhaps God truly had worked a miracle to save her. For an instant, she pictured an angel in the water beside Alan, his strong arms pushing her free from the water's pull. She smiled and shook her head. "However You did it, Lord," she whispered, too soft for Alan to hear, "thank You."

## twelve

The autumn months swept Bandy into a flurry of activities. Her boutique team pulled off the Gilchrist wedding with a grandeur befitting the occasion. Bandy had never been so proud of her business and her employees, and Mr. and Mrs. Gilchrist lauded them with praise. Nan didn't seem to be the happiest bride Bandy had ever met, but even she was thrilled with the way the tiniest details were handled, and she made it a point to tell Bandy so. The week after the wedding, two more accounts came through from Harwood Heights; Bandy was ecstatic.

She had seen Alan at both the engagement party and the wedding, but she barely had time to even nod to him. He'd called several times since Labor Day, wanting her to go out with him, but she truly had no time. She was at the point where another full-time employee was desperately needed, and yet the budget didn't quite cover it. Finally, she had hired on a girl part-time to help Ellen.

The problem, like any problem that deals with business growth, was both good and bad. She was heartened to know that the accounts were coming in. The frustrating point seemed to be with Denise. The more jobs she assigned to Denise, the more the bookkeeper balked. In the past few weeks, she'd taken off a number of days, giving first one excuse and then another. Bandy knew she needed to address the problem directly—but she was so swamped with work, she constantly put the problem out of her mind. Right now her focus was all on the upcoming Bridal Fair, and past that, her trip to market in Dallas.

116

Confronting Denise, she knew from experience, was nearly impossible. Denise always had an excuse or a well-thought-out line of defense. Bandy didn't relish hearing what the excuses were this time. Mentally, she made a decision that if the situation had not changed by the new year, she'd be forced to let Denise go. She dreaded the slowdown of having to train a new person, but she seemed to have no alternative.

She remembered back to when she had first met Denise. Bandy had just taken the big step to open her boutique in its first site in the little shopping center. Denise had been fresh from a messy divorce and struggling to support herself. Although Bandy hadn't been in a position to afford an employee at that time, she agreed to take Denise on and give her a chance. Until the past few months, it had seemed to be a good decision, but now she was beginning to wonder.

The other thorn in her flesh, one that rankled nearly as much as Denise, was her stepmother Claire.

Not long after the Gilchrist wedding, Denise had announced over the speaker phone, "Claire O'Sullivan. Are you going to take it?"

In the past, Bandy had on occasion instructed Denise to tell Claire she was out, but she knew that was wrong. She hesitated, then sighed. "I'll take it."

She felt her stomach muscles tighten as she picked up the receiver. "Hello, Claire. Good to hear from you again. How have you been?"

"I don't need any of your syrupy salutations, Bandy O'Sullivan. I understand that now y'all are thinking of doing weddings for the families up in Harwood. Is that correct?"

"Not correct."

"What?"

"I said it's not correct. I've not been *thinking* of it, I've been *doing* it. We just finished up the Gilchrists' and now there are two more contracts lying here on my desk."

Bandy heard a groan on the other end of the line. "Oh, lands, not the Gilchrists."

Such theatrics. Did Claire think Bandy moved the boutique to Harwood Heights for her health?

"I can't believe what you've done to me since your father died," Claire went on, her voice as tinny as though she were coming out of a faint. "If only he were still here to help me with this unspeakable situation."

"And what unspeakable situation are you referring to?"

"Those people up there. . ." She paused and began again. "Those Harwood families know me. I mean, they know my family, my parents and my grandparents. What must they think of me? That my own stepdaughter is now one of their servants."

"Claire. . ."

"Don't try to defend yourself. You don't even care what happens to me. You don't care what my friends think of me."

"You should have thought about that a long time ago."

Claire was silent for a moment. "Why, whatever do you mean by that?"

"I mean that you should have thought of that when you decided to marry an Irish Yankee who just happened to have a Yankee daughter." She started to hang up, but then added, "Tell me, Claire, did all your Harwood friends come to your wedding? I don't remember seeing them."

The only answer was a click on the other end.

Bandy stared at the receiver a moment before replacing it. She shouldn't try to give a reasonable retort to Claire's unreasonable behavior. Her attitudes were incomprehensible, so far as Bandy was concerned.

Millie had tried to explain Claire to her more than once.

She had outlined in precise detail the family from which Claire was descended, explaining how important family lines were in the Pembrooke community. How, in spite of financial setbacks, Claire's mother had struggled to keep up the appearance of being wealthy, when in fact they were nearly destitute.

As touching as that story might be, living in the past was not part of Bandy's thinking. For perhaps the millionth time, she wished her father had never married Claire.

a

The fall bridal fair was held in Pembrooke's newly refurbished civic center. The fair opened on Friday evening and ran through Sunday evening. Friday afternoon, as Bandy and Gena were bringing in the boxes of materials needed to set up the booth, Bandy happened to see the name in the booth across the aisle.

"Look there, Gena," she said. "Brockhurst Photography will be here, just across the way."

"I could have told you that."

"Really?" Bandy put down the box she was carrying and pushed it to the back of the booth area. "How did you know?"

Gena smiled. "Hayden and I have been spending some time together at school."

"I see."

"I mean, I knew they would be here. I sure didn't know they'd be so close. Hayden's really a great guy once you get to know him."

Bandy pulled the table covers out of a box. "I won't argue with that. The guy helped save my life, remember?" She spread out the dusky rose cloths and covered them with lace drapes. "You stay here and put up your flowers. I'll go back out and bring in the mannequin."

She was wrestling to get the mannequin out of the van when a familiar voice sounded behind her. "Looks like she's not cooperating. May I give you a hand?"

Bandy was surprised to feel her pulse pounding as she turned around to face Alan. She couldn't allow herself to admit how eager she'd been to see those clear blue eyes again. He seemed to radiate a sense of vitality that excited her. Without waiting for her to respond, he moved to help her. His nearness brought a flashback of the ride in the ambulance when he was there beside her, praying for her.

"They have carts for you to use. Want me to get you one?"

The mannequin was now standing on the ground by the van. Bandy still had several boxes to unload, and the dress for the mannequin was lying in its protective bag across the back seat. "I'll need one, I guess."

"Don't go away." He turned to go get a cart. Over his shoulder he said, "I was lucky to get the booth across from yours."

"Lucky?"

"Well, not really lucky. I asked for it. I knew you'd know the best spot." He shot her a sweet grin and left to get the cart.

She hadn't planned to work the entire fair, but she had such fun with Alan and Hayden right there. During the lulls, they talked and bantered jokes back and forth. Gena was right, Hayden was a nice guy.

Bandy gauged the turnout to be better than the predicted numbers. Their booth, mostly designed by Gena, was one of the more beautiful ones there. The box of names and addresses was filling up quickly as the visitors signed up to win the honeymoon cruise to the Bahamas.

Millie was there on Saturday morning, and Gena was able to help during the busiest time on Saturday afternoon. By Saturday night, however, both Bandy and Alan were alone in their booths.

Every once in a while she glanced through the crowd to

watch him. She saw he was personable with the potential clients, carefully showing his catalogs and the price sheets he'd prepared for the fair. The portraits hanging about the booth were indeed professional quality, and interspersed with the portraits were landscapes and nature scenes. Two were breathtaking sunsets taken at the Swannanoa Lodge on Labor Day weekend.

When the doors closed at nine-thirty, Bandy was exhausted. As she was emptying out the box of names to take with her, Alan came up beside her and touched her shoulder. The mere touch sent shivers racing through her.

"Want to go with me to get something to eat?" he asked. "You're probably starved."

She gave a soft laugh. 'My body doesn't know if it's more hungry, or more tired. It must be a toss up."

"I'll make sure you rest while you're being served. How about it?"

She studied his face a moment. Why had she been so defiant to him before now? "I think it's a great idea. I need to put a few things in the van and I'll be ready."

She wasn't surprised when he drove back out to Giustino's. She remembered the last time they'd been here when she'd acted so rudely. Why did she let Denise disturb her so?

Papa Giustino was at his usual post by the door, happily greeting each customer "Ah," he bellowed with a wave of his hand. "These two I have not seen in a very long time. So, you are together again? All is made up, no?"

They looked at one another and laughed, but made no comment. The air was still warm enough to have the terrace open, and Bandy was pleased when Papa Giustino led them that direction. Alan put his arm gently about her as they followed, and once again, Bandy felt shivers race along her nerves.

They both ordered salads along with hot Italian bread and

cups of steaming tea. "The fair is a success, don't you think?" Alan asked after they were served.

She nodded. "I'm pleased. I think everyone within the four-county area was there today. We'll see if it continues tomorrow. It's a great way to make customer contacts."

"But not exactly the type of clients you look for, right?"

She came out of her easy comfort, feeling suddenly defensive. "What's that supposed to mean?"

His eyes were twinkling. He put up his hands. "I was making a simple statement, not an accusation. Your goals are in a different direction, am I correct?"

"I assume you're referring to higher income clientele, and you're right. Is there anything wrong with that?" Claire's words still echoed in her brain. She knew she shouldn't respond to Alan out of her wounding from Claire, but she couldn't help herself.

"Not if that's the way the Lord is directing you," he said as he spread butter on a chunk of the soft, warm bread.

"If? Are you saying I might not be following what the Lord is calling me to do?"

He shrugged. "I don't know. Sometimes the extremely wealthy can be a rather ungrateful lot. I'd hate to see you get hurt."

"Mrs. Gilchrist seemed overly grateful if you ask me."

"Yes, she did. She and Nan both were very appreciative." He gazed out into the distance for a moment. "I guess I should keep quiet. I'm speaking from experiences that have nothing to do with the Gilchrists. Or anyone in Pembrooke for that matter."

"Family?"

He nodded. "It was their wealth that gave them license to treat people as though they owned them."

"Someone would have to get up pretty early in the morning to think they ever owned me—other than the Lord, that is."

The remark sparked a hearty laugh from Alan. "I can see that! I guess that's what I find so fascinating about you." He leaned over, took her face in his hands, and kissed her softly on the lips. "I've been wanting to do that ever since I gave you mouth-to-mouth resuscitation on the banks of the Swansea River."

"You have? I mean, you did?" She felt weak, like a little kid with a stomach full of butterflies.

"Mm hm. I have, and I did. Both."

# thirteen

Alan suggested she leave the van at the civic center, and allow him to drive her home. "I'll come over in the morning and take you to church, and from there to the Bridal Fair. How does that sound?"

"Fine. That's fine."

The truth was, she really didn't want to go get her van. She wanted Alan to take her home. To walk her to her front door. And she wasn't disappointed.

As they stood at the steps, he gathered her into his arms and held her snugly but gently. The evening air was sweet and cool, the fat harvest moon draped in a thin bridal veil of wispy clouds. Bandy relaxed into his embrace. They stood there in a comfortable silence.

"Thank you for taking the time to be with me tonight," he whispered into her hair. "I enjoyed every moment of it."

Before she could answer, he lifted her face to his and pressed a soft kiss onto each cheek, then softly on her waiting lips. She kissed him back, her lips eager as she inhaled his sweetness. Her senses reeled, and her knees weakened.

Ever so gently, he released her and took a small step back, still holding her arms. "Sleep well, Bandy. I'll see you in the morning."

She tried to speak, but only nodded. He reached past her to pull open the screen door. She opened the front door and let herself in. "Goodnight," she managed to say. "And thank you."

Surprisingly, Millie was not waiting up. Quietly, Bandy went up the stairs. Her mind was a swirl of childlike giddiness and very adult confusion. What was happening to her? She'd thought Alan Brockhurst an arrogant snob, but since Labor Day weekend, he'd shown himself to be totally the opposite. He was sensitive, gentle, and caring. Why had she been trying so hard to avoid him? Quickly, she changed into her nightgown and slipped between the cool sheets. As she lay looking at the moonlight casting shadows across her bed, she had visions of her limp body lying on the ground, and a handsome, strong Alan breathing life back into her mouth. Was she now enamored with him because he had saved her life? Or were her feelings genuine? How could she know?

❧

She watched him closely the next day in church. He attended most Sundays when he was in town, but he usually served as an usher, and their paths seldom crossed. Today he was impeccably dressed in a trim navy suit with a pale blue shirt and dark tie. A few heads turned as they arrived together for the worship service.

Millie taught a children's Sunday School class and had left early, but she had left a note on the kitchen table by the freshly baked muffins:

> *The van didn't come home, but you did. Could it*
> *be you found another ride? Perhaps with a hand-*
> *some photographer we all know?*
>
> > *Love, Millie*

*Wonderful, sweet Millie,* Bandy thought as she and Alan found seats in a pew near the center of the church. Every time Bandy had refused to go out with Alan, Millie was there to rebuke her. "For heaven's sake, girl, go with the guy. You never have any fun. You work too hard. You need to take time to enjoy yourself."

Well, she had definitely enjoyed herself last night. And as

she and Alan held the hymnbook together for the first hymn, she realized she was enjoying herself just as much now as their voices blended in praise to God.

Before the day was over, Bandy found an opportunity to ask Alan about helping her with the boutique's catalogs. In the slow time early in the afternoon, before the crowds arrived for the last day of the Bridal Fair, he took the time to show her several samples of his indoor photography. They sat together in her boutique booth, studying her old catalogs and his samples.

Bandy quickly saw that his work was flawless. She was impressed with the attention to detail, in both color and lighting, but also in arrangement. This was exactly what she needed. She listened with rapt attention as he explained to her what he could offer and how he would go about getting the needed photographs.

"It may mean we'll need to spend quite a bit of time together." He stood up to return to his own booth, as the visitors were beginning to arrive.

She looked up at his open expression and his lopsided grin. "I think we can manage that."

Before she could react, he leaned over and kissed the top of her head. "Have I told you I think your red curls are ravishing?"

The red curls she fought with daily? He thought they were ravishing? What a thought! She'd have to mull that one over. "Thanks," she said and reached up to touch his hand that lingered on her shoulder.

Denise was supposed to come in to relieve Bandy that afternoon, but she called at the last minute to say something had come up. Funny, but it was Denise who had first encouraged Bandy to use Alan to work on their catalogs, and Bandy had vetoed the idea. What a ninny she'd been. She would make a point to apologize to Denise first thing

Monday morning.

Throughout the afternoon, she kept glancing across the aisle to where Alan was working. She'd never realized before how infectious his smile was. Nor how straight he stood. Nor how bright his eyes sparkled when he laughed. She fought to keep her mind on the business at hand, but she had little success.

Millie was all smiles when she arrived at the fair late Sunday afternoon. "I saw the two of you in church together," she said in a low voice, as though Alan could hear from across the busy aisle. "I knew it had to happen sooner or later."

"What had to happen?"

"You couldn't keep running forever. He was bound to catch you."

"Hey, wait a minute. I've not been caught!"

"Well, that's a simple matter, my dear. Just let yourself *get* caught."

"Millie, I swear. You're impossible."

Millie fussed with the veil on the mannequin, spreading it out and smoothing the folds in the back. "You'd look lovely in a little number like this, Bandy. That red hair would glow like a crown of gold!"

"Now, Millie, stop it."

But there was no stopping Millie once her mind was set. The teasing went on throughout the day until Bandy was wishing Gena had come in to help instead. But then she realized that once Gena found out she'd spent time with Alan, Gena too would be teasing. Bandy made up her mind to get used to it.

Hayden showed up as the fair was closing and all of them worked together to close out the booths and load the items in Alan's car and Bandy's van.

"I'll see you next week, right?" Alan said as she was ready

to get in the van.

"Next week Millie and I will be in Dallas at market. I won't be back until Friday. We'll have to wait until the week after to get started."

A brief look of disappointment crossed his face, then he smiled. "Ah, shopping and buying. What women love."

"Most shopping I loathe. This shopping, I admit, I do love it."

He slipped his arm around her waist. "I'll talk to you Friday then." He leaned down and brushed her lips with a soft kiss. She stood on tiptoe to receive it, hoping Millie wouldn't see.

"On Friday," she whispered.

❧

When Bandy arrived at the boutique early Monday morning, she was surprised to see Denise's car already there; usually Denise never arrived until after nine. Something was up.

Ellen must have known what was going on, for she gave Bandy a strange look as she came in the door. "What is it?" Bandy asked.

Ellen only shook her head and threw a glance toward the mezzanine offices. Bandy hurried upstairs and found Denise clearing personal items out of her desk.

"Denise, what are you doing? It's Monday morning!"

"My resignation is on your desk. I'm leaving."

"Today? This morning? But you can't." Bandy's mind flew to the bundle of names and addresses gleaned over the weekend. She desperately needed Denise's help on the follow-up. She couldn't bear the thought of hiring strangers to take care of it.

"Watch me." Denise's pale, well-manicured fingers continued to take items from the desk and place them in a shopping bag.

"But why? Why are you quitting?"

Denise's dark eyes flashed. "I don't have to give you a reason, Miss O'Sullivan. It's a free country. I have better things to do."

"But don't you think you owe. . ."

Whirling around in the office chair, Denise stood to her feet. "Owe? I swear, you people are all alike. I've worked hard for you all these years, and all I've ever gotten in return was the demand to do more work. I don't owe you a thing."

Bandy thought of the raises and bonuses she'd lavished upon this woman. Money she could never really afford, but always considered an investment in building good employee relations. She wanted to scream out and defend herself. But what was the use? Denise was unfair to leave her in such a tight squeeze, but perhaps this was best after all.

"I'll go make out your last week's check."

Denise held up the check. "I made it out myself. All you have to do is sign it."

Bandy shook her head in disbelief. She took the check from Denise's hand and slowly walked into her own office to sit down and sign it. She had to do something to calm the storm seething inside. She took a moment to double check the figures to see if they were accurate. Would Denise try to cheat her? Had she perhaps messed up the books before leaving? Bandy would have their CPA come in to go over everything as soon as she returned from Dallas. The amount on the check was accurate as far as she could ascertain.

She forced herself to sit still a moment, hoping the anger would subside. Why should Denise be treating her this way? And why was she so defensive? None of this made any sense.

After a moment, Bandy rose and went back to where Denise stood waiting beside her desk. "I'm sorry you feel you haven't been treated fairly, Denise," Bandy said. "I wish. . ."

"Forget the speech. If you don't want to hand me the check, just drop it in the mail."

Without another word, Bandy handed her the check and watched as the slim figure picked up her bag and walked to the stairway. Denise's short black hair seemed more severe, her steps more determined. She marched through the store and pushed through the front door without a backward glance.

❧

Bandy was fidgety on the flight to Dallas. She couldn't calm her jumpy nerves. Everything had suddenly turned topsy-turvy. Millie graciously agreed to stay behind and spend time in the office answering the phone and keeping abreast of the mail, so Bandy had left for Dallas alone.

She was still preoccupied with Denise's sudden departure. Gena and Ellen both said, "Good riddance," and seemed to feel no remorse at all that Denise had left in such a huff. So why didn't Bandy feel the same relief? But the gnawing deep inside continued to eat at her as she attempted to conduct business at market.

She missed having Millie at her side. The older woman's keen insight and nose for sniffing out great bargains was invaluable. Denise was to blame for Millie not being here, and Bandy's anger against Denise grew.

She waded through the grand arrays of new products, her mind still snagged on Denise. She had more available money to spend on new inventory than at any time since she'd been in business, and this should have been the happiest market trip ever. But it wasn't.

Wednesday night late, she was in her hotel room just ready to collapse into bed when the phone rang. "Did I wake you?" Millie wanted to know.

"No. I'm not in bed yet. Just ready to fall in. Is everything all right?"

"Fine. A real busy day. I can't believe the traffic in the store."

They had talked each evening as Millie reported details that had transpired at the boutique. But tonight Millie's voice sounded strained. "What is it, Millie. Is something wrong?"

"What do you mean?"

"I can hear it in your voice. What's up? The place didn't burn down, did it?"

Millie laughed. "Nothing that bad."

"Then there *is* something. Spit it out."

"I thought about just waiting to tell you when you got back. Or just let you see for yourself."

"See what?"

"Remember that little jewelry store that vacated on the corner next to the plus-sizes dress shop?"

Bandy thought a moment, picturing the Harwood Heights Shopping Center. The center was laid out in rustic little streets with quaint globed street lights, and old South charm. "I remember. What about it?"

"A new proprietor is moving in."

"So what does that have to do with us?"

"It's a bridal boutique."

"You're kidding. Just when I'm beginning to make a little headway."

"Bandy, it's Denise. Denise is the new proprietor. There's been a flurry of electricians and carpenters going in and out ever since you left. And she's been right in there directing the whole thing."

Slowly, Bandy sat down on the edge of the mammoth king-sized bed. Pain shot through her midsection as though she'd been hit with a fist. Every nerve in her body went taut. Was this why she'd felt like a bundle of nerves all week? Was the Lord somehow trying to tell her?

"Bandy, are you there?"

"I'm in shock. I can't believe it. How could she? Where would she ever get the money?" But even as she asked the question, Bandy remembered the rich, little man named Wendell that Denise hung around with. And then the fact that she was chumming around with the owner of the Swannanoa Lodge. The woman knew how to attract money. That was no problem for Denise.

Millie was probably thinking the same thing. "Someone obviously bankrolled her," she said.

"Obviously."

"I don't want to make things sound worse than they are, Bandy, but I have reason to believe she garbled messages from your newest clients."

Bandy squeezed her eyes shut. This couldn't be happening. Not now. Not after all these months of such hard work to carefully lay the groundwork. For a moment she thought she was going to be sick. Carefully, she pulled the phone into the bathroom and wet a cool cloth to press to her face. "How bad do you think it is?"

"I'm not sure. It'll take time to figure all that out. Don't fret, Bandy. Your clients know you and love you." Then she added, "And never forget that the Lord is in total control."

"Thanks, Millie."

She knew that was true—but it didn't *feel* true.

# fourteen

Sleep eluded Bandy for most of the night. She tossed and turned, rose to pace, then lay back down to try again to sleep. Her emotions vacillated from fear to anger to deep sadness. How could Denise do this? How much harm had she already done by undercutting Bandy to existing clients? This explained Denise's strange actions in recent months—slipping out, refusing to help at the fair, various doctor and dentist appointments. All that time she was probably working hard to lay the foundation for her own boutique. What a traitor!

Denise would never be able to run a business by herself. What did she know about inventory and buying? On the other hand, if money was no object, she could easily hire buyers and business managers.

Bandy didn't for a moment believe that Denise could build a solid, long-lasting business on such a weak foundation. But on the other hand, even if her business had only a brief stint, it could bring ruin to Bandy's boutique. Especially, if Denise decided to play dirty—and from what Millie said, this was definitely her intent. Suddenly Bandy felt very alone and very frightened. How could the Lord have let this happen, after all the hard work and sacrifices she'd made?

Should she go ahead with the large orders she was placing for inventory, or pull back and work on a more reserved margin for the next six months?

Bandy tried to pray, but Denise's unsmiling face and cold eyes loomed big in her mind. What an ungrateful, hateful, spiteful woman she was!

Bandy spent one more day at market and arrived back in Pembrooke a day early. She had cut back on her buying just to stay on the safe side, and now, before talking to anyone, she had to see Denise's new shop for herself. Slowly, she drove through the tree-lined streets of the Harwood Heights Shopping Center.

From a block away, she saw the new sign: "Denise's Bridal Designs." Beneath this sign was another which said, "Fine Photography." A large sign inside the window announced: "Opening soon. Watch for Grand Opening Celebration!"

If Bandy had still been in the Valley Shopping Center, this would have been a small matter. But up here, at this time, she was still on such shaky footing. The overhead was enormous. Would she have enough of an edge to survive this?

Denise was smart to begin by offering a photography service. Bandy wondered what other services she planned to offer? Would she too have catering and flowers?

Bandy parked in an out-of-the-way spot to sit and think. As she sat there, she saw Alan Brockhurst's car drive by. Obviously he hadn't seen her. But then she wasn't expected back until tomorrow. His car pulled in directly in front of Denise's new shop. Bandy watched as his tall, handsome form emerged from the car and entered the shop.

So that was it. That was the "Fine Photography" referred to by the sign. Mr. Brockhurst had finally found a spot for his business. Bandy could easily imagine how eager Denise was to have him come in and make himself at home. But how long had this cozy little merger been simmering? Had Alan been planning this move even as he held Bandy in his arms and kissed her? Was he so blind as to think this competition wouldn't affect her business?

Slowly she drove home without even stopping at the boutique. She fought a losing battle with a cold numbness that crept over her entire body. Suddenly, she felt totally exhausted. She wanted to crawl in a warm bed and never get up.

≈

"Bandy O'Sullivan!"

The words yanked Bandy out of fitful dreams of wars and battles with Denise Jepson.

"What in heaven's name are you doing home? And in bed?" Millie's tone was one of total disbelief.

Bandy attempted to bury her body deeper under the pillow and covers. Why did she have to be disturbed?

Millie sat down on the edge of the bed and tried to pull the covers from Bandy's face. "What's ailing you, girl? Talk to me."

"Leave me alone. I'm tired. I just want to sleep."

"In the middle of the day? That's not like you." Millie pulled back the covers enough to feel Bandy's face. "Mm. No fever. Shall I bring you hot soup? I can make up a batch quicker than scat."

"I don't need soup, I just need to be left alone." Bandy pulled the covers up even more tightly. She felt the bed go up slightly as Millie rose.

"Suit yourself. I'll be downstairs if you need me. But if you're in a tizzy just because of that little snit Denise, I'm ashamed of you. She's no more threat than a gnat on an alligator's hide." Her voice was moving toward the door. "Just remember, Bandy O'Sullivan, God's not in the business of catering to your whims. He wants to guide you into His perfect will."

≈

Alan attempted to call and talk several times in the next few weeks, but Bandy refused his calls. He left messages that he was ready to talk business regarding the catalogs. How dare he think she would go ahead on that project now? Bandy couldn't help but wonder if some of the Longmont money had been invested into Denise's new shop. Much to Millie's concern, Bandy began arriving at church late and leaving early to avoid meeting Alan.

Bandy counteracted her pain and anger by working hard to undergird the business as tightly as she knew how. As quickly as she could, she found a new secretary/bookkeeper who was qualified and came with exemplary references. Marla Sue was immediately accepted by the rest of the staff. Bandy explained to her that business was slow at the present time, to which Marla Sue cheerfully replied that this way she would have more time to learn the ropes.

Under the close scrutiny of both Marla Sue and Bandy's accountant, the books and records were inspected. No clandestine evidence was uncovered. But Bandy was sure Denise had taken plenty of names, addresses, and phone numbers with her.

In spite of everything Bandy did, December and January were dismal months. The weather did nothing to cooperate. An intense cold wave gripped the South in an unprecedented icebox of winter weather. Residents of the area, unaccustomed as they were to frigid weather, went out as little as possible. Traffic in the store slowed to a standstill. In spite of all the contacts made at the Bridal Fair, the slow months were even slower than usual. The days dragged by.

Through the grapevine, which was never frozen even by the weather, Bandy learned that Denise had indeed been undermining the integrity of the boutique. Two potential clients from Harwood called and backed out of their contracts.

Bandy wasn't sure how things could get any worse. But then she learned from Gena that Professor Jordan Wyler and Professor Lena Brookneal were an "item" on campus. Much as she hated to admit it, Bandy's heart broke at the news. Even though nothing had ever blossomed in their relationship, still Jordan had always been there for her. Now, just at the time when she longed for his friendship, she hesitated to contact him.

Bandy felt hollow and lifeless. She couldn't shake off her weariness and despair.

One evening as she and Millie were leaving the boutique together, Alan met them in front of the store. Bandy gasped as panic gripped her. She hadn't allowed herself to even think of Alan—to remember his face, or his touch, or his gentle kisses. Now he was standing tall before her in the dim winter twilight. The soft streetlights reflected on what was left of day-old snow and ice and on Alan's soft blond hair.

"Bandy," he began, "I need to talk to you. Please."

Bandy cringed at the pleading tone of his voice. "I can't. We've got to get home." She pushed past him to the van parked at the side of the boutique. He followed. Thankfully, Millie kept quiet and simply walked to her side, unlocked the door, and got in.

"Just for a moment. Please. There's something I need to tell you."

She'd reached her side of the van and quickly unlocked the door and stepped up inside. "It's too late for talking, Alan." She closed the door, started the motor, and drove off.

Millie held her peace half the way home, then said, "That's a pretty cruel way to treat someone you care for."

"It's called self defense. I'm protecting myself from further woundings."

"And how could Alan Brockhurst hurt you? He's the one who saved your life, remember?"

An involuntary shiver swept over her. "I remember."

"Can't you at least listen to what he wants to say? He

sounded so. . .so sincere."

Bandy was fighting to get the sound of his voice out of her mind. "He chose his place. If he wants to aid and abet the enemy that's his choice."

She could feel Millie's eyes boring through her. "What are you talking about? Do you have reason to suspect he's involved with Denise?"

"With Denise, I don't know. With her business, yes. He's set up his photography studio in her shop, just like he wanted to do in the boutique, but I refused. He needed a spot. I guess it didn't matter to him which spot he chose."

Millie cleared her throat in a way that infuriated Bandy. "Are you sure this is true?"

"Have you seen the shop? Have you been over to that part of the shopping center to see?"

"I was the one who reported the news to you."

"Then you saw the sign 'Fine Photography.' When I came back from market early, I drove over there and saw him there. He may even be one of her investors. Who knows?"

"Obviously you don't. Shame on you for jumping to conclusions. You don't know anything and you've let evil imaginations take over your brain. I never thought I'd see you like this—Bandy the Fighter, curled up in a little ball of self pity."

Millie's usually soft voice grew harsher. It grated on Bandy's tender nerves. Had she not been driving, she would have considered jumping out of the van to get free of that accusing voice.

"Even if he did decide to set up his studio in her facilities," Millie went on, "that doesn't mean he's a criminal. Shame on you for treating him like one."

Bandy steered the van up into the drive. As they approached the front door, Millie turned and said, "And one more thing. Until you make up your mind to forgive Denise

Jepson, your profits are going to continue to nosedive. If you think God will bless an unforgiving spirit, you're just plain daft. That's all I have to say in the matter."

Bandy went up to her room and closed the door. How could she ever forgive someone who had not only sabo- aged her business, but stabbed her in the back with ruthless gossip? That was impossible.

❧

The next Sunday, she arrived late at church as usual and slipped into a pew in the back. She'd barely sat down when Alan came over and folded his tall frame into the pew be- side her.

"This seat taken?" he asked with a slight smile.

The fragrance of his cologne swept back all the memo- ies she'd been trying to forget.

The congregation stood for a hymn. He held out the hym- nal, but she took her own out of the rack and turned away from him.

Later, as the sermon began, Alan wrote a note on the back of the bulletin and handed it to her. His handwriting was bold and round, with soft swirls:

> *The biggest engagement of the decade in Harwood Heights is about to take place. The families of Prouteau and Marsden. Because of family, I'm invited to the engagement announce- ment party on Valentine's Day. I can bring a guest. If you attend you might corner the account. Will you go with me?*

Bandy studied the note. The names of Prouteau and Marsden were well known. She would never have known his on her own. She sighed as she thought of how she was osing her grip on the area. Perhaps this could help her regain her position. It was worth a try. Better than curling up in a ball of self pity as Millie had accused.

Beneath his writing, she penciled in:

*I'll go. Thanks.*

To her surprise, he took the bulletin, folded it, and put it inside his coat pocket, then rose to join the ushers as they took up the offering. She thought surely he would come back to his seat beside her afterward, but she didn't see him again.

The sermon that morning spoke of the parable of the sower, and how the cares of this world can choke out the clarity of the Word of God. Bandy stared down at her hands her mind on Alan's note. Valentine's Day was two weeks away.

# Fifteen

A wedding between the Frouteau and Marsden families was sure to be mammoth. In the back of her mind, she wondered why Alan hadn't given the news to Denise. She decided not to mention the party to her staff members. After all, it was a shot in the dark. But if they did get the contract, she'd take them all out for dinner to celebrate. After all, they'd hung in there with her through this slow time.

By early February, the terrible cold was all but forgotten, and the green tips of the jonquils could be seen poking their noses through the ground. The purple crocuses had been in bloom for a number of days. Waldo constantly fumed and fussed about how many old plants had died as a result of the terrible cold. Bandy silently wondered if her boutique would be added to the list.

Because of her copper-colored hair, Bandy could never wear red, but she searched through the back room stock of dresses for a suitable number for a formal gathering on Valentine's Day. She settled on a cranberry sheath with puffs of frothy white organza ruffles at the shoulders. It was perfect.

Luckily, Millie had a meeting at the church the night of the party. Bandy left her a note saying she would be out until late. Of course, Millie would wonder, but she wouldn't meddle.

The evening was chilly, and Bandy wished she had a long fur to wear, but all she had was a shoulder wrap. It would have to do.

She was ready early and found herself pacing. Was she so

nervous because of the possibility of netting this large account? Or was she nervous because she would be seeing Alan again? She wasn't sure. How confusing that he should want to give her this edge, when he could just as easily have given it to Denise. It didn't make much sense.

She took another look at herself in the hall mirror. She had piled her curls high atop her head and fashioned trailing tendrils at the temples and neckline. The cranberry dress fit perfectly. Hopefully, she would look like she belonged at this prestigious event.

Her heart stopped as the doorbell sounded. With an air of calmness that was only pretended, she opened the door to see Alan looking more dashing than ever in a gray tux. The sparkling blue eyes registered surprise as he looked at her.

"I always knew you were pretty, Bandy O'Sullivan. But tonight you are ravishing. I've never seen you look so beautiful."

As she said her thanks, he held out a small box containing a wrist corsage of tiny pink rosebuds and carnations. Suddenly, she felt like a high school girl—and ten times as giddy.

❧

The Prouteau mansion was notably the most magnificent one in Harwood. Although Bandy had driven by it, she had never paid it much attention. It had been built on the back side of a large hill, and only the massive, tiled roof was visible from the road.

She and Alan had talked very little after he had helped her into his car, and now they were silent as he stopped at the gate to the estate. A voice asked Alan his name. Once he had given it, the iron gates swung open, and they proceeded up the winding drive banked by formal gardens and thick stands of trees. Bandy found herself imagining how colorful it soon would be when all the spring flowers were in bloom.

She shivered as Alan helped her from the car. He carefully put his arm around her fur-clad shoulders as they walked up the vast stairway to the front entrance.

The opulence of the home was greater than Bandy had ever imagined. "Yankee money," Waldo would have said. The grand, marble entrance hall was accented with gold stencils, and vaulted ceilings were trimmed with hand-carved walnut. Two matching crystal chandeliers glittered in the center of the vaulted ceiling.

They were greeted at the door and shown to the ballroom where other guests were mingling. For the most part, the evening was somewhat awkward, but thankfully, Alan never left her side. He requested non-alcoholic drinks for the two of them, taking pressure off Bandy. They nibbled at hors d'oeuvres and made small talk as Alan moved them among the tightly-formed groups.

He was careful to introduce her to both sets of parents of the prospective couple. He was also careful to announce that she was the proprietor of Bandy's Bridal Boutique in the Harwood Heights Shopping Center, but there seemed to be little response. Until Carmen Prouteau breezed into the room, Bandy was sure the evening had been totally wasted.

The moment Alan introduced Bandy to this charming young lady, something seemed to click between them. Unlike the others in the room, Carmen exuded a sweet joy and warmth that was like a soft flower blooming in a rock wall.

As soon as Carmen learned who Bandy was, she took her aside where they could sit down and talk. She wanted to know all about what Bandy could provide. Alan stood nearby with a slight smile on his lips.

"Mother and Daddy want to bring people in from New York City to do the wedding, and I'm aghast," Carmen explained. "I have my own tastes, and my own ideas. If you can show them you have everything we need right here,

I'm sure they'll agree."

Briefly Bandy explained the boutique and all that was available. She took a business card from her satin bag. "Call me Monday morning, Carmen. I'll show you everything we have available. Let me know what you want, and we'll try to oblige."

Carmen leaned over and gave Bandy a light hug. "You may have saved me a world of grief, Bandy. I'm so glad you were here tonight. Now maybe I'll have a chance at doing at least part of this wedding like I want it." She waved the card. "I'll call you Monday."

Later in the evening, the formal announcement was made of the engagement of Carmen Prouteau and Michael Marsden. Bandy studied the couple as they moved to the center of the ballroom to waltz together to the strains of the orchestra. Michael and Carmen appeared to be the perfect storybook couple.

As they were driving home, Bandy asked Alan, "Do you think it will be difficult for Carmen to convince her parents not to do the New York thing?"

"I'm not sure. They adore her, but they also smother her. It depends on how badly they want to show off with this social affair." He loosened the gray-blue bow tie at his neck. "Once you show them the best you have to offer, then that's all you can do."

Suddenly she realized she still hadn't updated the catalogs. "Oh no! My catalogs," she said with a little gasp.

Alan shook his head. "I tried."

"You tried?" she snapped. "Tried what? Tried your best to help Denise get her business off the ground?"

"Denise's business? Her shop is of no interest to me. What makes you think I would help Denise?"

Her throat suddenly went paper-dry. "But the sign outside the shop says, 'Fine Photography.'"

"That it does."

"And I saw you going into her shop the day I came back from market."

Alan had pulled up into her driveway and shut off the ignition. "Oh, you did? So you added two and two and got five? Is this why you've been so put out with me?"

"You haven't set up your photography studio in her shop?"

Alan shook his head. "No, ma'am. And if you want to know the whole truth, I was invited to do just that, but I refused. Somehow, it just didn't seem right that she should open a competitive business so close to yours. I didn't agree with her actions, so I said no."

"Then who. . ."

"The photographer? Actually, it's a guy named Fine. Jack Fine. And if you ask me, he's not very good at what he does. I'll be surprised if he lasts in there six months. If that long."

"Jack Fine? Fine Photography." Bandy couldn't remember ever before feeling so small and so ashamed. "I was so hurt and angry, I guess I let the bitterness take the upper hand. Millie tried to warn me."

"Millie's a smart gal. You should listen to her."

Hot tears were burning in Bandy's eyes, and she didn't even have a tissue.

Alan reached across her to open the glove box. "There are usually a few napkins in here—from when I eat lunch in the car." He pulled out a paper napkin and handed it to her so she could dab at her eyes.

"I'm sorry," she told him. "I've been such an idiot."

He touched her lips with his fingers. "Shh. Don't say that. You've been through a rather traumatic experience. I've been so worried about you. Especially since Denise pulled her little coup. But more than that. . ." He reached down to take her hand. "I was worried that I'd somehow hurt you. And I wouldn't do that for anything in the world."

Suddenly, she was immersed in his embrace and his sweet kisses. She let out her breath in a long sigh and pushed closer against him. Her world had been set right side up again.

※

Carmen did not call Bandy on Monday. Instead, she was at the boutique before the doors were open, waiting out front in her little blue Mercedes coupe. She and Bandy had a delightful time that morning as Bandy showed her around the shop and introduced her to the staff. Bandy took copious notes as Carmen revealed her preferences in styles and colors. If the parents were as easy to please as Carmen, this job would be a breeze.

Within the week, Alan and Bandy were working on the catalog photography. Although still nothing was said about actually giving Alan space for his own studio, he did begin working some in a spot in the storeroom. He set up drapes and lighting equipment and began to photograph several of the bouquets that Gena was working on at the time. Bandy could see that the project might take quite a while. In the meantime, she enjoyed having Alan nearby, even more so now that Denise was gone.

The possibility of having the Prouteau-Marsden account looked more promising with each passing day. Carmen stopped by the boutique several times to look at dresses, and just to talk. From everything Bandy could tell, these two families might well hold the key to her success in Harwood Heights. She had no doubt she could do a great job for them, once she had the contract in hand. That is, *if* she could get the contract in hand. That remained to be seen.

Finally, after two weeks of negotiations and much talk with both families, Bandy was invited to a dinner at the Prouteau mansion. She wanted Alan to attend with her, but he told her, "I wasn't invited. This is your show, Bandy. I got the ball rolling, now it's all yours."

Bandy was nervous as a cat the night she maneuvered the curving streets in Harwood Heights up to the massive iron gates of the Prouteau estate. She announced her name at the gate as she had watched Alan do, and saw the gate swing slowly open.

Thankfully, it was Carmen who met her at the door. The girl grabbed Bandy's hand. "I think we've won them over, Bandy," she said. "Finally, it looks like I have a say in this event." She led Bandy past the entry with the elegant chandeliers and vaulted ceiling, and down a back hallway. "Michael's parents are here too. We're eating in the Green Room. Don't let them rattle you, Bandy. I like you, and I like your boutique. The people from New York don't have anything on you, and I keep telling them that."

Carmen's voice was so fast and breathless that she gave Bandy no chance to answer. "This is a shortcut," she explained as they walked through a room circled with large arch windows and a white grand piano in the center, with several music stands scattered about.

One more long hallway and Bandy was ushered into the Green Room where dinner was about to be served. Carmen made sure Bandy was seated by her side, but dinner was still uncomfortable and awkward for Bandy. She felt as though she didn't belong there, and she wondered why she had even been invited. Nothing was said to her about the wedding until dessert had been served. Then, it was Mrs. Prouteau who spoke, explaining that they had found a boutique in New York City that they favored greatly.

"Mother," Carmen said quickly.

"Wait until your mother finishes" Mr. Prouteau chided his daughter, and she held her peace.

Bandy wondered how the sprightly Carmen could stand all this stuffiness.

"It should be made clear," Mrs. Prouteau continued in her monotone voice, "that we do not favor your boutique, but since Carmen has insisted repeatedly that your services be procured, we have decided to grant her this wish."

"In other words," Mrs. Marsden put in, "we can't see that it will do that much harm for you to provide the services, although we know the gentleman in New York much better."

Bandy started to answer, but there was no place to jump in. The conversation continued to swirl about her as she heard how important it was to maintain certain connections and for everything to look just right, but that they didn't mind making an exception for once as a sort of gift to Carmen.

Before Bandy left that evening, she was beginning to feel sorry for Carmen. But Mr. Prouteau handed her the signed contract along with the retainer check in the amount she had requested. Thank heaven, she was in!

# sixteen

"Carmen doesn't love him, you know," Gena said. She twirled a white silk boutonniere in her fingers, deftly weaving in bits of baby's breath. They had been discussing the Prouteau-Marsden wedding in great detail. Carmen would have fresh flowers. No silks for this wedding. Nothing but the best!

"What do you mean?" Bandy wanted to know. "Have you seen Michael Marsden? He's a knockout."

"I don't have to see the guy. I've seen *her*."

Bandy was sitting in Gena's workroom watching her work as they reviewed the massive number of flowers needed, not only for Carmen's wedding, but for the showers that would precede the wedding. The clipboard in Bandy's lap held the worksheets she'd drawn up for the project.

Gena's remarks about Carmen disturbed Bandy. "You should be careful—talking about things you know nothing about, Gena. That's not like you."

Carefully, Gena placed the boutonniere on a rack with several others. She whirled around and looked at Bandy. "Come on. You've been with her a lot more than I have. Don't tell me you haven't seen it too. You're not blind."

"Why would a smart, independent girl like Carmen marry someone she doesn't love? That doesn't make sense."

Gena rolled her eyes as though she'd suddenly lost all patience with her respected employer. "She is smart, and she is independent. But she can be smart and independent only in certain areas. Marriage is not one of those areas. That matter is out of her hands."

"Are you talking about an arranged marriage? That's crazy. People don't do that. . ."

"I'm not saying it happens in every high society family, but I can guarantee it's happening in this situation. They're not your typical kids next door, you know. Do you think it's a coincidence that the offspring of the two most wealthy and influential families in Pembrooke just happen to be getting hitched? To one another, that is."

"I never gave it a thought."

"No need for you to, I guess," Gena said with a shrug.

"You guess? What are you insinuating?"

"Carmen respects you, Bandy. She admires your spunk. Maybe you could help her."

"Help her what? I just endured the most intense scrutiny of my life just to get this account secured. What are you suggesting I do?"

"Help her avoid the worst mistake of her entire life."

Bandy rose from her chair and placed her arm around Gena's shoulders. "All this sounds very noble, Gena. But I'm in the wedding business, not the pre-marital counseling business. And I've been around long enough to know not to meddle in the affairs of my clients. Who Carmen Prouteau marries or does not marry is none of my concern."

"You're having lunch with her today, right?"

"I am."

"Maybe it will come up."

Bandy turned to go. "And maybe it won't." Ah, the idealism of youth!

❧

Bandy was scheduled to meet Carmen at Victoria's Tea Room a mile or so from the shopping center. By the time she arrived, Carmen was already there sipping a cup of herbal tea from a delicate china cup. She was dressed in an understated jade wool crepe suit, and she flashed Bandy a big smile when she saw her.

They ordered turkey sandwiches on homemade bread with bunches of alfalfa sprouts tucked in, sprouts which would not stay in the sandwich, nor on the plate, but seemed to want to sprinkle about everywhere. Of course Carmen had no trouble: the alfalfa sprouts seemed not to dare fall from her sandwich onto the meticulous jade suit.

The bride-to-be was obviously thrilled at her conquest, having won the two sets of parents over to retain Bandy's services. As they discussed the list of details—which seemed to grow bigger each day—Bandy could sense no hesitancy in Carmen's voice nor her actions. She seemed as happy as any bride.

As lunch and the conversation was concluding, Bandy felt encouraged at the progress they'd made. Carmen was easy to work with, and she certainly knew her own mind.

As she was slipping her credit card back into her clutch bag, Carmen looked at Bandy and suddenly asked, "Have you ever been in love, Miss O'Sullivan?"

The question threw Bandy completely off guard. "Who, me?" She laughed uncomfortably. Had she been in love with Jordan? Not really. Was she now falling in love with Alan? She hadn't a clue. "Well, not since junior high when I fell head over heels for my biology teacher. He was new that year—fresh out of college. What a great looking guy he was."

"You've never really fallen in love then?"

Bandy shook her head. "Not the real thing. Not yet, anyway."

"But you'll know the real thing when it comes along, won't you?"

"I certainly hope so."

"How? How will you know? Do you believe there should be romantic love involved?"

Bandy felt she was being pushed into a corner. Had Gena been right after all? "I've been in this business a long time. I've seen all kinds. Some couples seemed to be so wildly in love yet, after a couple of years their names would pop up in the divorce statistics page of the *Chronicle*."

"I wasn't asking about your clients," Carmen said softly, not taking her eyes off Bandy for a moment. "I was asking what you believe."

Bandy felt herself squirm. "Why, Carmen? Why are you asking me? What difference does it make to you what I think or believe?"

Only then did Carmen's eyes leave Bandy's face, and momentarily, Bandy saw her façade slip. Carmen gazed out the windows at the garden courtyard. "You seem to be so much your own person," she said, articulating each word carefully. "So independent. You must love having your own business."

"It has its ups and downs, but for the most part I enjoy it."

"That's why I feel sure you have definite ideas about what you would want in a marriage relationship. Because you've seen so many couples pass through your boutique, and because you're so decisive, so sure of yourself."

Bandy gave a little sigh and leaned back in her chair. "Those are flattering remarks. Although I've more often been accused of being bull-headed than being sure of myself."

Carmen gave a light laugh at this comeback. "Then I admire your bull-headedness."

"But I would be worse than a liar if I didn't explain to you where my confidence comes from."

"What do you mean?"

"I'm a Christian, Carmen. My confidence is not in me. It's in the One I love and serve. I surrendered my life to Christ many years ago. He's the One who leads and guides me."

Carmen gave a slight nod. "I thought so. You remind me of my college roommate. She was a Christian, too. But you're still not answering my first question."

"Oh, but I am. You see, when I meet the man whom I am to marry, I will be seeking God's guidance and direction just as I do in all the matters of my life. He'll never lead me astray. And I can't imagine my loving God guiding me to marry someone in whom I have no romantic interest. After all, God is the Author of love and marriage in the first place."

Carmen's soft, gray-green eyes were once again gazing out the window. She said nothing. After a moment, she picked up her clutch and stood to leave. "Thank you, Miss O'Sullivan." She reached out for Bandy's hand and clasped it firmly. "You're a truly good and wonderful person." With that, she turned and walked out.

Bandy sat there a while wondering what she had just done. She brushed two alfalfa sprouts from her skirt, then she too left the tea room.

In the parking lot as she approached her car, another car pulled up beside her. In it was Mrs. Lavercomb, the biggest gossip in Pembrooke next to Millie's cousin Waldo. Bandy hurried to get in her car before she could be seen, but she was too late. "Miss O'Sullivan. Say there, Miss O'Sullivan." The plump matron was quickly getting out of her car, while Bandy just as quickly got into hers. Bandy had no time for this, but before she could get the key in the ignition, Mrs. Lavercomb was at the car window with her hand reaching in to give Bandy's a shake.

"Why, Miss O'Sullivan, hello there. Mercy me, I've not seen much of you since you moved your little shop up on the hill. How's everything going up there?"

"Splendidly, Mrs. Lavercomb. Why don't you come up and have a look?"

"Why, Sugar, I have no need for wedding niceties."

"Surely you know we have a line of formal dresses for all occasions. I have a lavender satin and organza that would look simply stunning on you. Just your size, too."

Mrs. Lavercomb waved a glove-clad hand. "Ah now, go on, Miss O'Sullivan. You're such a flatterer. No wonder you have so many customers. And now two stores, even. Mercy me, I just don't see how you do it all."

"No, ma'am. I closed the store in the Valley Shopping Center when we moved." Bandy turned the key and started the car, hoping Mrs. Lavercomb would get the hint.

"No, no, I'm talking about the other new one, the branch you opened in Harwood."

"Branch? That's silly. Why would I want a branch?" Didn't these people know anything about the retailing business?

"The one Claire helped you with."

Now Bandy was incredulous. Imagine anyone in Pembrooke thinking Claire helped her with anything. She thought their strained relationship was common knowledge. "Mrs. Lavercomb, excuse me, I have a lot of work to do. I really must be going."

"Well, I know what I know, and I know that Claire offered to help you open another store with your secretary as the manager."

Bandy felt her cheeks grow fiery. She shoved the gear back up into park. "What did you just say?"

Obviously, this was the kind of attention Mrs. Lavercomb had been seeking all along. She gave a wry smile and the plump cheeks bulged. "So you *do* have a branch store?"

"Exactly what do you know about my stepmother *helping* me, Mrs. Lavercomb?"

"Just that she wanted to see you become a genuine success, so she put up part of the money—along with several other investors, of course—to help your secretary, Diane Jettison or something. . ."

"Denise Jepson."

"That's it. That's the one. Claire put up money for her to help you run another store."

"And who else helped me open my *branch* store?"

"Why, you silly girl. Are y'all teasing me? You ought to know your own investors."

"You would think so, wouldn't you." This time the gear went into reverse and the car rolled backward. Mrs. Lavercomb quickly pulled her arm out of the way. "I must go now, Mrs. Lavercomb. Ta ta. So good to see you again."

Hot tears burned Bandy's eyes so that she could hardly see to drive back to the boutique. Of all the ruthless, mean, lowdown tricks she'd ever heard of in her life, this one certainly won grand prize. So Claire was that desperate to have her name protected in this town. So desperate she would actually help Denise open a competitive store. Such hate was beyond comprehension. And here Bandy had thought it might be Alan who had helped Denise, but instead it was her own step-mother.

That information, plus the conversation with Carmen at lunch, was almost too much to handle at one time. What was coming next?

# seventeen

A few days later, Bandy was working late in her office when she heard a tap at the door. Since Marla Sue had gone for the day, she assumed it was Gena. "Come in."

The door opened to reveal Alan standing there. He stood still for a moment, then stepped inside. His eyes were smiling, though his face was not. He sat down in the chair nearest her desk.

Bandy had never seen him look this serious. "Is something wrong?"

"I've just come from the *Chronicle*. There's a late breaking story that will hit the headlines early in the morning. I thought you'd want to know before that."

"What? Was someone hurt?"

"I think someone is trying to avoid getting hurt. The Prouteau-Marsden engagement is off."

Bandy leaned back in her chair and lifted the heavy copper curls off her neck. "I figured as much. So what else can go wrong?"

"You're not surprised?"

"Why should I be surprised? I practically talked her out of marrying the guy—all by myself. It was an arrangement, Alan. The parents just arrange these things. What a crazy world this is. She asked me about romantic love. In a nutshell, I told her about God's guidance and how I would search for a mate, and I guess she really listened. I mean, *really* listened. Can you beat that?"

She held her breath for a moment. This account was big for Alan as well. And he was the one who had set the whole thing up in the first place. She was surprised to see a smile now light up his face.

"What a gallant thing to do, Bandy. You practically saved the girl's life."

"And pulled the plug on mine."

"Her wedding wasn't your life."

"Well, at the moment, it seemed to be a big hunk of it."

"Maybe your vision is getting blurred."

She sat up in the chair. "And what's that remark supposed to mean?"

"You explained to this girl about God's guidance in the most important step in her life, and yet you talk like God just checked out of the guidance business in your own life."

"Alan, please. I don't need a sermon. Everything is unraveling around me and the last thing I need is somebody on a soapbox. Denise dealt the first blow by sabotaging my business and stabbing me in the back. Then I learn that my own step-mother was the instigator of the entire scheme. Now the account that could have secured the entire region has just blown up in my face. I'm not sure at this point if I can even keep the doors open through the next few months."

"I knew about Claire O'Sullivan being one of Denise's backers. In fact, Denise said the woman approached her originally with the idea."

"What a sick, desperate woman she is."

Alan shook his head as he stood to his feet. "You know the answer, Bandy. It's so simple." He came over and knelt down by her chair. "It's called forgiveness. That's how you can release Claire and Denise and everything they've done." He put his hands around her face and brushed away her tears.

She pulled back from him and turned in the swivel chair. "You don't understand, Alan. That money that Claire dumped into Denise's shaky business—however much or little it was—had to be money my father left her. She didn't have much of her own." Bandy pushed the chair back and stood up. "After Daddy died, she was so wickedly cruel. Many of the things he wanted me to have, she sold or gave away to her family and friends. Not expensive things, but little, sweet, sentimental things. Things that would have mattered only to me. She continually did deliberate things to hurt me. But worst of all, I feel like I've let Daddy down. Like I've deserted him somehow."

"Bandy, those are hurts and wounds only God can heal. Just let go of them. Give them all over to Him."

"You make it sound so easy."

"Bandy, I grew up around people who make your stepmother look like Mother Theresa. Thick-headed people who have little or no forward vision. They live mired down in the muck of the past and all that goes with it." He stood and moved toward the door. "But I serve a God Who's much bigger than all that." He paused as he opened the door. "I guess I thought you did too." And he was gone.

Bandy remained motionless, fighting the urge to call him back. Within moments, she heard the side door of the storeroom slam shut. He was gone. Slowly she gathered her things and walked down the stairs to the store. She laid her coat and purse in one of the velvet mauve chairs and turned to step up into the viewing platform. Plush carpeting muffled her steps. The series of triple mirrors multiplied the grief that lined her face.

"I'm so sorry, Daddy," she whispered to the stillness. "I've let you down again. I've worked so hard to follow what I thought was right, but everything's falling apart. What am I going to do?"

The jangling of the phone exploded into the silence and startled her. Millie was probably wondering where she was. Bandy stepped down from the viewing platform and grabbed the wall phone behind the counter.

"Bandy's Bridal Boutique. Bandy speaking."

"Miss O'Sullivan, this is Mrs. Prouteau. Working rather late, aren't you?"

A wave of fear swept over her. Did this mother know yet about the breakup? "I was just ready to lock up. How can I help you?" She strained to keep her voice calm.

"Nothing now. You seem to have spoiled your chances to help us. Perhaps you were unaware, but Carmen has decided not to marry Michael. There will be no wedding, so your services are no longer needed here."

"Yes, Mrs. Prouteau. I did know. Perhaps it's for the best."

"How would someone like you know what's best for a girl like Carmen? I understand it was your influence that helped her to change her mind. Some religious talk about looking for the will of God. Whatever it was, it seemed to work well to serve as the excuse she needed."

"Your daughter has too much on the ball to lean on excuses. Or haven't you noticed?"

"I've only noticed that our two families bent low to acquiesce to use your services, Miss O'Sullivan, and all we received in exchange for our charity was an act of mutiny. Had I known how conniving you were, I never would have allowed you in my home in the first place."

"Why are you afraid to let your daughter lead her own life?"

"And furthermore," Mrs. Prouteau continued, ignoring the pointed question, "you may rest assured all of our friends and family will learn of your meddling ways. I shall be compelled to inform them that it would lie in their best interest to avoid patronizing your boutique. Good evening, Miss O'Sullivan."

The phone clicked and went dead. Bandy's hands were shaking so she could hardly replace the receiver. The trembling grasped her entire body, and her hands covered her face as she felt assaulted by loss. A loss that was deep— much deeper even than her father's death, for now she had lost her sense of God's love and guidance in her life. Sensations of intense sickness and desolation swept over her, while heavy sobs racked her insides. She slumped to the floor and lay there sobbing until her strength was spent.

She had no idea how much time had passed when she finally rose up, gathered her strength, and drove home. Somehow she had to find the composure to break the news to her staff. Clearly, now she would not be able to hold onto her boutique in Harwood Heights. She hoped Claire was satisfied.

❧

She called a staff meeting early the next morning. Millie was there with a grave look of concern on her face. Bandy had refused to talk the night before. Although she knew Millie was hurt, she simply couldn't let her blood spill out yet. She had tried early that morning to repair her red, puffy eyes, but she might as well not have tried.

They were gathered in the mezzanine office around Marla Sue's desk. Bandy explained as best she could that not only had they lost the Prouteau-Marsden account, but that their reputation was so threatened in the area she would begin immediately to take steps to move their location. She had no intention of staying on and taking her chances that everything would gloss over. That wouldn't be fair to any of them. Better to cut and run now while she still was in the black. Not much in the black, but some.

Each person was silent, and yet Bandy felt the love coming back toward her. Even Marla Sue, in the short time she'd been with them, had become intensely loyal.

"You told her, didn't you," Gena stated flatly. "I knew it. I knew you would. When I saw the headlines this morning, it was awesome!"

"Told her what?" Millie wanted to know. "Is there something more here you're not telling us?"

"There's more all right," Gena said. "She won't tell you that she's the one who convinced Carmen not to marry Michael Marsden—seeing as how the poor girl was being forced into a marriage of convenience."

Ellen's eyes lit up. "Bandy! Did you really?"

"Gena's a bit dramatic," Bandy said in her own defense. "I simply told her a bit about following the Lord's leading. Knowing Carmen, I think she would have made the right decision on her own."

"Maybe," Gena countered. "But when? Five years into the marriage?"

Millie, who was sitting next to Bandy, reached out to give her a motherly pat. 'Bandy, I'm so proud of you. That couldn't have been easy for you. You knew what it might cost."

Bandy was fighting another losing battle with tears. She dared not look out the windows to the store below. To her beautiful, beloved boutique.

"Whatever happens," Ellen said, "I'm with you. I'll take a cut in pay, a cut in hours, whatever. If we hang together, this will work wherever we might go."

The others echoed her sentiments. Their words sounded good, but Bandy knew it would take so much more than that. How she could get financing to make a major move, she had no earthly idea.

They all made valiant attempts to conduct business as usual for the remainder of the day. Bandy had never been so proud of her crew. Maybe they *could* make it in a new location. But where? And how?

The next morning a call was put through to Bandy. "It sounds like a young girl," Marla Sue's voice came over the speaker phone, "but she won't give her name."

Bandy was surprised when she picked up her phone, to hear Carmen's voice on the other end. "Miss O'Sullivan, thank goodness you're there."

"Carmen, where are you? Isn't your family about ready to throttle you?"

"I'm not sure. I'm trying to stay as far away as possible. I've more or less been kicked out and disowned."

"Oh, I'm sorry."

"Please don't be. I've never been happier in my life. I called to ask a favor of you."

"Sure. Anything. Provided we now operate on first name basis."

"Fine with me, Bandy. I need your services."

"Services? For a wedding? But you. . ."

"This isn't Michael. His name is Gary, and I've been in love with him for over a year, and never truly realized it until you explained to me about God's guidance. I met him at college. Oh, Bandy, he's such a sweet Christian man, and he's explained how to commit my life to the Lord and ask Jesus into my heart. But I can tell you those details later."

Her voice sounded absolutely jubilant. Bandy could hardly believe this was the same girl. "Can you drive out to Westridge this afternoon," Carmen continued, "and meet me at the little church where we plan to have the wedding? This is Gary's church where he grew up."

Bandy thought for a minute. This was crazy. Just plain crazy. "I'll be there. Where and when?" She grabbed pen and pad and scribbled fast, taking down the time and directions.

"I can't afford anything compared to what Mother and Father were planning for me," Carmen explained. "It'll be a simple affair with a few of my college friends. But I still want it to be nice."

"Of course you do. And we'll do a first-rate job for you. See you at three."

"Bandy? One more thing."

"Yes."

"Please bring Mr. Brockhurst with you. We'll need a photographer."

"Of course."

&

Bandy and Alan didn't talk much as they drove the ten-mile stretch to the small town of Westridge. Bandy's mind was flooded with thoughts of Carmen, how one little word of direction and encouragement had changed the girl's life around. Bandy began to ask herself about God's true call in her life. Had she been so busy and out of touch these past few months, that she'd lost her vision? Proverbs 16:3 ran through her mind like a broken record. At what point had she ceased to roll her works over onto the Lord? She felt the confusion swirling. Even though it would be nice to help Carmen with her wedding, it was no answer for Bandy's mammoth problems.

Gary's home church was a typical small-town, stone church that had stood on this corner for decades. The interior was warm and filled with love. Gary and Carmen were there, arm in arm. He appeared to Bandy to be every bit the Christian young man that Carmen had described. She and Alan were introduced to the congenial pastor, who seemed thrilled with this interesting event taking place in his church.

They spent an hour with an excited, beaming Carmen, discussing her new plans. She was still very much the classy young lady, but with a new sparkle and a new dimension. Seeing the change in Carmen gave Bandy a warm feeling that dispelled some of her despair and worry.

Before Carmen and Gary departed, Carmen asked Bandy and Alan and the pastor to pray with them. They joined in a circle near the altar and prayed for this young couple's successful marriage, for their continued service to God, as well as for their lifelong happiness.

Bandy couldn't remember a time when she had shed so many tears, and now she was crying again. As the couple prepared to leave, Carmen hugged Bandy, repeatedly thanking her for all her help. Later, the pastor also excused himself as he was needed in his office. Alan took Bandy's hand as though he too were ready to leave, but she pulled back.

"I need to stay here a few moments," she told him. She moved toward the front pew and sat down. The stillness was so sweet and the presence of the Lord so real, she wanted to greedily drink it in. Reluctantly, she had to admit she'd not experienced the presence of the Lord much in the past few months.

Seeing the change in Carmen had done something inexplicable deep inside her heart. She was weeping freely now. Alan came to put his arms around her.

"I've been so blind, Alan. I've been following my own selfish agendas—which included being wrapped up in hate and bitterness. I can't believe I've been so dense. God had to allow me to lose my entire dream just to get my attention."

"Not the entire dream, Bandy, but maybe a part of it that needed to be pruned away."

"Millie told me that God doesn't cater to my whims, but that He gives me the desires of my heart. But I've not been still long enough to learn what those desires truly are. I've not even checked in with Him to see if I was staying on the right track." Alan pulled a handkerchief from his pocket and pressed it into her hand. She dabbed at the tears running down her cheeks. He patiently, quietly, let her talk. "I came so close to missing this precious blessing with Carmen. I didn't want to say anything to her at first, because I didn't want to lose my chance with her family. Oh, Alan, God spared my life from drowning, and I've not even been grateful to Him. No wonder He had to shake my life up." She buried her face in his chest, and he held her close.

Presently he pulled her to her feet and led her to the wooden altar where they both knelt together. There Bandy poured her heart out to God and found the refreshing cleansing she so desperately needed. She came away from that altar knowing with an inner surety that it would not matter from here on out what Claire O'Sullivan did—nor anyone else for that matter. God was once again in control of her life.

# eighteen

Bandy was armed with a spray of skillfully arranged fresh flowers, designed especially by Gena for this occasion. She carried the arrangement out the front door of the boutique and walked slowly down the street two blocks and around the corner to Denise's shop.

She found her former secretary in the back inventorying stock. The dark eyes surveyed her suspiciously.

"These are for you," Bandy explained. "I want to apologize for anything I've ever done to hurt you."

Denise didn't make a move to take the flowers, so Bandy set them on a nearby table. "I apologize for the anger I've held against you. You were right. It is a free country, and you're free to open whatever business you choose, wherever you choose to open it. I want to wish you great success in your new venture."

She stood for a minute waiting. Nothing. Slowly she turned to walk away.

"Bandy?"

Bandy paused and turned. Denise's face was strained. She managed a slight smile. "Running a business is a lot tougher than it looks."

Bandy nodded, turned again, and walked out.

With Claire, Bandy knew it wouldn't be quite so simple, but she did write a short letter expressing her forgiveness and asking for Claire's in return. She received no answer, but Bandy didn't need one.

❧

The day of Carmen's wedding was the most glorious spring

day Bandy had ever seen. She and Millie were in great spirits as they unloaded the van and began preparations. Presently Hayden arrived with Gena. Shyly, Gena showed Bandy the friendship ring she had received from him. Bandy gave her a hug. "He really is a nice guy, you know," Bandy said, "once you get to know him." They laughed together at the stale joke.

The wedding was small but perfect. The most important Guest was present and that was what mattered.

Bandy watched from the kitchen as Hayden and Alan worked deftly together to take quality photos of the reception. Alan had been right: the boy just needed a chance.

The bride was radiant, the groom beaming. Even Gena gave Gary her approval! The couple drove away in the groom's late model Chevy—a far cry from the little blue Mercedes coupe. And Bandy was willing to bet Carmen would never want to trade back.

As they were busy cleaning and repacking the van, Alan came and grabbed Bandy by the arm. "Keep on with the work, girls," he said to Millie and Gena, "I'm kidnapping the boss."

"Go for it," Millie said with a laugh. "You should have done that a long time ago."

"Millie!" Bandy protested as she was pulled out the back door of the church. Alan opened the door of his car and ushered her inside. "What's going on?" she asked.

"You'll see. I have something to show you."

The car wound through the small town of Westridge, in the direction of Pembrooke, then Alan turned down a side street. After a few blocks, he pulled up in a driveway and stopped.

Bandy stared in disbelief. Standing before her was the most delightful white two-story house she'd ever seen. On one side was a stately, pointed gable and, on the other, a turret. The porch stretched across the front of the house and curved around the turret side, extending on around to the back. Delicate gingerbread woodwork spindles decorated the pillars of the porch and were repeated on the second-story balcony where french doors opened out of the gable.

White lattice panels fitted around the bottom of the raised porch, enhancing the delicate appearance. A pale blue front door added to the inviting atmosphere. In the front yard, pink impatiens grew in gay profusion, and white wrought iron chairs were set about as though a garden party were about to begin. Mammoth shade trees stood sentry on both sides, draping Spanish moss with an air of aristocracy. And a realtor's sign was stuck solidly into the front lawn.

Bandy had never seen anything so sweet, so lovely, so inviting. "Why are you showing me this?" she wanted to know.

Rather than answer, Alan came around to help her out of the car. He led her up the walk past the chairs, past the flowers, to the blue front door.

"Wouldn't this front porch make a marvelous setting for wedding pictures?" he asked.

"It would," she agreed.

"It's zoned for business here."

"Is it?"

"There's a full basement. A marvelous place for a photography studio, and even darkroom if a person wanted one. There's space in the back to build a warehouse, if a person needed one for merchandise storage. The upstairs could be used until the warehouse is built."

"I see. And what other plans have you made for this place, Mr. Brockhurst?"

"It's close enough to Pembrooke to drive each day, and yet you're centrally located in the county to be accessible."

"Anything else?"

He drew her over to the front door. "Look in."

She did and saw a lovely curving staircase, ornate woodwork, and a glittering chandelier. Perfect. Everything about this house was perfect.

"We can call the realtor later if you want to see the inside."

She smiled up at him. "You mean I'm going to have a say in this?"

He grabbed her hands. "Together we can swing it, Bandy. I've already asked the price, and it's unbelievable. You can be up and running again in no time. Don't give Harwood Heights another thought. Perhaps you were there only for Carmen Prouteau, who knows? But here—here you can build the solid business you've always dreamed of. There are hundreds of kids like Gary and Carmen. They need you, Bandy."

She looked around at the peaceful surroundings. It was better than any refurbished ante-bellum mansion she could ever imagine. Alan was right, she wouldn't need much capital to get a fresh start here in Westridge. "How did you find this place?"

"Ever since the news broke about Carmen's split up with Michael, I've scoured the countryside searching for the right place. I kept praying for the Lord to guide my steps and direct me. And when I saw this, it seemed. . . Well, it seemed right. Do you like it?"

"It's beautiful. It's perfect." She reached up to touch his face. She was amazed to see the gentle love shining in his eyes. To think he'd cared enough to spend his time to find this house—this exquisite house. "And I suppose you're thinking I should now have a business with photography on the side, right?"

He pulled her close. "What I had in mind was to put the photography smack in the middle, as opposed to being 'on the side.'" He gently kissed her nose. "But there will be two conditions before we can enter into this little business merger."

"Conditions? Now the truth is coming out. There's a catch to this offer."

"The first condition is that we change the name of the business."

"Change it? To what?"

"Bandy Brockhurst's Bridal Cottage. Bandy Brockhurst," he repeated softly. "It has a nice ring to it, don't you agree?" He kissed her again, a long lingering kiss full on the mouth.

When she could catch her breath, she asked, "And the other condition?"

"That our wedding be the first client of this new business venture."

She looked up at his smiling blue eyes and brushed the blond shock of hair off his forehead. "What a sneaky way to become my business partner! You are without a doubt the most nervy guy I've ever met." But when she tried to tell him she agreed to the conditions, her words were smothered in more kisses. Her arms closed around his neck, as she willingly returned the kisses.

Later, as Alan led her around the house to view the rest of the property, Bandy's feet felt light as air. She looked at this ideal location for the boutique and then looked up at Alan's face, and exhilaration filled her heart.

At last God had shown her the difference between her selfish whims and His perfect will. And as always, His will was so much better than anything she could ever have imagined.

# *A Letter To Our Readers*

Dear Reader:

In order that we might better contribute to your reading enjoyment, we would appreciate your taking a few minutes to respond to the following questions. When completed, please return to the following:

Rebecca Germany, Editor
Heartsong Presents
P.O. Box 719
Uhrichsville, Ohio 44683

1. Did you enjoy reading *Cater to a Whim*?
   ☐ Very much. I would like to see more books
      by this author!
   ☐ Moderately
      I would have enjoyed it more if _____

   _____

2. Are you a member of *Heartsong Presents*? Yes   No
   If no, where did you purchase this book? _____

   _____

3. What influenced your decision to purchase this
   book? (Check those that apply.)

   ☐ Cover            ☐ Back cover copy

   ☐ Title            ☐ Friends

   ☐ Publicity        ☐ Other _____

4. On a scale from 1 (poor) to 10 (superior), please rate the following elements.

___Heroine     ___Plot

___Hero     ___Inspirational theme

___Setting     ___Secondary characters

5. What settings would you like to see covered in *Heartsong Presents* books?

_____

_____

6. What are some inspirational themes you would like to see treated in future books?_____

_____

_____

7. Would you be interested in reading other *Heartsong Presents* titles?    ❏ Yes    ❏ No

8. Please check your age range:
❏ Under 18    ❏ 18-24    ❏ 25-34
❏ 35-45    ❏ 46-55    ❏ Over 55

9. How many hours per week do you read? _____

Name _____

Occupation _____

Address _____

City _____ State _____ Zip _____

*Don't miss these favorite* Heartsong Presents *titles
by some of our most distinguished authors!*

**Your price is only $2.95 each!**

\_\_\_HP01 A TORCH FOR TRINITY, *Colleen L. Reece*
\_\_\_HP02 WILDFLOWER HARVEST, *Colleen L. Reece*
\_\_\_HP03 RESTORE THE JOY, *Sara Mitchell*
\_\_\_HP04 REFLECTIONS OF THE HEART, *Sally Laity*
\_\_\_HP10 SONG OF LAUGHTER, *Lauraine Snelling*
\_\_\_HP17 LLAMA LADY, *VeraLee Wiggins*
\_\_\_HP18 ESCORT HOMEWARD, *Eileen M. Berger*
\_\_\_HP19 A PLACE TO BELONG, *Janelle Jamison*
\_\_\_HP23 GONE WEST, *Kathleen Karr*
\_\_\_HP28 DAKOTA DAWN, *Lauraine Snelling*
\_\_\_HP36 THE SURE PROMISE, *JoAnn A. Grote*
\_\_\_HP39 GOVERNOR'S DAUGHTER, *Veda Boyd Jones*
\_\_\_HP41 FIELDS OF SWEET CONTENT, *Norma Jean Lutz*
\_\_\_HP42 SEARCH FOR TOMORROW, *Mary Hawkins*
\_\_\_HP43 VEILED JOY, *Colleen L. Reece*
\_\_\_HP44 DAKOTA DREAM, *Lauraine Snelling*

# ...Hearts ♥ong...

# .... Presents ........

\_\_HP54 HOME TO HER HEART, *Lena Nelson Dooley*
\_\_HP57 LOVE'S SILKEN MELODY, *Norma Jean Lutz*
\_\_HP58 FREE TO LOVE, *Doris English*
\_\_HP61 PICTURE PERFECT, *Susan Kirby*
\_\_HP62 A REAL AND PRECIOUS THING, *Brenda Bancroft*
\_\_HP65 ANGEL FACE *Frances Carfi Matranga*
\_\_HP66 AUTUMN LOVE, *Ann Bell*
\_\_HP69 BETWEEN LOVE AND LOYALTY, *Susannah Hayden*
\_\_HP70 A NEW SONG *Kathleen Yapp*
\_\_HP73 MIDSUMMER'S DREAM, *Rena Eastman*
\_\_HP74 SANTANONI SUNRISE, *Hope Irvin Marston and*
                                        *Claire M. Coughlin*
\_\_HP77 THE ROAD BEFORE ME, *Susannah Hayden*
\_\_HP78 A SIGN OF LOVE, *Veda Boyd Jones*
\_\_HP81 BETTER THAN FRIENDS, *Sally Laity*
\_\_HP82 SOUTHERN GENTLEMEN, *Yvonne Lehman*
\_\_HP85 LAMP IN DARKNESS, *Connie Loraine*
\_\_HP86 POCKETFUL OF LOVE, *Loree Lough*
\_\_HP89 CONTAGIOUS LOVE, *Ann Bell*
\_\_HP90 CATER TO A WHIM, *Norma Jean Lutz*

### Great Inspirational Romance at a Great Price!

Heartsong Presents books are inspirational romances in contemporary and historical settings, designed to give you an enjoyable, spirit-lifting reading experience. You can choose from 92 wonderfully written titles from some of today's best authors like Colleen L. Reece, Brenda Bancroft, Janelle Jamison, and many others.

*When ordering quantities less than twelve, above titles are $2.95 each.*

# LOVE A GREAT LOVE STORY?

*Introducing Heartsong Presents —*
*Your Inspirational Book Club*

Heartsong Presents Christian romance reader's service will provide you with four never before published romance titles every month! In fact, your books will be mailed to you at the same time advance copies are sent to book reviewers. You'll preview each of these new and unabridged books before they are released to the general public.

These books are filled with the kind of stories you have been longing for—stories of courtship, chivalry, honor, and virtue. Strong characters and riveting plot lines will make you want to read on and on. Romance is not dead, and each of these romantic tales will remind you that Christian faith is still the vital ingredient in an intimate relationship filled with true love and honest devotion.

Sign up today to receive your first set. Send no money now. We'll bill you only $9.97 post-paid with your shipment. Then every month you'll automatically receive the latest four "hot off the press" titles for the same low post-paid price of $9.97. That's a savings of 50% off the $4.95 cover price. When you consider the exaggerated shipping charges of other book clubs, your savings are even greater!

**THERE IS NO RISK**—you may cancel at any time without obligation. And if you aren't completely satisfied with any selection, return it for an immediate refund.

**TO JOIN,** just complete the coupon below, mail it today, and get ready for hours of wholesome entertainment.

Now you can curl up, relax, and enjoy some great reading full of the warmhearted spirit of romance.

Spying one of the refueling nozzles, I went over to it. The long hose had been draped over the three-story walkway to thaw out. Below me steamed an open vat of lox, the impossibly cold liquid boiling off into the atmosphere.

Even the metal railing on the walkway had turned cold from the arctic storm boiling beneath my feet. Checking the nozzle, I saw nothing to tell me anything was amiss.

Sometimes the most effective approach is the best. The saboteur had only to carry the thermite bomb over to the rocket, clamp it onto the side of the fuel tank with a special magnetic limpet catch and then wait. There wasn't even the need for hiding the procedure. Anyone passing by would mistake it for part of the fueling.

Sighing, I leaned forward onto the railing and stared down into the furiously boiling vat of liquid oxygen. As I thought about the sabotage, I heard a faint metallic scraping noise.

I turned in time to see one of the eerie silver-suited figures advancing on me. With gloves on and hood securely in place, an anonymity had been achieved more effectively than any mask. That was all I saw before powerful hands gripped me under my armpits and lifted me bodily into the air.

I yelled once, then fell through the air toward the deadly sea of liquid oxygen . . .

# NICK CARTER
## IS IT!

# THE SOLAR MENACE

**CHARTER**
NEW YORK

A Division of Charter Communications Inc.
A GROSSET & DUNLAP COMPANY
51 Madison Avenue
New York, New York 10010

An Ace Charter Original.

First Ace Charter Printing August 1981
Published simultaneously in Canada
Manufactured in the United States of America

2 4 6 8 0 9 7 5 3 1

# THE SOLAR MENACE

Dedicated to the men of the
Secret Services of the
United States of America

# PROLOGUE

The cold morning wind whipped across the Gobi Desert, stinging the guards' eyes and making them water. The Chinese Army colonel peered into the west, the wan sun at his back, and wondered what the Soviets were up to. Their troop movements had been extreme during the night. An entire division had abandoned their posts in favor of the warmer barracks in Ulan Bator.

Colonel Chun Li doubted the obvious. The Mongolians were a satellite country of the USSR, true, but they had little love for their too-European overlords. Given the chance, Chun thought, the Mongolians would overthrow their revisionist masters and join the People's Republic of China in forming a world-spanning socialist state.

But propaganda didn't explain the Soviet's mysterious retreat. At this time of year, their activities leaned more toward taunting their Chinese counterparts into firing upon them. Chun sighed. Some of his younger men responded in the way the more seasoned Russians desired. But what were a few green soldiers? Mother China held millions more—hundreds of millions—to match every Soviet soldier.

"Comrade Colonel," spoke his aide. "The Soviets retreat on all fronts. They leave the desert country totally unguarded. A sudden movement on our part

1

would make it appear they are in rapid retreat from our forces.''

"Invade Mongolia?'' mused Chun. "No, I think not. This is a stratetgic decision to be made by our Board of Notable Generals. But there is a germ of an idea in what you say. Call up the heavy armor. Mass the tanks forty kilometers to the west from their present position. Make it appear that *our* movement has caused *them* to retreat. But under no circumstance will you allow any of our units to give chase or fire.''

"Understood, Comrade Colonel!'' The sallow, flat-faced man saluted smartly, spun and hurried off to the communications tent.

Colonel Chun peered through his powerful binoculars wondering at what the Soviets really did. Afghanistan had hurt them. It was the Russian Vietnam. But their troops along the Chinese border had not been reduced due to that particular imperialistic venture. If anything, their vigilance increased, as if they waited for a Chinese assault because of their occupation elsewhere.

Chun had advised General Hu Low that such an expedition could succeed. And Colonel Chun Li was the commander to execute perfectly such an invasion of the Soviet-occupied territory. The People's Republic stood an excellent chance of regaining the lands stolen away so many years ago. But the Comrade General had other, more political, concerns.

The accursed round-eye white capitalists from America now supplied much food to starving peasants. Any action against the Soviets threatened that influx of grain.

Chun shook his head in bewilderment. Did not the American capitalist dogs hate the Soviets also? Mutual friendship could never blossom between the People's

Republic and the U.S. but mutual hatred might allow both to prosper and grow—at Russia's expense. Chun grew confused at such convoluted logic. It seemed perfectly sensible to him that the Americans would support a Chinese invasion of Siberia. Promise Kamchatka and the Sakhalin Islands to Japan and the most potent manufacturing nation in the world would supply all the ordnance needed. No, Chun was best at military maneuvering, not political games.

The sun rose steadily but carried no warmth with it. The bitter wind picked up energy and sent icy knives slashing through the colonel's heavy jacket. He hardly noticed. His heart raced at the sight of the Russians retreating, the sight of his own heavy armor advancing to the demarcation line. His troops performed admirably. None was battle-seasoned, yet they went about their tasks efficiently, with verve. Holding back a few stray mortar rounds might prove impossible. He would have to issue specific orders concerning fire across the invisible line drawn on the cold desert sands.

"They run!" laughed a nearby tank commander, his head bobbing out of the turret for a better view of the distant Russian column.

Chun smiled. The smile faded as a sudden gust of wind whipped off his fur-lined hat. It was as if someone had opened a blast furnace door. The second blast came like a thunderclap. Heat.

Intense, searing heat.

In the middle of the Gobi Desert in midwinter, searing, awful, blistering heat.

Colonel Chun lifted his arm and peered back along his ranks. His soldiers' parkas had burst into flame. They ran into the weak morning sun attempting to stifle the flames licking at their bodies.

Another burst of heat, then another and another.

Chun swatted out tiny fires springing into being on his own body. The flesh had been parboiled on his face. He barked orders but none heard. The roar of a growing windstorm shoved the commands back down his throat, choking him.

Chun fell to his knees, the terrible heat draining all energy from him. He peered through burned eyelids at his own magnificent column of soldiers. Fires smouldered on dead backs. Armored personnel carriers burst into flame. Tanks appeared strangely melted.

Then Colonel Chun Li knew.

"The Soviets!" he groaned. "The unexpected from those Communist bastards!"

He fell forward dead, and he was burned beyond recognition when a final super-heated windstorm erupted.

\* \* \* \* \*

"This is Goldstone Four, over," said the efficient radio technician. "Tracking the satellite Mark Seven-Zero-Four over—"

He broke off in mid-sentence. All his equipment had gone dead. Jiggling switches, slamming the palm of his hand against the front of the panel and cursing did nothing to restore working order. He ripped off his headphones and spun in his swivel chair to yell over his console.

"Hey, Fred, you do something dumb again? The whole damned panel's down."

"Mine, too," came the immediate reply. "I lost the microwave link over the Sierra Madres, as well. Whole shooting match folded up on us. What gives?"

The supervisor came up behind the men and stared at the dead panels in disbelief. Not a single warning light had flared before the entire array went down. Good money—big money—had been spent on fail-safe systems to prevent this. Even if the unit malfunctioned, it should have given twenty-three different kinds of warnings.

"Isn't it a little hot in here?" asked the first technician. "I bet the air conditioning for the entire trailer went out, too."

"Check it, Bobby. Though I doubt if any more damage can be done. This looks dead, dead, dead." He reached over and dutifully flipped a toggle switch, as if this would make it all right again

Bobby went to the door and threw it open. The Mojave Desert in midwinter got cold at night, but in the middle of the day temperatures soared into the seventies. The gust of wind striking the technician came from the bowels of hell. His clothes burst into flames. He fell forward, dead before he struck the parched ground.

"Mother of God, I don't believe this!" exclaimed Fred, peering out a small observation port. "The entire antenna's melted. The whole damned thing's in a giant puddle!"

The supervisor never made it to the door as the trailer exploded in a cataclysmic eruption. Fiery pieces rained down on the somber desert for fifteen minutes.

* * * * *

"This is General Denton," the tall, white-haired man barked into the microphone. "Get that idiot McLeod up here on the double!"

Buried far under Cheyenne Mountain in the Rockies outside of Colorado Springs, NORAD Headquarters was impervious to even the most sustained nuclear attack. But for the past hour, one after another of the far-flung monitoring stations feeding their data to NORAD had winked off mysteriously. Without the sensitive electronic ears to listen in on the Soviets, a preemptive strike loomed large.

Before a decision was made to launch America's own Minutemen and Trident missiles, more information had to be accumulated. Time was of vital importance.

"Major McLeod, reporting as ordered, sir." The slender, sandy-haired officer appeared more pale than normal. He obviously realized what the general wanted.

"Give it to me straight, major. How many posts have we lost?"

"Fourteen inside the U.S., sir. And—"

"And?" prompted the general. "How many worldwide?"

"Another seventy-three."

General Denton sank to the edge of his desk, stunned. Eighty-seven electronic spy posts out of order meant that less than a quarter of America's defense listening capability remained. The Russians wouldn't have to launch a sneak attack. They could drive a dogcart through the early-warning network undetected.

"All outages occurred within ninety minutes, sir," the younger officer continued. "We have teams parachuting down to find out what's happened. 'It . . . it's weird, sir!" he blurted. "The posts have been melted. Just like they'd been made out of ice cream and left in the sun. Melted!"

The general said nothing to the frightened major. He

reached across his desk to the red phone and took it off the hook, his hand trembling. He took a deep-steadying breath before speaking into the device.

"This is General Denton, NORAD. Red Alert, I say again, Red Alert. Connect me with the President." He peered up, his eyes slate-cold now as he said to McLeod, "Order Air Force One prepared for the President. Issue a Condition Two standby, to go to Condition Red on Presidential command."

"Yes, sir." Major McLeod saluted and left, trembling like a racehorse at the starting gate. All his military life had been directed toward this single moment. He wasn't sure whether he liked it or not. The reality of possible nuclear war hit him like a pile driver. And he no longer thought of himself as some romantic, modern-day knight about to rush forth and do battle with the godless Commies.

But he did his duty. Air Force One scrambled at Andrews AFB. The entire hidden NORAD Headquarters prepared for war, even though it was more deaf and blind than it had ever been before. And missile silos throughout the U.S. armed potent warheads and aimed then over the pole for distant Russian cities.

*     *     *     *     *

"Mission Control to Shuttle *Columbia*, how do you read?"

"We're reading you five-by-five, over," came the crisp response from the space shuttle pilot. He glanced over the array of lights winking on and off in front of him. Everything was in readiness for the launch. In spite of the training he'd been through for the past three years, he felt himself tensing as he watched the chronometer begin its slow decline to zero-zero-zero.

"Ten seconds to launch. Good luck. Eight, seven, six. . . ."

He worked rapidly, checking everything twice to insure a perfect liftoff. His copilot leaned back, snuggled into the formfitting couch, gave a brief thumbs-up and a smile, then six men sat on their chests.

Slowly, majestically, the shuttle lifted from Launch Pad 38 at Cape Canaveral. Then all hell broke loose.

The pilot saw the red lights flashing even as he strained to move his hand against the potent force of acceleration. The boosters had somehow overheated. They sat atop a giant bomb. Panic flared and lent strength to his movement. His thumb flicked the safety. Distant solenoids clicked and armed the rocket engines on the shuttle for escape. But he was too late.

Ground control had already initiated the backup safety mechanism. Even harder fists of acceleration pounded into his body as the *Columbia* left the doomed booster rockets. Seconds later the entire shuttle rocked with the explosion just yards behind them.

The pilot blacked out before the drogue chutes opened to gently drop the shuttle into the turbulent Atlantic.

# ONE

I don't know how it is with other agents. Perhaps they get nervous when the proper instant comes. I don't. I've been in this dirty rotten business too long to be anything but professional in outlook. There comes a small rush of excitement, adrenaline flowing, then a curious calmness, a rightness, a knowing everything is perfect.

The sight picture through the rifle's scope firmed up to show a tired old man in a rumpled gray business suit. He looked as if he'd slept in that suit for a month. His hair flew wildly in all directions and the bags under his eyes showed the strain.

He knew Nick Carter, Killmaster of AXE, stalked him. I took a deep breath, relaxed and tightened up on the trigger. The sudden bucking of the weapon took me by surprise. That's the best way of firing; each shot is unexpected which reduces anticipatory flinching. I didn't have to take a second shot. The man crumpled into a wasted gray heap on the steps of the mansion.

Silently, I packed away the rifle in a special carrying case, glad that the mission was over. I ordinarily turn down simple assassinations, but this one appealed to me. The insignificant old man had a career that would have made Hitler envious. Setting himself up in an emerging African nation, he had raped the land, murdered hundreds of thousands—and then he'd done the unforgivable. Through his intelligence network he had supplied information to the Russians allowing them to permanently remove eighteen of AXE's top agents inside the USSR.

One of them had been a good friend, and more.

In this business it doesn't pay to develop friendships. We are all expendable; we all know that tomorrow may never occur for any of us. But Barbara had been a special friend, a very special one.

I stowed the attaché case containing the rifle in the trunk of my rented Ford and returned to the beach. The day was deceptively mild, but the sun shone brightly above. Miami can be a scorcher in the winter time if you're not expecting it. I draped the towel around my neck and debated taking another quick plunge into the ocean.

A soft voice stopped me.

"Nick darling, you're ignoring me." I mentally pictured the beautiful pout on her ruby lips, the slight crinkling around the eyes as merriment danced, the delightful dimples making a beautiful face into one that was breathtakingly gorgeous.

"Is that you under that huge, floppy sun hat?" I asked needlessly, teasing her. I'd met Michelle Brooks two days ago, almost exactly in this same spot of beach. She had decided that New York City and the constant push for her to model took second place to sunning herself for a week in Miami. I'm glad she gave up that thousand-a-day modelling career, at least for a while.

She was delightful.

A slender-fingered hand pushed back the brim of the straw hat and Brazilian topaz green eyes peered up at me. The lips, the smile, all were as I'd mentally envisioned them.

"Do join me," she invited, patting the warm sand beside her blanket. "It gets lonely out here."

"Liar," I said. "You're hiding under that hat so a dozen bronzed lifeguards won't come over and make fools out of themselves trying to impress you."

"It happens," she admitted candidly. "And I'm bored with it. Men who have to posture like that are . . . boorish. Don't you agree?"

I shrugged. I felt a definite letdown now from my mission. What would this stunning high-fashion model think if I told her that ten minutes ago I'd just assassinated one of the world's leading butchers? I knew the answer. She'd think it was a poor joke.

"Take you, for instance. You don't go around trying to impress the hell out of me. Just by sitting there you do it just fine." She reached out and lightly drew her fingertips over one of the larger scars on my chest. It'd been left behind after an Arab in Tripoli had tried to perform a little surgery on me. "So many scars," she wondered aloud. "What do you do for a living, Nick? Really?"

"I told you. I'm a deep-sea diver. Scuba, hard-hat, you name it. Getting caught in sunken ships is chancy at best. Rusty iron braces, jutting wood planks, all are potential sources for cuts and scars."

She looked skeptical.

"And then there's coral. I've got a dozen coral scrapes from swimming too close to reefs. Nasty stuff underwater."

"But it's so beautiful," she said softly, her eyes locking with mine.

I didn't know if she meant the coral I'd just mentioned or the scar. For whatever reason, women find my scars exciting. Maybe it hints at a life of danger. I've earned those scars, each and every one of them reminding me of a near brush with death. It was about time they gave me more pleasant memories.

If Michelle liked my scars, fine.

She gave a delicate little shiver and said, "It's getting chilly out here. Let's go to my cabana for a drink."

It was almost eighty degrees out on the sand, definitely not chilly. But the insistent way her fingers played over my chest and the way her eyes sought and held mine so boldly told me she had more in mind than a single drink.

I've read all the psychiatrists' theories about how the nearness of death increases sexual need. For all I know, they might be right. Perhaps the simple act of pulling a trigger and killing a mass-murderer and betrayer of our most valiant agents inside Russia had heightened my desires. I prefer to think that Michelle was all woman and my desire was motivated by simpler, more primitive yearnings.

"Race you to the cabana," she said brightly. I let her beat me. I enjoyed watching the way her behind rolled like a pair of well-oiled ball bearings as she ran. There was none of the mincing stride to her movement, either. She flowed smoothly, every muscle playing strongly under her bronzed skin in a delectable fashion. It was easy to see why this tall, elegant, green-eyed blonde commanded such a fantastic price in New York fashion circles.

"You beat me," I panted, not really out of breath. Neither was Michelle, as she turned and looked frankly at me.

"Let's have that drink," she said, closing the door to the high-walled patio just outside the cabana. Michelle moved away, dropping her towel as she went. Before she reached the sliding glass door leading inside, the top of her string bikini was gone, her breasts firmly bobbing in front of her, the ruddy aureoles tracing out invisible figure eights in the air.

"What would you like?" she asked wickedly, the tip of her pink tongue making a slow circuit of her lips.

"The same as you," I said, discarding my own towel and sitting down on a chaise lounge.

"Two rum screwdrivers coming up," she said, turning coquettishly and making sure he saw the way her fingers worked under the flimsy waistband of her bikini bottom. She lithely stepped out of it, treating him to a hind view of twin bronzed globes. There was no way of mistaking that Michelle sunbathed in the nude.

She returned with the drinks. The blonde appeared totally unaffected by her lack of clothing. Whether this was a teasing facade on her part or whether nudity was an accepted part of modelling, I didn't know. All that I was sure of was that her lissome body aroused me visibly. Her eyes latched onto my groin and witnessed the slow, painful tenting in my swim briefs.

"You look so uncomfortable," she said, taking a small sip of her drink, then placing it on the chair seat between her slender thighs. My eyes followed the drink downward. Puffs of crinkly fur peered up over the rim of her glass.

I felt an insatiable thirst.

Draining my drink in one long, cold gulp, I put the empty glass on a small metal table beside the chaise lounge.

"Let me get more comfortable," I said, lifting up to skin off the swim trunks.

"Let me help," Michelle said eagerly. Like a bronze flash she straddled the lower portion of the aluminum and nylon-webbing chaise, her fingers working over mine to help me off with the trunks. I kicked the useless garment free and started to pull her down to the lounge. She surprised me by powerfully shoving me flat.

"Wha—?" I started. Then she showed me in the

most delightful manner possible.

Lying back on the lounge caused my erection to jut boldly upward. The blonde model gripped it firmly in her warm hand and began stroking it. I moaned softly as I felt intense stabs of stark desire course through my loins. I wanted more than her hand surrounding me. I reached out and cupped her breasts in my hands. The red nipples throbbed with lust. I tweaked them hard enough to make her shove her chest forward. Both my hands filled with tender, suntanned flesh.

"I need you inside me, Nick. I need it so!"

She moved like a snake slithering up a tree. In a slinky, boneless fashion she knelt over my waist, her legs widely spread, her hand guiding my pulsating manhood toward the furred crevice I'd seen before over the edge of her glass.

We both gasped as she shoved downward with her hips. I sank fully into hot, moist womanflesh. I felt the blonde, crinkly pubic bush crushing down into my crotch. And then she began a slow, circular motion with her hips that almost drove me out of my mind.

Still fully buried to the hilt in her cavern of desire, I felt myself growing larger and larger as she moved. Michelle had closed her eyes and tossed her head back as she ground herself downward. I reached up again and took a secure hold of her firm, high-placed breasts. They just filled my hands; nothing wasted here. Like the rest of her divinely gorgeous body, she was perfectly proportioned in every way.

She made this even more apparent when the velvety grip around my erection tightened and she began moving up and down with the same deliberation she'd begun with.

"You're so big inside me, Nick," she moaned

softly. "So big, so swollen. You're a man, a real man!"

I said nothing. My hands said all there was to be said. From the hot mushroom-sized nipples, I lightly stroked down to the broad bases of her breasts. I lifted upward slightly to indicate she should rise up once more. She did, my hardness slipping from her hotly greased interior until only the crown remained hidden inside the delicately scalloped pinkness. When I allowed my hands to rove along her flanks, she dropped back down, once again filling herself to overflowing.

"Y-you don't mind it this way. Nick?" she asked, her voice curiously like a little girl's.

"Mind?" I asked, surprised. "I love it!"

"Most men—so-called men—have to get on top. I . . . ummm, oh! I've found that men secure in their sexuality don't care."

"I care," I said. "I care about us both enjoying this to the maximum." My hands curled around the bronzed buttocks and cupped them firmly. This way I guided her rhythm as she moved up and down faster and faster.

I enjoyed peering down between my legs and watching the erotic activity. But the sight of her long, lustrous honey-blonde hair flying in wild disarray as passion seized her also thrilled me. And the way her breasts jostled around, bobbing firmly, decisively, made me even harder. And most of all the carnal friction of her clutching female sheath around my fleshy masculine sword convinced me we would both enjoy this to the utmost.

Struggling joyously, her hands pressed down into my chest, and she began bucking and thrusting wildly. I found myself arching powerfully upward to sink as deeply as possible into Michelle's yearning hot center. She gasped, shuddered like a leaf in a high wind, then shrieked out her untrammeled ecstasy. The hot spurt of my own passion followed seconds later.

She shivered once again, sighed and bent forward, her cheek resting against my shoulder. Slowly, we repositioned so that we lay side by side on the narrow lounge. Her fingers idly worked over my scars again and I knew she was building up her desires for another love bout. The way her hand occasionally strayed between my legs to check told me she wanted to try it all over again right now.

I was game. But it'd take a few minutes.

"You are one of the most beautiful women I've ever seen, Michelle," I told her, stroking the lustrous mane of blonde hair. She giggled, then bit me. "Ouch!" I exclaimed. "That hurt. Why'd you bite me?"

"You said I was 'one of the most beautiful women' you'd ever seen. That means I'm not *the most* beautiful."

"Quit fishing for compliments. You're one in a million—a billion."

"That still means there are three others out there who're at least my equal and maybe even better."

I snorted in disgust, then slapped her across one of those silky smooth buttocks. She yelped delightedly.

"Is it going to be like that next time?" she asked eagerly. "I want to prove to you I'm the best, bar none."

"You're the best," I told her, meaning it. There had been many women in my life, but the current one is always the best. The rest are just memories. Like Barbara.

"That's better. And so is your response."

I moaned softly as her hand worked between my

muscular thighs until she found the rock-hard pillar she desired so. Stroking it up and down a few times returned it to its former needy state.

I turned toward her, my lips crushing hard into hers. Our tongues duelled and I felt the tide of desire rising in her. I played with it, teasing it into full blossom, then denying it so that I could resurrect it to an even more potent level.

"Ummm, Nick darling, now, do it now!" she begged.

A pounding noise sounded. At first, I thought it was the roar of my own pulse in my temples. Then I realized someone enthusiastically knocked at the closed door to the cabana patio. My first impulse was to ignore it, but some hidden computer buried in my brain began going click-click-click. This wasn't an over-agressive aluminum siding salesman at Michelle's door.

I knew it and cursed it.

"Don't," she protested, her eyes half-lidded and her lips puffy from the kisses I'd lavished on them. "Let 'em go screw themselves. I want you, Nick. Now!"

"Just take a second, beautiful," I said, swinging up off the chaise lounge in a smooth motion. I moaned as I bent to pick up my discarded towel. I wrapped it around my middle and went quickly to the tall wooden gate where someone still knocked feverishly.

"What do you want?" I asked in a less-than-friendly tone.

"Ah, Mr. Carter," said the young man outside. That he recognized me was another piece of the overall picture. The use of the name "Carter" told me even more. The rest of it came when he said, "I just wanted you to know that the game's over. You won."

"How much?"

"N3," he said in a softer voice. Then, louder, in

case Michelle had overheard even the sotto voce identifying code, "Eighty-three dollars. Betting on the Patriots instead of the Reds worked out fine for you. Of course, you didn't do as well on the Hawks game."

I eyed him again, wondering where they recruit these days. He wasn't more than twenty, had a decidedly feminine aspect to him, even to smelling of French perfume. But his hands weren't soft and the slight bulge at his right hip told of the .38 revolver he carried there. I had the impression he could unbutton his jacket, draw and fire before my towel could fall to the sand.

He'd said all the right code words needed to get me to abandon lovely, blonde, lissome, willing, wanton Michelle. What had been the deciding stroke was the mention of the Hawks. Not the Seattle Seahawks but David Hawk, my boss at AXE.

He needed his N3, Killmaster again.

"I'll be right there," I said.

"Don't be too long. You'll miss the payoff. I'll be waiting in the car." He motioned toward a Land Rover parked a few yards away on the sand. I nodded and went back to Michelle to tell her I had to go collect on a football bet.

From her reaction, I doubted she'd be interested in seeing me again.

The memories are always the best for one in my line of work, anyway.

# TWO

The bright, young, well-perfumed man took me to a motel just off A1A. We pulled in and he turned off the Land Rover's engine. He smiled, flashing perfect white teeth.

"Capped?" I asked, still angry at being dragged away from Michelle's passionate embrace. The muscles in his face didn't move but the smile turned icy cold. I decided this man was a cold-blooded killer, one without soul or conscience, the kind that has been showing up in our ranks lately. I don't like the type. I feel you have to do this kind of dirty work for a purpose, a goal higher than simply the sick thrill of killing. Call it patriotism or whatever there had to be more to this job than the simple removal of one's adversaries.

"Inside," he said, the smile as frozen as any arctic dawn. "Number seventeen."

I got out of the Land Rover, wondering if I should strain to hear the soft rustle of a coat opening, the gentle hissing of leather and blued steel revolver caressing one another. The .38 he carried would be double action. I'd never hear him cocking the piece. Walking to the indicated door as if I hadn't a care in the world, I reached the indicated door, turned and waved.

He keyed the Rover to life and left dual smudges of rubber in his haste to depart. Bad form. Someone might be annoyed at the noise and complain about "kids" to the local authorities, who might actually decide to act on the complaint, who could foul up an important mission. Such minor things spell the difference between life and death.

But with the cold-eyed, pretty boy type, death was often preferable to a continued existence in a world hardly appreciating their murderous skills.

Inside the room David Hawk sat on the bed, rolling the stub of his cigar from one side of his mouth to the other. Except for this small indication of nervousness, he stayed perfectly stationary as I entered.

"I just finished a mission, Hawk," I began. He cut me off with an impatient hand gesture.

"I know, N3. Good job, as usual. Valletorres deserved it for what he'd done to the department. But that's not what I wanted to speak to you about."

"I hope not," I said under my breath. A vision of lovely, long-legged Michelle flashed in my head. Louder, I said, "I was engaged in delicate exploratory maneuvers when you sent pretty-boy after me. Where'd you dig him up? From the morgue?"

Hawk screwed his face up into a sour expression. He spat out the cigar and fumbled out a new, unsmoked one from his coat pocket. He bit off the end, spat it after the other cigar stub, then began gently gnawing on it without lighting.

"He's one of the newer recruits sent over by *them*." His distaste for the other security agencies radiated powerfully now. "They used him in Europe for a while, but he had a tendency to—"

"Shoot first and never ask questions," I finished. "I won't work with him. Or any like him."

"Not asking you to, N3. This is too big for the likes of him, anyway. Take a look." He turned and aimed the television remote controller at the set. It blinked once, then came on showing a vapid, tired-looking weatherperson going through her poorly memorized spiel. Hawk did something else to the controller and the picture scrambled, then reformed to show a powerful multi-engined rocket lifting off from a launch pad.

"This is a bit of film shot at Cape Canaveral. The space shuttle launch earlier today. Watch carefully."

At first I saw nothing. I moved closer to the set and peered at the fuzzy picture. The concrete pad around the base of the missile appeared to waver, a mirage caused by the intense heat billowing from the nozzles of the rocket.

"Let me stop it for you, right about . . . here!"

The shuttle hung suspended in midair, captured on the freeze-frame like a bug in electronic amber. Visible on one side of the booster fuel tank was a small hole, the liquid oxygen pluming outward in a furiously cold feather.

"One of our men ran an optical pyrometer on that spot. The tank was at the right temperature just a few milliseconds prior to this. Then came intense heat and the hole appeared. Got up to almost a thousand degrees Celsius. Obvious sabotage. Someone planted a bomb on that booster fuel tank."

"What happened to the shuttle?"

He ran the rest of the videotape, showing the emergency firing of the shuttle engines to pull apart the rocket and send the manned portion tumbling free.

"The crew is injured, not seriously. A concussion, two broken legs, that sort of thing. The *Columbia,* however, is another six months behind schedule. Let me run it back to the point where the hole appears in the fuel tank again."

The tape reversed until he came to the appropriate spot, then freeze-framed it again. From the jagged metal, even a cursory glance showed it to be the produce of a bomb, a powerful one planted at precisely the spot to cause the most damage.

"Thermite?" I asked. "Is it possible someone planted thermite on the outer skin of the rocket, then timed it to ignite while the launch was in progress?"

"That seems most likely. The booster is made of a titanium alloy, with aluminum parts throughout the engines. Best physical chemists doing the analysis on this, too. But we won't find anything more conclusive than those pictures.

"So say your experts?"

Hawk nodded.

I sat back in one of the uncomfortable chairs and thought hard. When Hawk said the AXE experts had agreed, that meant a one-hundred percent certainty it was a fact. Those scientists buried in their vaults in Maryland were good, damned good.

"Whoever did it was an expert. The hole in the fuel tank is bad news, especially during a lift-off, but it's not necessarily fatal to the mission. But this was planted just right for an added effect. The externally applied heat—the bomb—produced eddy currents in the fuel tanks on the boosters. These eddy currents set up a thermal instability that literally wrenched the booster apart."

"A real pro," I said with conviction. "Do you know how the bomb was planted? When it might have occurred!"

"No."

I knew again his experts had given him a full rundown. The only problem was that the sabotage had been so simple. Straightforward and deadly. I waited for Hawk to continue, then I'd get to work on finding who did it.

"We don't know how it was done, N3. All we can be sure of is a professional saboteur inside the Kennedy launch complex at Cape Canaveral."

"This doesn't sound like the other problems the spy outposts have been having. Intense heat melting metal until it flows like putty. Any possibility that it's all the same thing?"

"We're not sure it's not the same method. We're also sure that a spy has infiltrated Cape Canaveral. Certain information has been leaking out, planted information. And we haven't been able to get a handle on how it's leaving the U.S. The man inside is good, too damned good for the security people out there to find easily."

"So I stop him. But it sounds as if the destruction of the electronic listening posts is more important. The grapevine said NORAD actually scrambled Air Force One to get the President away from Andrews Air Force Base and up safely into the air "

"I should ask you how you came about that highly classified datum, N3, but I won't. You accumulate such information in a reflex action by now."

I smiled, knowing that Hawk was secretly pleased that he didn't have to brief me on the other occurrences. In a way, he was right. Collecting information had become second nature to me. It no longer mattered whether it was a U.S. secret or a Soviet one. I listened when people spoke, I deduced, read between the lines, then conjectured. I'd stayed alive because my conjectures were superior to everyone else's who'd been sent against me.

"We are replacing the listening rigs as quickly as possible. Our information from overseas indicates the

People's Republic has had even more serious problems. An entire battalion on the Mongolian border has been eliminated.''

"Heat waves? Or a bomb like that?'' I asked, pointing to the TV screen.

"Sources are vague but the answer appears to be heat.''

"And you're sure it isn't a laser?'' I asked again. His scowl told me he was positive and that I was being bullheaded. Another answer would suit him.

"Check this out, N3. Immediately. We need action.''

"The space program's interesting enough,'' I said, ''but it can't be that high a priority. Not any more. Look at the way Congress has gouged out the heart of the NASA budget. We get pretty pictures from Saturn and that's about it for another ten years. Why the rush on something that might be an accident when listening posts are melting down all over the world?''

"First, this was no accident. I've explained that. Second, the space shuttle is becoming more and more vital to our national security. The existence of a saboteur at Cape Canaveral proves that. While the scientific missions are not to be ignored, however, the new mission of the shuttle is more military.''

"Putting up spy satellites?''

"That, but even this takes a backseat to a Department of Defense memo. The cargo bay of the shuttle has been designed to hold no fewer than a dozen atomic MIRV'd warheads.''

"That's a violation of the Outer Space Treaty signed back in 1962,'' I protested.

"Of course it is. But times change, N3. You know that. That particular treaty was hurriedly signed when we detonated an H-bomb in orbit and scrambled both the Van Allen radiation belt and the ionosphere, causing certain officials to fear we'd permanently disrupted communication on earth, perhaps even destroyed life on this planet by allowing in solar radiation through the normal shielding of the Van Allen belt.''

"That doesn't hold now?''

"We've learned much in the ensuing twenty years. Also, the Russians have done huge amounts of near earth orbit research, most of it military in nature on their Salyut-6 space station. Salyut-7 is to be launched soon, quickly followed by an even larger Salyut-8, one with decided military capabilities. To counter this, we need a space shuttle able to reach orbit, launch atomic weapons if the need arises, then return. A suggestion has been advanced and is seriously being considered that the shuttle launch these weapons into polar orbits.''

"To give us an atomic Sword of Damocles to hang over the Soviets' head?''

"Precisely. We can call down the orbiting bombs in less than ten minutes, which is obviously faster than even the Trident submarine-launched missiles. The orbiting bombs, though, are vulnerable because their orbits can be calculated. Hence, a space shuttle is required to reposition them from time to time.''

"The MX shell-game in orbit?''

"That is an imprecise way of stating it.'' Hawk began chewing more vigorously on his cigar and soon demolished it so that it resembled the one he'd just spit out.

"But accurate enough.''

"We need the space shuttle operating soon, Nick. Get that saboteur. Stop him—or her—and find out for certain how that was done.'' He lifted his head so his chin pointed in the direction of the TV screen. I blinked as I watched the giant booster rockets flower and split, spewing forth kerosene and liquid oxygen fuel.

The screen momentarily blinked out in intense heat. A cold shiver crept up my spine.

# THREE

All my time in Miami had been spent previously on the beaches soaking up sun and trying to unwind. Driving the twenty-three miles northward toward Cape Canaveral from Satellite Beach and through Titusville convinced me there was more to Florida than Miami Beach and Disney World. This was the heart of the "Space Coast" and every sign proclaimed that over and over again.

I drove along the Indian River and sighted an incredible number of huge aerospace production plants in the Gateway Center. Just about every major company in the space business had a building, all filled with thousands of antlike workers busily producing more hardware to shoot off into space.

Still, I realized more than most, that the space program had impact far beyond bringing back a few rocks from the moon. Half of the communications gear I routinely used in the field had been developed for NASA. I relied on their satellite weather reports and spy satellite recon for infiltration. The new look-down Landsat even showed what types of rock underlay the terrain, important details when you can't personally make an examination before a mission. And without the Vela satellites, we'd have never known about the Soviet atomic submarine pen at Cienfuegos on the southern side of Cuba. And communication—the TV scrambler unit now routinely used by AXE agents did away with older models of radio. Why only get a voice when you can see pictures at the same time, even get a hard copy of material over the TV waves if needed? All that came from the microelectronics of the space world.

Besides, if Hawk told me the space shuttle mission was more important than losing most of our electronic spy stations around the world, it had to be vital to our national defense. He wasn't a man to lose track of priorities.

I turned onto the four-mile-long bridge going over to the Kennedy Space Center, breathing deeply and going over my cover story. I smiled at it; this was a corker, one of the best I'd ever had. Before slowing down for the guard shack, I put on horn-rimmed glasses and took a quick glance into the rearview mirror to make sure my hair was parted right down the center.

"Identification, please," came the brisk request from the guard at the entry point. I flipped open my wallet and passed it out to him. He peered at it, squinted, then moved into the bright Florida sun from under the roof of his guard shack. He looked up, compared the picture with my face, then glanced back at my phony credentials in disbelief.

"I'll have to call ahead, Mr. Crane. This is beyond me."

"What's beyond you? I'm a duly certified agent of the Occupational Safety and Health Administration— OSHA. I am empowered to investigate the recent space shuttle accident to determine if further launchings endanger the crew's life. If so, I am likewise empowered to prevent further launchings until the problems are rectified." I tried to sound as smug and bureaucratic as possible. It worked. The guard hastily handed back the wallet and vanished into his guard hut.

In less than a minute, he came back, waving me on through. Out of his hearing, I laughed. The OSHA inspectors had tried to investigate working conditions in AXE several months ago. They refused to take "national security" as a reason for denying them access to our files. By the time Hawk had finished with that team of bureaucrats, they were sure that AXE was little more than a Boy Scout troop. Hawk's counterfeiters had duplicated enough records to keep the officious bureaucrats happy—and it had provided those same forgers the chance to photograph the credentials used by field agents of OSHA.

While a simple request from Hawk to the proper official would have been enough to obtain those same photos, this appealed to his sense of humor. And it guaranteed that the proper official would never mention passing along those credentials to one of the most secret spy organizations in the world.

I drove through the Florida countryside, taking in the swampy lands and the cypress growing so near the launch complex. Cape Canaveral hadn't ruined the ecology as so many doomsayers had predicted twenty years earlier. Ducks paddled idly on a pond less than a thousand yards from the major launch pad and the profusion of greenery told of constant battles keeping it down rather than worry about restoring it.

I pulled the car into a convenient parking spot just outside the main office building and was immediately confronted with three men in business suits and worried expressions. Smiling broadly, I climbed from the car and shoved out my hand.

"Martin Crane, Field Representative, OSHA," I said loudly. "Here to check up on that launch problem the other day. And you are," I bent down a little peering through the thick lenses of my fake glasses to read his security badge, "Dr. Samuelson. Right?"

"Uh, yes, right. Arnold Samuelson. And this is my administrative assistant, Dr. Paul Bretain." He didn't bother introducing the third man. He didn't have to . I recognized him from the National Security Agency files I'd read about Cape Canaveral. Ross Jacobs had a formidable background. While serving as a Green Beret captain in Vietnam, he'd won two Silver Stars plus dozens of lesser medals for heroism. After returning to the U.S. he had joined NASA as assistant head of security at the Johnson Space Center in Houston. He'd worked his way up until four months ago he'd been placed in charge of launch security at Cape Canaveral.

"What brings your particular administration into the picture, Mr. Crane?" asked Paul Bretain. "We've never had occasion to deal with OSHA in this capacity before."

"Not so," I said briskly, checking my small black notebook. "OSHA representatives have followed all aspects of construction on this site. I have the full documentation to back me up in this."

"That's not what I meant," said Bretain in exasperation. "That's building. That's actual construction you're talking about. I mean why should you meddle in NASA launches?"

"Meddle?" I said in a stunned voice. "You dare accuse OSHA of meddling? Improper, sir, very improper. We are entrusted by the Congress of this United States to maintain safety throughout our great land, no matter the cost. If I find that this space shuttle of yours is unsafe for the human crews, I will be forced to shut down the entire facility until that particular project is either scrapped or made into a safe one."

"You can't shut down the entire Kennedy Space

Center over one failed launch," said Arnold Samuelson, his eyes bright.

"I can and will, if necessary. Here is my authority." I thrust out the thick sheaf of papers, knowing it would take a lawyer a month to work through all the ramifications of my supposed mission, not to mention the powers I claimed.

Ross Jacobs took the papers and tossed them on the ground, the sea breeze riffling through them like cards being shuffled.

"Take it and stuff it!" he snapped. "We're able to handle things on the premises without the likes of you nosing around."

"Then I have no other alternative but to shut down the entire complex."

"You'll need a court order to do that," said Paul Bretain.

"Easily obtained. In fact, foreseeing such recalcitrance on your part, I had one prepared. Here it is. If one more bit of work is done on the shuttle program—or anything else in the confines of this complex—you are in contempt of court and face possible punitive action by Congress, as well."

"What?" asked Arnold Samuelson, stunned.

"You might see your budget cut," I said, pushing up the fake glasses onto my nose. "On the other hand, this court order need never be served if you cooperate."

"Show the bastard around," snapped Bretain. "And don't let him get into anything where he might hurt himself." His words didn't match his tone. He obviously wished I'd fall into the sea and never be seen around the Cape again.

"Uh, Dr. Bretain, please," said Arnold Samuelson in a mild voice. "He's only doing his job. I know we're all very upset over the failure the other day, but there's no need to take it out on him.''

I smiled knowingly. They were over a barrel and knew it. I turned to face the security man for the complex.

Glancing into Ross Jacobs' cold eyes, I saw that he wanted to take out all his frustrations on my head—using a monkey wrench. But that was what I'd hoped for. If I made the man angry enough, he'd concentrate more on that anger than my snooping.

He wasn't the sort to take usurpation of his power as security chief lightly.

''Come along, Paul,'' said Samuelson. ''I want to go over the figures on the launch again.'' It sounded like a routine that had worn on both of them over the past two days. I suspected that they were tired of debriefings and security meetings and everything else tied to the shuttle launch that had ended so badly.

''And you, Crane, what do you want to see?'' demanded Ross Jacobs. ''The boss told me to show you what you wanted—and I will. But I don't want to hear anymore of this closing down the launch facility bull out of you.''

''It's Mr. Crane,'' I said, smiling broadly. As I followed behind his hulking, silent form, I quickly checked to make sure my two weapons were securely placed and ready for immediate action.

Wilhelmina, my Luger, rested easily in the suede holster under my left arm. A quick scissoring motion with my right arm assured me that my steel stiletto, Hugo, still hung in his sheath ready to snap into my hand at the flick of my wrist. Knowing my two trusted companions were ready for action allowed me to turn my attention from the hulking Ross Jacobs and toward the launch facility itself.

"Are those the fuel tanks?" I asked, pointing to huge cylinders laying along one of the outbuildings.

"Of course not," said Ross Jacobs in disgust. "How are you supposed to check out safety if you don't know anything about the operation? Those are sewage tanks. The liquid oxygen is generated straight out of the atmosphere in yonder cooling towers. The kerosene is stored away from it so the two can't mix. Not that it matters much. If the lox ever got out, it'd freeze you solid or explode just about anything combustible it touched."

I nodded. I knew enough about the process to fake it when talking with Ross Jacobs. He was a security man; it told me much about the pressure on the staff here that they hadn't sent a technical consultant along with us. Instead, they relied solely on Jacobs making sure I saw only what they wanted.

"I'd like to meet some of the crew working on the lox facility. Especially the crew that is responsible for fueling the bird."

"The bird?" Ross Jacobs asked quizzically. "You pick up the lingo pretty fast."

I cursed under my breath at the mistake. It's always difficult telling how much to reveal and what to keep under your hat. I'd been around launch facilities in half a dozen countries. Sometimes it's impossible to keep slips like that from occurring. All I could do was cover the best way possible.

"I watch TV a lot. Science fiction stuff. Lots of rockets blasting off for Andromeda, things like that. Guess I picked it up off one of them."

"Science fiction," scoffed Ross Jacobs. "This is the real thing. This is science fiction coming true." The way he said it convinced me he was hooked. He'd do anything to protect his precious launch facility. While it was nice that he'd become so devoted to his work, it posed new problems. Keeping him angry as a diversion probably wouldn't work much longer.

"Call it fact, if you will, but I must determine if your science fictional facility is safe. I don't think it is. Look how that shuttle crew was almost killed."

"Almost. And exploring space is risky. They knew it. They're volunteers."

"Even volunteers must be protected from themselves, if their lives are in jeopardy."

He "harumped" and pointed to a pair of alien-looking creatures clumsily moving along a scaffolding overhead.

"That's the pair that loaded in the lox the other day. Kowalchowski and Campbell. They got work to do checking over the new tanks. Don't bug 'em too much, Crane."

"Mr. Crane," I corrected. Then to the pair, I called out, "A word with you two. Come on down!"

They exchanged glances through the thick plastic shields in the hoods they wore, then closed off the liquid oxygen valves and slowly descended the ladder. They wore heavily padded suits, silvered on the outside, giving them the appearance of creatures from outer space. Heavy insulated gloves came off revealing unexpectedly slender fingers on the first person. The second pair of gloves coming off revealed what I'd expected to see—big hairy hands, powerful and competent.

When their hoods came off, I was in for an even bigger surprise. Kowalchowski might have been a model for all her good looks. Campbell, on the other hand, had heavy bony ridges above his eyes making him appear to be a Neanderthal. Both tossed their hoods and gloves into a pile and came over.

"What is it, Jacobs?" demanded Kowalchowski. "We've got a lot of work to do before quitting time."

"This is Martin Crane with OSHA. He wants to make sure the next shuttle launch doesn't end up in the drink, too."

"OSHA?" asked the woman. "Hell of a bunch to be checking us out. Damn near had to push one of you guys into the liquid oxygen to keep him off my back while I was setting up the facility."

"You set it up?" I asked.

"Dr. Harriet Kowalchowski, head of the fuelling fadility at Cape Canaveral." She thrust out the slender hand. I took it in mine and felt the icy coldness. She laughed and said, "Comes from being so near the lox. Even with the gloves, it gets to you."

"I see," I said, writing down gibberish in my notebook to keep with my official guise.

"And this is Max Campbell. Best fuel technician in the place." I dutifully shook hands. He was one of the bruiser types who thought it impressed and intimidated people to break bones with his grip. I tightened up just enough to keep from getting hurt, then yelped.

Harriet Kowalchowski smiled, Ross Jacobs smirked and Max Campbell showed no reaction at all. I rubbed my injured hand and stepped back a half pace.

"Nice to meet you." I said insincerely.

"Yeah," was all he said. I wondered if he could be house-trained and taught to fetch balls.

"What is it you want—exactly?" asked Kowalchowski. "Something about the shuttle tanks? The way they're welded? Best welding in the world. All work up to ASME standards."

"They seem to have come apart in flight," I pointed out. "If there is any problem in the welding, that poses a potential safety hazard for the welders, too."

"Give it up, will you?" groaned Ross Jacobs. "These are highly skilled people working with the fuel, not hourly workers running seams on tanks."

"Cool off, Ross," advised Kowalchowski. "Look, Mr. Crane, we're under a bit of strain right now. Something went wrong with one of the liquid oxygen tanks and that caused the entire mission to fail. We feel a hell of a lot of pressure over this. We're being blamed, even though it's not our fault. And now you come around sticking your big fat nose into—" Harriet Kowalchowski broke off, her face flushed.

I glanced from her to Max Campbell. His expression hadn't changed, but I felt a tension in the air, and it was due to him. A tiny flicker of something more than stupidity flashed across those slate gray eyes, then vanished, as if he'd shown a light and quickly shuttered it. I found my hand involuntarily drifting toward Wilhelmina.

"Ross Jacobs. Mr. Ross Jacobs to the administration building immediately," blared one of the PA speakers strung high overhead on the scaffolding.

"I've got to go," he said gruffly. "Will you two look after him? Make sure he doesn't get into anything important."

"I resent your attitude, Jacobs," I said in as huffy a voice as possible. Jacobs grunted and stalked off without another word. I checked how my injured dignity act had gone over. Harriet Kowalchowski hadn't noticed it, and I had the definite feeling Campbell saw through it.

"Come on up the ladder and we'll give you a quick tour of the liquid oxygen compressor, the storage tank area and the fuel truck loading docks. This way, Crane," invited Kowalchowski with ill grace.

They picked up their hoods and gloves and followed

me up the ladder. No one said a word as the three of us climbed erect onto the walkway over the lox compressors.

"Do I need a suit like yours?" I finally asked.

"Not for an inspection tour. We require it if you're working here."

I nodded sagely and began following the petite woman along the catwalk.

"These are the compressors. Suck the atmosphere clean of oxygen and nitrogen, then we liquefy and fractionate it off. Simple distillation process. We use the liquid nitrogen for research stuff. Ship it to the other side of the complex. And we keep the lox."

"How cold is it?" I asked, feeling the chill rising from the frosted-over conduits on the compressors.

"Very," she answered. "Liquid oxygen boils at minus 297 degrees Fahrenheit. Liquid nitrogen boils around minus 321 degrees Fahrenheit. We use that temperature difference to separate the two, as I said before. We boil off the oxygen, then recool it using a cooling bath circled by tubes running liquid nitrogen. Simple operation."

I looked behind me at Max Campbell. He stood impassively, his hands dangling loosely at his sides. I had the feeling that he didn't understand a single word of what Kowalchowski was saying, yet he had to. He worked with this impossibly frigid substance all day long. And Ross Jacobs had said Campbell was one of the top technicians working at this facility. I didn't see the security man making idle statements like that, even to impress the likes of me.

"What does the lox do?" I asked Kowalchowski.

"It's the oxidant," she replied, as if I were the world's stupidest human and her simple statement supplied all the information to be had. When she saw that I didn't understand, she added, "There's no oxygen in outer space to make the kerosene burn. The shuttle's rocket engines have to carry along their own supply. This is it."

I nodded again and made a few more meaningless squiggles in my notebook to cover the time I needed to think. Anyone working on this part of the fuel supply could have planted the thermite bomb on the booster engines. All I had to do was find out who.

Remembering something else that Hawk had said about information leaking from Cape Canaveral, I asked Kowalchowski, "How much time do you spend out here working? Compared with desk time?"

"Almost all my time's out here," she said proudly. "I hate the paper shuffling. Max, here, takes the load off me in that respect. He knows I prefer to get my hands dirty with the rest of the gang." She held out those lovely, slender hands that might have belonged to a model and stared at them. The fingernails were chipped and broken, but other than that the hands were perfect.

"What're you exact duties, Mr. Campbell?" I asked.

He shrugged. "Whatever I'm told. This week's busy out here. Last month I was a gopher."

"Gopher?"

"Sure. Gofer this, gofer that. I shuffled a lot of papers back and forth to the administration building."

"Any of it having to do with safety handling procedures on the fueling?"

"Nope. I just plug the hoses in. Dr. Kowalchowski okays everything."

"You mean you have to crawl all the way up the side of the rocket to fuel it?" I asked, my voice carrying a tinge of awe.

"Somebody's got to do it."

I started to ask Dr. Kowalchowski another question when the loud speaker boomed forth another of its endless messages.

"All lox handlers to the main assembly area. All lox handlers to the VAB immediately."

"VAB?" I asked.

"Vehicle Assembly Building," supplied Kowalchowski. "World's biggest single-story building. Has its own rain showers inside and much more. It's huge. We've got to go. They're beginning work on another booster engine there, Mr. Crane. Feel free to wander around. Just don't stick your fingers into anything that looks smoky. It'll freeze 'em off instantly, turn 'em into glass. Come on, Max. We've got to make tracks."

I watched the two suited, inhuman figures descend from the catwalk. I stared down into the compressors and saw other silver-clad creatures making their way outside. This was more to my liking. I'd have a chance to look around on my own before they returned and I had to play-act the bureaucrat again.

Wandering along the catwalk gave me a perfect view of the floor area. Spying one of the refueling nozzles, I went over to it. The long hose had been draped over the three-story walkway to thaw out. Below me steamed an open vat of lox, the impossibly cold liquid boiling off into the atmosphere. I guessed this was the way they drained fueling hoses, by draping them over the walkway, any lox remaining would drain down into the vat.

Even the metal railing on the walkway had turned cold from the arctic storm boiling beneath my feet. Checking the nozzle, I saw nothing to tell me anything was amiss.

Sometimes the most effective approach is the best. The saboteur had only to carry the thermite bomb over to the rocket, clamp it onto the side of the fuel tank with a special magnetic limpet catch and then wait. There wasn't even the need for hiding the procedure. Anyone passing by would mistake it for part of the fueling.

Sighing, I leaned forward onto the railing and stared down into the furiously boiling vat of liquid oxygen. As I thought about the sabotage, I heard a faint metallic scraping noise.

I turned in time to see one of the eerie silver-suited figures advancing on me. With gloves on and hood securely in place, an anonymity had been achieved more effectively than any mask. That was all I saw before powerful hands gripped me under my armpits and lifted me bodily into the air.

I yelled once, then fell through the air toward the deadly sea of liquid oxygen.

# FOUR

I twisted and turned helplessly, flailing wildly as I fell. My arms and legs cartwheeled outward—and this is what saved me.

I felt something intensely cold under my fingers—the still-frozen fueling hose dangling over the vat. I grabbed for it, desperation giving me the strength and agility needed.

Pain shot into my hands and up my arms. The hose was *cold*. But the vat of liquid oxygen just inches under my shoe soles was colder, deadlier. I hung on for dear life. I felt icicles forming on my wrists as my body heat melted the ice on the outer surface of the hose, only to have it trickle down and refreeze instantly on my precious flesh.

Goaded by the need to get away from the lox sucking my body heat out through my feet, I began to climb. In this I was lucky. The hose proved stiff enough to give me some purchase.

But the numbing cold affected my hands more and more as I frantically climbed. I felt my strength quickly fading as frostbite turned my fingers blue.

Kicking as hard as I could, I swung up and locked my legs around the metal walkway from which I'd been thrown. Through the metal grating on its floor, I saw silver-soled boots swiftly walking away. Whoever had tried to toss me into the liquid oxygen apparently thought he'd succeeded and had decided not to stay around to watch the human icicle forming in the tank. And I knew that mistaken idea would turn to truth if I didn't get away from the hose, the vat and the awful cold seeping into my body like a cautiously invading army of killers.

Every part of me ached, hurt, tickled with the loss of circulation from the cold. When I felt my hands turning warm, I knew I had to hurry. Loss of sensation would doom me.

Glancing downward into the bubbling, churning vat, a moment of surprise seized me. How could anything that seemed so hot be so intensely frigid?

My hands gave way. I fell headfirst toward the vat. Tensing my legs allowed me to keep my tenuous hold on the catwalk, but I hung upside down in the air, my hair only inches from the surface of the vat. I felt the cold winds gusting upward, sucking out my breath, freezing my lungs. Panic flared for an instant, then I allowed the icy coldness to take hold of my mind.

Panic meant death. I would not panic.

Calming myself in spite of the predicament helped me to think through the perilous situation to find an answer. I knew my legs were strong enough to support me like this for several more minutes. Only then would my muscles begin to knot. I pulled my hands inward and tucked them under my arms, just as if I'd been caught out on the tundra in Norway on a long winter's night.

Tiny needles of pain danced along my fingers. Circulation slowly returned. And just in time. My legs were tiring faster than I'd thought. Another convulsive jerk allowed me to reach up and grip the bottom of the catwalk. Fingers still hurting from the frostbite but adequate for the task, I pulled—hard.

I swung up to one side of the walkway. Another kick, a grunt to coordinate the effort, then I slid belly down onto the rough metal flooring of the catwalk.

Safe.

For the moment.

Sitting up on the ragged metal grating, I peered around the liquid oxygen compressor complex. Only automatic, mechanical sounds came to my ears. No human moved, not even one clad in the obscuring silver of an insulated suit. With the damned visor and gloves, all of the workers looked alike. I hadn't even been able to tell the dainty Harriet Kowalchowski from the Neanderthal Max Campbell until I'd seen their faces and hands.

I moved away from the vat and its constant updraft of chilly air to a spot near one of the compressor vents. Hot air from the constantly running machinery gusted out, warming me, restoring a feeling of life to my deadened limbs. Checking hands and feet decided me that nothing was permanently damaged. I hadn't been near the deadly liquid oxygen long enough for that to happen.

A sudden crash sent me spinning into action.

Wilhelmina was in my hand in a flash. But no danger stalked me now. It was only the fueling hose falling over the railing. It had finally drained, thawed and slipped off the side of the catwalk. No doubt my hot body had speeded the thawing process. Putting the Luger back into its holster under my arm, I straightened, wondering how long it would take to find whoever had tried to toss me into the vat—and make them pay for it.

\*    \*    \*    \*    \*

"I fail to see why you should bother him at all," said Arnold Samuelson in a distracted tone. I could tell his mind was worlds away, maybe already up in near earth orbit. He was more a scientist than a politician and didn't handle bureaucratic types like I pretended to be very well.

"He's one of the astronauts, he's going up in the shuttle. I have to know his feelings on this. I have to know if he feels anything might go wrong."

"Do you think Tom Queensbury would go up in that," asked Paul Bretain, pointing out to the rocket being loaded onto the pad, complete with space shuttle atop it, "if he thought he'd die inside?"

"Did Grissom, Chaffee and White think they'd die?" I asked. "If OSHA had been in existence then, they might not have died."

"If OSHA had been in existence a million years ago," snapped Paul Bretain, "we'd still be living in the caves—or worse. No, it'd be a damn sight worse than that. You'd be chasing us out of the caves if we wanted a warm fire, warm because of the smoke. With near-sighted, frightened types like you, the chimney would never have been invented."

I ignored Paul Bretain. I understood his contempt for what he thought to be a useless agency. Basically, though, I only used the credentials to get closer to a saboteur. If I hadn't suspected him of being capable of the sabotage, I might have taken him aside to assure him I'd do nothing to prevent his precious space shuttle from blasting off.

"Dr. Samuelson, please allow me to talk with Queensbury."

"Very well. But only for a while. He has work to do, important work to finish before the launch. And his peace of mind is vital prior to a launch. He must feel absolutely confident about everything before lift-off. Otherwise. . . ."

He gestured toward the air-conditioned trailer in which the astronauts stayed until being ferried out to the launch site. I went in, put on stiff cloth protectors for the soles of my shoes and relented as they gowned and capped me like a surgeon for an operation. No dust, no dirt, no contamination of any sort, they explained. When I went through the tiny air lock into the main part of the trailer, I felt a slight breeze blowing into my face. The overpressure, I guessed, helped keep out the dust ordinarily in the air.

Sitting on softly padded seats, already suited up, were the three astronauts, Tom Queensbury, George Wyatt and Rob Edwards, according to their nametags. Queensbury was the crew commander and had spent the most time around the Cape. The other two were rookies, their first time for real launching. One was a backup while the other would actually go with Queensbury.

"What's this about you being a snoop?" asked Queensbury in an amiable manner. His wide grin took any possible sting from the words.

"You know what happened when the *Columbia* went up," I said. "I'm a field investigator sent down from Washington to make sure it doesn't happen with this launch."

"It won't," he said confidently. And I believed him.

Shaking my head, I had to get out of my role of investigating a safety problem and into the area where real data—on a saboteur—could be gained.

"Not good enough," I said. "There are distinct problems with the engines, for instance."

"Well," Queensbury said thoughtfully, "the shuttle engine is a brand new concept. Sure, the hydrogen pump system is dangerous since we've never tried it in free fall. But—"

"I mean on the booster engines, not on the shuttle itself. Look what happened with the last launch. *Blooie!*"

The man appeared perplexed.

Finally he said, "The booster engines are fine. Now and then something goes wrong. Human error, an act of God, call it what you will. Nothing's perfect. But those engines have been tested for long hours. They're good. It's the shuttle engine that is relatively untested; it's the one that kept blowing up in the tests in Huntsville."

I pressed the point. After what had happened to me in the liquid oxygen compressor plant, I had decided the saboteur had to be one of that crew.

"The liquid oxygen's dangerous," I accused.

"Of course it is. But Doc Kowalchowski's the best there is. I trust her to make sure everything's loaded and ready to roll."

"You're trusting her with your life."

"Hell, man, I'm trusting a million *lowest bidders* with my life. How'd you like to sit out there on top of a bloody twenty-story tall bomb knowing the government built that thing by going to the companies who did it for cut rates?"

"Zero defect analysis insures good performance," I said, trying to get him back to the fueling crew. "But tell me, how many of the fueling people do you actually meet? This is just for my own information. This is the first time I've ever been to a launch site."

He snorted and looked over at his copilot. The third man, the backup, turned and looked out the window toward the launch pad. They obviously had heard this routine before and had grown bored with it. I'd become

another of their admirers, not a fly in their launch
ointment.

"I make a point of meeting most of the people. Good
for my ego, plus it gives everyone a sense of belonging
to the team. Most all of them want to go up with me and
damn few ever even qualify. So the ground crews hang
around, wishing they were up there on top of that bird,
hating me and envying me at the same time."

He paused, then a quizzical expression crossed his
face. He shifted in his seat, pulling the air conditioning
hose around to loop over his left knee.

"Yes?" I prodded.

"Thinking about it, I've seen one of the crew working for Kowalchowski around somewhere. Hmmm,
hadn't given it much thought since I travel so much, but
this was an odd place."

"Where?"

"Can't remember."

"Which of Dr. Kowalchowski's crew is it?" I had a
feeling I knew. Max Campbell stuck me as an anomaly.
I don't like round pegs in square holes; that produces
friction. And with Campbell there was no sign of any
friction at all. That didn't fit the picture; he didn't
belong, somehow.

"Big dude, heavyset, looks like a monkey. Doesn't
quite drag his knuckles on the ground as he walks, but
close."

That description fit Max Campbell as good as any.

"Surely these technical people would follow the
project from beginning to end. Maybe you saw him
before in one of the factories where the engines were
assembled."

"Didn't go to any of them. No, it's like I met him at
some scientific conference. But that's silly. Except for

Doc Kowalchowski, they're all just technicians.''

"Two hours until launch," boomed the omnipresent loudspeaker. I felt the entire vehicle begin to tremble as the powerful diesel engine coughed to life before beginning to move the huge vehicle out to the launch pad.

"Better get out of here," I said.

"I'll join you," said Edwards, getting up and plugging himself into a portable air conditioning unit. "I'm obviously scrubbed for another flight, dammit."

"What? Why?" I asked, surprised.

"Only two in each launch. I'm the backup in case one of them gets sick. They never get sick. Too damn healthy. But just you wait, guys, I'll be thumbing my nose at you from orbit yet."

"Sure you will, Rob," laughed Queensbury, awkwardly slapping the man's shoulder with a gloved hand. "But until you do, George and I will send you a postcard."

"Do that," he said, nodding toward the door indicating we should leave before the trailer left.

Edwards and I stood outside in the bright, hot sun watching the trailer ponderously roll out to the giant booster rocket already trailing cold plumes of vented liquid oxygen. I wondered how this flight would end and if Rob Edwards would thank his lucky stars that he hadn't been aboard.

*   *   *   *   *

"Come in, Hawk," I repeated into the small communications unit disguised inside the lining of my attaché case. "I need some quick information."

"Yes, N3," came the imperturbable voice from the tiny speaker hidden in the attaché case.

"Max Campbell. All the dope you can get me on him. And on Harriet Kowalchowski, too." I felt a large nagging doubt about the woman. She seemed almost too good to be true, yet more small things pointed to Max Campbell.

"Are they the ones?" demanded Hawk.

"One is. I doubt if they are working together. I just need the data on Kowalchowski for corroboration. What scientific conferences has she attended recently that were also attended by Tom Queensbury, the astronaut?"

"None," came back the answer a few seconds later. I'm always amazed at the information stored in the AXE computers.

"And the same with Max Campbell."

"None," the answer returned even faster. "Max Campbell has never attended a scientific conference; several seminars on fuel technology, but none of the hard science ones."

"Give me a complete rundown on Max Campbell."

"Pretty dull stuff. Ready for a printout?"

"Ready," I said, closing the top of the attaché case. From inside came a deep humming noise, noticeable to anyone within a few feet. But I'd chosen my spot carefully. No one was near enough to wonder why my briefcase purred like a kitten.

Opening the lid when the humming noise ceased, I pulled out a damp copy of Max Campbell's file. It had been completely transmitted to the mechanism in the case, which had then used a thermocopy process to produce the hardcopy.

Scanning the page told me nothing. But the feeling

kept gnawing at my insides. This was too common, too ordinary a life. People like the one portrayed on the page in front of me existed, but usually something somewhere in their life seemed peculiar or out of place. Nothing of the sort existed for Max Campbell. While it was not impossible, it was suspicious. It was almost as if someone wanted to construct a completely nondescript personality.

"Hawk, go ahead and let me have the list of all the scientific conferences Queensbury has attended, especially those with Russian delegates in attendance."

Again the purring noise. The list was a long one.

"Just about every space science convention Queensbury has gone to in the past three years has had a healthy contingent of Russians in attendance," came Hawk's voice from the speaker. "It wasn't until Afghanistan and Poland that they were no longer welcome at the international conferences."

I studied the list but saw nothing on it the least bit suspicious. Certainly nothing on it linked Max Campbell to the mysterious man Queensbury vaguely thought he remembered as having seen at one of the conferences.

A dead end.

Cursing, I put away the printouts, still chaffing at the lack of information and the need for speed. I glanced up and saw the fueling crews preparing to go out to the rocket and top off the tanks with a last minute gush of liquid oxygen.

I slammed shut my case on Hawk's voice and tossed it aside, running out onto the tarmac, shouting at the top of my lungs.

One of the silver-suited figures turned and made a gesture of disgust and resignation. I knew that was Harriet Kowalchowski.

"What do you want, Crane?" came the muffled voice through her hood, as I ran up beside the truck carrying her crew.

"I want to watch the final fueling up close. I demand it!"

"Damn," came the muttered curse. "Hey, Max, get this fool a suit." Turning to me, she said sternly, "And you'll wear it every second we're out there. I don't want any damned government safety inspector croaking because of a damnfool accident."

I hastily donned one of the spare suits while the crew glowered at me. The last thing in the world I wanted was to go near the lox hoses without a suit. I remembered my near brush with death over that icy cold vat in the compressor room.

"All suited up and ready to go."

"Why are you along?" demanded Max Campbell with ill grace.

"To observe," I said, eyeing him through the visor. This time we were both anonymous. I wished I could take a few minutes to search him. I felt the nexus of a dangerous situation arriving—and I was in the middle of it.

All through the fueling, I stood close to Max Campbell. Twice he tried to move me away as he worked beside the bayonet junction that accepted the lox hose. And twice I simply moved out of his way, never taking my eyes off him. If Kowalchowski were the saboteur, she could have dismantled the rocket engine under my nose. I was putting all my chips on Max Campbell. That might prove foolish later, but I had to operate on instinct.

Harriet Kowalchowski was strong enough to have tossed me over the railing in the compressor plant. The way she lugged the heavy, half-frozen hoses around with the men on her crew told me that. But more subtle feelings of pride in her work, fear and disgust at what had happened to the prior launch vehicle, and a driving need to do better pervaded her personality.

I didn't see her wrecking something she loved.

Remembering what Queensbury had said about all the people on the ground feeling both hatred and envy for the lucky few who blasted into orbit, convinced me Harriet Kowalchowski was one of the envious. But working on a successful launch fed her ego enough to prevent her from sabotaging all those men and women who had passed through astronaut training.

That left the nondescript record of Max Campbell the only thorn in my mental processes.

As he worked, he became more and more nervous and jerky in his actions. I felt the tension mounting unbearably, then almost burst when Kowalchowski called out, "All done. Everyone back to the truck. Everyone back!"

Campbell finished clearing the hose from the side of the engine, then descended the ladder with me clumsily following. He never left my sight for an instant, even when he wrestled with the frozen hose getting it back out of the direct line of blast from the rocket engine. As we climbed into the truck, I heard huge fuel pumps in the booster begin their doleful operation. The bird readied itself for takeoff in less than one hour.

I'd done all I could to insure that Max Campbell—if he was the saboteur—hadn't planted another thermite bomb.

Cold fear caused me to shiver inside the insulated suit as I considered the possibility that I had bird-dogged the wrong man. If that were true, two vital space shuttle launches in a row were kaput.

\*　\*　\*　\*　\*

"See enough to keep you happy, Crane?" demanded Kowalchowski as we climbed out of the truck.

"Enough," I admitted. "And I have to give your crew a clean bill of health. You observed all the safety regulations to the letter. It'll be in my report."

"Thanks," said Kowalchowski sarcastically. "I can use the good news."

Turning, I noticed that the rest of the crew had skinned out of their insulated suits. But Max Campbell was missing.

"Where's Campbell?" I asked.

The woman shrugged, busy getting her own suit off.

"Where's he likely to have gone?" I demanded.

Startled, Kowalchowski looked up. Her brown eyes widened a little. I'd dropped the officious attitude totally and a slash of command had entered my voice. The role I'd created now ruined, I asked her again, more harshly.

"I don't know, Mr. Crane," she answered crisply. Then she started studying me more carefully.

"Think, dammit," I exclaimed. "This is important." My mind raced. With Max Campbell off somewhere, it might be necessary for me to reveal who I was to Ross Jacobs. The security man wouldn't like having AXE muscling in on his domain, but if I was right about Campbell, it'd be necessary. Any number of other things besides a simple bomb might be done to sabotage the launch.

"I remember he mentioned that he likes to go out to a nearby hill and watch the launches through binoculars. I always thought that was silly since we're all allowed into the viewing bunker. High resolution TV cameras make it like we're just a few feet away."

"This hill. Where is it?"

"Who are you?" she demanded suddenly. "You're

not a safety expert. I wondered about that from the way you stumbled around.''

"Tell me where that hill is," I said through clenched teeth.

This woman didn't cow easily, but the look in my eyes must have convinced her I'd stop at nothing to get the information.

Hand shaking, she pointed. "Over that way. About five miles."

"Five miles," I mused. Too far for a rifle. "Where else might he be? Closer up to the bird? Say, within a mile."

"That's mighty close. No one's allowed close-in without a concrete bunker around them. Too dangerous, except maybe. . . ."

"Where?"

"Scrubby Knoll," she said finally. "Look, what's this about? That little hill gets a good blast over it if anything happens to the rocket. I don't want Max Campbell hurt. If you think he's out there—"

I was already on my way. Max Campbell might not be there. I thought he was. Since I'd prevented him from planting his bomb by watching his every move during the fuel topping, he had to wreck the launch in some other way. The most convenient was a high-powered rifle. But a shot of five miles was too great a risk, even for a trained marksman. One mile was stretching it, but certainly possible if he was any kind of a shot. All Max Campbell needed to do was hit the missile anywhere, accuracy not meaning a thing. The leak would take care of the rest.

If he had something more sophisticated, like a surface-to-air missile, knocking down that rocket would be like dynamiting the proverbial fish in a barrel.

Jumping into the truck, I gunned it to life and left the

fueling crew standing beside the bunker, watching in
confusion as I raced off. I wondered how long it would
be before Kowalchowski phoned Ross Jacobs and reported this. Not long, I thought.

I had memorized a map of the entire Cape Canaveral
area. The Scrubby Knoll that Harriet Kowalchowski
mentioned was off several miles to the right at the end
of a lot of lonely dirt roads. I pulled off the tarmac and
screeched along an unpaved road leading to it. Low
hills covered with salt cedar and sickly looking cypress
and sand dunes dotted the area. Some swampy regions
existed in treacherous locations on either shoulder of
the road, making me drive more slowly than I'd have
wished, and the hill I sought was little more than a lump
in the middle of a lot of emptiness. Finding it among all
the other look-alikes might prove to be impossible.
About all I really knew about it was that it would be
enough to protect Max Campbell from a missile explosion should he be successful in whatever sabotage
scheme he'd concocted.

I cursed my lack of knowledge. This might be a wild
goose chase. I might have blown my cover at the Cape
for nothing. But instinct told me differently. Max
Campbell had been upset and uptight out at the fuel
topping such a short time ago. Sure, he might be having
woman problems or had gotten drunk last night and
sported a hangover today, but that didn't explain my
intuition.

Most of the cases I was assigned to came down to
little more than educated guesswork. I was one of the
best because my guesses were better than most.

A glint of light shone ahead, a small reflection off the
silver bolt of a hunting rifle.

I felt a surge of relief, of vindication. Quickly following it came fear. The launch was only minutes away

now. And Max Campbell had the missile lined up perfectly for his shot.

Slamming the truck into a skid, I slewed around and came out the door. All I got were fleeting impressions of the scene, but it was enough to make me realize how close to sabotaging the second shuttle launch my man was.

The powerful rifle—no mere deer rifle, I realized now—was put into a sandbagged brace to insure maximum accuracy. The massive scope on the top seemed almost superfluous. The rifle itself was a .44-40 magnum, a potent weapon easily capable of holing the fuel tanks in that rocket, even at a mile away.

The man sighting so carefully hardly seemed to take note of me as I pulled out Wilhelmina and slipped back the cocking toggles. I heard the 9 mm Parabellum round click into the chamber.

Nick Carter, Killmaster, was about to earn his keep.

"Put your hands up!" I barked, bringing Wilhelmina to bear on the prone target.

A single shot boomed forth across the swampy lands. The rifle bucked against the sandbags and the muzzle lifted upward under the tremendous push of the heavy bullet as it fled the barrel.

My shot was only milliseconds later—too late.

The saboteur rolled just enough to allow my first shot to miss him by scant inches. My second shot hit empty sand. My quarry bounded over the rise and down the other side.

I hesitated. Finally deciding on my course of action, I jumped to the roof of the truck and pulled out a pair of binoculars that had lain inside. Carefully studying the distant missile, I couldn't tell if the shot had done any damage or not. Plumes of the normally venting liquid oxygen covered any possible hole in the tank. If I called off the launch, or ever held it up for a few minutes, with all the press coverage there'd be hell to pay if I failed to produce a hole.

If the saboteur had hit the rocket, I might be saving the lives of two men.

My eyes worked quickly over the booster engines. I saw nothing amiss. That left me with just one final duty.

Catch the saboteur.

Dropping the binoculars, I jumped to the sandy ground and sprinted up to the top of the rise. My man had fled, leaving behind only small, indistinct impressions in the sand.

Wilhelmina firmly in hand, I started the tedious, dangerous job of tracking him down.

# FIVE

I stalked through the tangle of underbrush careful not to make even the tiniest of noises. That came from pure habit. It seemed impossible that anyone could really hear me unless I was right on top of them. The distant thunder of the rocket engines as they started into their final five minutes of earthbound glory came rumbling over the low hills like a deadly storm building, drowning out any small noises I made. When the rocket actually launched, those engines would be blasting out enough noise to deafen me.

I had to use all my senses to find the wily saboteur. He couldn't escape under the cover of the space shuttle launch.

Taking a deep whiff of the air convinced me that tracking by this type of spoor was useless. The thick, moist air felt like a sponge stuffed in my nostrils. Sound and smell useless, that left only vision. I'd have to be doubly careful not to be sighted first. The sandy Florida loam crunching slightly underfoot, I stepped up my pace of following the track laid down by the fleeing man.

A sixth sense has kept me alive for a long time. And it aided me now. A tension in the air, a feeling of ''difference'' assailed me. I dived low and off to one side just as the heart-stopping powerful cannon-roar of the man's rifle filled my ears. The massive slug ripped feverishly at a tangle of vines to one side, hit a buried rock, then whistled off into the distance.

If he'd hit me with that bullet anywhere in the body, the hydrostatic shock alone would have killed me. I didn't even want to think of the damage it would have done to a kidney, a liver, or a spleen. Better to be dead than crippled for life with a shattered gut.

I didn't think he would miss a second time. I didn't dare give him the opportunity. Staying low, I duck-walked behind a low rise and circled back the way I'd come. Trying to second guess the man was impossible. I had to play this on my own, using techniques that had worked well for me in the past. If I'd tried to advance, most men would have been waiting patiently for me. By doubling back, it gave me time to quell the shaking I felt inside from the nearness of the miss—and give him time to become nervous.

He knew he hadn't hit me. But he also had to know he couldn't scare me off. When I didn't appear on schedule from behind the sandy rise, he'd begin to wonder, to think, to reconsider his position. And he might even become hasty and make a mistake. I didn't count on it since he'd been letter-perfect up till now, but it improved my chances if I forced him into action.

The rocket's majestic beauty was cloaked in a constant updraft of exhaust fumes now. The booster engines were being cranked up to top performance to prepare the shuttle for its final seconds on earth. Then huge locking snap-blocks would break away and the entire rocket would hurl into space like a rock from a slingshot.

I pushed the shuttle's imminent departure from my mind. I wasn't a tourist. I couldn't afford the luxury of daydreaming about the romance of space travel, the fantasy of flying off this planet. I engaged in deadly business among the sandy dunes, business amounting to more than just my own continued survival. The man who'd tried to toss me into the liquid oxygen vat carried a magnum rifle. He was an expert saboteur and assassin. He didn't make mistakes. I couldn't allow him to force me into making one with a second's ill-advised inattention to our deadly game. I continued backtracking, trying to catch a brief glimpse of him again, and failing.

The sudden roar of the truck engine startled me.

"Damn!" I cursed. He'd circled around while I was circling in the opposite direction, had gotten behind me and was now stealing the truck.

Throwing caution to the wind, I leaped up to the top of the rise, saw the truck spinning around, kicking up an obscuring cloud of sand, then assumed the marksman's pose. Both hands on my Luger, my eyes both open to sight along the barrel, I let Wilhelmina speak once, twice, three times.

A loud bang reached my ears. One of the 9 mm bullets had punctured a large rear tire. Then came a gaseous whooshing I recognized. Another of the bullets had smashed through and ruptured the gas tank. I fired a fourth time. A sudden burst of flame engulfed the rear end of the truck.

And again I cursed my bad luck. The man had seen the danger, dived across the front seat of the truck and was out the opposite side before I changed my position to cover him. I fired three more times, in vain. Two quick motions pulled the empty clip from the Wilhelmina's butt and just as quickly I rammed in a fresh one.

Then it was my turn to go for cover. Putting the burning truck between me and that impossibly powerful rifle, I worked my way silently to a point I hoped would deliver my quarry to me.

Victory!

A dark lump lay sprawled on the dune, the rifle loosely held in steady hands. He obviously waited for me to repeat the sneak-technique I'd used before. I had fooled him this time and circled around to him from his blind side. Wilhelmina lifted, the sights centered on the man's spine, and my finger tightened.

The Luger jammed.

The delicate mechanism had to be cleaned repeatedly to prevent sand from jamming the slide. During all my rolling, dodging and running on the sandy beaches of Cape Canaveral, a few grains had gotten into the precision-machined tracks. While it would take only a few seconds to clean, I didn't have those seconds. He had heard the slide clicking and grinding futilely, the firing pin just a fraction of an inch from successfully firing the round.

As I dived, Wilhelmina dropped to one side and Hugo's handle came firmly into my hand. The heavy-grain bullet from the rifle ripped through the air a hair's breadth above my head. Then I fell heavily onto the man, forcing the magnum away and bringing up the knife to poke firmly into his ribs.

Something hard turned away Hugo's needle point. He wore a flak vest under the work overalls.

Before I changed the direction of my slash to cut his throat, his powerful hand clamped my wrist and twisted. Still off balance from the leap, I fell heavily as he managed to jerk me to one side. Hugo buried point first into the soft sand.

I kicked free and stood ready for hand-to-hand combat.

"So, Campbell, at least you're out in the open now," I said. "Your cover is blown. Why not give it up?"

The heavy-set man came to his feet with surprising agility. This was no ordinary man. I realized he was neither slow nor stupid. And from firsthand experience, I knew he was considerably stronger than I was.

"Mr. Crane—or should I call you Nick Carter?" he said taunting me as he slowly moved to his right in the proper fashion, one leg never crossing the other for even an instant.

Calling out my name like he'd done startled me. I rose slightly. He rushed. My body responded automatically. My fingers closed on his groping hands, I bent double, my leg coming between us. Foot planted firmly in his belly, I rolled backward using his momentum to add power to the throw and tossed him overhead using a *tomoe-nage*—the stomach throw. I kept rolling and came up straddling his chest.

I grabbed a double handful of fabric at the neckline of his overall and began choking down hard on that muscular neck. The cloth ripped and the choke failed long enough to allow him to hammer wildly at my upper arms and ribs. He unseated me.

Again we faced each other. But this time I'd been able to get a closer look at his face. Tiny scars networked the area around his eyes, behind his ears, over his forehead just under the hairline. Extensive plastic surgery had been performed within the past year on him. No matter how good the surgery, the scars would always show. I know. I carry many scars from past missions requiring plastic rebuilding of my own features.

But the basic bone structure, the sheer animal power, the cunning locked behind those slate gray eyes, told me who I faced.

"Well done, Colonel Kolakovich," I said, my hands

extended slightly in front of me in a defensive position. Again we circled.

"So the fabulous N3 recognizes me at last, eh?" he chuckled. His bland American accent faded slightly to be replaced by a more guttural Russian pronunciation.

"At last. Colonel Gregor Kolakovich, cosmonaut and bureau chief for the KGB in the Balkan countries. I hardly expected to see you here, on a mission usually performed by younger men." He didn't seem surprised that I knew all about him. It had been worth the effort trying to surprise him; it hadn't cost me anything but a little wind.

"It is a mark of the importance we attach to your space shuttle that I personally should see to its demise," he said. The words came effortlessly, as did his every movement. For a large man, he moved well, almost bonelessly, like a striking snake. I didn't let his words hypnotize me. I watched a spot on his sternum for clues to his movement. The very best can deceive with eye-feints, tiny glances in the wrong direction before real movement. The body must move for anything to be done; I concentrated on a spot just above his solar plexus, letting peripheral vision take in hands and feet, as well as head position.

He twitched slightly. I acted. And caught him slightly off balance. With all the power I could muster, I gripped his upper arms and knocked his feet out from under him with a powerful sweeping motion. He fell heavily, spinning as he dropped.

This time I was ready. No cloth would tear and allow him to escape. My right arm locked around his exposed windpipe, my right hand gripping behind my left forearm. The palm of my left hand pressed down into the back of his head. I applied pressure. More. Even

more. I felt his bull-sized neck weakening under the
onslaught. His chin tipped forward allowing me to
increase the pressure to the point where no man could
stand it. I felt life slipping from his body.

Then a powerful hand lifted me upward and casually
tossed me aside as if I were nothing more than a rag
doll. Hot, harsh winds gusted above me, filling the sky
with fire and debris. Molten bits of titanium alloy
rained down while an acrid burned odor infiltrated its
way to my nostrils.

The space shuttle booster engines had blown.
Kolakovich's single shot had punctured the fuel tanks.
During the maximum dynamic stress of takeoff, the
entire liquid oxygen tank had ruptured, destroying the
missile and shuttle.

Burning fuel sprayed down seconds later, threatening to set me on fire. I rolled through the dry sand until I
found a swampy section of the landscape. Burrowing
down, I waited until the worst of the deadly shower had
passed.

I rose and squinted into the holocaust in front of me.
The rocket hadn't gotten more than five hundred feet
into the air when the tanks had exploded. I only had to
see the crumpled remains of the blunted prow of the
space shuttle to know that this launch had ended in total
tragedy. Queensbury and his copilot Wyatt were dead.
No one could possibly have survived that raging inferno.

Worse, looking around for Kolakovich told me he
was long gone. He'd probably gotten to the car he'd
used to drive out here and was barreling over the sand
dunes toward the miles-distant beach. With his mission
so successfully completed, the KGB High Command
no doubt wanted him back inside the USSR.

Dejected, I retrieved Hugo and found Wilhelmina

where I had so carelessly dropped her. A few swipes with the tatters of one of my sleeves cleaned out the action. I replaced her in the soft leather holster and began walking back to the control bunker. I'd have to report in full to Ross Jacobs.

And David Hawk.

*   *   *   *   *

I plugged in the special television adapter invented by the geniuses in AXE laboratories, wincing as I moved. More of the fiery debris from the sabotaged rocket had touched me than I'd thought. My back and arms were covered with blisters and charred flesh. Just sitting was painful but lying back flat on the bed was altogether impossible. I needed a doctor, but that had to wait.

Reporting to Hawk came first.

Using the remote controller, I activated the TV and got a poor picture of one of the daytime soap operas. The scrambler took hold, sought out the AXE communications satellite poised somewhere over the equator—Ecuador, I'd been told—and sent my request on to Washington D.C. and Hawk's office.

The crystal clarity of the reception told me that Hawk had been waiting for my call and had cleared a top priority channel for our exclusive use. His impassive face peered out from the TV set, the butt end of a well-chewed cigar rolling from one side of his mouth to the other.

"Well, N3, what's happened? I have reports . . ." He pointed down at a huge stack of papers on his desk. There wasn't any need for me to be told what was contained in them. AXE has information gathering capabilities that astound me. Word of the shuttle failure had already reached Hawk's desk in just the time it took me to drive back to the motel.

"They're accurate. I failed. Colonel Gregor Kolakovich had received plastic surgery and used counterfeited papers and a constructed persona as Max Campbell to get the job on the fueling crew. Of course he knew the job perfectly, possibly better than Harriet Kowalchowski. He is one of Russia's most decorated cosmonauts."

"Kolakovich?" mused Hawk. "What happened? Did you remove him from the game?"

"I failed at that, too. He used a high-powered rifle to put a hole in one of the booster's fuel tanks. I stopped him from placing his thermite bomb during fueling, but was too late afterward to prevent the rifle shot."

"He *is* dead?" demanded Hawk.

"He escaped." I didn't go into the whys and wherefores. Hawk wasn't interested that I'd been within seconds of killing Kolakovich with my bare hands. I'd failed. That was all that mattered.

Hawk's expression turned dour. He sat back in the swivel chair hidden by that massive oak desk of his and laced his fingers behind his head. His eyes got a far-off look. I knew better than to disturb him while he thought out the entire matter.

Finally he broke the long silence.

"This has to be turned to our advantage since the scope of the Soviet activity is widening drastically. You already know about the destruction of our electronic listening posts. The Russians did it."

"How?"

"I'll get to that in a moment. They have increased their space activities. They have their delta wing space shuttle about ready to go into full-time operation, which from their point of view, is a good thing. Their Soyuz-T3 is hardly capable of supplying the newly orbited Salyut-8 space station."

"It's not just an orbiting laboratory, is it?" I asked. The press releases all lauded the Soviet scientific effort. The Salyut-8 was too huge for just a simple lab.

"Don't believe all you read, N3. Don't believe *anything* you read about the Soviets." Hawk swiveled around, his eyes glowing with feverish intensity now. "They have built a very sophisticated military post in one end of the Salyut-8. Apparently, Gregor Kolakovich's mission was to prevent development of our own space shuttle to keep us from investigating on the spot. The atomic bomb scheme dreamed up for our space shuttle was a secondary goal, I'm now told by the Pentagon."

"One of these days, they'll keep us better informed as to what they're doing."

"The left hand never knows what the right is doing," said Hawk, stating the aphorism that ruled government. "What we now know is that the Pentagon would have docked with Salyut-8 and conducted an on-site inspection. With the space shuttle now hopelessly behind schedule due to the sabotages, the Russians have bought themselves another year of hidden activity in orbit."

"What's all this got to do with the destruction of our listening posts?"

"They've constructed a simple reflecting mirror outside the Salyut. By turning the mirror and focusing it on certain spots on the earth, they can create an intense heat."

"Just like a laser!"

"Not as hot or as concentrated, but vastly easier to do. Their electronic and technical sophistication still doesn't match ours. Getting one of their lasers into orbit would have required too much work. It probably wouldn't have worked as well, and certain other complicated scientific considerations have to be taken into account. Beam dispersion problems that we've solved and they haven't, for instance. With a simple concave mirror, however, they could take it up a piece at a time. And the actual construction wouldn't require much skill, only tedious work in orbit.

"And they've been in that station—or the Salyut-6 and 7—continuously for almost two years."

"Three years, N3," he corrected. "And three years is more than enough time for even the Soviets to construct such a large, bulky structure," Hawk said authoritatively. I knew the AXE experts had briefed him fully on it.

"I didn't think it was possible to concentrate enough sunlight at the earth's orbit to do that kind of damage. Too low a solar constant and other scientific reasons. They melted steel."

"And incinerated that Chinese battalion, tanks and all. Well, to be frank, our experts are unsure how it was done. But they know it was. While the Soviets lack certain of our microelectronics and advanced computers, they do not lack ingenuity. But the use of the mirror might be put to more devious ends."

I thought about it, then light dawned.

"That's right, N3," said Hawk solemnly. "There's nothing to stop them from beaming down a diffuse version of their melting ray, but doing it over a large area. Say they bathe the entire Midwestern part of the U.S. with their weakened sunlight."

"The grain belt!"

"They alter the weather with continual heating. The dust bowl returns. Massive crop failures cause worldwide starvation—we do supply almost a third of the world's foodstuffs. The Russians capitalize on this, excuse the pun.''

''All they have to do is raise the ambient temperature along the Mississippi River by a few degrees.''

''Or they can aim their mirror at the Gulf Stream. Alter its course and melt the northern polar cap. We'd drown inside ten years.''

''But they could use the mirror for their own benefit. Imagine a Siberia heated and turned into usable farm-lands.''

''The Russians do not think in those terms. Their thinking processes most closely match the way a chess knight moves. Nothing is straight, direct; it's always slightly askew. Perhaps some day, after they have removed what they perceive as the Chinese threat—and the Western threat—they will turn to such develop-ment. At present, they use the mirror in an aggressive and hostile fashion. Definitely against the best interests of the U.S.''

''All this sounds more and more like Kolakovich,'' I said heatedly. ''He's a genius, a warped genius. But subtle.''

''I concur. It is a shame you failed to remove him when you had the opportunity.''

I shook my head. Getting the chance to kill Kolakovich wouldn't be as easy the second time—and the first effort had ended in failure. Sure, he'd been lucky. Wilhelmina had jammed at the most opportune time for him. The rocket taking off and exploding had come at the time best for the KGB colonel. But luck didn't explain my own failure to finish him off with Hugo when I'd had the chance.

''But,'' continued Hawk, ''we must make plans to proceed as if nothing had happened.''

''Then there'll be another shuttle launch soon?''

''I'm afraid not. The Department of Defense could not convince certain key senators that Congress should appropriate emergency funds. The entire matter is being put into committee.''

''But that'll slow the entire program.''

''It will bring it to a dead halt for as long as a year,'' said Hawk grimly. ''You were impersonating an OSHA official. It seems that particular agency is officially getting into the act. They smell free publicity. And astronauts did die.''

''They'll kill the entire program!'' I cried, realizing now that the importance of the space shuttle program was vastly greater than putting a few more communications satellites into orbit or peering at light-years distant stars through a telescope not hidden behind earth's obscuring atmosphere.

''That won't happen, but they will hinder it. The Russians are progressing. Their use of the mirror at this time indicates ambitious expansion plans elsewhere. With our listening posts silenced temporarily, they will be able to move with impunity.''

''Or see how quickly we regain our abilities—so they'll know how long they have if they do it again.''

''A good point, N3. Yes, the Soviets are opportunistic when it comes to expanding their empire. Ah, here's the latest message coming in now.'' Hawk peered down at the top of his desk at a TV console invisible to me. He frowned. ''It's bad, N3. Kolakovich apparently was picked up by an atomic submarine off Cape Canaveral and taken directly to the atomic sub pens in Cienfuegos, Cuba. From there, he was transferred to one of their Backfire bombers. He's flying up the Atlantic coast and over the pole. He'll be in Moscow before you could take Amtrak from Florida to Washington.''

"We could order the bomber shot down."

Hawk hesitated. He obviously considered the proposal seriously. Then he shook his head.

"Too risky. They probably have their TU-94s pacing the jet so that it's always within observation distance."

"It seems to me the key to all this isn't so much Kolakovich as it is the Salyut-8 with its mirror. Why not launch a Minuteman and blow it the hell out of space?"

"That was suggested and soundly rejected by the President. We are signatories to the Outer Space Treaty preventing us from using atomic devices in orbit."

"But you said earlier the shuttle was being considered for an orbiting shell game with hundreds of warheads."

"There is a difference between detonating a device in space and calling it down to earth. Some of our scientists feel that further explosions will damage the ozone layer, as well as scrambling more earthly communications."

"It wouldn't destroy the Van Allen Belt, though?"

"No."

"But the detonation of the atomic bomb destroying the Salyut-8 with its crew might be seen as an act of war?" I didn't want to even consider that. With the U.S. military preparedness so tenuous in many respects, it would be touch and go if we got into a real shooting war with Russia. We'd win eventually, but the cost might be more than the country could endure.

"The destruction of the Salyut-8 might be looked upon favorably, however, if done without a nuclear device, N3."

From the expression on his face, I read my next assignment.

"It must appear accidental?"

"Naturally. We cannot be held accountable if, say, the Soviets accidentally put nitrous oxide into their oxygen tanks destined to supply the space station. Or if food intended for consumption aboard turns out to be infested with botulinus bacilla. Or perhaps they might experience a problem similar to the ones we have been having recently at Cape Canaveral. The explosion of one of the Soyuz-T3 engines while docked in space might do grievous harm to the station. That, of course, would be a tragedy as it would remove permanently the entire station. But this is up to you."

I considered the alternatives. Killing the crew made sense only if the Russians wouldn't send up others to finish the diabolical task of aiming that mirror at the U.S. I couldn't see it working that way. Whatever I did had to be of a more permanent nature.

I noticed that Hawk's attention was already shifting to some other message coming in on the hidden desk console. He reminded me of a big spider in the middle of a web. The strands would jiggle and he'd pounce. I had no idea how many strands ran directly to him, either. All I did know is that he demanded results.

And I would deliver. The future of the United States of America was at stake.

# SIX

The constant hum of planes flying overhead made me nervous. While I wasn't technically here in the middle of the Turkish desert, physically I was very much in real danger. The almost daily escalation of the fighting in the Middle East had spread from a border skirmish between Iran and Iraq to shooting between Syria and Jordan. Even Israel was arming, preparing for the PLO to take advantage of the unrest in the area. The Saudis supplied the Iraqis arms and the Turks favored the Kurds in their fight for independence. The politics and ins and outs of the situation were too complex.

I preferred my assignments simpler and without outside complications intruding on the work at hand.

Still, I had to rely on the good graces of the Turkish Air Force to get me near the Soviet-Turkish border. At that point I'd be on my own. Until then I had to listen to the NATO armed exercises going on all around me. The Turks took these maneuvers seriously; they had to. With Russia a constant companion along their northeastern borders, eternal vigilance was the only way they maintained their sovereignty.

"We are ready," came the guttural words of the Turkish NATO commander for this protracted military exercise. I was only supercargo to them, hardly more than a bother, certainly nothing to get upset over if I lived or died.

"Let's go, commander," I replied. Hitching up the small pack on my back, I trooped off behind the swarthy, small-statured man. But from the way he walked I knew he wasn't one to pick a fight with. He might have been small but the determination, the steely glint in his dark eyes, told of intense loyalty to his nation, his cause.

The small troop plane seemed primitive by U.S. standards. The rattletrap DC-3 had seen better days forty years ago, but for the Turks it was ideal for getting back into areas of their mountainous country not easily reached by road.

"Why don't you use helicopters?" I called out over the whistle of the wind through the sides of the plane. Some of the rivets had popped out and left gaping holes. But the engines hummed smoothly and the plane lifted easily from the runway. It might have been old, but it was still dependable.

"In desert?" he laughed. "You Americans never learn. The helicopter did not work so good in cold, wet Korea, but it was new to the enemy and it sufficed. In Vietnam jungles it proved a liability. To die in one was too easy. And for this part of the world, pah! We have sandstorms. Remember the Sea Stallions as they landed inside Iran to rescue your hostages?"

"Poor maintenance," I said. "But the Soviets use their helicopter gunships well in Afghanistan. I've seen the reports."

"With a rock you can knock them from the sky. Give me rocks!" He subsided, leaning back against the quaking sides of the plane, his arms crossed.

I nodded and shut up. The Russians had their own problems but simple rockets took out their vaunted gunships with ease. Newer "smart bombs" proved even more effective, although none of these had been given to the Afghan rebels. Still, without airfoils to hold up the plane should the engines quit, helicopters proved very vulnerable to even the slightest damage.

The ancient DC-3 lumbered along, slowly gaining altitude until I gasped for air. The frigid upper atmosphere turned my nose red. Each breath cut deep into my chest and made me feel as if I'd been dipped in the liquid oxygen vat back at Cape Canaveral. The plane continued to climb until we were near the fifteen thousand-foot level. Just sucking in enough oxygen proved difficult now. I hoped the pilot wore an oxygen mask, but I somehow doubted it. These Turks were fiercely proud of their fighting prowess. Wearing a sissy thing like an oxygen mask to keep from passing out might be an affront to their *machismo*.

"Here. Drink." A heavy crockery bottle passed along the line of soldiers and was thrust into my hands. The ceramic warmed my hands but I didn't try the liquid.

"What is it?" I asked.

"Good!"

I drank. Gagging on the fierce hot liquor produced laughter in the Turkish ranks. I swallowed, smiled wanly and leaned back. But the fiery liquor dribbled down my gullet and left a burning path behind. In a few minutes the intense cold inside the DC-3 no longer mattered. Closing my eyes, I leaned back and let my mind drift forward to the work I had to do inside Russia.

I hated clandestine activities inside the Soviet Union. There's only one country more tightly controlled by the police and military than Russia: East Germany. I speak good Russian, having learned it from a British translator at the United Nations. And Russian wasn't all I'd learned from Mandy. She'd been adept at many things, both intellectual and physical.

No, speaking the language, even if I did have a slight British accent, wasn't the biggest problem. The Communists are one of the most paranoid of all political groups in the world. Travel papers are always required; they change forms according to some magical formula only the Soviet bureaucrats understand. The forged papers safely tucked inside my pocket might be a month out of date. The only way of telling was to give them to a guard and find out the hard way.

Still, bluffing played a large part in my job. Guards are bored people looking for a little excitement. If I played the role well, I'd seem too dull to bother with. And one little trick I'd learned years ago was to always cut into line in front of the most beautiful woman. If the guard was male, as most were in Soviet-block countries, he would pass me through as quickly as possible to examine the woman's papers with the most intense of all scrutinies. The longer he dallied with her papers, the longer he could ogle her.

By the time he'd finished, I was always long gone.

I knew all the rules for travelling inside the Soviet Union; I still didn't like it. The liberals in the U.S. complain about lack of respect for an accused's legal rights. In Russia there are no rights. Any citizen can be arrested arbitrarily by the KGB—and no charge given, ever. If the local commandment of police feels the urge, he might go through the streets pulling people in at random to torture and kill, and worse, ship them to Siberia. This didn't happen often. The people wouldn't have stood for a constant diet of it, but the promise of it occurring rode on the backs of everyone, making them fearful, causing them to jump at small noises and shifting shadows.

The Soviet Union isn't even a good place to visit, much less live in.

My pack contained little more than a change of clothing and a very sophisticated communication device. Disassembled, it appeared to be only buckles for the pack and the straps. Inside the straps were the electronics; the buckle acted as a directional antenna. Other than this—and Wilhelmina, Hugo, and Pierre—I was on my own. The Turks would deliver me to the Sino-Turkish border and I'd parachute in. Then I was totally on my own.

Travelling almost seven hundred miles to the Caspian Sea launch facility at Baikonur might take as long as four days, depending on my luck in hitching rides and making the proper connections. And once there, my mission began.

Thoughts of explosive devices rippled across the surface of my mind. I had no idea right now what I'd do once at Baikonur. But any missile launch site had chemicals, electronic timers—materials useful to a saboteur. They could be put together in cunning ways to destroy the entire launch facility. Cripple Baikonur, cripple the entire Russian space program. Gregor Kolakovich had done it at Cape Canaveral. I had been ordered to duplicate his efforts at Baikonur.

Simple.

An added bonus in preventing launches from Baikonur would be the stranding of their astronauts in orbit. Without new food, oxygen, water and other essentials, they would soon perish. Since there seemed to be no sure way of wrecking the Salyut-8 while in orbit, the next best thing appeared to be destroying the supply site on the ground.

The Turkish commander shook my shoulder. My eyes opened slowly, focused on him, and saw the brilliant white smile peeking through the thin lips.

"We are now over the Soviet border. Prepare to jump."

I nodded and rose, getting into my parachute. As the last buckle snapped shut, the plane suddenly banked. I slammed into one of the flimsy walls. Peering out, I saw the flexible wings flapping up and down like a wounded albatross. The pilot wildly banked in the other direction, flinging me toward the door. Since this was where I'd intended to go anyway, I didn't even attempt to stop myself from vanishing through the open door.

And it was a good thing. Seconds after I left the plane, I saw the smoking trail of a high velocity surface-to-air missile ripping upward. Somehow, the Turkish pilot had failed to avoid the Soviet radar network. They'd spotted him and fired.

The missile smashed into the left wing of the plane. For a crazy second, the entire world moved in slow motion for me. The missile lightly caressed the fluttering wing, then expanded in an eye-searingly brilliant supernova. The sound, heat and blast wave hit me and sent me tumbling through the air.

I spun out of control and this saved me. If I'd opened my chute then, the secondary explosion from the DC-3's fuel tanks would have set my parachute on fire. As it was, the superheated wave of air passed by me, starting only tiny fires on my heavy jacket. I whirled around and straightened myself as I patted out the tiny flames trying to gain a foothold on my body; then I pulled my ripcord.

I opened less than a thousand feet above the steppes. The sudden jerk rocked me to and fro, but the chute didn't spill any air and the airplane had tumbled off in the opposite direction toward the south. I doubted I would show up on radar. All that threatened was possible sighting from the ground.

Smashing down hard, I tucked my knees under me and rolled, tangling slightly in the shroud lines. After coming to a halt, I lay flat on my back. Every joint and bone in my body aching, I rolled over and got free of the chute. I bundled it up and buried it before looking around.

The sight wasn't too awe-inspiring.

Steppes stretched outward for miles. To my back, in the direction of Turkey, rose the mountains we'd strained to get over in the DC-3. But across the rolling plains lay Baikonur. Not seeing a road, I knew the only way I'd get there would be to walk.

So I started.

*     *     *     *     *

The dawn promised cold but fair weather as the sky turned pink around the edges. I'd been lucky. So far the infamous Russian weather hadn't dumped snow or sleet on my head. While I hadn't been so lucky in getting motorized transport, I still averaged close to forty miles a day across open country. My meals had been meager, consisting mostly of slow rabbits and boiled weeds, but it wasn't anything I hadn't done before. All I really had to fear was the omnipresent overflights by the Russian reconnaissance planes. I hoped they were more intent on the Iranian and Turkish borders than they were on the terrain in their heartland.

A tiny fire of dried dung warmed my hands. I pulled out the single tiny cooking pot I had, boiled some snow into water and fixed a bitter herb tea. Making a face as I drank it, I considered how much luckier I was than the Turkish commander with his heated liquor. The liquor was good; being alive to drink the awful tea was better.

Suddenly vibrations coming through the half-frozen ground alerted me. I pressed my ear down trying to determine the source. Although skills are less refined than the average American Indian, I was able to ascertain that the disturbance *was* equine and not mechanical in nature.

Checking under my jacket, I loosened Wilhelmina in her holster. Hugo rested in a sheath secured to my left forearm and Pierre, on my upper thigh. Not much but they'd proved faithful companions in the past. They would prove equally trustworthy in the near future, I knew.

The tiny gray dots against the rising sun told me the position of the danger confronting me. I stamped out the dung fire, pushed cold earth over it and slung my pack for travel. By heading due north I might be able to avoid the horsemen.

As dawn stretched into midmorning, I realized this wouldn't work. If they had sighted me, they made no big production of coming after me. Yet no matter how many times I altered my course, they always seemed to change direction in such a fashion that they would eventually cross my path.

By noon, I'd run my race. Exhausted, I could only sit on the cold ground and wait to see what they wanted. Something about the manner in which they tracked me told me they weren't Soviet troops. The Russian military, like their leaders, are seemingly devious to Western minds, but in field maneuvers are blunt, direct, no-nonsense conquerors. The entire Russian strategy is a quick strike with overwhelming force, then consolidation. In spite of Stalingrad, they do not fight well when forced into prolonged engagements.

The riders continued to circle me, as if I could somehow sprout wings on my feet and do a Mercury number on them, running fleetingly away. At a half hour past noon, the riders finally circled me.

I could hardly believe my eyes. Cossacks. They sat arrogantly astraddle their powerful mounts, rifles slung over their shoulders and crossed ammunition belts on their chests.

Whoever they were, they rode in violation of one of the most basic of all Soviet rules: no personal firearms. The only weapons allowed Soviet citizens, except for shotguns, were rifles—and the only citizens allowed these were the Siberian wolf hunters. A disgruntled citizenry with arms might decide the Communist workers' paradise wasn't all it was cracked up to be and overthrow their masters.

No. Arms control inside the Soviet Union was absolute. Yet these twenty-plus riders all sported hunting rifles.

We were a long way from Siberia or Siberian wolves.

"*Kto?*" snapped the hairiest, most muscular of the riders. He asked who I was.

"*Yah zahblooddeelsah,* I'm lost," I started. A quick hand movement from his second-in-command silenced me. They obviously didn't care about my problems.

"Who are you to walk these steppes without permission?" he asked in harsh, rapid-fire Russian.

"I have permission!" I cried, hoping to appear fearful. It didn't take too much acting on my part. I reached inside my jacket, my fingers lightly touching Wilhelmina's trigger. But the few shots I'd be allowed hardly seemed worth it. With so many, I'd be dead before the third shot, no matter how fast I was. Instead, I came out with my counterfeit papers. I waved them in the air.

"Papers? What do we care about those?" scoffed their leader. "Those are for peasants. We are Cossacks."

That stopped me dead in my tracks for a few seconds. I'd thought all of the Cossacks had been purged by Stalin in the 1930s. There were no good records of how many millions of people Stalin had slaughtered, but I knew he made Hitler appear a piker in comparison. All the Cossacks had gone the way of the dodo.

Except a band of twenty-three confronted me now.

"What do you want of me. I have no money," I said. I hardly wanted them to know that I did have a few rubles, though not enough to cause suspicion should I be caught, but enough to bribe and buy my way through to Baikonur, if necessary.

"What do we want of your money? It is worthless scraps of paper, nothing more."

"Well, then?" I asked. I saw instantly my boldness had been a mistake. These proud men took any show of courage as defiance. It goaded their *machismo* and turned them into killers.

The closest one reared his horse. The animal kicked out viciously. I dropped and rolled away from those brutal, slashing metal-clad hooves. Coming to my feet, hand resting on Wilhelmina, I again wondered if I should open fire. I might be able to kill as many as five before they killed me.

The Salyut-8 swinging slowly through space, a giant mirror focusing its deadly rays on the United States, came into my mind. With no way of protecting against such an insidious weapon, the U.S. lay helpless under the Soviet attacks. If I died here and now on the steppes, that mirror continued to exist and destroy listening posts—and ultimately, the grain lands of the Midwest.

"Please!" I sobbed out, hoping I sounded frightened and contrite enough for them to allow me to live. "Don't!"

"Listen to the worm. He crawls. Wiggle, my little worm. Wiggle for Dmitri Petrakovich!"

I lay down on my belly and began an inchworm progress across the freezing steppes. I swallowed bile as my anger rose, but I masked all expression on my face. They got sick amusement from this. But my mission came before personal pride.

Dmitri Petrakovich would one day pay for this humiliation. I didn't know how or where, but he would.

"See, my comrades, see how he crawls. Eat dirt, worm. All worms eat dirt."

That was too much for me.

I waited until he spurred his horse closer, then I acted. Still flat on the ground, I rolled my legs around and pinioned the horse's two front legs. The creature reared but I'd thrown it off balance. It fell heavily, throwing Petrakovich.

Almost as soon as I began moving, his fellows acted. Rifles came unslung and their horses all reared. I got to my feet in a hurry and kicked powerfully at Petrakovich's struggling mount. Again I unbalanced it. The frightened horse stumbled and went down heavily again, this time knocking over four nearby horses like dominoes. Not satisfied, I kicked out and caught another animal just behind the knees. It went down as if poleaxed.

The sound of the rifle bolts closing on chambers filled with heavy lead slugs convinced me I'd be cooling meat if I stayed around here much longer. I dived, a pair of nasty bullets humming just inches over my head. I rolled down the slight incline into a ravine, got my feet under me and ran like hell.

A man can outrun a horse—if you consider only distance. Any marathon runner is able to drive a horse to exhaustion. But over short distances a horse is much faster. I knew I'd have to make good use of my superior stamina to avoid the horses until I got out of the Cossacks' firing range.

It wasn't easy.

Dodging, ducking, I kept moving as fast as I could along the bottom of the half-frozen ravine. My feet were turning into lumps of snow as I broke through the thin sheet of ice over the stream. Sloshing loudly, I knew this wasn't the right thing to do.

But there wasn't much choice. The steppes were flat and open. If I got up and out of the small ravine the Cossacks would spot me in an instant. My only hope lay in running in the same direction. Yet that hardly seemed too bright. These men knew the steppes intimately. They had to if they'd avoided Soviet military patrols over the years. And the superior numbers, and anger, of the horse-riding Russians insured they'd find me.

I had to outsmart them.

My brain clicked into overdrive. While my sodden feet pounded along the edge of the stream bed, my feet cold and growing colder, I thought hard.

When I saw the slight depression on the cutbank an idea came to me. The Cossacks trailed me by sight, not by stealth. They figured I provided only a diverting sport hunt, nothing else.

With a powerful leap I cleared the far bank of the semi-frozen stream, scrambled up the slope without disturbing much of the coarse grass covering the embankment, and pulled myself up and under the root system of a scrawny tree that was threatened with immediate extinction the next time the ravine filled with water and cut away a little more of the soft dirt bank.

I curled up into a fetal position, my hands going under my arms for warmth. I listened intently. Just a few feet away I heard the pounding of shod hooves. A few seconds later came the guttural curses of the Cossacks.

Petrakovich was not happy that they had lost me. I heard him demanding a more careful search. As long as they remained mounted, I was relatively safe. If they dismounted and searched along the bottom of the ravine, they could glance up and see my huddled form under the scrawny tree.

I don't remember how long I stayed like this. It might have been just a few minutes. It felt like days. The Cossacks were persistent in their searching. Again and again, I felt the dull thudding of their horses' hooves through the layer of dirt at my back. Somewhere toward late afternoon, I drifted off to sleep, thoughts of Baikonur and the space shuttle and Salyut-8 in my mind.

I should never have allowed my body to dictate policy to my mind like that. As I slept, my muscles relaxed, I leaned forward precipitously and then fell from my perch. Scrambling, half awake, I felt the earth giving way under my feet. By the time I was fully awake and sure of where I was, I looked up and saw Petrakovich standing on the bank, his well-used rifle aimed at me.

The bore was the size of a firehose.

"Come up, burrowing worm," he commanded.

I knew there wasn't any chance to escape. I obeyed.

"You have given us quite a hunt, little one," he said. The "little one" was especially appropriate. On the ground the man was a giant, while on horseback he hadn't appeared so large.

Easily six feet eight inches and three hundred pounds—none of it fat from the way he moved—Petrakovich might have been a weight lifter. My hand wasn't too steady as I evaluated my chances of getting out Wilhelmina and dropping him before the others killed me.

Seeing his ominous bulk, I wasn't sure even a full clip of the 9 mm Parabellum rounds would faze him. He seemed more like a bull elk than a man.

"Why do you harass me so?" I asked. "I am only a poor peasant. I seek work along the Black Sea, at one of the resorts."

"Resorts? For the tyrants running this country?"

I nodded.

"What do you do for a living? Kiss Communist ass?"

"I . . . I'm a waiter. I can cook, a little, and when I get the work, carry bags at the hotels."

"You speak with a funny accent," he accused. Moving closer to me, Petrakovich loomed above me until I smelled the sour milk odor coming off his body like the fumes from a chemical dump. This Cossack and modern sanitation were strangers.

"I am Estonian. I learned Russian from a Britisher."

"Estonian, eh? You allow the Communist dogs to keep your country. You, the Poles, the Czechs, all the Eastern countries, pah!" He spat on the ground between my boots.

I turned slightly, then swung as hard as I could, my fist landing on the side of his head. Pain shot all the way up my arm and into my shoulder as hard knuckles

smashed into even harder cheekbone. I had decked
Petrakovich but wondered if I hadn't broken my hand in
the process. Yet I knew I'd done the right thing by the
look on his face.

I'd have been killed outright if I'd allowed an insult
to my supposedly native country go unchallenged. The
Cossack was fiercely patriotic—to his native, non-
Communist homeland. He expected a true man to be
likewise willing to die defending his home country.

"So the worm has fight in him, eh?" he said, sitting
up and rubbing the spot on his face. I'd cut him through
the skin and a steady stream of blood ran from the
wound. Tiny plumes of steam rose from the cut as the
hot blood touched the frigid air caressing this polar,
barren steppe country.

"Call me worm, if you will. Do not insult my country." I kept the words cold and crisp, my hand still
balled into a tight fist. But I felt the reaction setting in.
My hand uncurled of its own volition and pain jarred
me into a state of acute awareness.

"Very well, worm. For what I said of Estonia, I
apologize."

This surprised me. What followed didn't.

"And I accept your challenge. To the death, of
course."

"And when I win your lackeys cut me down, is that
it?" I asked looking around the tight circle of Cossacks
astride their horses. All kept their rifles across their
laps, ready for instant use.

"You malign my honor. You best me—ha!—and
you go on your way to serve the Commie pigs in their
fancy pleasure resorts along the Black Sea."

He began stripping off his heavy fur coat. The wool
tunic underneath came off with a flourish, too. He
stood in the wan afternoon light, a giant of a man, his

powerful muscles rippling. He pulled back his shoulders and for a moment I thought he was going to beat his breast. Instead he threw back his head and laughed. The deep, resonant laugh rolled over the empty steppes until he almost unnerved me.

I flexed my right hand a few times and felt sensation returning. Carefully removing my own jacket so that none saw Wilhelmina, I put it by my pack. My simple peasant shirt followed. I'm well muscled but compared to Petrakovich, I was a midget. My muscles strained taut skin. His bulged twice as large.

But a wary look came into the Cossack's eyes as he studied my build. While he probably thought me a weakling, the scars crisscrossing my body told stories of ancient fights, all won. He'd thought me a soft Communist servant; the scars told a different story.

Also, the fact that I carried Hugo sheathed along my left forearm warned him I knew how to use the weapon.

"We fight in the traditional manner. Take this rag in your mouth. Drop it and die. And keep it in your mouth and die!"

I knotted the end and bit down on the dirty brown kerchief. It was greasy and made me want to vomit. But the sight of Petrakovich's gleaming nine-inch steel blade wickedly reflecting back the pale afternoon sunlight worried me more. I held Hugo easily in the knife fighter's position.

With one end of the handkerchief in my teeth and the other end securely between Petrakovich's yellowed, broken teeth, we circled one another less than three feet apart. All around us stood the ring of Cossacks, their fingers nervously moving on the triggers of their rifles. Somehow, I knew that if Petrakovich should drop his end, they'd be just as swift to shoot him as they would me. Honor demanded it and above all these proud, fearless men valued honor.

We circled slowly, feinting with our blades, cautiously trying to create an opening and failing. Petrakovich was an old hand at this style of fighting. I'm no stranger to knives, but the restriction of fighting in close bothered me. I prefer room to work, to dance around, then attack. I had only one option open to me as long as I kept the kerchief in my teeth: straight ahead, frontal attack.

I feinted, feinted again and finally launched an attack meant to go home. It almost worked. Hugo's tip lightly raked Petrakovich's side. He yelped in surprise and twisted away before I could inflict further damage. His own blade lashed forth and almost caught me in the throat. Only catlike reflexes allowed me to parry the blow.

"You fight well," he grunted between his teeth. "For a Commie lover."

I feinted again, then kicked with my left foot as he tried to parry my pretended knife attack. I connected with his right knee. He fell heavily. I tried to finish the fight but his superior strength prevented it. He surged forward using impossible amounts of muscle, caught me up in a bear hug and tossed me high into the air. My head snapped down as the kerchief ended the sudden flight.

I jerked to one side to prevent myself falling downward onto the point of his knife.

As it was, I got another scar to join the dozens of others on my chest. Or it would be a new scar if I lived long enough for the cut to heal.

On my own knees, I fought hard to prevent the taller, stronger man from ending the fight in his favor. His knife pressed down into Hugo. I gripped his tree-trunk thick wrist and tried to move him from his attack. He bored onward, downward, forcing me to use more and more of my precious strength.

Trooping across the frozen steppes all day had tired me. The flight from the Cossacks had further drained my reserves. And the hiding under the tree amid the roots had taken even more out of me. His knife point came closer and closer. He had the wicked point aimed directly between my eyes.

He forced me down onto the ground so hard my knees actually dented the frozen steppes. The knife point cut into my forehead. His overwhelming strength allowed him to drag the knife point downward past my eyes and lips and chin to my throat. I arched my back to avoid it. But my strength faded faster and faster. He was too strong, too tall, too much in command of the situation.

As the nine-inch blade moved inexorably toward my Adam's apple, a sharp command echoed out.

"Stop, Dmitri Petrakovich! Do not be more of a fool than you have to be!"

The overpowering grip kept the blade at my throat—but he didn't push it home. Not yet.

# SEVEN

"Halt! I command you, do not kill him!" came the woman's voice, loud, strong, dominant.

"Martina, you overstep this time," snarled Petrakovich, dropping the end of the kerchief from his broken, uneven teeth to answer. But the impossible grip on my wrist lessened and the knife moved from my throat. I debated driving Hugo into his unprotected groin but decided against it. If I failed to make a clean kill with one cut, I'd be dead. And the weakness pouring over me in waves told me that a kitten might be stronger than I currently was.

"Do it, Dmitri. Do it and *we* fight."

"I don't fight women," Petrakovich said sullenly. He stepped back out of range of Hugo. I sank gratefully to the ground, the brown handkerchief still between my teeth. I spat it out and fell forward, gasping for breath. Strength returned slowly as I straightened to look at my benefactor.

My breath gusted out harshly at the sight of the woman. She sat astride an Arabian horse that almost matched her in haughtiness. The woman wore a scarlet babushka that accentuated the ravens-wing darkness of her lustrous hair. Although the sun was almost set, her hair caught the remaining sunbeams and cast them back with a vigor and brilliance that took my breath away again.

The fur-lined jacket she wore was open and revealed

a thin silk tunic underneath. I wondered how she kept
from freezing to death dressed in such a manner. But I
didn't complain. The tunic had pulled back to outline
ample breasts impudently thrusting outward. Tiny
wrinkles appeared in the fabric to mark the spots where
her nipples sprouted like tiny mushrooms. Strong legs
encased in leather trousers gripped the heaving sides of
her horse. Brilliantly polished boots finished the bar-
baric, outlandish, yet gorgeous trappings.

"You do not recognize him, Dmitri?" she demanded, pointing at me with the riding crop she held
lightly between her fingers. "Even you cannot be so
stupid."

Petrakovich muttered something under his breath.
He moved and began putting on his tunic and coat. I
heaved myself to my feet and also dressed. The butt of
my Luger had become cold from being away from my
body's warmth. I shivered anew as I felt the cold steel.

"He could have cut you down at any time, Dmitri,"
the woman continued. "He is not one of *them*."

I didn't have to be told who "them" referred to. A
band like this had to stay mobile—and one step ahead
of the Soviet military.

"I know that. But who *is* he?" demanded the giant.
"He fights well, that I'll give him, but he talks like one
of their ass-kissing toadies. All he wants from life is to
bow to his Communist masters."

"He is Estonian, is he not?" the woman continued. I
studied her more carefully. She hadn't been around
when I'd told that particular lie. "His entrance permit is
numbered 1076-N3. He lives in Tallinn at number N3
Lenin Place. Is this not so? He is the one I told you to
seek out. And you fight him! Dmitri, you have the
brains of an *ootkoo*, a silly duck."

At the dual mention of N3 I knew who this lovely

woman had to be. AXE puts "moles" into Russian government all the time. These are agents who do not report, who do nothing until it is time for them to perform one vital mission. Then they act, and after they complete their mission, they are spirited away out of the country—if they survive.

"Thank you, Martina," I said, still not sure of her role in all of this. It seemed plausible for me to claim to know her—she obviously knew of me.

"You fought well," she said, smiling. Her perfect white teeth were startling in contrast to the yellowed and broken ones in Petrakovich's mouth. If she had ridden much with these modern-day pirates of the steppes, she had taken better care of herself than they did.

"For survival, anyone fights well."

"Not so. And thank you for not killing him." She tossed her head in Dmitri's direction. "He bumbles around but he means well."

I felt the man's hot stare boring into the middle of my back. I had to respond.

"He had me. No question about it. If you hadn't stepped in, his knife would have buried itself in my throat."

A hard slap to my back almost knocked me flat. Petrakovich laughed loudly and said, "I like you. Damn, but you fight well and you know how to lie! If you can drink vodka, we might even become friends."

"Let's ride and discuss all this later," said the woman. "The patrols are heading in our direction. I saw one of their helicopter gunships less than an hour ago. It flies a checkerboard pattern northward and should be over this area within the hour." She glanced down at me, her piercing blue eyes shone brilliantly. "Can you ride?"

"If it means not being caught by the Communists."

With that I held on to the back of her mount and heaved myself up behind her with ease.

"Then let's race the wind. Ride, Cossacks, ride!"

She was a natural. She rode the Arabian with a firm hand, yet at the same time she was graceful. I held onto her slender waist and admired the scenery from the rear.

* * * * *

The frigid wind whipped through the camp and threatened to freeze my arms to my body. My teeth rattled together in a chattering that might have been heard all the way to the Turkish border and the faint light and heat from the small fire only tantalized. It promised warmth and failed to deliver.

"Well, N3, you can thank your lucky stars I came along when I did. If I hadn't found Dmitri when I did, he'd have skewered you."

"No question about it. The man is a giant."

"You eluded the entire band for over four hours. That is unheard of. These men know the steppes like their own horses. And nothing is more important to a Cossack than his horse. You are shrewd, N3, but that is the message I received from Hawk."

"From Hawk?" I asked mildly, trying to keep from shivering in the cold wind.

"David Hawk, of AXE," she added. "I have been a mole for nine years."

"You must have been recruited early. When you were ten?"

"Twelve," she answered, moving closer to me. The heat radiating through her leather trousers gave me more than simple warmth. She was very lovely, and very close.

"A bit young for such a job," I observed, staring into her cobalt blue eyes. She only nodded. A thin sheen of moisture touched those blue orbs. I reached out and wiped away a tear before it ran down her cheek and froze.

"What happened?"

"My parents. They were killed . . purged. I was with an uncle at the time, in Gorki. I was virtually in exile and the KGB chose to ignore me. It was then I vowed to do what I could to see those butchers all dead and Russia returned to Russians!"

"I'm glad you are here," I said, lifting her chin. She gazed into my eyes and a silent communication told her exactly how happy I was with her.

"It is my duty."

"Only duty? Nothing more?" I asked gently. I saw the slight trembling in her lips and knew it wasn't from the cold, not this time. She seemed totally unaffected by the bone-chilling breeze sweeping across the deserted steppes. Even the tiny fires burning around the Cossack encampment provided scant heat to offset the cold.

"Duty takes many forms," she said in an oblique fashion before averting her eyes. She stared into the dancing flames in front of us but moved perceptibly closer. The entire length of her upper thigh now pressed into mine. I shrugged my shoulders so that the blanket covering me engulfed both of us. She moved even closer when my arm snaked around her waist.

"Duty doesn't always have to be onerous."

"Dmitri enjoys playing hide and seek with the Soviet forces," she said, again her words oblique. But I caught her meaning.

"What's Dmitri to you? Or what are you to him?"

"Friends—more. But not for some time," she said frankly. "Our lives have taken divergent paths. It happens. Like Dmitri, I was born on the steppes. Unlike him, I know that we can never be free of the Communists by fighting them out here on this desolate wasteland. They must be defeated in other places, in other ways."

"The people must want it. No small revolution will successfully overthrow a group as well entrenched."

"The Communist Party numbers only two or three percent of the total population of all the Russians, yet their hand is strong," she agreed. "But burrowing from within is not the answer, either. To become like your enemy is to become indistinguishable from the evil we fight."

"Do you know why I'm here?"

She gazed again at me, then shook her head. Tiny strands of the luxurious black mane sneaked down from under the scarf she wore. The firelight highlighted her face and cast shadows along the soft planes of her cheekbones. Seldom had I seen a woman so vital, so alive and so beautiful.

"I must get to Baikonur."

"Oh."

"I expected more of a reaction."

"I am not stupid. None of us is. We would die quickly if we were facing the entire might of what was once our beloved Mother Russia. No, I understand. You are to destroy the space launch complex there. You will disgrace the country in the eyes of the world."

"It's not the political coup I'm after. It's more a

matter of defense." I briefly sketched what the mirror in orbit was doing to the U.S. listening posts, how the KGB sabotaged our space shuttle program to keep us from making an in-orbit inspection of their Salyut-8 space station. Finishing, I added, "We must maintain a watch. Without good electronic surveillance, the hardliners in the Kremlin might opt for an all-out attacks."

"A preemptive strike," she said, nodding in understanding. "I have heard it mentioned in passing. Few took it seriously until Kosygin was retired from office. Now the neo-Stalinists are gaining a foothold. Luckily the ones like Mikhail Suslov are too old, but the newcomers—they are evil men. They would destroy this country in order to further dreams that should have died with Stalin."

"Will there be any trouble getting me into the Baikonur facility?"

"None. Or very little. The inner security of Russia is directed more against black marketeers than spies and saboteurs. So you are safe as long as you do not smuggle a bushel of potatoes!"

"No potatoes," I said. I suddenly felt her long-fingered hand moving up my leg, stopping for a moment on muscular thigh, then moving between.

"Are you the fresh produce inspector?" I asked.

"I might be."

I kissed her. Our lips were cold at first, but passion quickly warmed them. Her fingers tightened on my manhood until I felt as if my turgid length would turn cartwheels inside my pants. My arm around her pulled her lush body closer still. My other hand worked under her tunic. She flinched at first from the coldness of my hand, but the warmth of her body quickly warmed my fingers. I moved upward until I cupped her trembling breast. It trembled not from the cold but from lust.

The nipple I had seen silhouetted against her thin silk tunic now throbbed with life. The hard little button pulsed and beat in syncopation with her racing heart. I kissed her more deeply, more passionately. I knew then that there could be no stopping. We had allowed ourselves to go over the line where control was possible.

"We . . . a tent. Let's go to my tent," she said. "Dmitri?"

"We are adults. We are Cossacks. He does not own me or tell me what to do. If he tried, he would regret it. I promise you that."

I believed her. She was fierce, passionate, this woman. And that aroused me even more.

We rose, my blanket around both of us. The simple hide tent pitched in the lee of a small rise hardly seemed adequate but I was pleasantly surprised to find a warm down-filled sleeping bag inside. They might lead rough, primitive lives on their horses, but they knew the value of a good night's sleep. And more than sleep.

"Seems small," I said, crawling next to Martina.

"Do you object?" she asked. Already she was stripping off her tunic. The pale light filtering into the hide tent caught those firm, high-placed breasts and cast shadows into the deep valley between them. She tossed her silk tunic aside and lifted her hips upward off the ground. "Help me please," she said simply.

And I did.

The leather pants slipped off her like a snake shedding a skin. She wore nothing under them. Martina kicked off her boots while I began stripping. The cold wind from the steppes blew in the open tent flap. I pulled the hide hanging shut and turned the dimly lit tent into a totally dark cavern.

"Are you like so many Americans? Do you have to make love in the darkness?"

"I know where everything is," I assured her. "Light isn't necessary."

And to prove it, I slid into the down-filled sleeping bag beside her. The fit was snug—in many ways.

She groaned softly as I began moving with gentle, slow thrusts. Her long, well-proportioned legs parted even more and circled my body. Her heels came up and locked behind my knees. In this position she was able to hunch upward and grind her pelvis in a most delightful fashion against my groin.

Her heated interior turned damper and damper as we moved in slow, deliberate motions. She gasped when I bent down and covered one of those delicately formed, throbbing nipples with my mouth and sucked. Her fingers raked along my back but she said nothing. I could tell by the way her body tensed around me that she was approaching her climax.

I abandoned my oral post at her breast and worked my soft, demanding lips upward to the hollow of her throat. She sucked in her breath and shook all over like a leaf in a high wind. The tightness of her around my manhood almost caused me to respond like a teenaged boy in bed with a lover for the first time.

My lips kissed and caressed her flesh as I moved up to her perfectly formed shelllike ear. Thrusting my tongue in and out with the same rhythm I used on her breast produced another quaking in her body. This time she gasped louder.

"Faster, Nick darling. Faster! Take me hard!"

My own control was fading. The seething wetness of her center caused me to tighten into an almost painful steel-rod rigidity. The top of the sleeping bag prevented me from rising up and thrusting into her with all the speed and force I'd have liked to use, but the very confining feeling given by the sleeping bag added a new and stimulatingly different dimension to our lovemaking.

Tiny gasps escaped constantly from her lips now. I began thrusting with more force, with more need. Her fingers stroked over my upper arms, across my back, then tensed and turned into claws as she climaxed again. I ignored the tiny scratches she'd given me. They were nothing compared to the intense feelings mounting in my own loins.

Falling into the age-old rhythm, I drove forward and buried myself to the hilt in her hotly clinging female sheath. She let out a tiny trapped animal noise and her entire body tensed. She clutched feverishly at me and I knew there was no holding back. Locked together in the confining sleeping bag, we both experienced the ultimate in human pleasure.

All too soon it was over. Relaxing afterward, I slipped to one side so that we lay facing each other. Her breasts were pleasantly compressed against my chest. My own hands snaked around to cup her buttocks. The sweat from our passionate wrestling seeped into the down surrounding us and kept us from feeling cold. That was good. Nothing should disturb the warm afterglow of such a fine act.

"We are good together," she said in the Stygian darkness. I barely saw her ruby lips moving even though they were scant inches away. Only when she slowly licked them did they shine enough for me to catch the movement.

"It's a shame we had to meet under these circumstances. After I get into Baikonur, we won't see each other again."

She sighed, realizing how true this was. "A terrible business. People should not be forced to part when given such a nice beginning."

Martina moved closer. My hand strayed between her legs and found the damp swamp of her still-churning sex there. She sighed more deeply as I started running my hand up and down over her mound of Venus.

I thought back to all the friends—and more—lost because I stayed with AXE.

"How long before I reach Baikonur?"

"Two days, three at the most. You have come far on your own—and almost tracelessly. That is why it has taken me so long to find you after I received my activation orders."

"I know so little about you, " I said, realizing for the first time that I didn't even know her last name. "What do you do? What hold do you have over Petrakovich? I don't even know your full name."

She laughed delightedly.

"You, the master spy, you do not know these things? Ha! I am Martina Ludonova Dubrovnik, a woman dedicated to returning Russia to better times."

"Under a new czar?" I asked.

"That would be better than the present government," she said. "But I am no monarchist like Dmitri. I want only that Russia be free of tyranny, that we do not continually send forth our young men to die in enslaving other countries."

"What do you do for a living?" I felt her tense and try to pull away. I held her close, to reassure her that no matter what she did it didn't affect our relationship.

"I am a whore "

"What?" I said, stunned. 'Explain that. I can't see you out on a street corner selling yourself for a few rubles."

"Not a whore like you mean. Such women are executed in this country. Our Soviet masters are very prudish. No, I am the mistress of the local commissar. I prostitute myself to be close to the lines of information flowing through him. While I do not send any of this out of the country, I do what I can to help ones like Dmitri.''

I thought about that. Martina played a dangerous game, one Hawk wouldn't like if he knew. The idea of a "sleeper" was to lead as ordinary a life as possible and only act when told to do so. Martina might make a slip in her desire to aid Petrakovich and others like him and jeopardize her usefulness to AXE.

I shook myself at the thought. This was a woman I'd just shared the most intense of all human feeling with and already I turned into a machine, a killing machine intent only on my mission.

Sometimes I think being N3, Killmaster for AXE, is dehumanizing me.

"You disapprove."

"We all do what we have to. It's just that keeping such a deception going is difficult and you might slip and be caught. Your position is in constant danger.''

"And I would no longer be of use to you," she finished for me. "I take the risk. But waiting for this moment was so difficult. I *hate* them. I hate them with all my soul. They've robbed me of my parents, my religion—and what they've robbed my country of is even more terrible. We remain in the nineteenth century while the West forges ahead into the twenty-first. We are little better off than the peasants were under the czar. For that, I hate them all. I had to act.''

"And Dmitri was doing something."

"They commit petty sabotage, tie up many troops, keep the tyrants confused and occupied with matters other than oppressing the local population. Dmitri is like—who is your folk hero?''

"Robin Hood," I said.

"Yes, he is like Robin Hood, stealing and destroying—for Russia."

Patriotism comes in all guises. What I do for the United States is patriotism. What Martina did for her Russia was patriotism, too.

"I feel something—it's growing," she said teasingly, her fingers working over my new erection.

"You're cooling off," I accused. "Let me slip something hot into you." And I did.

*　*　*　*　*

"You can stay on top of it?" demanded Dmitri.

I looked skeptically at the shaggy horse. I've done many things in my career as an agent for AXE but this was the first time I'd ever been required to ride a horse like a bandit across the steppes.

"I can do it," I assured him. I allowed one of the Cossacks to hold the reins for me as I stepped into the stirrup and swung aloft. The horse reared slightly, almost unseating me, but I hung on and got myself properly set in the saddle.

I patted the horse alongside the head and calmed him. Then I was off racing the wind with Dmitri leading the charge, Martina at my side smiling at the ease with which I rode the beast.

"You ride well," called Martina, her long black hair streaming away from her face. "You worried me at the start. Was that only for Dmitri's benefit?"

I nodded and winked. My training has been rigorous; my coordination, physical strength and agility are those of the best trained athlete. Without top performance at all times, I'd have been dead a long time ago. Riding a horse was simply another athletic skill. I might never match the flawless ease with which these Cossacks rode, but I made sure that I came pretty close.

We rode until just after noon when Dmitri called a halt. I reined in, thankful for the chance to dismount. My muscles were stiff and I moved clumsily.

Dmitri chuckled. "How do you feel?" he asked.

"A little sore," I admitted.

"You ride almost as well as a Cossack, but you are not nearly as hard," he cackled, obviously pleased at his own joke as he pointed to my backside. "But we'll make you a Cossack yet."

"Where are we headed?" I asked, wanting to change the subject. Offending Dmitri by telling him what I thought of becoming a Cossack like him wasn't a smart move. Better to change the subject.

"A small village," answered Martina. "It has only minimal communication with the outside world. While Dmitri and the others harass the small troop encampment there, we will steal a vehicle able to get you to Baikonur. From there you are on your own."

I nodded. Martina Dubrovnik would provide the jeep, bid me a fond farewell, then go back to her commissar, her mission for AXE accomplished. It's a cruel business we're in. I wished there was some way we could have stayed together longer, but I knew better.

"Airplane," came the shouted warning from one of the sentries. "They have spotted us!"

"Do we run?" I asked, thinking how improbable it all seemed. A modern reconnaissance plane chasing a band of horse-mounted Cossacks across the steppes seemed like something out of a 1930's movie.

"No," said Martina. "They have radioed back to

their base camp already. Running would only cause the commander to file a report with his superiors. And they might call out a few helicopter gunships. We haven't the firepower to knock one of them down."

I thought about the dead Turkish NATO commander and what he'd said about the vulnerability of the gunships. With a SAM they were sitting ducks. But Martina and her Cossacks had nothing like that. All they carried were bolt-action rifles, hardly adequate for anything more than sniping. It seemed a shame we couldn't supply them with a few smart bombs. But of course that was ridiculous. The U.S. didn't meddle in the internal affairs of other nations, not to that extent, even when confronted with the Soviet bear.

"What of your rifles?" I asked, knowing that to be caught with them meant immediate execution.

"What rifles?" she responded innocently. I glanced around and all the rifles had vanished as if by magic.

"They are hidden well," said Dmitri. "This is old hat for us. It happens all the time."

"Here they come!" cried the sentry.

Squinting into the sun, I saw the glint of light off an armored personnel carrier. The APC moved at breakneck speed over the semi-frozen land. I moved closer to Martina and opened my jacket to reveal Wilhelmina.

"Take the Luger and put it with your rifle," I said.

Her eyes widened slightly at the sight of the blued 9 mm automatic.

"You have had this since your fight with Dmitri? And you did not use it?"

"Wouldn't have done me any good."

"You *are* a remarkable man, Nick Carter," she said, obviously meaning it. Among the Cossacks, the gun would have been used.

She took Wilhelmina and lifted a piece of the frozen turf. Under it rested her rifle. The Luger dropped in beside.

"There is no danger of getting dirty," she assured me. "The sod is so firm at this time of year that it is like a brick. If we need the weapons, we can retrieve them quickly."

I said nothing, content to watch the rapidly approaching Soviet APC. I tried to estimate how many soldiers might be riding inside. Anything up to a full platoon, I guessed. But this was out in the boondocks. Maybe they kept the post understaffed.

I hoped that was so. Fewer soldiers meant fewer eyes to deceive, fewer minds to confuse.

The personnel carrier driver downshifted and wheeled the heavy vehicle around to disgorge a full dozen armed troops. Fewer than I'd thought. This might actually work out all right.

"Who is in charge?" demanded the Soviet lieutenant.

"In charge, captain?" asked Dmitri carelessly, obviously promoting the young officer to bloat his ego. "Why, you are. You have your weapons on us."

The lieutenant smashed the butt of his pistol into Dmitri's head. The huge Cossack fell to one knee, hot blood oozing from the wound. He lightly touched the wound, shook his head as if dazed, but said and did nothing. I let out my pent-up breath. If Petrakovich had attacked, the soldiers would have used those AK-47s on all of us.

The lieutenant and all his men were young, green, inexperienced and nervous. And they were eager, too, which made them more dangerous than seasoned troops.

"Do not mock me," said the lieutenant in a voice

that almost broke in adolescent shrillness. "What do you do out here?"

"We are horse raisers. We seek out escaped horses from our breeding farm," said Dmitri, remaining on one knee. My estimation of his intelligence soared. He had pegged the lieutenant properly. If Dmitri had spoken from his six foot, eight inch height, the lieutenant would have turned more brutal from fear. As it was, he could speak down to a beaten adversary.

"The nearest such farm is fifty kilometers from here," accused the young officer. "Why do you stray so far?"

"We stray because the horses have strayed, nothing more."

While the lieutenant continued with his inept interrogation, one of the soldiers nudged his companion. They'd seen Martina. She neither tried to hide the shapeliness of her body nor did she try to display it. I figured these men had been on duty for a long time; even if they'd just come back from a two week leave, Martina's beauty would have sent their pulses racing.

Of course they ogled her.

What worried me was the older Soviet sergeant who remained in the bed of the APC. He neither ogled Martina nor paid the least attention to the dialogue between his lieutenant and Petrakovich. He stared at the ground, straight at the spot where Martina's rifle and my Wilhelmina were hidden.

I moved forward a few paces to try and head him off. He impatiently brushed past me and looked down. He knelt, his fingers slipping under the frozen turf. Before he lifted the sod all the way up to reveal the guns, I acted.

Hugo flashed into my hand. I dragged the razor-sharp edge across the sergeant's throat. A fountain of hot blood gushed out over my hand. I spun the instant I knew the man was dead and tossed Hugo. The steel spike of death entered the lieutenant's back, slipped easily between two ribs and sank into his heart. He was dead before he slumped to the cold ground.

The inexperience of the troops became obvious. With their sergeant and lieutenant both dead, they froze. Then they panicked. By this time the Cossacks had retrieved their rifles. I heard bolts snicking shut on chambered shells, then a half dozen loud reports.

All hell broke loose around us.

I caught up Martina in my arms and dived for the ground. Fumbling to get Wilhelmina out from the frozen hiding spot, I immediately tested Martina's contention that dirt didn't affect the workings of the gun. She was right. The Luger spoke decisively five times and five of the young soldiers died. The Cossacks finished off the last of the troops amid the deadly chatter of the AK-47s.

Silence fell as suddenly as the firefight had started. I felt the usual letdown—and exhilaration. The feelings inside are too complicated to put into words. The release of tension and knowing that I still lived soaked up excess adrenaline in my body and took me off "fight" status. But the thrill of a job well done and the nearness of violent death remained.

"You are fast," said Martina, awe in her voice. "You knew the sergeant would find our guns and you acted. And you killed more than half of the entire squad."

"AXE sends only the best." This wasn't the time for false modesty. If I hadn't acted in exactly the manner I had, we would all have been lined up, hands tied behind our backs and blindfolds over our eyes, then executed.

"I felt cheated when Martina did not allow me to kill you last night," said Dmitri, his eyes fixed on Wilhelmina's still-smoking barrel. "I think I am lucky you did not kill me."

"We need men like you, Dmitri," I said, slapping him on the shoulder. The tension broken, he threw back his head, bared his yellowed teeth to the sky and roared with laughter. When he slapped me on the back, he rattled my senses.

"Yes! And we need more men like you, eh!"

"What do we do now?" asked Martina. I glanced around to see what she meant. Six of the horses had been killed by the automatic weapons carried by the soldiers. Three of the Cossacks were dead. And worst of all, when the patrol failed to report back, another reconnaissance plane would be sent. The next time would also bring more troops, lots more—and probably better trained.

"You clear out," I said, my mind racing. "I'll take the APC until I can get something less noticeable. With luck, I can be at Baikonur before the higher-ups even hear about this. In any event, I doubt they'd connect what I'll be doing with the elimination of a squad on the steppes until it's too late."

"Dmitri, go!" commanded Martina.

The huge Cossack turned glum but obeyed.

"Goodbye, Martina," I said, taking her in my arms and kissing her.

"Goodbye, Nick?" she laughed, pushing away. "Hardly. I will show you where to get a new vehicle. Come, don't stand there gaping. Flies might crawl into your mouth."

She swung up into the cab of the APC and waited for me. I knew better than to stand and argue. Gears clashing, we drove off at full speed across the steppes while Dmitri and the remaining Cossacks rode in the opposite direction.

Only the dead remained behind to mark the spot where the firefight had occurred.

# EIGHT

The bumpy ride across the steppes rattled my teeth together until I thought they'd end up as chipped and broken as Dmitri Petrakovich's. But if I thought it was rough going, Martina seemed to love every minute of it. For a while I didn't understand.

Then realization dawned on me.

This was the big time for her. She was taking part in a mission to help subvert the control of the hated Communist masters. Martina treated this as part of a giant game, a lark, something hardly more than a Sunday outing that would turn out just fine, even if a little rain did dampen the spirits and get the sandwiches a bit soggy.

Taking it as the life and death struggle that it was hadn't occurred to her, even when all twelve of the Soviet soldiers had been killed—and some of her own Cossacks had been killed along with them. I knew I'd have to do something to convince her that this was for all the marbles; there wasn't any quitting once we got going.

The only way out of the game was death.

That didn't appeal to me and I didn't want it happening to someone as lovely as Martina Dubrovnik.

"Where's this village you were telling me about?" I asked, shouting over the ping-ping of the motor and the constant clanking of chains and panels throughout the vehicle.

"About ten kilometers ahead," she answered, her eyes glowing. She definitely thought of this as her chance to strike a blow for freedom. I shook my head in dismay. Amateurs will get you killed every time. I'd seen it happen over the years to some of my best friends. I didn't want it happening to me, especially not on a mission of such grave importance to the U.S. I mentally steeled myself to sacrifice Martina instantly if she got in the way of my goal at Baikonur.

"What's the name?"

"Novosirk," she responded. Turning, she looked at me again and asked, "Can I come along? To Baikonur? You'll need help. I know it. Especially after what has happened on the steppes. The Soviets will be swarming like ants with boiling water poured into their anthill. The distance isn't great but the terrain can be tricky this time of year."

"You stay with me only as far as Baikonur. Then we split. I'll go on in and you return to Dmitri."

"Dmitri?" she said, her voice growing soft and distant. "Him? Hardly. I thought he was a man, but you—"

"He *is* a man, quite a man," I said. "But he's different from me. I kill when I have to without a second thought. Dmitri would have second thoughts and that's what almost got him killed back there. If the soldiers had been battle-trained, Dmitri would be dead now. He isn't the cold-blooded murderer he makes out to be."

"And so you, Mr. Nick Carter, are?"

"Yes." And I knew she didn't believe me. She was right. I wasn't a cold-blooded murderer—just a Killmaster. The mission came first; it always did. Personal feelings couldn't get in my way. I just hoped that she didn't try something stupid and make it necessary for me to eliminate her.

"There," she said brightly, pointing out the dirty window of the APC. "There is the edge of the Soviet camp in Novosirk."

There's something grim about a Russian military base, even the small ones. I've never been able to pinpoint why. One army camp looks much like another, no matter whose country has pitched the tents, put up the barbed wire, or has soldiers smartly making their rounds. But there was a grimness to this that told me instantly that the Soviets were responsible for it.

I braked and killed the engine. Studying the perimeter of the camp showed it wasn't worth the effort of getting inside. While there were only a few soldiers left—not so many that I couldn't take them all out with Wilhelmina and Hugo—I decided to let them remain. A chance existed that their radioman might get a call through to one of the gunships or another, larger base.

I had to reach Baikonur before the squad out on the steppes was discovered.

"Can we get some transportation to Astrakhan from here?" If I reached the city at the mouth of the Volga River, getting over to Baikonur would be easy.

"That will not be so easy," she said, gainsaying my thoughts. "Better to steal a jeep here and drive all the way. A stolen jeep is commonplace these days. The black marketeers do it all the time to strip them for parts, to take the tires and gasoline, even to resell the entire machine to unscrupulous peasants."

I considered what Martina said. She was probably right. The use of my few rubles to buy a train ticket left a trail wide enough for the paranoid Soviet secret police to follow. Any transaction inside Russia, even on the black market, left tracks. I had to get into Baikonur, do my job, and leave. The leaving part was the hardest— and how well I succeeded in that part depended on what I did now.

"We've got to get rid of this APC fast. Just being seen in it is arousing suspicion."

"The peasants will say nothing."

"They'll squawk their heads off if threatened with working in a coal mine in Siberia," I told her. She turned and stared straight ahead, offended by my opinion of her countrymen. I didn't bother telling her that anyone, anyone at all, can be made to talk. The old days of the KGB using rubber hoses over the kidneys had long passed. Sophisticated mind control drugs, electronics, and the most advanced psychological theories on how to break down an agent's will were all commonplace in interrogation both in the USSR and in the U.S. This wasn't one of the prettier aspects of intelligence work, but it went on.

"There," I said, trying to distract her. "There's a jeep. Think we can hotwire it?"

"Of course. They are such simple machines."

She was out of the cab of the APC before I'd fully stopped it. Gears clashing, I killed the engine and joined Martina beside the parked jeep. She already had a handful of wires pulled out from under the dashboard. She touched two of them together and produced a fat blue spark an inch long. The motor coughed asthmatically. When she held the wires together and pushed down on the starter button, the jeep kicked over and roared into life.

"You're good. You should come to the U.S. and be a used car salesman," I told her.

"Really?" she said brightly. I didn't bother telling her what I thought of car thieves and used car salesmen.

"Go on, Martina, go back to your people," I said. "I have to go to Baikonur on my own."

"I am going with you, Nick." She climbed in and sat in the other seat as if daring me to say anything different. I debated the point mentally and lost. Martina stayed. And I didn't know why I made that decision. She would only be a hindrance to me. I work solo, period. I have to. The job's dangerous and having a green partner makes it even more deadly. In a way, I'm a professional gambler playing the odds. Whenever possible. I stack the deck in my favor, mark the cards, and then deal off the bottom to make certain I survive. With Martina Dubrovnik along, the cards in my deck got all shuffled and confused.

"Hang on," I said, pushing the accelerator pedal to the floorboard. The jeep leaped away, screeching in protest under the strain I placed on the drive train. The Russians have begun buying some autos and trucks from the Japanese. I wish they'd left one of those fine products around where I could have stolen it. This clunker was born in Magnitogorsk; it should have been still-born. But I managed to coax it into continued life long enough to get around the suburbs of Astrakahn. Stealing fuel for the jeep proved easier than I'd thought and by nightfall we neared the perimeter of Baikonur.

I'd expected something like Cape Canaveral and the Kennedy Space Center. But this was Russia and in Russia things have lots of rough edges; the seams show and brute force is used where finesse is called for. The steppe had been plowed flat and a double barbed wire fence marched around the outlying areas of the launch facility. In the distance I saw a spotlighted rocket ready to blast off. From the briefing I'd received, this was one of the supply rockets going up to Salyut-8. I might not be able to get inside in time to prevent the launch, but I vowed to make sure that that was the last bottle of oxygen, the last morsel of food, those cosmonauts received for a long, long time.

The mirror had to be put out of action. At any cost.

"Here's where I earn my money," I said, slipping out of the jeep and stretching tired, cramped legs. I went to the outer fence and examined it, then whistled low and long. Expecting a simple alarm system, the sight of one of the most elaborate ones in the world astounded me. The Soviets had spent a lot of hard yellow gold to buy this model. I wondered if they told their people they bought security equipment from U.S. companies. Somehow, I doubted it.

"This is most fancy, isn't it?" asked Martina, her fingers hovering just inches above the sensor wire. "I have seen similar ones in compounds near Moscow. It is difficult to subvert, but not impossible."

"You've done it before?" I asked in surprise.

"Yes. The grain storage area outside of Moscow used to be protected with this identical system."

"Used to be?"

"Dmitri and I got in, destroyed the grain elevators with a few well-placed bombs, then left. A piece of cake, I think is your expression, no?"

"That is the expression, yes. But how did you get through the outer alarm area? This wire, if broken or even bent, will set off the alarm. And I'm sure they have motion sensors just inside this fence. I have no idea what's on the inner fence."

"Just barbed wire," she said so positively that I believed her. The Russians had minds that worked in peculiar ways, but once that way was deciphered, they were quite predictable. Almost too predictable.

"So show me how to get through the fence," I said, watching her pull tools from the tool kit in the back of the stolen jeep. It took forty minutes of uninterrupted work until Martina sat back on her haunches, satisfied.

"We now cut the wire, like so."

I cringed, waiting for the distant alarms to go off, the spotlights to pinpoint us, the guards and dogs to come running. Nothing of the sort occurred. We'd gotten around the alarm system in the outer fence. Cutting through the barbed wire was simple. That left only the motion sensors between us and the inner fence.

We crawled through the hole snipped in the outer fence. I kept an eagle eye out for the location of the motion sensor heads inside the scrapped area leading to the inner fence. I found one. Studying it with great care, I wondered what would happen if it suddenly went dead.

"Martina," I asked quietly, staying flat on my stomach, "what happens if the sensor is knocked out?"

"Shot out?" she replied. "I do not know. Like most things in Russia, this might not even be working. A tiny red indicator light should be glowing on the side. I see nothing."

That struck me as ridiculous, then I remembered the problems the snipers had in Vietnam. Their Starlight scopes had tiny red indicator lights on them that the enemy picked up easily. We lost a lot of good marksmen simply because they didn't bother to hide the telltale glow from their intended targets.

"If it's working, all hell might break loose. But if it's not working, then this won't matter, will it?" I pulled out Wilhelmina, sighted and fired off one of the powerful rounds. The bullet struck the casing of the sensor head squarely, then ricocheted with a high-pitched whining.

I waited, listening intently for any sound in the night. After the gunshot and the ricochet, all the tiny animal noises had ceased. Now they slowly returned. And there wasn't any roar of powerful engines or the curse of soldiers intent on finding an intruder.

I marvelled at a military mind that can spend hundreds of thousands of dollars for a state of the art electronic system on the outer fence, then not even bother to maintain a simpler system inside the compound. Yet it fit what I knew of the Russian mentality. The pieces of the puzzle were oddly shaped and the completed picture seemed odd to a Western mind, but it hung together in a logical fashion.

"Let's go. And make it fast."

We sprinted across the ten yards of plowed and scrapped field to the inner fence. A dozen quick snips got us under this fence. And all that remained between us and the bulky launch vehicle out on the pad was a half dozen miles. I figured Martina would return to the jeep outside the fence and leave. It wasn't that much of a jolt, though, when I found her running alongside me, easily pacing me, her finely sculpted nostrils flaring white plumes into the cold winter night. Like her Arabian, she appeared able to run all night long.

I didn't want to tell her that simple running wouldn't get us out of here after I finished. We'd have to be a lot more fleet than possible afoot.

\*    \*    \*    \*    \*

"I must rest, Nick," she panted heavily, bending over, her hands on her knees. "You are a superman. You run and run and run and do not tire. How is that possible?"

"I am in perfect condition, Martina. I have to be," I said. I was tired, but not on the brink of exhaustion like she was. Cursing myself for allowing her to come this far, I looked around the small cluster of buildings we'd found temporary shelter among.

One of the larger sheds held blankets, some foodstuffs, items for use by the ground crews. I didn't have to check the others to know they contained similar equipment. What I wanted would be separate, and distant enough so that an explosion or fire wouldn't take out the rest. I wanted the chemical storage depot.

"There," I said, pointing into the night at a dimly lit building some yards away. "Is that what we want?"

Martina looked up, peered at the building, her lips moving slowly as she read the sign.

"It makes no sense to me. I cannot read all of it. All I see is part of a warning."

"Good enough. Let's go."

I flitted from one shadowy area to another, fading out of sight when a patrol drove by. They passed within fifty feet and never suspected my presence. I didn't bother with Martina now. I scented the goal for my searching. The building had something within it that required a warning sign. No matter what it was, that warning sign indicated potential destruction for the Soyuz-T3 now out on the launch pad preparing for blastoff.

The door to the building was sturdier than that on the others. I knew this was the payoff. Glancing around assured me that no patrols came close to this spot. I had time to work. I pulled out a thin picklock from a seam of my shirt, drove the slender spring steel sliver into the lock tumblers, and began the tedious work of tripping them one by one. When I had them all in the proper position, I turned the pick around and used the hooked end in a twisting fashion. The heavy padlock snapped open.

"You are good," congratulated Martina from behind me. "Maybe you, too, should be a used car salesman."

I smiled and silently entered the building, wary of alarms. But inside the compound the Russians hadn't bothered setting traps or tripwires. I wondered how long it would be before they discovered the holes in their fences and the out-of-order sensor head. They seemed as tangled up in their bureaucracy as we were. It might take hours to discover. I hoped it would take days.

By then I'd be long gone.

"Read some of the signs to me," I said. My spoken Russian is good; reading it is more difficult since I have to phonetically sound out each word. I can do it but it's time consuming. Martina was able to do it quickly, easily. For that I was glad she had come this far.

"Another, stronger warning on this room. Explosive chemicals," she said, pointing to the storeroom I'd already pegged for the one I wanted. A noxious aroma wafted under the ill-fitting door. And I recognized those odors as ones useful to me.

The lock came off as easily as the outer one and I pushed into the room. From floor to ceiling, stacks of cardboard cannisters littered the room. I quickly checked through them until I found the ones I wanted.

"Keep a watch while I do a little mixing," I told Martina.

Choking on the fumes from my crude chemistry, I put together six bombs hardly larger than the palm of my hand. But size meant little. These were going to go off and burn forever. They'd make Colonel

Kolakovich's simple thermite bomb on the *Columbia* launch booster appear to be a wet firecracker.

I put all six of them into my pack and motioned for Martina to follow.

"Listen carefully. I am going to plant these in the fuel area and anywhere else I can find that they'll do the most good. I want you to drift around, listen to anything being said, but don't intrude. Don't get caught. Meet me back here in one hour. Understand?"

Her bright blue eyes stared at me in the dim light. They seemed to bore right through me.

"And if I'm not back, you will leave me." She made it a flat statement.

"You know that's the way the game's played, Martina. This is for keeps. No time cuts, no King's X. And if I'm not back here in one hour, you get the hell out, because this place is going to be on fire five minutes after."

"Goodbye, Nick," she said, kissing me with surprising passion.

Returning the kiss, I touched her cheek lightly, then melted into the shadows. She complicated my mission. I didn't want to think about her safety when success was within my grasp. I had to concentrate fully on planting the bombs.

I scouted the skyline for the telltale plumes of liquid oxygen boiling off. In the cold night, they stood out like silver beacons. I moved swiftly to the compressor plant, glad that I'd spent so much time in the one at Cape Canaveral. This appeared to be an exact duplicate. They'd probably stolen the design.

I got up onto the catwalk I remembered so well, made sure I wasn't seen, then duckwalked along to a point directly above the monstrous compressor, which was sucking oxygen and nitrogen from the atmosphere, condensing the gases down to their liquification point, and piping it along to special low temperature Dewar storage tanks. I singled out the liquid oxygen lines for my incendiary bombs. Two of them were planted where they would rupture the lines and spew the lox into electrical equipment. I broke the tiny wax cylinder on the top and allowed the nitric acid within to begin chewing into the thin sheet of plastic over the main portion of the bomb. In about forty minutes, give or take several minutes, the acid would combine with my makeshift bomb and produce a lovely blast. The resulting explosion and fire would quickly take out this entire facility.

Not satisfied, I did a quick reconnaissance and found the hydrazine tanks used as the other component of the Russian rocket fuel. Two more of my bombs went onto hydrazine lines and tanks just past the valves necessary to stop the flow. I broke the acid fuses and looked around for a likely spot to plant my remaining two bombs.

I smiled grimly when the thought of how nice it would be to stuff it into the exhaust nozzle of the Soyuz-T3 on the launch pad hit me. But I couldn't get out and away in time. I had to opt for a fully loaded gasoline tanker truck parked near the rocket engine assembly area. I planted one of the bombs, keeping the other in case I came across another likely target. With any luck, this fire would spread quickly and take out the capsule and rocket ready for launch.

If not, then it'd be the last supplies the men in the Salyut received for at least four months.

That ought to be adequate time to starve them to death or allow them to suffocate. Without constant fine-tuning of the mirror's position, I'd been told, the solar wind would gently push it out of focus and remove the danger. Even if the Soviets got another crew up after the currently orbiting ones had died, the warning would have been clear; Don't use the solar mirror.

I made my way back to the chemical storage area and found Martina waiting for me. She had a grim expression on her face that I didn't like. It boded ill for the mission.

"What's wrong?" I demanded. "Did someone see you?" I had visions of a full security alert being called just as we got to the fence. With the entire launch facility in flames, we might escape. But we'd be trapped like rats if they started searching before the bombs went off. Worse still, if she'd been seen, they might begin a check of all the most sensitive parts of the complex.

They might find and defuse my bombs.

"Your plan, it won't work," she said breathlessly.

"They found the bombs already?"

"No, Nick, not that. But I overheard part of the briefing that Colonel Kolakovich is giving to the crew to go up in that." She pointed in the direction of the launch pad. "He said that the crew already aloft has supplies able to last for at least six months. More, if they ration themselves."

"They can't have enough oxygen up there for that," I said. AXE experts had assured me on that point.

"They have a new recycling system. They are now virtually self-reliant. Some type of new algae developed at Moscow State University provides a closed system for them. It is a miniature earth when it comes to breathing. Their food and water supplies are sufficient to withstand even the longest cutoff from earth."

I considered the type of explosion I'd be creating in less than twenty minutes. The destruction would be great, but the entire facility could be functional again in

three or four months. That left a large enough safety
margin. Considering the absolute Soviet control over
the press, the outside world would never even know of
the sabotage. For all intents and purposes, Baikonur
would never be shut down. Four months between
launches was not unusual and the Russians were secre-
tive even during the best of times.

"The mirror won't even be in jeopardy," I sighed.
My mind raced, searching for the proper course to
follow now. Even if the Soyuz-T3 on the launch pad
were completely destroyed and the Baikonur facility
devastated, it meant the solar mirror continued its
deadly operation.

Blasts of super-heat would wash the Midwest. The
climate would change. Crops would fail. All our listening posts throughout the world became even more vulnerable to the solar attack. And Baikonur would be
quietly rebuilt.

Bile burned in my mouth. I had failed.

"Take me to the briefing room," I demanded of
Martina. "I want to hear more of this."

"But the bombs!" she exclaimed. "They will go off
soon!"

"Dammit, don't you think I know that? I set the
damn things. But they don't matter. The mission is
what counts. If that mirror continues to operate, I've
failed, no matter what I do to Baikonur. If I have to
disable this place for longer than six months, I have to
do more than set fire to it. I have to find out what else is
possible. Take me to the briefing."

"This way," she said, silently moving into the
heavy shadows.

I followed, my brain rebelling at the thought of
failure. *To come this far to fail!* I refused to believe it.
Something had to turn up that changed defeat into

victory. I was N3. I was AXE's Killmaster. David Hawk depended on me to do a thorough, workmanlike job.

I wouldn't fail.

"Here. Inside."

I moved behind Martina, my hands circling her waist as I peered over her shoulder and into the brightly lit room. The sharp contrasts again struck me between the Soviet space procedures and our own. No clean room with a delicately controlled atmosphere, this. The two cosmonauts sat around on wooden chairs without their suits while Gregor Kolakovich lectured at a chalk board.

Straining, I made out his words.

"Comrades, in a short while you will don your suits and be launched into space for the glory of Russia. Your mission is one of utmost importance. I hardly have to tell you two this, yet I cannot stress too much what is riding on your performance.

"The solar mirror is only our first step." He pulled down a map showing the American Midwest. Spots marked in red indicated the richest farmland in the world. "These are the areas to be devastated first. The mirror will continually focus on them and change the rainfall patterns. Your part is more complex. In the military end of the Salyut, you will put together the optical observation equipment needed for sighting in our ICBMs."

"What's that for?" whispered Martina. "I don't understand."

I did. The Soviet electronics industry lagged far behind the U.S. in sophistication. As a result, their guidance systems were inferior to ours. While we had sold them ball-bearing plants that had dramatically improved their targeting ability, they lacked the microelectronics to fully cash in on it. With an orbiting observation post, however, they could sight-in their missiles perfectly, perhaps even directing the missiles from the Salyut.

Launch the missiles in the general direction of their targets, then allow the crew on board the Salyut to guide them directly into their targets. Maybe they used a laser communications device, or perhaps just simple radio devices. Ingenious—and it used a bit of Soviet technology where they were already superior to us. They knew the long-term effects and conditions in earth orbit. They held all the space endurance records and they maintained the first permanent space station. The reasons behind Kolakovich's sabotage of our space shuttle became even clearer.

The Russians held the edge in space habitation and were determined to keep it.

What bothered me the most was their development of the optical targeting system. Such things aren't invented, funded, built and tested unless they're meant to be used. Everything coming out of Russia these days hinted at growing imperialism. The neo-Stalinists were waiting for Brezhnev to die before taking over, but once dead, the last of the moderates following Khrushchev would be gone. A harder line toward the United States, bolder military ventures throughout the world, and increased pressure on the West apparently lay ahead for us.

"Then they talk of nuclear war!" the woman whispered hotly. Her breath gusted forth into feathery kinetic sculptures. She was incensed that anyone, even the hated Communists, threatened the world with atomic destruction.

"You're beginning to understand the importance of

my mission. That solar mirror is only the start. They can use it with impunity now because it hardly seems a weapon. After all, who'd take us seriously if we complained that a simple mirror was being pointed at us? The neo-Stalinists are using it to soften us up. They'll produce crop failures, maybe food riots inside the U.S., melt down our radar sites—and then, when they've got the power at home, use the Salyut to send in their missiles. Without sufficient food, with civil unrest and no way of detecting the missiles, we'd be sitting ducks. Everyone had predicted a very short nuclear war. The ones like Kolakovich want it to be over in a few minutes."

I pictured all the Minuteman silos blowing up. Only fifty percent of the missiles were in condition to fire at any given time. With precision guidance from orbit, none would leave their silos. And our Trident submarine was years behind schedule. The U.S.S. Ohio wouldn't part the waves for another year. And the older Poseidon subs could be detected using orbital observation and computer-enhanced sonar.

I shivered, but not from the cold. I was witnessing the first small step in the destruction of the United States. And I'd failed in my mission to stop it.

Or had I?

The bombs hadn't gone off yet. My presence was still unknown to the Soviets. There had to be more that I could do to snatch victory from the jaws of defeat.

It came to me in a rush. I knew what I had to do. It was impetuous, bold, foolish. But it would work. It had to.

"Listen carefully, Martina. There may not be time for us to go over this again." I huddled down in the shadows and pulled her closer so that our words couldn't be heard more than a few steps away. "Where do the cosmonauts suit up for their mission? What building?"

"In the room adjoining this one," she said, vaguely pointing to the area of the building at my back.

"Good. I'm going to suit up like a cosmonaut. When they come in to get into their suits, I'll take one out." I patted Hugo to indicate how. "Then I'll go through with the launch and—"

"And that'll never work," she finished. "You haven't thought this out very well."

"So?"

"So there are *two* cosmonauts. And if you hadn't noticed, one is a woman. That means you can only replace the man. That reduces your chances."

I hadn't noticed one of them had been a woman. Russian women tended to be powerfully built weightlifter types. Martina was obviously a delightful exception to that.

"And do you think you can go through the entire launch countdown and not make a mistake? They are highly trained. Have you astronaut training?"

I admitted I didn't, then added, "But the cosmonauts are little more than passengers. All the control work is done via remote control from the ground. I can fake it."

"You can't. If everything else went well, your slight accent would give you away."

"I'll mumble. Look, Martina, what you're saying is valid but I don't have any other choice. I've got to go up to the Salyut-8. I can destroy it in orbit."

"You will die."

"Probably," I admitted grimly. "But that's my job. You heard Kolakovich. This is the beginning of a long, determined plan to launch a nuclear war. If they're stopped now, it'll be years before they come up with another plan. And Kolakovich himself might be purged. That would be a big boost for the U.S. He's smart, cunning, one of the KGB's brightest strategists. No, regardless of what happens to me, both the space station and Kolakovich have to be stopped—now.''

"Your plan requires a woman—me," she said determinedly.

I knew by the set of her jaw she meant it. As I started to tense my fist to land it on the point of her chin, I hesitated. What she said was correct. The mission's success came first. She was just a "sleeper" but she'd been activated by Hawk. That made her a full agent, an agent who should take the same risks as I took.

I doubted her judgment, her ability, but I didn't doubt her devotion to an ideal. She aided AXE not out of patriotism for the U.S., but out of patriotism for her own homeland, for Russia without the Communist regime in power. I understood that; I counted on her being dedicated enough to go through with the wild scheme already coalescing in my head.

"Okay," I said. "We both try it. And if anything goes wrong, create as much chaos as you can and try to escape. Otherwise, let's ride that rocket all the way up to space!"

She smiled her brilliant smile and gripped my upper arm with fervor. I just hoped she actually realized what she was doing to herself by agreeing to this.

We sneaked into the ready-room adjoining the lecture hall where Kolakovich still pumped the cosmonauts full of propaganda. We found the racks holding the pressure suits. I went up and down the line trying to find one that would fit my tall frame. It seemed that the Russians were built like most Eastern Europeans, short and bulky. Only one of the space suits came close to fitting and even then I had to walk slightly hunched over after I donned it. Martina had better luck. She fitted one as easily as if Halston had created it just for her.

"Not *haute couture* but it'll do," I told her. "Help me fit the helmet on." She moved quickly to help with the bayonet fitting. The helmet snapped down firmly. I fought a momentary surge of irrational claustrophobia. Normally, such fears don't share my head with the coldly calculated need to accomplish an assignment, but this was new for me.

"Fifteen minutes until launch," blared the loudspeaker. "Cosmonaut crew to the Soyuz."

I glanced up at the speaker, my mind ticking off the seconds left until the fuses detonated my crude bombs. Using acid in homemade bombs is tricky. The exact instant of detonation can never be determined. I figured I had anywhere from five to twenty minutes before hell blossomed all around the launch facility.

"Let me call Hawk," I said, pulling off the buckle and straps from my knapsack. I quickly fitted them together so that the metal tongue touched the buckle. A surge of electrical power produced a tiny spark. I began using this crude but adequate telegraph key to code out a message. I had no idea if this particular frequency was being monitored; it hardly mattered.

By the time the Russians triangulated on me, I'd be circling the earth a hundred and twenty miles up.

"That's it. I hope Hawk understands the message," I said, slipping the straps and buckle into a convenient zippered pocket on the outside of the space suit. Thinking about it, I put in the remaining incendiary bomb I'd made. It might come in very handy when in orbit. Hefting Wilhelmina, I considered leaving her behind. But I couldn't. We were old friends. Wilhelmina followed the buckle and strap radio into the pocket. Hugo was strapped to my arm inside the space suit.

"They come," said Martina, pointing to the door. "Act quickly."

But I saw instantly that we weren't going to be able to make this work the way I'd planned. With the two cosmonauts came Colonel Kolakovich—and beside him came a half dozen heavily armed guards sporting their submachine guns.

I looked around for a way out of the room and saw none.

Martina and I were trapped. And from the way those guards fingered the triggers on their weapons, we were also going to be very dead.

# NINE

"Nick, we can't escape! They've got us trapped!" cried Martina, starting to panic.

Awkwardly, I tried to grab and shake her. With the thick gloves on and the clumsy space suit hindering my movement, I couldn't do more than shove her against the wall. But that motion gave me the germ of an idea on how to survive. Not by running. That way meant suicide. But if we pretended to be a pair of empty suits hanging in their racks, we might be able to avoid detection.

"Quiet," I hissed. "Just stand in the slot you took the suit from. Don't move. Don't even breathe. You might fog up your faceplate that way. Pretend to be an empty suit."

I didn't have any more time to caution her. Kolakovich and the two cosmonauts were already entering the room, flanked by the soldiers. I spun around, shoved my broad shoulders into the narrow confines of the rack and tried to look lifeless. I must have succeeded well enough because no one paid me any attention.

This worked out better than it had any right to. I had lowered the blast visor on the helmet. This hid my face from anyone in the room. But I was able to hear fairly well through the thick plastic. I'd worked on assignments requiring me to listen through motel walls; the sound quality had been worse than this.

"You do the State great honor, comrades," pontificated Kolakovich. "You will be given medals upon your return."

The male cosmonaut snorted as he stripped to a pair of woolen long johns. The woman nodded and smiled, but I had the feeling she and Kolakovich didn't see eye to eye on much of anything. While he was stocky, built like a weight lifter, she was even heavier, stronger, bulkier.

"Yes, comrades," the KGB colonel continued, "this work you do on the Salyut is of vital importance to our future plans. Keep the secret well and your promotions will be assured. And when the new regime is firmly in power . . ." His voice trailed off. I caught the corners of his mouth turning upward in a combination of smile and sneer.

He obviously figured prominently in this new regime. The neo-Stalinists were growing in influence. Killing Kolakovich turned into a top-priority job. I wished I'd had time to tell Hawk this. If I didn't make it back—which looked more and more likely—someone would have to permanently remove Colonel Gregor Kolakovich from the game. That would put a dent in the new Soviet expansionist plans, since I had a gut level feeling this arrogant colonel spearheaded the group plotting the downfall of the U.S.

"The targeting computer is aboard the capsule?" asked the woman cosmonaut. "I will not have it banged around like the last one. I don't care if the optical system is chipped; the computer must work if we are to successfully guide the down range launch next week."

"The missile is ready for launch now," said Kolakovich. "Our trawlers are currently steaming into the impact area in the south Pacific. When they are ready to photograph the reentry, we fire."

"Don't rush it," cautioned the woman. "Everything must be readied in orbit."

"Comrade Zolotov, you will prepare for the test launch as soon as possible. Work double shifts, if necessary."

"Comrade Kolakovich, *I* am the scientist. You are a . . . military man, nothing more. You do not rush science. No one does. When I am satisfied that everything is perfect, we will shoot the missile. Not one second before."

"For the glory of Communism you will accomplish it as soon as possible," the KGB colonel said in a cold, level voice. "And my scientific credentials are not to be questioned. I have made four successful flights aloft and performed many valuable scientific tests while in orbit. This, Comrade Zolotov, is your first flight. I *know* what can be done. You do not."

"Will someone help me with my helmet?" broke in the male cosmonaut. "The launch is pre-timed. It will not wait for us."

I heard a short, sharp sound as if someone had exploded a tiny firecracker. The noise puzzled me for a moment. Then I realized what both its source and cause was. Turning my head inside the helmet without shifting the suit's position, I saw Martina's space suit shaking. She'd sneezed.

"What was that?" asked Kolakovich. He glanced at the guards, who stood impassively, machine guns ready.

"Who cares about that?" said Zolotov. "What are these?" She poked the pile of Martina's and my coats with the tip of her space-booted foot. "These are not ours."

"Gu—" began Kolakovich. I silenced him quickly. If I hadn't had the clumsy space suit on, I'd have finished him. As it was, I managed to knock him unconscious. He slumped into a pile on the floor. The momentary confusion of seeing one of the space suits come alive saved me. Before the guards could train their guns on me, I had Wilhelmina out and firing.

Four quick shots drove the remaining guards from the room. A single burst from a submachine gun killed Zolotov. The guard commander barked an order to stop firing; he didn't want to kill the other cosmonaut or Kolakovich.

"Come on, Martina," I cried. "We've got to get the hell out of here."

"What are we going to do, Nick?" she asked fearfully.

"First of all, get rid of him." I put Wilhelmina away and scooped up one of the fallen machine guns. The cosmonaut awkwardly tried to train one on us; I cut him down before he had the AK-47 halfway up. I turned to finish off Kolakovich, but the guard had seen me kill the last cosmonaut and decided to be brave.

He rushed. We both fired at the same time, but I was a better shot, even inside the space suit.

"They'll be radioing for more men," said Martina, trying to calm herself. She picked up the fallen guard's machine gun and backed toward the window. A quick glance outside convinced her it was safe—for the moment.

I started once more to finish off Kolakovich, but the rain of bullets through the open doorway forced me to run for it. I dived through the window without bothering to open it. It gave way surprisingly easy, though I bore the brunt of the force on the thick plastic helmet.

Martina tumbled after me, the machine gun slowing her down a little. I took in the entire scene. Already spotlights winked on. Overhead a pair of helicopter gunships hovered, their 20 mm cannon a definite threat. In the silvered space suits we wore, we stood out like an orange bandage on a hitchhiker's thumb.

"A truck. It goes to the launch pad." Martina pointed.

If the truck hadn't been going to the rocket before, it was when I got there. I stuffed the machine gun muzzle under the young driver's chin and ordered him out. He turned pasty white. For a ghastly second I thought he might faint on me. I didn't want a limp body to get rid of. But he overcame his fright enough to slide out and then run like the devil was after him. I sprayed a few rounds in his general direction to lend speed to his feet and confusion to the troops slowly forming into ranks around the building.

I wondered how the cosmonauts ever accomplished anything inside those suits. The sweat poured down my body and turned my clothing into a sticky quagmire. Thinking back to Cape Canaveral, I remembered how our astronauts had carried portable air conditioning units. I understood why now. I wished I was plugged into one.

"Where now?" asked Martina, her face cast into a frown. "We cannot go directly to the rocket. Look ahead."

Already, troops put up barricades. I debated about making it through with the truck, then decided against it. They'd shoot out the tires. We needed something else, something armored enough to bull through even that deadly barrier.

I spied it. Without hesitation, I gunned the truck to life and spun the wheel the best I could. I wished for a suicide knob to be able to turn the wheel faster. But the truck slewed around on the proper course. Cutting off an armored half-truck, I went past it, then slammed the truck into reverse.

Martina screamed as we smashed into the tracked vehicle. I was out and clumsily running, the machine gun held in my thick fingers. A few quick bursts took out the few troops aboard.

"Inside. Get in back with your machine gun," I ordered her. "Shoot at anyone coming up from behind. And don't miss. And don't stick your head up too far."

As if some sniper had heard me, I felt a sudden hard blow on my helmet. A bullet had glanced off. For a moment I lost my balance. I stumbled a couple paces, then righted myself. Glancing upward showed me the track the bullet had taken. A gouge of plastic as thick as my finger had been reamed from the tough clear acrylic helmet. Without the protection I'd have been cooling meat on the ground. I didn't even think to check to see if the helmet remained spaceworthy.

Just staying alive kept me too busy.

My finger tensed on the trigger and I wildly sprayed heavy bullets in all directions. When the machine gun jammed on a spent piece of brass, I tossed the weapon aside and climbed into the half-track. I kicked the starter and got the powerful diesel engine running. Hoping Martina was in back but not looking to see, I ground the gears and got the mechanical behemoth moving.

I aimed it straight at the manned barricade separating us from the Soyuz-T3.

Hitting the barrier at thirty kilometers an hour still jarred me. The front wheels went up and over, then the tracks bit into the asphalt tarmac. Like a miniature rocket, the front end of the half-track came up, pointed off into space, then surged forward. We landed heavily and I gunned the engine again.

From behind, I heard Martina's machine gun spitting out leaden death. That kept the soldiers from getting too close. But some of their bullets still pinged around inside the cab. At least they couldn't shoot out the back tires—there weren't any. The metal treads continued grinding out the distance between us and the rocket long after the front tires had been flattened.

"Out of ammunition!" I heard Martina cry. But it was okay. We were close enough to the base of the rocket that it didn't matter. I only hoped that the automatic sequencing was similar to that used in the U.S. Atlas Centaurs and Saturns. Once the countdown reaches a certain point, the launch continues, regardless of what happens. If something goes wrong, the entire rocket is destroyed.

Destroyed.

The thought prodded distant, vague memories in the back of my mind, but I didn't have time to examine it more carefully right now. Later. When we were aboard the Soyuz.

"What's happening, Com—?" started the technician at the base of the rocket. He didn't get any farther. I kicked him in the face. He went down, spitting blood and teeth.

I half-dragged Martina toward a steel doorway near the base of the rocket. I didn't have enough neck mobility wearing the helmet to turn my head to see what was attached to it above.

Luck was definitely with me. The room was a staging area for the cosmonauts. Leading off toward the rocket itself was a metal cage—an elevator leading to the capsule perched high atop the three-stage booster rocket.

"Who are you?" demanded a man inside the room. I grabbed him by the collar of his overalls and heaved.

He bounced against one of the metal walls, then slumped. I kicked him through the open door, ducking at the last instant as a bullet came zinging inward from arriving troops. The man's last words before I slammed the heavy metal door were, "Launch in only ten minutes. Don't—"

I did.

I turned the dogs on the door as I listened to the hail of bullets against the thick metal.

"Get that elevator cage down here now, Martina!" I shouted. The words echoed around inside the confines of the helmet and made me dizzy. I wondered if the bullet glancing off that thick helmet earlier hadn't given me a mild concussion. Everything appeared in double vision and blurred out of focus. But I didn't have time to stop and wait for the symptoms to cease. Our lives would be forfeit if I didn't act decisively—right now.

Martina punched frantically at a large red button. For a few seconds nothing happened. Then I heard the distant whine of an electric motor starting up. The cage was descending from its position next to the capsule.

I worried about the timing. Less than ten minutes. Could we get all the way to the top in time? Then I stopped worrying about that to think about the Soviet soldiers getting through the dogged door. The space suit made me too clumsy to hold those metal handles against the attack from outside.

My mind shifted into overdrive and things snapped into crystal clarity. I knew how to stop the soldiers dead. I fumbled in the outer zippered pocket of my suit and found the bomb I'd been saving for the Salyut space station. I needed it more at this moment.

I ripped off my crude fuse and twisted open the tiny clay tube of nitric acid. I pushed aside the plastic "timing" plate so the acid wouldn't have to chew through it. The hissing and foaming as the acid touched the chemicals underneath told me I had just seconds to get rid of the bomb before it went off.

Smashing the claylike substance against the metal door, I turned and ran to Martina, who now held open the protective grating of the elevator. As I dived inside, a powerful shock wave of superheated air followed me. The bomb had gone off.

"Get this thing going up," I called out to her. But the woman was already acting. I thanked my lucky stars that she had gotten over her panic. Martina may not have been a trained agent, but she was responding well to all the problems confronting us. I admired that in a woman—in anyone of either sex.

The blast had killed a full dozen of the Russian soldiers. They milled in confusion, wondering what else might be coming out of that staging area. But one of their non-coms heard the electric motor on the elevator and pointed up at us. They began firing, the bullets pinging off the side of the cage.

I hoped none of those bullets would hit the fuel tanks. I remembered too vividly what had happened to our second space shuttle when Kolakovich had holed one of the fuel tanks with his well-placed shot.

Chaffing at the delay that seemed to stretch into an eternity, I waited until the cage reached the top of the twenty-story rocket. The door opened with agonizing slowness. But my fist came shooting out like the speed of light. I smashed the technician to the floor and quickly dragged him into the elevator cage.

"Anyone else up here?" I called out. Martina's quick circuit around the capsule assured our privacy now.

The hatch of the Soyuz-T3 opened like the mouth of a hungry rhino. I looked into the interior, saw the multi-hued indicator lights winking on and off and hesitated. Only Martina crowding in beside me overcame my instant of—what?

Fear? Perhaps. But I think it was more a feeling of awe. I remembered what astronaut Queensbury had said. Those that worked around Cape Canaveral did so with both hatred and envy in their hearts. I'd been caught up in the euphoria gripping the U.S. back in July of 1969 when Armstrong, Aldrin and Collins had reached the moon.

I'd wanted to be there with Armstrong, to be the one taking that first step. I'd shared that fantasy with millions of Americans. Now I was on the brink of actually going into orbit, of fulfilling a dream I had never seriously considered possible.

Gripping the convenient bar over the hatch, I swung both feet upward and kicked inside. I fit into the pilot's seat like fingers going into a glove. Martina came in beside me and the hatch slammed shut.

A timer on the control panel showed the status of the countdown.

Three minutes and counting.

*     *     *     *     *

"We made it, Nick. we made it!" crowed Martina.

I didn't want to tell her we hadn't made it, not yet. But her joy was too real to bring her down with the possibility of being yanked out of the capsule by the troops, or having the ground control blow the entire rocket up rather than let it be hijacked by a couple of interlopers.

Destroyed. Again came the niggling thought. But

this time it became stronger, more insistent, like a nova exploding in a nighttime sky. It finally hit me.

A secret report that had crossed Hawk's desk some years ago had been shown to me. The Russians put a bomb inside each of their rockets. In case the launch strayed—over China—they would detonate while still in mid-flight. This had been designed to prevent the Chinese from learning the secrets of the Soviet space capsules. Of course, it worked just as well in preventing the United States scientists from determining the exact state of Russian space science if the Soyuz passed over China and crash-landed into the Pacific, also.

The Soviets were paranoid about their inadequate science. And the more I was around them, the more I realized to what lengths they would go to protect themselves from exposure.

This time it would kill both Martina and me.

Looking over the complicated control panel was confusing. I'm kept abreast of all the current electronic gadgets AXE turns out. The knapsack radio was one of those. The array of buttons and blinking lights confronting me now was totally beyond my experience. I hesitated to touch even one of the buttons or switches. The entire missile might go up in a cloud of smoke if I made a tiny error.

Somehow, sitting aloft now in the Soyuz capsule, the idea of stowing away and going into orbit to destroy the space station didn't seem feasible.

"What do we do, Nick?" asked Martina, her voice trembling.

"I'm not sure," I said. I saw her face lighten perceptibly, even though the obscuring plastic of her helmet dimmed my vision. A comforting word, a lying phrase telling her everything would be just fine, a hope, is what I should have mouthed.

I didn't feel like holding her hand right now. Survival came first and I needed my full attention on the situation.

"Air. We need oxygen. Look around for the hoses to hook into our suits."

The dual oxygen feed and exhaust tubes were near the base of our thickly padded acceleration couches. We managed to get one another hooked into the air system. For a brief second I wondered if the Russians could shut this off from the ground. Then I figured that even they wouldn't go that far. Their cosmonauts could be trusted to do minor things like this.

The helium-oxygen mixture rushing into our suits cooled us and gave added confidence that things might work out in the end. Martina relaxed visibly when she felt the soothing rush of air over her body.

"Now what?" she asked, her voice lighter and less tension-filled than before.

I again studied the winking lights on the control panel. One clock in particular caught my eye. I assumed it was the countdown clock. Less than two minutes remained.

"Check out the panels for any red lights," I said. "I don't know if that means danger like it does in the U.S., but it'll give us somewhere to start."

I found one light blinking balefully. I thumbed the switch under it. For a long, worried heartbeat the light burned constantly red, then flashed green. I tried to read the Cyrillic markings on the control panel and found my sight dimmed too much by the helmet. I doubted I could decipher the writing in time to do much anyway. If the Soviets arranged their panels like the U.S., the markings would have been little more than cryptic nudge-words, mnemonic symbols to help out the crew who had trained for long hours inside mock-ups. Figuring them out for myself would take longer than two minutes.

Or a minute and four seconds.

"Fasten the safety harness," I said. "The harness!"

Martina did as she was told while I worked the thick-webbed material around my own shoulders. My eye strayed to the clock. Fifty-eight seconds until we were hurled into space.

"This is Colonel Kolakovich," came the scratchy voice over the radio. "To those spies barricaded inside our Soyuz, give yourselves up before it's too late. If you do not leave the capsule immediately, you will die."

"Nick!" exclaimed Martina, her hand reaching over to rest on my arm.

"Take it easy. If we do leave, that's sure death. These things are set to automatically fire after a certain point's reached. They can't hold this baby back. Not now. We open the hatch and we'll die as the rocket goes off."

"No good, Kolakovich," I said into my helmet microphone. Somewhere along the way, I had activated it—probably a dual connect when I plugged the oxygen hose into the chest panel of my suit.

"Carter?" came the strangled voice of the KGB colonel. "Nick Carter?"

"None other than, Gregor. Wish me luck. My sequencing clock says you've just got thirty seconds."

"You won't survive this, Carter, I assure you of that. Surrender now."

"Better clear your troops away. The rocket wash will melt them all down into undifferentiated protoplasm in twenty seconds."

I felt my eyes lock onto that hypnotic clock. Each

flash of the LED display brought us another second closer to lifting out of earth's gravity well.

"We will take this to the United Nations, Carter! The United States imperialist warmongers will not be allowed to steal one of our top-secret space capsules!"

"Five seconds, Nick," said Martina in a choked voice.

Solenoids clicked deep in the heart of the rocket engines. For almost a minute the fuel pumps had been working, pumping liquid oxygen and hydrazine into the firing chambers. As Martina spoke, ignition occurred. I felt the tremendous power building just under me.

And as the LED clock flashed to zero-zero-zero, a giant jumped onto my chest. At first the pressure was bearable. In less than five seconds it became intolerable. I felt the rocket lifting slowly from Baikonur, the fiery tail licking out and melting concrete and steel as if they were snowballs tossed into the furnace of hell.

Then more than physical torture assailed me. I heard Kolakovich's voice coming over my headset. He'd probably forgotten he'd left his microphone open in the control bunker.

". . . detonate at forty seconds. Make it appear the missile came apart in the maximum dynamic stress portion of flight."

My mind raced even as my body was pinioned helplessly by the six gravities of acceleration. The Russians *did* plant a bomb inside their manned launch vehicles to insure that the secrets inside were never recovered by the Chinese or anyone else should a mission abort. A bomb was inside the capsule and I was held down like a fly under a schoolboy's thumb.

My eyes rolled wildly as I examined the control

panel for some clue. Nothing. The LED clock timer now flashed a different message. It showed elapsed flight time. Five seconds. Only thirty-five left for me to find the bomb and disable it.

But how? Acceleration crushed me. And the Soviets would not put the bomb where their own cosmonauts might disarm it. Their cosmonauts were not stupid; they wouldn't want to end up like Grissom, Chaffee and White.

The names of our own three astronauts blazed brilliant pathways through my mind. They'd died on the ground, during training. And the reason for their death was the use of almost pure oxygen—a tiny fire, pure oxygen, raging inferno—a deadly equation.

And one the Russian KGB would know about.

If the bomb was located anywhere I could reach inside the space capsule, it had to be next to the oxygen bottles supplying both Martina and me.

"Martina, help me!" I called out. But I saw the still-increasing acceleration had caused her to pass out. The equivalent of eight men sat on my chest now. I felt the seat cushions flattening under the intense weight—my weight—pressing into them.

But I had to move. I had to seek out that diabolical bomb. My arm weighed tons, hundreds of millions of tons. The strain was immense but I moved it. Against the acceleration, I moved inch by slow inch. But while I moved as if dipped in molasses, the elapsed time clock raced faster than thought.

Kolakovich would detonate at forty seconds. The clock read twenty-three.

My leaden hand moved to the hose supplying my oxygen. I followed the hose downward. This part proved easier than anticipated. I simply relaxed and allowed the monstrous acceleration to help me. Under my fingers came cold metal fittings, cold fittings spewing forth their life-giving atmosphere—and something else.

It might have been anything. An emergency medical kit. Food storage. Anything. It had to be the bomb that was resting next to the oxygen bottle. It just had to be.

It was.

Fingers clumsily moving, I traced the outlines of a familiar land mine used by the Russian army. They hadn't even bothered to design a new casing for it. I knew how to defuse it.

The clock read thirty-one seconds.

Desperate need lent strength to my arm, my hand, my fingers. I found the tiny protuberance on the top of the mine. I twisted as hard as I could. The surplus weight on my body tore muscles, crushed the very breath from my lungs.

Thirty-three seconds.

I felt the black tide of unconsciousness rising. I fought it back. If I passed out now we were both doomed—and the solar mirror burned on, burning earth, charring wheat fields, turning acres of corn into burned remains not even suitable for hog feed.

Thirty-five seconds.

I strained harder. The shoulder muscles separated. I screamed in pain, but the acceleration forced the cries back into my throat. My fingers tightened. I turned another half rotation. Every joint in my body ruptured and sent searing waves of pain into my brain. Another half turn on the detonator atop the land mine.

Thirty-eight seconds.

I screamed. My lungs burned. My chest felt caved in. My arms were broken. My fingers were mangled beyond repair. My head threatened to split apart like a rotted melon. And I screamed louder. For a brief instant, every part of my body coordinated perfectly.

Forty seconds.

The detonator came free.

Beneath my seat I heard a deadly relay click shut.

I dropped the detonator and allowed the acceleration to press me back into my couch. The danger from destruction due to the bomb was gone. But then I found out what Kolakovich had meant about maximum dynamic stress. The engine of the main booster continued to burn. But the entire capsule shook like a paint mixer in a department store.

We were at the optimum point where air friction and velocity produced the most stress possible on the entire rocket.

Then, mercifully, it was as if we'd slipped into a safe harbor, a gentle sea, a glass-smooth ocean. A grating noise rumbled through the capsule to be followed almost instantly by a muffled explosion more felt than heard.

I knew the main booster had expended its fuel. BECO. Booster Engine Cut Off. Explosive bolts fired and we were free of the first stage. The second slammed us back into the couches, but the acceleration was like a love pat compared to the first brutal seconds aboard.

By the time the second stage jettisoned, I heard Martina moaning lightly. For several minutes we coasted free, no acceleration pinning us down at all. I reached over and gently shook her.

"You still in one piece?" I asked.

"I ache all over. I . . . I must have passed out. How embarrassing. Never have I done such a thing."

"And I'll bet you've never been shot off into space before, either," I said, holding back a chuckle.

The detonator from the land mine slowly drifted to a spot between us. Martina fixed her blue eyes on it, then reached out to touch it. I stopped her.

"Let me do that."

"But something's come loose. It might be dangerous."

"Dangerous?" I said, laughing aloud this time. "No, not now. Everything's just fine."

My gloved hand closed over the detonator device. I pulled it in slowly, marvelling at the effects of weightlessness on it. Pushing it into the zippered pocket of my suit, I felt more secure than at any time since hearing Kolakovich order the destruction of the Soyuz.

The final stage burned and gave us a brief taste of gravity again. My entire body glad for the weight but aching abominably, I snuggled down into the acceleration couch and closed my eyes. In seconds I was fast asleep.

# TEN

"Shouldn't we be doing something, Nick?" Martina asked anxiously. "It's getting on my nerves just sitting here. Just sitting here and floating!"

I knew what she meant. The people on the ground had probably taken complete control of the space capsule. I assumed that Kolakovich now wanted us alive, otherwise there seemed to be a million things he could have done to destroy us after the Soyuz had gotten out of the atmosphere. Or maybe there wasn't a damn thing he could do.

I didn't know that much about the Soviet control systems. It might have been that, once launched, the Soyuz went on its merry way and there was nothing anyone could do. That sounded a lot like the way the Russians might set it up. Like shooting a gun, after the bullet leaves the barrel, there's no way further the marksman can affect the trajectory.

After Kolakovich tried to detonate the land mine under my couch, I somehow thought he would have done all in his power to wreck the Soyuz space capsule in other ways. That we were still safe and sound strongly hinted that little or no control was possible from the ground during this part of the trip.

"There's nothing we can do unless we can learn a hell of a lot in just a few minutes." I glanced over the control panel with its myriad flashing lights and marvelled that anyone could learn what they all meant given any amount of training. The idea that our lives depended on what those lights meant worried me, but obviously not as much as it bothered Martina.

I rather enjoyed the weightless sensation. Cutting loose my harness, I drifted upward under the slight movement and hung suspended in midair. There was no feeling of weight whatsoever. For a few minutes after the Soyuz capsule engines had cut off I'd felt queasy—dropsickness. But the vertigo and upset had quickly passed. I was pleased to see that it didn't bother Martina at all. Even experienced astronauts had gotten space sick from the lack of gravity.

I reached out and grabbed a convenient handle placed just above the control panel. Instantly, I found that the rules of physics still applied. I tried to stop all my angular momentum with a simple handgrip. I nearly ripped my shoulder out of its socket.

Yelping, I let go. On the next rotation, I held on a bit longer and this brought me back safely to the couch.

"You were a sight," giggled Martina. I smiled at her. She had forgotten all about our plight for the moment.

But I hadn't. We were on the far side of the earth from the Salyut-8 space station. In less than forty-five minutes we'd be docking with it, if all the automatic equipment and pre-programmed onboard computer worked perfectly.

And on that station were cosmonauts and military personnel.

I checked the zippered pocket of my space suit and found Wilhelmina safely tucked inside. The detonator from the mine under my couch rested snugly next to my faithful friend. I wondered whether I'd be given the chance to use either. No matter what had happened on the ground at Baikonur, a radio message would have beaten us up to the Salyut. They'd be waiting for us.

My mind raced to figure out the best approach. The solar mirror might be vulnerable if I worked out the control system on the Soyuz. Instead of docking, I could fire the rockets and ram the mirror, shattering it. Or just ram the space station and kill all aboard. Barring that, opening the hatch of the space capsule and heaving the detonator—properly armed—toward the mirror would wreck it.

Satisfied that there were options open to me, I forced myself back down in the couch and checked my slight drifting motion. Refastening my harness, I studied the control panel. The more I tried to figure it out, however, the less comprehensible it became.

"Can you make heads or tails out of any of these controls, Martina?" I asked.

"No, Nick. It . . . it's all so strange to me. I grew up on the steppes. I am not used to such technical gadgetry."

"You got through the alarm system on the fence outside Baikonur pretty well," I told her. Watching that deactivation had been a thing of beauty. She had worked swiftly, expertly, doing just the right things at the right times. I couldn't have done better.

"Dmitri had known about it from an engineer friend of his who had shown us the secret. I really knew nothing about how the system worked, just about turning it off."

"Hmm," I said, mulling over the prospect of turning knobs and flipping switches at random. I knew it was impossible for us to blast free of the earth's gravity field, but I also knew it was possible for us to go into an orbit. If that happened, it would be years before we returned close enough to the earth for rescue.

By then, we'd be long dead from suffocation.

Tinkering with the controls didn't seem too logical a path to follow. Yet there had to be some fine controls for the rockets if docking with the Salyut was to be done without massive damage to both station and space capsule.

"Do you see anything looking like the engine ignition switch? What do all the controls say?" I pointed to a bank of lights and switches between us on the console. Martina slowly told me what each sign said.

No good. I still couldn't decipher the way the Soviets had this thing set up.

"Nick, the radar. Look!"

The radar screen was unmistakable. The slowly moving rod of green light beeped when it crossed a distant, tiny dot. The dot moved closer and the beeping grew louder.

"The space station," I said "That's got to be it."

I peered through one of the transparent quartz ports hoping to make a visual sighting. No go. The distance was still too great. But I did see a bright flash. That had to be the solar mirror condensing the light from the sun and pouring it like thick butterscotch down onto the earth below.

Was it destroying electronic listening posts? Warming up our croplands? Or had Kolakovich figured out some even more diabolical use for his toy?

"I have a sighting, Nick. The radar return is strange."

"What do you mean 'strange?' "

"It is so small compared to the size of the station." Martina peered through a small telescope she had found in one of the cabinets. I marvelled at the Russians' lack of miniaturization. Not only was the interior of the cabinet done in wood—their plastic industry is way behind ours—but the telescope itself was similar to those you buy in toy stores. Nothing sophisticated at all about their equipment.

"What experience have you had reading radar returns?" I asked.

"Not much. I listen. My . . . commissar was an air force officer. He has taken me many times and shown me the workings of the base near Volgograd. But this!" she exclaimed. "It covers almost all my field of vision!"

I took the telescope, drifted 'upward' enough to see through the window and worked the telescope around. The space station came into view and behind it was the solar mirror. This was what Martina had seen. I understood now why the radar blip was not the size it should have been. The station itself returned most of the radar impulse.

The mirror wasn't solid. It was strung together like a spiderweb with tiny planar mirrors placed along the strands. The entire structure had been pulled together slightly by the wires to form the concave shape necessary to focus the rays of the sun on the earth.

"They didn't launch an entire mirror," I whispered. "They did it one piece at a time and then picture puzzled it together in orbit. Incredible."

"The controls, Nick. The controls are working by themselves!"

I glanced at the console and saw Martina was right. Lights flashed on and off in a different cadence now. The ground control wasn't responsible; Baikonur was on the other side of the world right now. Either the cosmonauts in the Salyut-8 were in control or the capsule followed a preplanned route. I had the gut feeling that we were being reeled in like fish on a line by the crew inside the space station.

"I've got to try and destroy the mirror now," I said. "This may be our only chance."

"But how? We are so far away. And there is nothing we can do."

I hefted the detonator and realized she might be right. The weightless little blob of explosive seemed puny against that miles-wide array of mirror held together with piano wire. Even a large explosion would damage only portions of the solar menace.

But I had to try. That was my job.

"Are you all sealed up? Oxygen lines okay?"

"Yes, but what are you doing?"

I blew the hatch above us. The sudden outrushing of air snapped me solidly against my harness. The pressure was almost welcome after the weightlessness, but I didn't have long to enjoy it. The air vented into the almost perfect vacuum of space. I stared up at the diamond-hard points of the stars. Somehow, they seemed to be watching, judging. I had to succeed.

I carefully unfastened the harness and stood, my head outside the capsule. The detonator in hand, I took careful sighting on the mirror, then heaved the explosive as hard as I could. The tiny blob of metal vanished from sight almost immediately. I waited. Nothing. I waited and waited for what seemed eternity.

My only reward was one tiny silvered surface erupting in a tiny nova of glass shards. The bulk of the mirror remained unscathed.

I pulled out Wilhelmina. I thought a pistol should fire in outer space. After all, the bullet contains all the powder and oxidant necessary on Earth. Atmosphere isn't needed.

Aiming, I fired. The effect was eerie. I felt Wilhelmina's kick against my hand. The backward reaction of the slug leaving the barrel even forced me backward against the side of the hatch. But it all happened in total silence. Again and again I fired, the spent brass ejecting out into space and the heavy 9 mm Parabellum round flying soundlessly to smash into one of the planar mirrors comprising the entire huge solar array. I destroyed six of the component mirrors. Five with bullets and one with the detonator.

That only left thousands more, unscathed.

"Nick, we're almost docked."

I looked around and saw she was right. The darkly gaping hole in the side of the Salyut-8 was obviously designed to accept the front portion of the Soyuz. In a very short time we would be inside the station. Or dead. At that moment I regretted having fired my last rounds into the mirror.

We docked.

The mechanisms snapped firmly into place allowing us to leave via the hatch I'd opened and go directly into an air lock on the side of the Salyut.

"Should we, Nick?" Martina asked anxiously. "I know what's inside."

"I know, too, but staying here means certain death. Better to get inside where there's light and oxygen and a chance of fighting. Out here, we're sitting ducks."

We carefully drifted out of the hatch and to the space lock. We squeezed inside. Immediately, the thick outer door closed and air hissed in from hidden valves. Frost formed on my helmet. I scraped it off in time to see the inner door opening and three men crowd around us with guns in their hands.

The gestures they made with the weapons told me what they wanted us to do. We slowly left the airlock and began stripping off the space suits. In a few minutes we stood clad only in the clothes we'd worn on earth.

"We should kill them," snarled the largest of the cosmonauts, a man of definite Oriental descent. He might have been one of the Soviets' Mongolian cosmonauts.

"Orders," said another. "You know how Kolakovich is when someone fails to follow his orders to the last letter."

"Kolakovich is on earth, not here. We can throw them out from the airlock without their suits and say they failed in the transfer from the Soyuz. Who's to know?"

"He will. The man's able to read minds."

I looked over the inside of the Salyut while the three continued to debate our fate. The inside was more spacious than I'd counted on. Again the Russians used wood in places where we'd use plastic. Wood is lighter for its strength than most metals; plastic is better since it won't absorb water from the surrounding air and swell. But the parts of the station that mattered were all top-rate.

The telescope peering earthward was one of the finest made. The small computers arranged around the circular walls weren't up to U.S. standards, but I didn't doubt for an instant that they could perform the task of targetting ICBMs. Most of the remaining equipment was so arcane I couldn't even begin to guess its purpose.

I returned my attention to the three cosmonauts and the nametags on their uniforms. Chan, the Mongolian, was short, bandy-legged and was obviously the low man on the totem pole. He deferred to both the Russians in all important matters. Petrov was taller, not by much. He was stronger, bulkier, and looked a little like Kolakovich. The commander of the station, Major Mendenovich, appeared worried over our presence. I didn't blame him much. A hundred and twenty miles above the earth you don't often have uninvited guests dropping in.

Again, I wished I hadn't used all my ammunition in the attempt to destroy the solar mirror. A well-placed shot through the side of the station would decompress it and kill all of us in a few seconds.

That thought started running through my mind. All three held handguns. The bullets from any one of them would accomplish just that. With my foot braced on the side of the station, I timed the jump perfectly. When Chan drifted 'above' me, I kicked. My hand closed on his wrist and I twisted as hard as I could.

The weightlessness startled me but I corrected for it. But Chan had lived here for months and knew all the tricks. A quick twist and he was firmly anchored on a convenient hand-grip while I floundered helplessly in midair.

"Capitalist pig," he snarled. I saw his finger tighten on the trigger. The yellow skin turned white with the pressure. The roar almost deafened me as he fired.

The common myth is that your life passes before you instants before death. My mind worked in a different way. Survival couldn't take a backseat to nostalgia for life. But I was helpless and without any way of escaping. My thoughts as the trigger went back were dark ones of failure, of letting down Hawk, AXE and the United States.

The bullet hit me squarely in the middle of the chest.

I whooshed as the air rushed out of my lungs. Spinning like a gyroscope, I smashed into the far wall, bounced off and careened into the middle of the room again. Mendenovich kept me from endlessly bouncing from wall to wall.

"Rubber bullets," he said. "We can't risk a puncture."

Breathing was too difficult for me to answer. I felt the bruise on my chest spreading; I wanted to ask Major Mendenovich where the real bullets were kept. He was the station commander; he had to keep order. The Russians wouldn't have brought up guns with only rubber bullets. That wasn't like them. These might keep order should one of the cosmonauts get funny ideas and need a moment's disciplining. The real bullets would be used if the station were in danger from a renegade cosmonaut.

"Petrov, put them in the storage compartment for safe keeping. There's nothing in there that they can harm."

Still gasping like a fish out of water, I allowed Petrov to pull me along like a captive helium-filled balloon. Martina was shoved in beside me. The thick metal door slammed shut behind us. We were prisoners awaiting execution.

\* \* \* \* \*

"Will we suffocate in here?" Martina asked nervously. She clung to one of the supporting beams on the outer portion of the curving wall. Her face was white and she obviously didn't think we would leave this room alive.

"There's plenty of oxygen coming in. Don't worry about that."

"What if they cut it off? There're valves all over the place. What then?"

"We can turn on this one," I said, pointing to a valve nearby. The Cryllic lettering had been difficult to decipher but it read "oxygen." All I had to do was open it and the air would come spilling into the small storage area.

"It's so dark in here. I'm afraid, Nick, really afraid. Hold me close."

I swam over to her; "swimming" being the only possible term for what I did. Arms flailing as if against water, I pushed myself through the dimly lit room to where Martina clung helplessly to the steel girder. I put my hand against her cheek and gently stroked. The smooth skin flowed and a hot tear trickled over my finger.

"Don't cry. We'll be all right. I promise."

"Things have been exciting up until now, haven't they?" she said, her voice choked with emotion. "But I didn't realize just how serious the situation was—or how dangerous. I've been a fool and nothing but trouble."

"You've done great. And we'll do even better. They didn't kill us outright. That means they want to save us for something."

"Kolakovich," she said bitterly.

Though I agreed, I had to keep her from worrying. We wouldn't get out of here easily and time had a way of dragging when in captivity. I silenced any further misgivings by kissing her.

At first she strained to break away, then she relaxed and threw herself into the kiss. Her arms circled my body and we floated free into the center of the room. It was an odd sensation being totally weightless, Martina's arms moving slowly up and down my body. She gripped at the back of my shirt for support. This alone would have held us together but I was also running my hands up and down her back, and they finally came to rest cupping her buttocks.

"Nick, should we?" she whispered hotly. "This hardly seems the time or place."

"You're wrong," I corrected her. "It is both the right time and the right place. We might not get out of this alive. This might be our last opportunity to be alone."

I pulled her closer. Her lushness thrilled me and sent life coursing through my veins. We needed this moment of escape. I didn't want Martina to know that in a few hours—minutes!—we both might be cast out from the airlock to drift forever in an airless, frigid orbit around earth.

My hands held her close. I felt her breasts crushing down against my chest, the nipples trying to poke holes in my flesh. She wiggled sinuously, like a snake dancing in midair. Martina managed to free her tunic and send it sailing away like some unfortunate bat that had lost its sonar. This allowed her breasts to float freely between us. The sight took my breath away.

I bent down and kissed the deep canyon between them. I felt the warm, vibrant female flesh on either side of my head. Needing more, I let my tongue roam slowly up one of the snowy white slopes until I reached the ruddy peak which was throbbing with lust. I sucked the nipple into my mouth and worked it around eagerly.

Martina moaned softly and leaned backward. Hands still on her behind, I guided her. The lack of gravity made our movements slow, making them appear almost like a ballet in midair. With all weight removed, I felt a freedom I had never experienced before at the bottom of the earth's gravity well.

I skinned her out of the leather pants she wore and exposed the dark mound of fur between her strong, firm thighs.

She gasped as I ran my hand between her legs. Her involuntary reaction sent both of us tumbling. I held on and she grabbed wildly for support. We lightly brushed the wall, then bounced into the middle of the room again.

"We'll have to get better coordinated," I whispered, my mouth kissing and working over her body.

"Ready for docking," she sighed in contentment. "I'm ready to accept your probe!"

I smiled at her. She was relaxing and enjoying herself, all our troubles momentarily forgotten. I moved away like a swimmer and began stripping off my clothing. Hugo remained in his sheath on my arm; the cosmonauts hadn't bothered searching me after they'd found the emptied Wilhelmina. But weapons were the farthest thing from my mind as I finally kicked free of my pants.

"Such a large missile," Martina joked, her hand reaching out to engulf me. She tugged lightly and I moved toward her. The delicacy of the movement would have been impossible on earth, in a gravity field.

"Target sighted," I replied. "Guide me into the target."

"Base ready for your ICBM," she said, still gripping my steely erection. Her legs parted delightfully and I effortlessly moved into the vee. We both gasped as our bodies lightly melted into one another. Never had I experienced such a sensation. My body was trembling like a rocket just before the launch.

"Oh, Nick, I need to feel you moving inside me. I need it so!"

She shuddered and I knew she needed what I had to offer. I needed what she had to offer. Locked together, we began a slow motion movement. On earth it wouldn't have meant a thing. In the liberating weightlessness of zero-gravity space, every delicate motion was felt and communicated. Gravity didn't muffle any of the thrusting, the stroking, the passionate kissing.

Her legs circled my waist and her ankles locked behind my back. I sank to the hilt in her superheated interior. I felt the dampness flowing and knew she was ready. My motion became stronger, more definite. She thrust her crotch down to meet mine. We gasped and sobbed and clung to one another as we glided through midair. There was complete freedom of movement. Nothing hindered us as we pushed our passion to the breaking point.

"You're so big, so swollen, Nick. I need it, ohhh, I need it!"

She gasped, arched her back and drove her hips down powerfully toward my groin. Using a circular motion, I moved in and out in a fashion impossible on earth. This pushed her over the brink again and again. And the feel of her tight muscles clamping down so powerfully on my hidden length caused me to move faster, demand more.

As I spewed out my seed into her hungrily awaiting center, Martina climaxed a final time. Sweat beading on our bodies, I was surprised to find that it didn't run. It couldn't. No gravity. Everything stayed right where it was until a vagrant air current moved it.

And that's just what happened with us. We hung in midair lightly touching one another, reveling in the warmth of the afterglow. It had been spectacular for us, a lovemaking that could never be duplicated on earth. But it had only been a diversion to get our minds off the problem at hand: escape.

Martina continued to sigh, her eyes half closed. But I worked on the problem of getting us out of here and ridding the U.S. of the threat of the solar mirror. I toyed with a few of our sweat globules as they condensed into spheres. They seemed elastic. The surface tension held them together until I batted them around. Then one larger drop would split into millions of tinier droplets that went sailing off to form a damp sheen on the walls of the room.

An idea tried to surface in my mind but it couldn't. Something about the lack of gravity, something about the weightlessness of everything. I finally shook my head. Whatever the idea was, it wouldn't come out right now.

But another idea did spring up. We were locked in a storeroom. And that storeroom had at least one oxygen valve inside it.

"Martina," I said, shaking her out of her delicious lethargy. "What kinds of gas bottles are stored in here?"

She checked.

"Carbon dioxide. It's marked 'For External Use Only.' "

"They use the $CO_2$ for jets when working outside the Salyut," I said. My mind raced. The gas wasn't poisonous, but it suggested a course of action that would free us.

"What are you doing, Nick?" she asked. I'd grabbed the carbon dioxide bottle and pulled it across the room to the oxygen valve.

"Get dressed. We're going to be leaving here real soon," I told her. I fitted the gas cylinder to the oxygen line, then opened the bottle valve wide. The gas hissed out. While it was doing its work, I dressed. Hugo came easily into my hand. I knew I'd have to be careful; in free fall I might hurt myself more with the sharp edge than with fighting any of the cosmonauts.

"I don't understand. The $CO_2$ isn't poisonous. It won't do anything to them."

"Wrong. Just wait and see what happens."

In less than a minute alarm bells sounded throughout the station. Chan was the first to poke his head into the storage room. And he was the first to die. I cut his throat, Hugo making one swift sweep just under his chin.

The blood drifted outward in a bizarre pattern. The liquid quickly formed droplets and hung like crimson balloons all around the dead cosmonaut's throat. He bounced lightly into the door. I kicked him back into the main part of the Salyut.

"Chan, what's—" Mendenovich cut off his sentence when he saw Martina and me coming out of the storage room. Hugo carried a small red cloud around his blade. Mendenovich took all this in and acted faster than I'd have thought possible.

His gun was out and aimed. But his earthly reflexes betrayed him. He fired one of the rubber bullets without bracing himself first. He went cartwheeling backward, ass over teakettle. The rubber bullet caromed off the steel stanchion beside me and soared around the room like a miniature meteor.

With Mendenovich momentarily out of commission, I searched for Petrov. He was curled around a post and trying to bring his gun to bear. I wondered if a quick throw of my knife would kill him, but I discarded the idea Hugo wouldn't tumble properly without gravity to act on him in flight. I was still a newcomer to this type of fighting; I'd have to play it conservatively until I learned to move as easily as the cosmonauts did.

I attacked by simply straightening out my legs and rocketing across the large common room. Holding Hugo ahead of me like the steel prow of an icebreaker, I speared toward Petrov. He panicked. The gun went off prematurely in his hand. While he was securely anchored, his grip on the gun wasn't good. The pistol blasted away toward the far side of the room.

As I aimed Hugo for Petrov's throat, my trajectory went a little off. The steel blade gouged a deep scar in the metal post Petrov held onto. But I managed to swing around, converting my linear momentum into angular. My knee drove into Petrov's kidney. He gasped, turned red in the face, and passed out from the pain.

"Nick, the other one!" cried Martina. She was attempting to throw loose items at Major Mendenovich. She wasn't getting anywhere. Newton's second law of motion kept confounding her. The woman hadn't realized yet that the slightest movement in one direction caused an equal and opposite reaction. As Martina threw a heavy book, she went backwards with the same momentum.

Mendenovich and I faced each other across the center of the room. The slight smile on his face told me he thought he would win. I'd have to show him how wrong he was. Time worked against me. The longer I fought, the greater the chance for my inexperience in the weightlessness to catch up with me. Besides that, Petrov would recover quickly. The Russian cosmonauts were like ours in one respect; they were in topflight physical condition.

A pencil floated by my head. I grabbed for it, then sent it zinging toward Mendenovich like a tiny spear. The man ducked to keep it from impaling his left eyeball, but hit his head on a metal post and went tumbling off into midair. This was all the opening I needed. I launched myself, did a neat flip in midflight and locked my legs around Mendenovich's neck. I twisted as hard as I could. The motion, coupled with the weightlessness, was enough to flop him around and smash his body into the side of the Salyut.

He was out cold.

"Let me help, Nick," said Martina, valiantly struggling to maneuver in the zero-gravity environment.

"Get him into the storage room. And put Petrov in with him." Petrov made weak gasping noises but I knew he was recovering quickly. I paddled over awkwardly and belted him as hard as I could. The punch lacked real impact since he flew away at first touch, but he banged his head against the desk fastened to the wall.

I let out my breath as I floated into the center of the room. The Salyut-3 was mine. Now it was time to complete my mission: destroy the space mirror.

\* \* \* \* \*

"I want to come with you, Nick," cried Martina. "I don't want to be left here with them."

"Maneuvering in space is tricky, Martina. You're learning well inside the station. Why not just watch?"

"I can help." Seeing that wasn't going to work with me, she added, "I have earned the right to be at your side. We have been through much together."

That got to me. I had a strong sense of duty, of fair play. Her presence here had been more accidental than anything else, but she had been useful. And she hadn't gotten in my way. Looked at in one perspective, she did deserve the opportunity to be there when the mirror was destroyed.

"It will be dangerous."

"Everything up here is dangerous," she scoffed. "Everything on earth is, too. We are not protected cradle to grave in cotton wool. I want to help."

"Finish getting your suit on," I said, giving in. "I might just need another set of hands to do what I intend doing."

"What is that? How are you going to destroy the mirror?"

"I've got all their bottles of $CO_2$ used for maneuvering in space. I intend to use them as tiny rockets to push against the mirror and knock it out of position."

"That'll work?"

"I hope so. At any rate, we've got to give it a try." I turned and glanced toward the storeroom. "They can't get loose until we let them out. Now, into the airlock."

We squeezed into the tiny lock and started the cycling, which pumped out the atmosphere and pushed it back into the space station. When the pressure had been lowered enough, I opened the outer door.

The feeling of being on the top step of infinity hit me all at once. As long as the Salyut had surrounded me, I had no sense of distance or of vastness. I did now.

The earth bulked under me, a gorgeous blue and brown ball covered with wax-paper clouds. A tiny storm brewed in the Atlantic—then I thought about it. The pattern was circular. That "tiny" storm was the birthing of a major hurricane. Distance diminished the woes it would cause below.

And above me whirled the entire hurricane of the heavenly stars!

Never have I seen stars so bright, so pin-point sharp, so harsh. The twinkle caused by the earth's atmosphere was gone, allowing the undimmed light to beam directly on us. I planted a safety line on a nearby ring and spun up and out of the air lock. For the first time, up close, I saw it. The solar mirror.

I'd thought it was vast before. But now I knew its true size. Approximately three miles around, it was an engineering marvel. It seemed almost a shame to destroy such a masterpiece of modern technology, but destroy it I would.

Starting right now.

# ELEVEN

I couldn't keep my gaze off the brilliantly shining stars completely circling my head or the earth slowly revolving below us. I had to irrationally assign "down" to the direction of the earth. It was the only possible thing to do, yet the feeling of continually falling told me the earth was no more down than the stars were up. I experienced a few seconds of vertigo as soon as I swung up and away from the air lock, then the feeling vanished.

The Salyut-8 provided me with the stable base I needed to keep my orientation.

"Nick, how can you possibly destroy that?"

Martina pointed out to the solar mirror. I had to admit my improvised plan seemed a little shaky now that the mirror heaved into view around the edge of the space station. The vastness of that three-mile-across structure awed me.

My eyes went to the burning disk of the sun and followed invisible rays to the slightly concave surface produced by the wire structure of the mirror. While all the flat mirrors lay on the curve of the wire support, it formed a parabola capable of focusing the light on a point down on earth. I tried to figure out where the mirror was sending those intensified rays. I made out the Great Lakes by finding Michigan. Below that reference point tiny arteries of brown flowed into a larger one; the tributaries of the mighty Mississippi River.

The focal spot where the solar mirror currently aimed was a little distance to the southwest of Chicago.

I shivered thinking what this device might do to a city. The asphalt in the streets running sticky and hot, even boiling. Automobiles exploding in wanton fury. Gasoline pumps erupting in fiery death. The very air sizzling from heat. Anyone caught outside would be fried alive. But all of this would be only minor compared to the other damage it would cause. The concrete buildings built with steel girders would heat up and soften. Huge skyscrapers would tumble killing millions of people and injuring millions more. And Kolakovich would be responsible.

My gloved hands clenched in unconscious rage. I turned at the light touch on my shoulder.

"Nick, are you all right?" came Martina's anxious voice. "You seemed to be hypnotized."

"I'm okay," I answered. "That mirror's got to go. Now."

"Why don't you just push it away? It doesn't weigh anything," she suggested.

Why not? What she said was certainly true. The mirror weighed nothing while in orbit.

"I'm going to give it a try. Hand me the maneuvering jet." Martina passed out a carbon dioxide gas bottle with a double jet fastened on it. The flaring nozzles pointed to either side. All I had to do was use the dual triggers to send out a stream of carbon dioxide in the proportion I wanted. If I wanted to go straight ahead, both triggers were pulled back in equal amounts. A turn in either direction was accomplished by letting up on the trigger on the side in which I wanted to turn. If one jet shut off entirely, I'd turn around one hundred eighty degrees. Or keep spinning if I didn't let off the trigger at the proper instant. Simple.

Only it took some time to learn to use it.

My first attempt to maneuver sent me tumbling like an acrobat in a circus. I'd kept my safety line cinched securely to the ring on the side of the space station for this reason. When I came to the end of the nylon line, I snapped out hard, stopped, then began slowly returning in the direction of the line. I shook my head to clear it, then began gently teasing the dual triggers to turn back in the direction I wanted to go.

This time my touch was more deft. The secret was not to go full out but rather to be content with what seemed to be slow motion. Without real points of reference, I misjudged both speed and direction. And a steady stream of the gas wasn't necessary. A tiny spurt served just as well and was easier to control.

My radio crackled with Martina's voice.

"You look like a sailfish trying to get away," she laughed. "Do you need to be reeled in?"

"Let me practice a bit more," I told her. "This bottle's almost empty. Do you have the backup ready to go?"

"I have all I found in the store room," she assured me, pointing to the stack of tiny bottles in the open air lock entrance.

I made my way back toward her. When I was about fifteen feet distant, I did a quick somersault so my feet were pointed toward the wall of the space station, then cut loose with a long burst from the $CO_2$ bottle. While the landing wasn't as soft or as neat as I would have liked, it would do. I took some of the shock of landing with bent legs. This kept me from bouncing back out into space.

"You did that nicely," Martina complimented.

"And I'm ready to give the mirror a try."

"Are you sure, Nick? It . . . it's a long way off.

And you'd have to do it without a safety line. One mistake and you'd go sailing off into space forever.''

"It doesn't work that way," I said. "I can't get enough velocity to leave earth orbit." I didn't add that I might become a frozen satellite, totally beyond anyone's rescue. Or that, if I failed to achieve orbit, I'd fall into the atmosphere and become part of the nighttime display of falling stars. That'd be my end if I made a mistake. I didn't intend to make one.

"If you say so." said Martina, obviously not convinced.

"Now cut me loose from the safety line when I tell you to," I told her. "I'll go to the end of the cable, align myself, then jet off after you've cut me loose. Fair enough?''

"Just do it, Nick. I'm getting nervous thinking about it.''

I was nervous myself. It was a gamble, but it had to be done.

A quick spurt of carbon dioxide sent me to the limit of the safety line. I fetched up against it, spun slowly, corrected using tiny squirts from the maneuvering jets. I steadied myself until I hung motionless. Lining up with the distant mirror seemed easy. It was huge.

"Cut me loose.''

"Be careful, Nick.''

She didn't have to tell me that. I pulled back strongly on both triggers and jetted smoothly in the direction desired. I turned off the feathery plumes of $CO_2$ as soon as I assured myself I was on the right course. But almost five minutes of travel caused a cold sweat to break out on my forehead. The mirror seemed no closer, yet the space station receded into the distance with frightening speed.

But I kept on my course.

Slowly, almost too slowly, the mirror grew in size. By this time the space station was only a tiny, bright dot of light reflected from the sun. Detail had long since faded away as distance diminished it. I wondered how fast I travelled, how far I'd gone. Time and distance meant nothing with no reference points.

I flipped the nozzles of my carbon dioxide bottle around and pulled both triggers. A gentle hand pushed the bottle into my chest, slowing me. The mirror approached even more slowly now. But I didn't want to overshoot. Even though I knew Martina's fears were groundless, the idea of sailing off to Canopus didn't thrill me.

The mirror showed scant damage done to it by my bullets and the detonator from the mine. One mirror showed spiderweb cracks where the bullet had gone through it. The reflecting quality of the mirror remained unscathed.

The planar mirror destroyed by the detonator hung in shards amid the piano wire skeleton. I jetted up into the center of the mirror, thinking to place my $CO_2$ bottles there. Then the danger of what I inadvertently did came to me. I couldn't see the sun's rays as they came into the mirror. I couldn't see them being concentrated to a focal point in front of the parabolic structure. But they were real, very real. Deadly real. Metal flowed like soft butter on earth due to those unseen rays. And I was drifting right into that area.

I frantically searched for where that focal point might be. I could tell only that I was crossing the face of the mirror. If I hit the wrong spot, I'd vaporize instantly. Even if I missed the focal point, which might be directed toward the earth right now, the thermal radiation accumulating and being concentrated in front of the solar mirror might fry me.

Aiming for the edge of the mirror, I pulled the two triggers of the maneuvering jet. Nothing happened. I pulled harder. Still nothing. My velocity was such that I'd have to really work to stop in midspace, much less alter my trajectory so drastically. Again and again I miscalculated both speed and how long it took to change directions using the puny little spurts of carbon dioxide rushing from the twin jets. I fired the gas jet continuously at full blast. It soon sputtered and died, as empty as the vacuum of space itself.

I still moved slowly across the face of the mirror. Fumbling, I got out another of the bottles and fitted the nozzles onto it. I wondered if it were my imagination, but I suddenly felt the temperature in my suit climbing. I was close to the center of the mirror structure. I thought I must be in the danger zone where the sun's rays were concentrated. The thermocouple on my suit told me I was. The outer temperature rose steadily from the three degrees absolute which was normal. I fired that gas jet clutched in my gloved hands as hard as I could, hoping this would speed the exhaust gases.

Heat caused sweat to pour from my body. I finally overrode the linear momentum I'd built up and managed to angle off, out of the deadly focal plane of the solar mirror. It took the remaining portion of the gas in the bottle to be able to slow me down enough in time to reach the edge of the mirror.

"Nick, come in. Is everything all right? I can't see you."

"Everything's okay, so far," I told her. No need to tell her how stupid I'd been aiming for the center of the mirror. "Why don't you go over to the Soyuz capsule and watch me on its radar? I can use the direction you give to insure I get this damned mirror out of line with the earth."

"I'm going over, Nick. It will be easy. I can use the safety line to ferry myself over to the Soyuz since it's still docked."

"Good. I'll plant the gas bottles I have remaining on the edge of the mirror."

"Save a couple to get back with," she cautioned.

"Will do," I replied. Then I didn't hear from her for a few minutes while she made her way to the capsule.

"Tracking you, Nick," Martina finally said, her radio signal weaker now that she was inside the Soyuz.

"Fixing the bottles to the rim of the mirror," I reported. Working as quickly as I could, I placed the four bottles remaining at twenty-foot intervals along the slightly curving rim. The bottles appeared so puny in comparison to the mirror's ten-mile circumference. But it was all I could do.

"About ready to give it a try," I said, taking a deep breath. Carefully jetting from one bottle to the next, I opened the valves on the fastened bottles wide. The cold gas rocketed out, twisting the structure of the mirror—I hoped.

"I don't see anything happening, Nick. In fact, I detect no change at all in the mirror's position."

The jets were firing full blast. And then I realized why they weren't going to accomplish the task. The flat mirrors were held together with the piano wire structure. As one mirror pulled out of position, it failed to communicate that displacement fully to the mirror next to it because of the flexibility of the wire. In airless, windless space, the mirror would stay in position for a long, long time. Only the tiny particles from the sun—the solar wind—would move it. And that would take months, even years.

My jets coughed, sputtered and died. Only a few of the small, flat mirrors at the very edge of the larger structure were affected. The mirror was as powerful as ever.

"Nothing, Nick. I see nothing at all being done. Well, perhaps a little change up near one side," came Martina's excited voice. "Is that it?"

"Yes, dammit, that's it." I floated disconsolately just above my handiwork. Moving a mirror three miles in diameter proved to be harder than I'd imagined. Even if the mirror had been rigid throughout, I knew now that I couldn't have moved it. Sure, it didn't weight anything. But that didn't affect the moment of inertia. I had to overcome the inertia before the monster mirror would budge. Being weightless only meant the mirror wasn't in a gravity field. The mass remained, with all the properties of that mass. Inertia had to be overcome before the mirror would move a fraction of an inch.

I didn't have the power to do that. All I had was one bottle of $CO_2$ left. And I needed that to get back to the Salyut.

"What are you going to do now?" came Martina's worried voice over my headphones.

"Cut the damn wires. I don't know if that'll do anything—it probably won't—but maybe after I get them cut I can think of something to get the component mirrors knocked loose."

I moved down toward the mirror with measured bursts of my maneuvering jets and took a pair of wire cutters from the tools strung at my belt. Snipping through the nearest strand of wire connecting two of the planar mirrors was easy. But the mirrors didn't move after I'd cut the wire. For a second this confused me. Then it hit me why they didn't move. My mind refused to think in space terms. Without gravity or wind, the mirrors would remain where they were. Inertia working against me again. I pushed gently against one. It slowly moved away—and I went in the opposite direction.

A tiny blast from my maneuvering jet brought me back into position. The next section of mirror cut loose easily. This time I braced myself before I pushed. The mirror floated out of focus while I remained anchored down firmly. I moved on.

The planar mirrors were only about three feet on a side. A ten-mile circumference meant over thirteen thousand mirrors just on the outer ring to cut loose, if I assumed only one foot of empty space between each. Seven square miles of mirror comprised the entire structure—and each individual mirror made up only nine square feet. A quick mental arithmetic problem with rounding off in my favor told me that I had thirty million square feet of surface to contend with, almost three million individual mirrors to knock out.

The Russians had been busy building this mirror for over three years. Destroying it wouldn't be possible for one with a pair of wire cutters.

I hung motionless above the vast silvered array and felt anger rising inside me. There had to be a way of destroying this mirror. There had to be!

"Nick, come in. Nick, this is urgent, over."

"What is it, Martina?"

"I'm picking up a blip. Coming around the curve of the earth. It looks like it might be a spaceship."

The cold lump formed in my belly again. I didn't have to be told who was in that spacecraft.

Colonel Gregor Kolakovich had rocketed up into orbit to join us.

\*     \*     \*     \*     \*

"Hurry, Nick, hurry!" Martina urged. But I couldn't speed up my painstakingly slow return. The single bottle of carbon dioxide I had left had to be nursed along carefully. If I ran out and missed the Salyut, I'd be dead within the hour. I had to make this journey right—the first time.

But the race was a losing one. Kolakovich's Soyuz space capsule had been a pinprick of light when Martina first warned me. I seemed to be stationary in space while the Soyuz grew to the size of pencil eraser. Then a dime. Then I could make out the bright red star and CCCP on the side. The automatic docking procedure aided Kolakovich since it allowed him to pull the capsule very quickly in beside the one Martina and I had stolen at Baikonur.

Martina had been quiet since sighting Kolakovich on her radar screen. She played it smart by not returning to the Salyut. I didn't see any way of preventing Kolakovich from breaking in; I was positive he brought equipment with him for just such a forced boarding, if it proved necessary Hiding in the other Soyuz capsule allowed us to be outside and in a position to take him by surprise.

My carbon dioxide finally ran out. But the practice I'd acquired paid off. Before the last feathery plumes of frozen gas left the end of the nozzles, I made a correction that sent me directly for the Soyuz with Martina hiding inside.

I touched lightly, bent my knees to absorb some of the momentum, but still bounced. Luckily, Martina had been awaiting my arrival. She tossed out the safety line. I caught it and quickly spun, wrapping it around my waist. I jerked out to the end, halted, then allowed her to reel me in.

She started to radio out her concerns to me. I motioned her to be silent. When I was crouched beside her in the hatch of the Soyuz, I pressed my helmet to hers. Shouting, the vibrations went through the thick plastic and allowed us to communicate without the use of the betraying radio.

"Kolakovich," I called out. "Is he inside the space station?"

"Yes," she replied. I saw her eyes widen with fear. "He and two others are inside. And they'll free Petrov and Mendenovich. That makes it five against two."

Numbers didn't bother me. I was the match for Kolakovich and any army. But he had the advantage of position on us. We were cut off from oxygen and other supplies. He could wait us out. I checked my oxygen level and found I had only about thirty minutes worth of air left. I glanced inside Martina's helmet and read her indicator. She had almost twice as much left; she hadn't been exerting herself as I had out at the mirror.

"Carter?" came the blare of Kolakovich's voice over my headphones. "I know you and the traitor-bitch are out there. Give it up. Surrender and I promise you a trial on earth."

I shook my head as Martina reached to reply.

"Where are you, Carter? I know you can't be far. We detected movement in the mirror. Our strain gauges showed one small section of it had been disturbed. It is nothing, Carter. The infamous N3 has failed. No one can ask you to give more than you've already given. Surrender."

"What are you going to do, Nick?" asked Martina, wisely not using her radio. We clung to one another to maintain helmet contact.

"Duty first. The mirror's destruction is top priority. If we die, we die. But Kolakovich will never allow us to set foot back on earth. I don't know what happened when all my bombs went off at Baikonur—obviously not enough to stop another launch—but the Soviets won't take kindly to any interference like that. And stealing one of their Soyuz and taking over their Salyut station was going a bit too far as far as they're concerned.''

"It's a long drop to the ocean," said Martina, her eyes rolling up to the earth hanging like a pendulous blue melon above us.

"There's got to be a way," I said. "Anything they can put into orbit can be destroyed. But how?''

"You wanted to smash the space capsule into it originally. Why not try that now?''

"No good," I said. I remembered how the wire structure had defeated my best efforts with wire cutters. It would take a potent explosion near the center of the mirror to destroy it.

Explosion. And I had no explosives. There are almost forty thousand U.S. nuclear devices hidden away in vaults and placed in nosecones atop Trident and Minuteman missiles, hidden in the bellies of B-52 bombers and on the fronts of cruise missiles. I'd settle for even a small fifty kiloton device right now.

Martina shifted around and sat down on her acceleration couch. The movement was simple, yet my mind began working.

The Soyuz still had most of its fuel. The two booster stages had accounted for most of the energy expended getting us into orbit. In fact, the Soyuz fuel tanks were almost full. Only a little had been used for maneuvering to dock with the Salyut.

Liquid oxygen. Hydrazine. Potent explosives when combined. Maybe not atomic bomb potent, but certainly enough to wreck a good portion of the mirror.

"Help me get the fuel lines restrung, Martina," I said to her via helmet contact. "We have to finish before Kolakovich decides to come looking for us."

"What are you going to do, Nick?"

I didn't bother explaining. It was a wild card of a chance, but it was all I had. The fuel lines were of copper instead of the stainless steel used in American capsules. That was lucky; they bent into their new shapes easily. I ran the lines outside and across the circumference of the space capsule so that they were exposed and vulnerable to what I was going to subject them to.

"Carter, give up," barked the KGB colonel over the radio. "You can't have much oxygen left by this time. I have checked with Major Mendenovich and he has conducted an inventory of his stock. All you took were carbon dioxide bottles. No oxygen. How much longer can you breathe? Ten minutes? Five? Is your air even now becoming stuffy? Are you sweating profusely? That's a sure sign you're running out. The oxygen jet inside the suit cools you off. You cannot radiate enough heat to stay cool in space and there are no convection currents as on earth. Are you feeling dizzy from lack of oxygen, Carter? Give up. Come in and eat, breathe, drink!"

"Nick. . . ."

"No, Martina, he's only trying to scare us. We've got more than enough oxygen left to finish the job. Don't worry."

The words came out so glibly. My supply of breathable oxygen was down to less than five minutes. Soon I'd be gasping like a fish out of water. I'd feel the heat building inside the suit, just as Kolakovich had said. But the anoxia would do me in quickly. After all my oxygen was gone, I'd last perhaps five minutes. Three? I didn't know. But I had the gut-level feeling I might find out all too soon.

"All the lines are moved to the outside, Nick," came Martina's voice. "But I do not understand the purpose."

"Wait and see. Help me get this baby unlatched from the Salyut."

Undocking proved very easy. The controls inside the Salyut either were circumvented or Kolakovich hadn't bothered to station anyone to watch them and override the manual controls. I shoved for all I was worth but couldn't budge the huge capsule. Mass and inertia again working against us. A tiny sput from the main engines would be required.

I quickly moved into the capsule's hatch after fastening my safety line to the safety ring on the side of the space station. I had figured out the engine controls on the capsule when I had gone digging under the control panel to trace out the fuel lines. A half second of blast moved the Soyuz away. Another half second aligned it with the mirror—directly at the center.

"Carter," came Kolakovich's worried voice. "You cannot escape back to earth. We will take over control and crash your Soyuz. Give up. Surrender. Now!"

I turned up the volume all the way on my radio before speaking.

"No way, Kolakovich. We're going to destroy your mirror. And there's no way you can stop us!"

"Don't be a fool. Suicide isn't your style, Carter. You're a professional. You know the rules. We are both in the same game. We respect one another. Don't do this. Don't throw your life away in a futile effort to—"

"Enough, Kolakovich. This is it. I'm going to take out that solar mirror of yours. And I'm doing it right now!"

As I spoke, I turned down the volume slightly. I kicked on the capsule's rockets. As the massive space craft began slowly moving away, the safety line fastened to the space station snapped taut and jerked both Martina and me out. The Soyuz continued to head for the center of the mirror while we remained behind, still tied to the side of the space station.

"Carter!"

"Too late, Colonel," I taunted, turning down my volume as I spoke to give the impression we'd remained inside the space capsule and that distance diminished the weak signal.

The Soyuz entered that deadly area near the center of the mirror where I'd almost roasted. Intense heat assaulted the capsule, but it was built to withstand the intense reentry friction generated by the earth's atmosphere. The nakedly exposed fuel lines weren't. They ruptured. And they spewed forth the liquid oxygen and hydrazine into the space surrounding the mirror.

A brilliant flare momentarily blinded me as the fuel tanks exploded.

"Carter!" screamed the KGB colonel. But the damage had been done. The fuel tanks erupting in a cataclysmic explosion ripped and tore at the mirrors and wires holding them together. It didn't destroy all three million planar mirrors in the array but it came close. After my eyes had fought off the brilliance of the explosion I saw only tattered remains left behind.

"Carter, you're heading out into interstellar space!" cried Kolakovich.

I peered in the direction of the empty Soyuz. The blast had damaged it severely and sent it tumbling. That tumbling motion through the mirror had added to the destruction wrought by the blast. But Kolakovich was wrong. The capsule spun out of control toward the sun. I doubted if it had achieved a high enough velocity to escape earth orbit, but it might eventually go into orbit around the sun, a new satellite worshipping the solar orb.

"Kolakovich," I said, my volume control turned as low as I could get it and still be heard. "It's done."

"Carter. You fool. We can build another mirror. This is nothing, nothing, I tell you! You've failed!" The colonel shrieked out his curses to the capsule thinking Martina and I were still aboard and hurtling outward to our deaths. "We can build another quickly. We know how to do it now. We can bring up entire sections in each capsule. Damn you, Carter, damn you to your capitalist hell!"

Martina pressed close as we clung to the hull of the space station. The Soyuz capsule was beyond vision now. I doubted if even the powerful telescope aboard the Salyut could pick it up now.

"What now?" she called out, helmet pressed hard against mine.

"We wait."

"For what, Nick?"

"For a chance." But I would have been the first to admit that the chance would have to come quickly to save me from a slow death by asphyxiation. My oxygen was down to less than two minutes. All the exertion of rerouting the fuel lines, the strain of dealing with the KGB colonel, the thrill of seeing the solar mirror finally destroyed, had taken their toll on my system. Every time my heart beat just a little faster, I used more oxygen. I was already feeling the effect of reduced oxygen in my bloodstream. Dizziness assailed me and I clung weakly to the safety line. If I'd been buried alive, the sensations wracking my lungs couldn't have been worse.

There was nothing I could do now but wait for the inevitable.

# TWELVE

"Die horribly, Carter. And take that traitorous bitch Dubrovnik with you. Die in space. Die without air or a planet beneath your feet. Know that the Russian Soyuz is your eternal tomb. Damn you, Carter, damn you!" cried Kolakovich.

I held onto Martina and pressed my helmet into hers so we could talk without using the radio.

"Don't give us away," I said. I felt my voice weakening. The sweat beaded on my forehead and I felt every breath as if sandpaper had coated my lungs. My air supply was quickly running out—and so was my time. "Wait. Take it easy. And let them make a mistake."

"Nick," she said, worry in her voice. "Your oxygen's almost gone. Share mine."

Scuba divers did this all the time. But we weren't underwater. We weren't even on earth. I glanced up and saw the bright blue of the earth's oceans swirling. It wasn't far—less than the distance from Boston to Washington, DC—but for me it might have been light years.

"No, Martina, it won't work up here like it does on earth. Rest. Lean back and relax," I ordered. "I'll be okay. If only. . . ." My voice trailed off as I consciously slowed the beating of my heart. I tried to gear down all my bodily functions. My breath came more slowly now. The entire universe actually seemed a warm place, a place where I fit into a nice little niche. It

was a long way to earth, but this no longer worried me.
I pushed all thoughts of home, of solid ground under
my feet, from my mind and calmed myself even more,
using the yoga tricks an Indian guru had taught me so
long ago.

"Nick!" she cried. But I ignored her. I had to. There
wasn't enough air left for me to answer. I felt the
warmth surrounding me, the warmth that meant either
life or death for me. The secrets of slowing my
metabolism using the East Indian techniques had to
work or I'd die. I was no master, no Houdini able to be
buried for long hours. But cutting my oxygen need
prolonged my life.

If only it kept me alive long enough.

It did.

Less than a minute after I'd totally run out of oxygen,
I felt vibrations through the bootsoles of my deoxygen-
ated space suit. The air lock door opened. The two
cosmonauts who had come up with Kolakovich poked
their heads outward, studying the damage done to their
precious solar mirror.

From this position, I couldn't properly attack.
They'd have to come out even farther. When I saw
Martina start to move, I held out my hand to stop her.
This had to be done right the first time. And the odds
were against me.

My breath came harshly now. I sucked in stale, used
air, air filled with my own carbon dioxide wastes. Hot
salty sweat ran down and flowed into my eyes. But my
instant of hesitation, of demanding a better shot at the
pair, paid off.

The first cosmonaut kicked outward and hung suspended less than five feet away. I looped my safety line
into a lariat and neatly snared him. He didn't even

notice he was drifting toward the station on a captive line until it was too late.

My fingers fumbled lightly with his oxygen bottle. Some of the gas leaked out on the valve and froze into solid ice, but I managed to get it free without sending the bottle rocketing off into the void. The cosmonaut realized something was amiss when his air supply suddenly stopped. He half turned. I kicked him away, making sure my safety line was free of his body now.

By the time he snapped to the end of his own line, I had his oxygen bottle fastened onto my suit. He flailed wildly as I juggled my empty gas bottle. I smiled suddenly, knowing what I could do with the empty. Like a pro football quarterback looking for his star down field receiver, I passed.

The metal bottle shot out of my hand, spinning around its long axis. The metal bullet drilled into the man's plastic faceplate, cracking it. I saw the tiny plume of what air remained inside his suit come gushing out. He convulsed once, then twitched slightly, and was dead.

Rupturing his faceplate had decompressed his suit. His body's inner pressure—used to sea level on earth—forced its way out into the newfound vacuum. He had exploded like a hot dog put in a microwave range. I saw his lewdly bulging eyes, the bloody nose and dripping ears as he spun by me.

The entire scene had taken place in eerie, utter silence.

I felt vibration under my feet. Turning, I saw the other cosmonaut grappling with Martina. He had been slower to respond but had moved with greater determination once he'd seen his danger. He was groping for the vulnerable air hose on her suit.

I whipped forth the safety line still fastened to my suit. Like a bullwhip it snapped just above the man's head. It broke off his radio antenna, cutting off all communication with Kolakovich inside. I didn't rest on this small victory. Martina would be dead in seconds unless I acted.

Sending the nylon safety rope out again, I managed to wrap the line around the cosmonaut's legs. I jerked strongly. He didn't fall "down" but he was pulled away. That was good enough.

Martina regained her poise long enough to get behind the man and unfasten his safety line. She wrestled away his carbon dioxide maneuvering jet. I snared it, turned the jet toward the man's chest and pulled both triggers back. The hard, solid ice plume rocketed out and hit him squarely, knocking him away from the station.

Tumbling like an acrobat, he cartwheeled off into black space. The oxygen bottle he carried, if it had been fully charged before he left the Salyut, would allow him to live for almost two hours. And then he'd become a frozen corpse for the rest of time.

Even as I watched, I knew those same thoughts had run through his mind. He was trained in the ways of space and knew the dangers. He wasn't going to linger for two hours, vainly hoping for rescue. He ended it all with one quick movement that opened his faceplate. I saw the intensely white cloud of oxygen and helium gust out and circle his body like a small nimbus. The sunlight refracted through the cloud and produced a momentary rainbow, then the man was lost to view, the brief expulsion of his personal atmosphere acting as a miniature rocket engine to propel him even deeper into space.

"Oh, Nick," moaned Martina, watching, too.

"How awful! What a terrible way of dying!"

Before I could answer, I heard the sharp crack of Kolakovich's voice over my headphones.

"What's happening out there? What's the condition of the mirror? Report."

I turned down the volume on my radio and spoke in a muffled voice hoping this would satisfy the KGB colonel.

"Colonel," I muttered, "it is bad. Very bad."

"I know that, fool. How bad is it? A total loss? Did Carter succeed in completely wrecking it? It costs millions of rubles to bring those mirrors into orbit. It'll be your head if you don't give me a good appraisal right now!"

"Bad," I said, motioning Martina into the air lock. We had to attack—and soon. "All inner mirrors are gone. Many of the outer ring."

"You sound distant, Pietr," he said. "Turn up the volume on your radio. Speak more distinctly."

"Am around curve of station," I said, saying the first thing that popped into my mind. I turned down the radio volume even more and kept up an abbreviated, whispered fictional commentary of what had happened to the solar mirror.

Martina was already inside the air lock waiting for me. I swung in, undid our safety lines and pulled shut the heavy outer door. It vibrated under my fingers. I'd still expected to hear the clang, even though I knew the airless vacuum around didn't carry sound waves.

Pressing my helmet to Martina's, I said, "Their indicator lights will probably show the air lock outer door is closed. We've got to hit them hard and fast. Ready?"

"Ready, Nick. Let's get 'em!"

It took forever to get the air lock up to station pressure. I hurriedly stripped off my helmet and the clumsy, padded gloves. I'd have liked to get out of the space suit, too, but time wouldn't permit it. I knew Kolakovich already wondered why his men were returning from their mission.

The inner door opened. My fist shot through the tiny crack to impact firmly on Major Mendenovich's jaw. The meaty thunk sent the man spinning backward, unconscious.

This was the last break we got. Kolakovich was quick on the uptake and had become suspicious over my impersonation of his men. He had known something was wrong; that N3 of AXE was what had gone wrong was only a momentary surprise for him. I had to hand it to the KGB colonel. He was a professional.

"Stop them!" he shouted.

A rubber bullet thwacked into the wall beside me. I leveled myself in midair and shoved, sending myself out into the room like a human battering ram. I smashed into Petrov and sent him into the nearest wall. The air gusted from his lungs. Rebounding, I tucked my legs under me and turned agilely in the air.

Kolakovich held a gun pointed straight at me. And I saw from the heavy slugs peering out of the sides of the cylinder that these weren't rubber bullets. This was life or death. He knew if he missed me, the bullet might go right on through one of the walls and jeopardize the station. The atmosphere inside would end up quickly on the outside.

"Don't try it, N3," he said in a monotone voice that was more threatening than if he'd shouted. "I might miss. The hole wouldn't be fatal, though. We have made provisions to guarantee that."

His eyes flickered slightly in the direction of balloons drifting with the air currents caused by the circulation system.

"Inside those are sturdy patches and a sealing compound. While it won't permanently fix a major leak, it will secure it temporarily. And this will give me more than enough time to kill you."

If he did puncture the hull of the Salyut, the balloons would be sucked toward the hole due to the outrush of the atmosphere. And inside those balloons were the patches and glue he spoke of. A sort of simpleminded automatic leak detection and repair system.

"I do not know whether to kill you outright or send you back to earth. My superiors are undecided."

"Sending us back to earth would be best."

"You might meet with an unfortunate accident in space," he continued, as if he hadn't heard me. "You might fall out of the air lock without a space suit. There would be no body to provide any evidence to the contrary later on."

"Where have I heard this before?" I muttered, thinking this was the identical conversation that now dead Cosmonaut Chan had carried on with Major Mendenovich.

"You are responsible for the destruction of the mirror."

"And the deaths of three of your men."

"That means nothing. The mirror is the crux of the matter. It took three long years to build. The cost was phenomenal. And it was my personal project. I conceived it, guided its approval through the upper echelons in the Kremlin, then personally worked on it. Destroying something I have helped construct with my own hands is personal affront, Carter. One I shall not allow to go unpunished."

I looked around for Martina, hoping she could throw

something at Kolakovich or at least distract him for a split second. But she hung limp in midair, her head lolling strangely.

Kolakovich follwed my gaze.

"She is not dead. Merely stunned. The curious effect of a seemingly broken neck is due to the weightlessness."

"Are you going to do the job right? Are you going to kill her?" I asked. My mind raced. I couldn't figure out any way of getting to Kolakovich before he fired. He was firmly anchored to a handhold and wouldn't lose his footing if he fired. And he obviously handled himself better in zero-gravity than I did. He had worked up here for many long months; this was a second home to him.

I still had to act. Using only my toes, I kicked out and sent myself in a flat trajectory at the man. He smiled wickedly, his finger pulling back on the trigger. But I had counted on this. My hands closed on a handhold. I felt the shock of my abrupt stop all the way down into my shoulders. But I was no longer the moving, easy target Kolakovich had counted on. He overcorrected his aim, fired wildly, sent a heavy lead slug ricocheting around the inside of the Salyut.

The bullet didn't puncture the hull.

But, I didn't have time to notice. I was busy collecting my feet under me. Then I shot them out, straightening them out directly at Kolakovich. The KGB colonel got both feet square in the middle of his stomach. The air whooshed out of him and he went sailing backwards into the wall.

But again my inexperience in space robbed me of an easy victory. A quick blow to his throat, his nose, the temple, any of those would have ended the fight. Instead, I found myself struggling in midair to find a handhold that would allow me to reach Kolakovich.

As I floundered like a beached whale, he regained his wind. The gun came up and sighted in on me. I saw the bullets, the bore of the gun, death.

He didn't fire.

"I have decided," Kolakovich said suddenly. "In the storage room again. And this time you shall not escape so easily. I have read the report given by *him*." The emphasis he placed on "him" told me he didn't think very highly of Major Mendenovich. "This time you deal with the KGB."

I reluctantly shed my space suit, then allowed myself to be led quietly into the storeroom. Martina's limp body was shoved in after me. The door clanging shut sounded like the peal of doom.

Suddenly the idea that had been niggling at my mind the last time I'd been in this room had finally surfaced. I knew now how to escape. All it would take was a little time.

\*     \*     \*     \*     \*

"What happened to me, Nick?" Martina rolled her head from side to side, her long black hair floating like an angelic halo around her pale oval face. "I . . . I tried to stop Kolakovich. I tried to hit him with a wrench but he was too fast. I missed and went spinning. I don't remember anything after that."

"He probably watched you smash your head against the wall," I said. "He's damned good, I'll give him that. But then he's been in orbit before. He's worked in weightlessness long enough to know how to move. With him, it's instinctive. We have to think about everything first."

"Where are we?" she asked, her head coming up and swivelling around. Any fear I'd had about a broken neck vanished in that moment. "Oh," she said, the sound similar to a leak in a tire. "We're back in the storeroom."

She voiced the dejection I felt. We'd come full circle, but the mirror had been destroyed. The mission was a success—regardless of whether or not we lived to report it.

"Prisoners again," I confirmed. "But don't worry. I have a plan. The last time I was in here something kept nagging at my mind. I finally got the message outside. We can get out of here any time we want—and destroy the station, too."

"What! How?"

"Allow me to conduct a small demonstration." I fumbled in my pocket and found a book of matches. I hoped they weren't too wet from all the sweating I'd done inside the space suit. "Tell me first what will happen." I held up the match preparing to light it.

"Why, it'll burn."

I struck the match and held it still. The head flared and burned until the cardboard caught fire and burned my fingers. I quickly put it out.

"So what?" asked Martina.

"So I positioned the match directly in front of the air duct. The space station's air circulating system made sure it was in a breeze. Now watch." I repeated the experiment, this time with my body blocking the flow of air from the duct. The match flared, sputtered and finally puffed out.

"You blocked the oxygen from the air duct?" she asked suspiciously.

"Not at all. What I did was block the current of air carrying away the waste products. As the match burns, it creates all kinds of waste gases. Down on earth, these gases are lighter than air and rise. In weightlessness, nothing is lighter than anything else; everything weighs the same—zero. The waste gas stays around the head of the match and eventually cuts off the oxygen. It snuffs itself out.''

I lit another match, this time moving it slowly. The gases trailed behind the brightly burning flame.

"This is the same as keeping the match in the air current from the space station's circulation system."

"This is all well and good, but so what?"

"I'm trying to show you that things combust differently in orbit. The laws of physics are the same, but the environment for them is different. That brings in new factors we usually don't think about on earth."

"So you're going to light a match and then snuff it out to impress Kolakovich?"

"Oh, ye of little faith. Here, help me grind up this aluminum plate." I took a file and made minute shavings of the aluminum but it was hard work. The aluminum galled under the rasp, and I was unaccustomed to working in zero-gravity. I had to curl one leg around a convenient post to keep from floating away from my work.

"Why?"

"Because it will get us out of here. In fact, you can grind up just about anything you want. Just make sure it's very finely ground. Like flour."

"There's no flour here."

"I know that. I meant grind up anything you can as fine as flour. The smaller the particles the better."

Martina wrinkled her brow but set to work on my arcane task. In a little while, she brightened and said, "I know! This will burn and fill the station with fire, or maybe with poisonous vapors. But . . . aluminum doesn't burn. Nor does this," she said, allowing a pile of powder from wood shavings off nearby stored crates and the wooden beams inside the room to float in midair.

"Try it," I said, tossing her the matches. I watched as she gathered the wood shavings into a tiny cloud and carefully molded and suspended it in front of her. She lit the match and stuck it into the center of the particles. The match sputtered and went out. She spun the matches back to me.

"Didn't work," she said glumly. "I have no idea what you are trying to do."

"You didn't learn from what I said before. The laws of physics are the same here as on earth, but the applications have to be changed due to weightlessness. The particles in that cloud just didn't get enough oxygen to burn."

"So?"

"So what we're doing is making enough powdery stuff to form a cloud. We'll go from there."

I had been working for what seemed hours and had gotten several kilos of aluminum filings. Martina's pile of wood shavings was even more impressive. I put it all into a handy cannister by the door.

"Now we wait," I said, patting my pocket to make sure I had my book of matches securely at hand.

"That's always the hardest part."

"Be ready, though. We'll have to get into the air lock and into the space suits as soon as possible."

"Why? Are we going somewhere? You forget that our capsule is sailing off into space."

"And you forget there's another capsule waiting for us out there. Kolakovich's. We can take it just as easily as we took the one from Baikonur."

"You sound so confident, Nick. I wish I were. I feel

we will die here. Kolakovich is toying with us. He will kill us and never let us go back to earth, even for burial. We'll drift frozen among the stars forever. Do you think Hawk will know our fate? Will he even care?"

"Hawk knows that dead's dead," I said. "But don't worry. This will work." I put my arm around her shoulders to comfort her. But I found myself needing the contact, too. I hoped this would work. I had just bet our lives on it.

We stayed like that, comforting each other, for what seemed hours. I had no idea when Kolakovich would order us out. Probably not until after he'd contacted his superiors in the Kremlin. I wondered what damage had been done at Baikonur. However extensive it had been, it was only a drop in the ocean compared to the havoc I'd wrought on their solar mirror. Even if they brought up a new one with advanced techniques they had learned constructing the first one, it would take a long time to get it going. By then, our own space shuttle program would be in full progress. I'd bought the United States the time it needed to counter the Soviet threat in orbit.

"Nick," whispered Martina as she clutched me even more tightly. "They're coming."

I released Martina in such a way that she drifted to the back of the storeroom. The container holding our carefully manufactured scrapings of wood and aluminum, plus other bits and pieces the size of dust particles, weighted zero. I hefted it and waited.

When the Russian started unlatching the door on the other side, I strained and heaved the minute particles directly at the door. They moved sluggishly in a solid stream. I saw the small eddy of currents forming as they crossed the spots where the air vents gusted out fresh oxygen. This produced internal movement in the cloud, dispersing the particles and scattering them.

By the time the door opened, the dust cloud was beyond stopping. One cosmonaut vanished behind the filings and scrapings.

*"Aieee!"* came the loud, guttural cry as the cloud engulfed him, getting in his eyes and nose. He flailed away. All I saw were arms and legs windmilling.

If Kolakovich had been expecting an escape attempt, he hadn't counted on one like this.

I motioned to Martina. I was already in motion following the cloaking dust cloud out into the room. The thick cloud was caught by the air circulation system and quickly dispersed throughout the main portion of the Salyut.

I smiled smugly to myself as I looked around and found the console I wanted. The high voltage transformers told me where the communications rig was located. I slipped over to it and slid the remaining matches between the contacts of the power relay. If that relay had power applied to it, the matches would ignite.

I hoped there wouldn't be any incoming messages. Not for a while.

"Get to the air lock," I hissed at Martina. The cloud of particles we'd produced veiled the interior of the space station. "Follow that wall around and you'll come to the air lock. Hurry, damn it! Hurry! You've got to get suited up."

"What about you, Nick? You're not going after Kolakovich, are you?"

I had to. That man was implacable. He wouldn't stand idly by and allow us to escape.

"Kolakovich!" I called out. "Where are you?"

I heard the telltale click of Wilhelmina's toggles being pulled back, then released so that a shell carried forward into the firing chamber. Kolakovich stalked

me through the dusty cloud. Before I went hunting, I
made sure that the last of the powder Martina and I had
created went into the air conditioning ducts. This would
keep the metallic cloud alive for hours. No matter how
efficient their air filtration system was, constant cleaning of the filters would now be necessary. By the time
the cosmonauts breathed clean air again, Martina and I
would be long gone—or dead.

"I'm going to kill you, Carter," came the KGB
man's cold voice from the other side of the dust cloud.
"I'm going to use your own pistol, too. That will be
ironic justice. Where are you, you murderous capitalist
pig? I will teach you the superiority of Russia. With
your death, I shall teach you!"

I began moving in the direction opposite to the one
Martina had taken, homing in on the KGB man's taunting voice. I wanted to decoy Kolakovich away from
her, if at all possible. On my way, my foot caught on a
writhing, twitching mass.

Petrov.

Kicking out, I sank my foot to the ankle in his belly.
He turned and weakly groped for my leg. I shook him
off but the cosmonaut was persistent, too persistent. I
flicked Hugo into my hand. I killed him with a powerful, quick jerk of the blade across his nakedly exposed
throat. The spray of blood fountaining out into the room
momentarily worried me. I didn't want it sucking up
the dust particles. I needed that cloud to obscure my
movements—and to carry out one final plan.

"Nick!" came Martina's voice. "I'm ready."

I nodded to myself. She'd be preparing my suit, too,
so that I could hurriedly climb into it when I reached the
air lock. Seconds would count then. But first came
Kolakovich.

The cloud of aluminum filings and wood shavings

made visibility inside the main room of the Salyut almost zero. I opted for staying put and listening. I heard Mendenovich yelling out. Kolakovich ordered him to be silent. Sighting in on the source of their voices, I hesitatated only a second, then launched myself. Hugo was the prow of my human battering ram.

I found flesh.

Slashing savagely, Wilhelmina spun away from the KGB colonel's grip. Rather than stay with Kolakovich and finish him off, I followed the flight path my gun had taken. Fumbling in the dancing mist of metallic particles, I found Wilhelmina and twisted, looking back into the silvery cloud. Two quick shots kept Kolakovich and Mendenovich busy. And then I was off for the air lock.

"What do we do, comrade?" came Mendenovich's voice. "How do we get this out of the air? It already clogs our filters."

"Turn the system off. Get a magnet and pull the metal filings out of the air."

I smiled. I'd used aluminum because it was non-magnetic. That trick suggested by Kolakovich wouldn't work. I imagined the KGB colonel hovering in the obscuring cloud, holding his cut arm, red in the face from frustration and anger.

"Nick," came Martina's voice again. "Hurry!"

I found the air lock and clambered through. I was working my feet into the suit even as I spun the wheel and started the evacuation process. I banked on her getting me suited up tight enough before the air leaked out. As it was, the race was close, damned close.

As the pressure dropped, I felt blood trickling from my ears. She spun the helmet into its bayonet fittings just as the outer door swung open. I stared out at the infinity of space as I felt the sweet rush of the oxygen-helium mixture from my own bottled little universe.

"To Kolakovich's space capsule," I ordered. "And no stopping. We have to make it before he radios earth."

"I see," she said. "Before he orders Baikonur to take control. Is that what you mean?"

"No, we've got to get out of here before he uses the radio at all. I put all the matches I had in the high voltage relay on his radio unit."

"But—"

I didn't give Martira time to argue over why this was significant or why we had to be outside and away from the station in a hurry. But she'd find out. Soon.

# THIRTEEN

"I can't do it, Nick," muttered Martina fearfully. She clung to the inside of the air lock door as if her life depended on it. Her helmeted gaze stretched across the emptiness between the lock and Kolakovich's spaceship held to the station by a long metal docking device. When we'd come up in the first Soyuz, we'd taken the single docking bay and forced Kolakovich to use the auxiliary device. Now that separation caused Martina to panic.

"You've been outside before. It's no big thing," I said, realizing that, for her it was a big thing. Martina had had time to think about what she was going to do—cross empty space to the other Soyuz—and as a result she had developed a real fear. I wished we had the time to go hand over hand along the docking arm, but we didn't. The only way we could reach the Soyuz in time would be to jump; and it would be a dangerous jump without the use of the nylon safety lines.

"But the line to the station. It anchored me. We . . . I'd have to cast off and drift."

"I did it to get to the mirror," I told her. "It's a little like hang gliding, only without the wind rushing into your face. You're absolutely free and the falling sensation is no different from the one you're experiencing now. Come on!" I glanced back at the inner air lock door, expecting it to fly open and seeing Colonel Gregor Kolakovich come rushing out.

That was absurd, of course. As long as we held the outer door open, he didn't dare open the inner one, not unless he was clad in a space suit. For my plan to work, though, the dust particles we'd worked so hard to create had to be kept suspended in the atmosphere.

"But I won't have anything solid under me. My feet are touching the station. It . . . it's the only solid thing in the universe, Nick. I don't know if I can do it."

The thought of what would happen when Kolakovich turned on his high power radio rig sent shivers up and down my spine. She might be truly fearful of what would happen if she stepped off into nothingness; I was terrified of our fate if we stayed aboard the Salyut for even one second longer than necessary.

"Martina, listen carefully. We don't have much time. This entire station is going to blow sky-high." I paused, considering the absurdity of that earth-bound cliché. We were already sky-high. "There's a time bomb inside and it's going to go off. We don't have time for you to be afraid. Fear's a luxury item right now. We have to get away if we're going to survive. You can be afraid all you want after we get on board the Soyuz."

"But Nick," she started. Turning and looking into my helmet, she asked "What time bomb? You didn't have any explosives with you. Except for the detonator off that land mine." She paused again, her mind working slowly. "Oh, you have to get the detonator out of Kolakovich's capsule. But—"

I didn't give her anymore time for "buts." While she talked I had undone her safety line. As soon as she noticed this and started to protest, I shoved her out into space. It was heartless, but I didn't have any choice. It was either leave her to die with Kolakovich and Mendenovich or scare her to death.

The latter was preferable.

*"Aieeee!"* came her shrieks over the suit radio. I followed immediately, kicking off and aiming myself.

Ice formed in my veins when I realized my inexperience in space had again caused me to make a dangerous mistake. Wild theories raced through my mind as to why I'd misjudged the jump so grievously. I'd jumped harder than Martina had been pushed; my speed was greater than hers and I overtook her within a few yards of the Soyuz. My speed took us right past it and the Soyuz became too distant for us to land aboard now. Grabbing her around the waist, I pulled the woman in to me.

"Listen," I said urgently. "I missed the jump by a couple of yards. We missed the Soyuz."

She turned in my arms and saw the spacecraft slowly diminishing in size behind us. It was obvious we were doomed to the same fate as the cosmonaut I'd thrown off the station earlier. We'd drift until our oxygen ran out, then we'd suffocate slowly. Or, like the man before us, we could open our faceplates to the infinite vacuum of space and be dead within seconds.

"The station. We can go back. Our safety lines . . ." Her voice trailed off when she realized I'd unfastened the lines to make the jump to the Soyuz space capsule.

"It doesn't work that way. We're heading outward at whatever velocity my legs launched me at from the station."

"We're dead, then?" Her voice sounded small, distant, a little girl's words. But she was strangely calm. The fear of jumping had been overwhelming. She now faced death with equanimity. For that I admired her greatly.

"Not if I can help it." I considered all that had

happened. I'd been so damn clever in my plans to wreck the space mirror and then destroy the Salyut station itself. I looked toward the Salyut, its long gleaming metallic cylinder still intact. Kolakovich hadn't yet turned on the high voltage radio rig. When he did, the book of matches would flare and—boom!

"What we need is a rocket," she said. Her eyes worked down over our suits in the vain hope that one of the $CO_2$ maneuvering jets would be attached to the belts. None was.

"What did you say?"

"A rocket. We need a rocket."

"And we've got one. How could I have been so stupid!" I grabbed downward and found the zippered pocket in which I'd stashed Wilhelmina. I pulled my trusty Luger out, sighted on a star and found one toward which we were directly headed, then fired.

Nothing seemed to happen. I fired again. And again and again. I fired five times as if I could put a perfect sight pattern into that distant star.

"Nothing's happening, Nick. It didn't work." I felt her strong arms close even more tightly around me. But she was wrong. Wilhelmina had done her work and done it well. I sighted on another star, one just at the edge of the obscuring haze of the earth's atmosphere. The sharp-edged light from that star moved outward slightly as our position changed. Soon enough, even Martina realized we were heading back toward the space station.

I hoped we were in time. Kolakovich would have rallied his forces and determined his exact situation. He'd be calling Baikonur for further instructions at any minute.

We had to be aboard the Soyuz and blasting away before that happened.

We had to wait agonizingly long minutes for the Soyuz capsule to slowly creep toward us. This was another effect I found strange in space. With no reference points by which to determine speed, it felt as if we were stationary and the Soyuz moving. But that didn't matter as long as we somehow got aboard it in time. I fired Wilhelmina once more to slightly alter our course. We headed directly for the spacecraft now.

We landed harder than I'd expected from the deceiving gradualness of our approach. I allowed my knees to buckle and absorb most of the momentum. Then I hurried Martina into the open hatch.

This Soyuz was even larger than the T3 model we'd arrived in. Definitely a three-man capsule, this one also had ample storage space located behind the passenger compartment. I suspected this was a newer model, one designed to bring more than just men to the near earth orbiting space station.

I slid down into the acceleration couch, studied the panel and was relieved to find it designed identically to the other Soyuz. I'd spent enough time tracing fuel lines and firing switches in the other craft to know what to do. I ignited the engines in such a fashion that we'd blast earthward and away from the Salyut.

The docking arm held us too firmly in place, however.

''What are we going to do, Nick? That metal strut is locked on too tightly for us to escape.''

Martin's concern was mine, too. I had no idea how to go about unlocking, either. I could fiddle with the controls until something unsnapped—and in the process of trial-and-error experimentation I might permanently cripple the Soyuz. Even worse, such an action might be totally futile if the locking arm was controlled totally from inside the Salyut space station. In that case, Colonel Kolakovich still controlled our destiny.

"We're playing for high stakes—our lives. It's time to gamble."

I flipped open the radio link on my space suit and called out, "Colonel Kolakovich, are you there? This is Nick Carter. We're inside your capsule."

"I'm suited up, Carter, and I'll be outside momentarily. You cannot escape." The KGB colonel's voice was tinny and weak. He used a space suit radio of his own. I cursed under my breath. He had to use the high power radio inside the station for my purposes.

"Don't worry about it, Kolakovich. We're already on our way back to earth. I just wanted to say goodbye."

"You can't land the Soyuz," he taunted. "The control from the ground is absolute."

"But you haven't told them we're coming. I can fake it long enough to get down, Kolakovich. So long." I sat back in the acceleration couch, waiting, wondering when he would turn on the high-power radio.

Then it happened. The silent blossoming of death as the Salyut-8 blew apart told me the exact instant he'd turned on his powerful station radio. The flying shrapnel might have holed the spacecraft we were in but I'd had to take that chance. We went tumbling away, the docking arm ripped from the station and still attached to the side of our Soyuz.

"Nick, what happened?" cried Martina. Her eyes had grown wide in fear as the station continued its silent fountain of death and destruction.

"The dust we put into the air. The aluminum filings, the wood shavings, all that combusted."

"But I tried to burn it in the storeroom. Remember? I

formed a little cloud of it and it put out the match.''

''And I told you that you're still thinking in earth terms. This is space. Weightlessness.''

''So?''

''On earth, we have grain elevator explosions all the time. The dust from the wheat hangs in the air, a light switch is thrown or some other spark—like a lit cigarette—ignites it. The grain itself won't burn. Yet the dust does.''

''Why?''

''Anything burns if it's small enough and there's enough oxygen to support the burning. I put the dust into the space station atmosphere both to cloud our escape and to act as the time bomb. With my matches across the contacts on the high power relay, the first surge of power would ignite them which would set off the dust. All the oxygen inside the Salyut went for the combustion. That would have snuffed out life aboard if it'd gone slowly enough. But it was fast, bomb-fast.''

''Wouldn't the spark from the relay itself have been enough to set off the blast?'' she asked.

''Maybe. I couldn't take the chance. I had to be sure the dust ignited.''

Only twisted scrap metal remained behind of the space station. It had been done in by a few kilograms of dust. It hardly seemed possible, yet it had happened.

''Nick, I'm getting sick to my stomach. Look out the hatch.''

I glanced ''up'' and saw what was affecting her so strongly. When the Soyuz had been ejected outward on the blast wave, we'd begun tumbling wildly. The earth flashed by in odd patterns so eye-confusing that my own equilibrium was threatened. I had to close my eyes and swallow hard to restore my sense of rightness.

"We're in trouble, Martina. But nothing AXE can't handle." I fumbled around in my zippered pocket in the space suit and found the buckle and straps from the knapsack I'd carried back on earth. This was the first chance I'd had to see if the tiny radio worked in space. If anything, it should perform even better than on earth. After all, there was no atmosphere to foul up the signal—and the AXE satellite was in orbit. A straight shot to the relay and I'd be in touch with Hawk in a few seconds.

"Nick, I'm going to be really sick."

"Don't. Not inside your helmet. Here, let me pressurize the cabin. There, that seems normal." My eyes flashed over the instruments on the control panel. I found a gauge that measured atmospheric pressure. As I opened the stopcocks on the air system, the needle slowly crept upward indicating enough to breathe. "Open your faceplate and see if you can relax a bit."

I watched as she hesitantly opened her helmet to the air carried inside this Soyuz. Seeing that Martina was going to be okay, I put together the buckle and straps. The tiny power supply in the strap was more than up to the task of reaching the KH-11 spy satellite AXE uses as an orbital relay.

I began tapping out my message in code. When I got no response, I tried a different code, a slightly different priority. The crackle of the speaker inside the Soyuz was my answer. The message on the buckle and strap radio had gotten through.

"Change frequency to mode twenty-three," came the stilted words of one of our radio monitors. I quickly readjusted the radio to the frequency dictated by the code message. Seconds later, Hawk's voice boomed out of the craft's speaker.

"Good work, N3. Our radar reports show that both the mirror and the Salyut were destroyed."

"Kolakovich, too," I added.

"It was a necessary elimination. I'll put it down as such in the report," said Hawk in a businesslike manner. "Now, to your immediate problem. We have recently obtained full schematics on the new model Soyuz you're in. Our technicians are working on an override system so that we can control your descent and prevent Soviet signals from reaching you to confuse a safe landing."

"Does this one have the bomb inside like the T3?"

"Affirmative. But we are jamming the detonation frequencies. The bomb in this model craft was placed in such a fashion that the crew cannot get to it without doing some extra-vehicular activity or spacewalking. It seems that many of the cosmonaut crews, as you'd done on your way up, deactivated the bombs rather than die for the glory of the State." Hawk's voice came out dry, wry, almost joking. I relaxed a bit. He continued, "This particular craft was designed to be used as both a personnel shuttle and a cargo carrier. Enjoy the extra room while we work."

"You can land us with no trouble, then?" I asked, more to hear the reassurance for Martina's sake than for my own. I knew Hawk. I'd already read between the lines of what he'd said—and how he'd said it—and come to the conclusion that he figured we had a ninety-nine percent chance of landing on earth safely.

"The experts can do it, N3. Anything else?"

"Yes, what happened at Baikonur? I never got a clear picture from Kolakovich. He did, after all, manage to launch the Soyuz afterwards and reach orbit."

"While the damage was greatest in their fueling

area, the rest was minimal. The fuel tank truck which exploded should have destroyed much of their launch pad area. It was quickly contained due to their readiness for possible explosion during the launch itself. Bad luck, N3. The lox compressors went down permanently, but such equipment is not custom-made. It's almost off the shelf They had a new liquid oxygen compressor working within hours. I will have photos of the damage for you when you return."

"Do we have to do anything on this end? The spinning of the capsule is affecting our stomachs."

"I'm putting on Dr. Goble," said Hawk. "He'll instruct you on the wiring changes that must be made for us to properly assume control from this end."

"Carter, are you there?" came the crisp voice. "Or do you have too many ions in the fire at the moment to do a little rewiring?"

"I'm ready."

"Good. We wouldn't want you to come down with an atomic ache. Just kidding. Now this is what you must do. Under the left-hand side of the control panel is a red and white striped wire. Break this and connect it to—" He droned on while I dutifully followed his instructions. Goble interspersed every third or fourth command with a wretched pun. But the man did know his job. In less than ten minutes I had a jury-rigged control panel ready to accept the override control from the U.S.

"Sit back and enjoy the ride," Dr. Goble told me. "And don't worry about reentry. We won't let you make an ash of yourself." Chuckling, he broke the connection.

"N3, Hawk here. You'll be in orbit for another hour, then we're bringing you in. This particular craft is designed to land on solid ground, just like our own shuttles. You'll be brought down at Edwards Air Force Base.''

''What do we have to do until reentry begins?'' I asked.

''Kill time. For you, the mission's over. Once more, N3, a job well done.''

Hawk's voice cut off and only the soft hissing of static remained. I turned over on the couch, noticing that the rockets had stopped firing for the moment. Once more in orbit, we were weightless. The feeling was superb, one of freedom.

And there was something I wanted to do one more time before the earth's ever-present gravity put its strong shackles around my body for the rest of my life.

''We have an hour to kill,'' I said. ''Have any ideas how to spend the time?''

Martina was already stripping off her tunic. Her breasts floated upward and swayed just enough to set my blood to boil. We'd made love once before in zero-gravity; this would be the last chance for either of us to do it again.

We gently docked in midair, floating free and experiencing the ultimate high. Our bodies performed acrobatic feats undreamed of on a gravity-ridden earth. We melted together as one, spinning slowly, enjoying the rapture set free by weightlessness. And when it was over, we rested contentedly for a little while, remaining in one another's arms, and then cautiously joined for one last taste of this unearthly bliss.

By the time the first touch of atmosphere began warming the heat shields protecting our capsule, we were both sated and ready for the return to earth. It had been a good mission for me, a successful one. The mirror had been removed as a potent weapon in the

Soviet military arsenal and their space station destroyed. Even better from one viewpoint was the death of Gregor Kolakovich. Hardware destruction is pointless unless the guiding genius behind it is also destroyed. This time, he had been. His death wouldn't stop their space program, but by the time they rebuilt it, our own space shuttle program would have forged ahead enough to take away the threat posed by theirs.

"Nick," said Martina from her couch. "I've got to go back to Russia."

"I know. I've known all along," I said, staring straight ahead out the hatch.

"It's not Dmitri. It's . . . more."

"You enjoyed this mission too much."

"Too much?" she asked.

"Too much to ever go back to being just a common, workaday citizen. The excitement got into your blood. You crave more and more. And besides, you feel you're doing something worthwhile in a world going to hell."

"That may be it, Nick."

"It is," I said positively. The skipping motion as we hit denser atmosphere made the insides of the Soyuz chatter. I fastened the broad straps of the safety harness around me, then I reached out and took Martina's hand. We'd land, she'd return to Russia, maybe die, maybe become one of AXE's top agents. Time would tell.

Time would tell.

# NICK CARTER

> "Nick Carter out-Bonds James Bond."
> —Buffalo Evening News

Exciting, international espionage adventure with Nick Carter, Killmaster N3 of AXE, the super-secret agency!